In Sickness and in Health

Karin Rose O'Callaghan

In Sickness and in Health is a work of fiction. Every name, place and incident are the product of the author's imagination or are real but used fictitiously. Any resemblance to actual persons, living or dead, events or locales, is entirely coincidental.

Chapter 1

Small towns are quiet, generally. But when you have a small town with two colleges, quiet happens mostly when the students are away on holiday breaks or summer or weekends. *Eight o'clock on a Friday night in a small town public library has to be the quietest time of all,* Cassie thought as she surveyed her tight little world. *Books shelved. Wanda pulling out her knitting over at the Circulation desk. A lone patron, probably a passing-through biker, at the computer. Both of the high school browsers long-gone for the night; student visitations, and problems, won't pick up until later in May as they finish last minute papers. Some things never change*, she thought with a secret smile, *at least not here. I like it this way,* Cassie told herself as she peered over the counter of the Reference desk. *I have Mich-the-diva to provide all the excitement I can handle*, she grinned at the thought of her former college roommate; really named Michela, her nickname was Mich, pronounced Mike.

"Here" is Lexington, Virginia, Cassie's hometown for most of her twenty-nine years. Born and raised here, went off to college and then worked in the big city, and now back, and very glad of it. Exceedingly glad. Right down to her toes glad. Dorothy was right, "there's no place like home and if I can't find it in my own backyard, I never really wanted it anyway." *No truer words were ever spoken* Cassie silently agreed.

As the ranking librarian tonight, Cassie was in charge. She knew that wasn't true though. Wanda had been working here since Cassie was little and used to walk to the library from her ballet lessons two doors away. And little kids still walk the streets of Lexington unattended, although Mom or Dad is usually close by. Even sleepy little Lexington is aware of what's going on in the world. Amber alerts. College shootings. After all, Virginia Tech is just 90 miles south of here. All these thoughts rambled through Cassie's mind as she stood up from her desk and stretched her back. Those were the days, getting lost in the children's section until Mom or Dad came to get me. *Maybe those days of contentment were a sign of what was to come; maybe I should have paid attention.*

Again Cassie heaved a contented sigh as she started to tidy the Reference area in preparation for the nine o'clock closing. *Yep, I'm just a small town girl. Always was, always will be. Learned that the hard way. Too bad I didn't admit it to myself sooner.*

She put the back-in-a-minute sign on the desk in the unlikely event someone might show up, waved to Wanda to keep an eye on things, and headed for the stacks behind the desk. Time to check for any stragglers – human or print. Her hands lovingly stroked the book bindings as she straightened shelves, bringing bindings into alignment with the edge of the shelves. *Nothing like a book in your hands,* she grinned. *Or the musty smell of full shelves.* She owned a Kindle, but only used it for travel so she didn't have to take an extra carry-on for her travel library; Cassie always had to have at least two books handy in case she got stuck in a plane or train station. And with the airlines' extra baggage fees, taking ten or twelve books for a long trip just wasn't practical any more, not to mention economical. And they got to be heavy, even paperbacks. Years before, she had started the habit of leaving the books behind when she finished them, even though it was very difficult to ever part with a book. *My own personal version of hoarding,* she giggled to herself, knowing it was almost true.

Cassie smiled happily as she took the four orphan books she'd found on the floor to the Circ desk and handed them to Wanda. "What are you so happy about?" Wanda asked brusquely. At 72 Wanda didn't miss a thing. Wanda had worked at the library since before her failed romance when she was 37. Now a "maiden spinster lady", as she was considered in the South, she knew more without her library degree than any of the librarians who had passed through these doors in her thirty-plus years...and she knew it.

"I'm just glad to be back," Cassie replied with an even wider smile.

"For heavens' sake, Cassie, you're been back for four years. That's more than enough time for you to see this library and this town as they are: small, nothing going on."

"I know, Wanda, and that's just the way I like it. I tried the big city, remember? First Nashville, then Chicago. I'll take Lexington any time."

"You're too young to be stuck here, Cassie Marie. You don't see other singles here in town do you? And especially not here in this barren public library and not on a Friday night. No, the young people get out of town as soon as they can, and you should, too."

Cassie and Wanda had this debate every time they worked the night shift together.
Fortunately that was only one week a month.

"At least you could have taken advantage of W&L's nepotism and gone to work over there, met some young faculty members."

"I know, Wanda, but a college library just didn't have the same appeal. Very few children come in there. Besides, working here, I can keep up on the local gossip, couldn't do that at W&L or VMI, at least not as well. Mom and Dad kept me up to date on the college gossip." Cassie was proud that she was finally able to mention her parents without tearing up.

"You could have worked at the hospital or Kroger and gotten the same gossip, and been more...accessible." Wanda glared at her like an angered mother hen, long skinny neck with her wattle wobbling.

"Thanks, Wanda, but I'm doing fine. I have books. I have Rosie. I have friends. What else is there?"

"Travel! See the world! Meet men."

Cassie chose to ignore the last remark. "I do travel. Mich and I take a trip every year, as you well know. Always some place exotic, too. Last year it was Malta, the year before Spain. What more do I need?"

Wanda hesitated, but only briefly before repeating herself, "A man? You're only 29. You could have children, a family. Don't bury yourself here like I did."

Cassie's face immediately took on a cold expression, her warm brown eyes turned dark and dangerous. Wanda had crossed the line, not even knowing there was a line. Cassie turned on her heel and headed toward the back of the library. "I'll get the lights and check the back door if you'll shut down the computers." She stalked off.

Wanda looked after her, crestfallen at the suddenly frigid treatment. She was only trying to help. She'd known Cassie since she was six, a bright, inquisitive little girl, staggering under the huge load of books she checked out each week. Now that her parents were gone, Wanda felt she should look out for her, shouldn't she? She started punching the keys to shut down the two computers on the circulation desk.

Wanda had her purse and knitting and was waiting at the front door when Cassie finished the nightly closing routine. "We're all set, Wanda." Cassie tried to sound cheerful, realizing guiltily that Wanda was just trying to be helpful in her own busybody way. "I'll lock up behind you. See you tomorrow." Cassie smiled a warm smile at the older woman and patted her shoulder as she nudged her out the door; she could only take so much *in loco parentis*, especially from Wanda. *By tomorrow it will have all blown over.* In a small town no one can stay mad at anyone for very long, there aren't enough people to go around. Except maybe for the Hatfields and McCoys. Cassie's good humor had returned and she was smiling to herself as she began the short walk to her family home, just a few blocks away on Jackson Avenue.

As Cassie climbed the steps to the 150 year old brick house with large white columns, she continued to mull over Wanda's comments. *Am I lonely? Am I hiding out here in Lexington?* Giving it further serious consideration while she unlocked the front door, she decided "no". And she sure as hell knew she did not need a man to make her happy. Tried that one, didn't work. She had Mich, her best friend and former college roommate, and she had Rosie. She grinned as Rosie came bounding to meet her, feet sliding on the polished wood floors, skidding to sit for a pat and a head scratch, a huge smile on her face. Cassie buried her face in the fluff surrounding Rosie's Golden head. "I've got you, don't I, Rosie? Who needs men?" Cassie walked down the central hall, Rosie hot on her heels, and opened the kitchen door for Rosie to go out. She kicked off her shoes and walked to the refrigerator to pour her evening glass of white wine. "I'll call Mich tomorrow and see how she's doing. Maybe we can start planning our next trip", Cassie said aloud as she took her first sip.

Chapter 2

November, previous year

Michela Ferncliff Merritt maneuvered the older-than-dirt Jeep Grand Wagoneer woody into the shrinking parking space. Most of the time she loved her old car, but trying to wedge it into narrow, short spaces built for minivans was like getting the proverbial square peg into the round hole.

"Good thing I like jigsaw puzzles, Tank, or you'd be long gone," she muttered to the car as she labored to turn the wheel. Even with power steering it was like turning an ocean liner.

Everybody told her to get rid of the stretch jeep, but she'd known this was the car for her the minute she saw it at the back of the Lakewood used car lot. The car had been part of the production crew for the old Perry Mason TV movies when they were filmed in Denver; of course it had been practically new then. But, it had lots of room and very little maintenance, even at its advanced age. She could lay her paintings down flat in the back and not have to worry about them.

Finally getting the car straight in the space, she turned off the engine and sat a moment, waiting for her pulse to slow from the exertion. "Phew, Tank, you are getting to be a bit much. Glad we don't have to park in parking garages every day. I'll stick to the 'burbs."

She climbed down from the seat and locked the door, patting the side of the car as she did so. "Don't worry, I'll never trade you in on a minivan." She frowned slightly at her own words, and moved on, literally and figuratively.

Not likely she thought to herself as she turned from the car. Glancing around the dim garage she realized she was practically surrounded by minivans. That's what I get for having a doctor in a suburban business park. *Maybe I can talk Doc into moving back downtown. Still parking garages, but a bigger variety of vehicles.*

She knew most of these vehicles belonged to working moms and young professionals using the gym in the Centrum Building on their way to work. Six-thirty in the morning was too early for them to be here for doctor appointments.

At that moment, Dr. Bill Harper was admiring the view of the front range from his medical office on the sixth floor of the Centrum Building in Denver's Tech Center. The mountains were snow-capped most of the year, and in early November he could see quite a bit of white. In the early morning light like this he always thought of "purple mountains majesty." He only had one patient who could get him into the office this early: Michela. A gentle smile touched his lips at the thought of her, but doubt still shadowed his deep blue eyes.

He had known Michela all her life, even before. He had been one of her mother's doctors through her pregnancy. He was a young oncologist then, one of the first full-time oncologists in Denver. Lillian's obstetrician had called him in as a consult when Lily, as Doc called her, had insisted on keeping her baby, even though she had stage three melanoma. Harper and Lily's now-deceased OB had strenuously tried to argue her out of continuing the pregnancy, explaining the strain of the pregnancy, coupled with the cancer and its treatment, could kill her, or the baby, or both. But Lily was just as stubborn as they come. She was pregnant and going to stay that way. She was elated, glowing with the vitality some women get with pregnancy, but her husband Tom was less enthralled, terrified of losing the love of his life.

Lillian fought her way through the cancer and the pregnancy, delivering a wonderfully healthy baby almost thirty years ago. Bill had been with her right up to the end, admiring her courage, loving her life. But it had all been too much for her. Lily died three days after Michela was born. He could still see the radiant smile on Lillian's face as she held her tiny daughter. He could hear her soft voice as she stroked the baby's head and whispered to him "She was worth it. Thanks for your help, Bill. Keep her safe for me."

Help! He raged inwardly. He had been helpless to stop the spread of the insidious disease that ate away at her strength and young life. Lily had been only 25 when she died. Much too young and lovely. But she had grown up when all the girls "worked on their tans" every chance they got, either beside a pool or out at Chatfield Reservoir. No one at the time had fully understood the future dangers that were lurking beneath the skin of those golden tans, made darker faster by Denver's mile higher proximity to the sun.

"Boy, you look a million miles away," Michela said from the open door of his office.

Turning his back on the mountain view, Bill Harper pushed his glasses further up on his nose as he focused on the young woman before him, reminding himself this was Michela, not Lily. The resemblance was unnerving in this shadowed light, both were on the tall side, long brown hair, deep-ocean blue eyes, but Michela wore her hair – when she had any – hanging loose and Lily had always worn it tied back, or almost always.

Walking across the room she gave her godfather a hug. "How 'bout if you move back downtown?"

"Still having a hard time parking Tank?" he asked as he draped his arm around her too- thin shoulder and walked her over to the burgundy leather sofa that faced the windows and the mountains.

"I'm sure the spaces are larger downtown than they are out here, and more of them."

That's it, he thought. The minivans. They hadn't registered with him when he had parked; he was so used to seeing them. He knew Michela's aversion to them, too; they always made her think of the children she could never have.

"I'll think about it, Toots," he said with a twinkle.

"I know that look. You're just saying that to appease me. You'd no more fight your way back downtown than you'd give up your practice. No, the Tech Center is fine. Besides, it's a closer drive for me and I get to see you more often."

"As much as I love you, I'd really like to see you more often socially and less often professionally."

Michela again hugged the silver-haired man, her best friend, and the closest thing to her idea of a father she'd ever known. Her biological father had shut her out of his life as soon as his wife died. He hired nannies and nurses and housekeepers to tend to "the girl" and packed her back east to boarding schools as soon as she was old enough. It hadn't been as bad as it was depicted in Dickens novels; she felt she had become very self-sufficient, if a bit of a loner. And there had always been books to console her when she got lonely. That love of books had created her bond with Cassie.

Fortunately, Doc had been waiting when she came home on vacations. He taught her to ski and to drive. Took her to all kinds of sports events; she grew up an avid Broncos fan, added being a Rockies fan when she was home, and even enjoyed the Avalanche hockey games when she could get tickets.

She knew they were as close as a father and daughter could be with no blood relationship. When Michela got older she realized the doctor had been in love with her mother, maybe still was. He had never married and Michela was the only family he had left.

Her "real" father's death when she was 16 had barely made a ripple in her life. The only difference was that Bill Harper was named her guardian and executor of the not-inconsiderable estate her father had left her. Tom Ferncliff may have been a non-entity as a father but not in the world of investments and business. Doc had taken on the management of her and her portfolio and both had prospered.

She sat back and took the hand of the man who had walked her down the aisle ten years ago, "What's up, Doc?"

Chapter 3

Dr. Bill Harper knew better than to hedge with his favorite patient, "Well, Michela, I'm sorry, but it's back." Michela looked around the well-appointed office. She didn't see the diplomas on the wall, not the coffee carafe on the side table, not the warm cherry furnishings. "Are you sure you don't want Larry here?" Bill Harper sympathetically looked through his wire-rimmed glasses at his goddaughter, knowing the answer, but still waiting for her to voice it.

Michela had known what Doc was going to say. She had felt it coming ever since the biopsy a week ago. She had steeled herself for this announcement; she couldn't let Doc see her fear.

"No, Doc, it's okay. He's busy at the shop anyway. Tell me the worst." Michela Merritt gripped his hand more tightly and smiled tentatively at her doctor, her friend.

"As you know from the last time, breast cancer is the most common cancer among women over 40."

"Yeah, I remember that. But I was only 26 the first time and I'm barely 30 this time; just lucky I guess." She smiled ruefully. "I thought since it had been over three years I was practically home free."

"Well, we all hoped that was the case, but it really takes five years before we can say it's gone, even then there is a possibility of recurrence."

"So, what? I missed the deadline by a few months?" Michela stared at the corner of the doctor's large cherry desk. Bill Harper was the most respected oncologist in the West. His office reflected his prestige and his inherited wealth. Not one to brag, diplomas and commendations were subtly displayed on tables behind the visitor chairs, no wall of fame for him.

Looking down at her chest, Michela spoke softly, "So what do we do now? I don't have any breasts left to cut on. They went the last time."

"It's not that easy, Mich. The cancer has spread. It's in your lungs.

It could spread to your bones or liver or even your brain."

"Wait a minute. How can breast cancer be in my lungs? Isn't that lung cancer? This doesn't make sense. Besides, I quit smoking four years ago."

"The cancer is determined by two things: where it starts and its makeup. No matter where the cancer appears, if it started someplace else and has the properties of the other place, it's still the original type of cancer. So breast cancer can occur anywhere in the body and still be called breast cancer."

"So what do we do? How do we fight it this time? Obviously the surgery didn't work."

Doc had always admired Mich's fighting spirit. He was glad it hadn't failed her now.

Michela stared straight at the doctor. His deep blue eyes and calm strength had brought comfort to many patients. Mich wasn't feeling too comfortable right now, though. She really hadn't been feeling herself for months. It had started with general tiredness; by seven o'clock at night she was ready for bed. Larry would have been okay with that if "bed" had included sex, but she was always too tired, truly bone weary. Then there was the weight loss. And the shortness of breath.

When the tiredness became weakness and she couldn't lift her paint brushes, she had decided she'd better get a check-up. Michela Merritt had never been one to avoid a challenge. In her brain, she knew the cancer had returned, she just had hoped she was wrong. That had been a few months ago.

Bill Harper stared silently at Mich. He'd treated her first bout with breast cancer, very unusual at such a young age. Only about four percent of breast cancers occur before the age of 40. Yet breast cancer continues as the leading cause of death in women younger than 40. Her OB/Gyn had picked up on the lumps when Mich went in for her annual check-up; Mich had hoped the hardness in her breasts was from a pregnancy. Boy was she wrong!

The cancer was advanced just too much for them to do anything less than radical mastectomies. Doc remembered Mich's stoicism at the time – and what a selfish pig Larry had been. While Michela cracked jokes and tried to make everyone around her feel comfortable, Larry had refused to accompany her to the hospital or Doc's office for consultations. He'd spent a lot of time drunk or in bed with someone else. Mich had made excuses for him, but Harper could only imagine the hurt she felt. Of course, as soon as her fame as a landscape artist started to take off, not long after the surgery, Larry became a doting husband once again.

"Doc? Are you there?"

"Sorry, Mich, I was just reviewing your case in my mind." Wearily the doctor got up and walked around his desk; he felt every one of his 62 years at that point. "It's not that easy this time, Mich."

"'Easy!' You think it was easy last time? Believe me, that was no walk in the park. The only good part was that for the first time in my life people were interested in my chest!" Michela giggled. "You may recall I wasn't exactly Dolly Parton, more like Peter Pan! After the reconstructive surgery the first thing everyone did was look at my chest to see the difference. It was hysterical..." she slowed to silence when she looked into the steady blue eyes.

"How bad is it, Doc?"

"It's bad, Mich. If we can't get it stopped, it will spread to your brain. You could be dead within a year."

Chapter 4

After leaving Doc's office, Michela sat a long time in her Jeep. The garage was dim, cool, and isolated. She was alone in her leather-and-dials world. She loved the smell of dried paint that always lingered in her car. It was a good place to contemplate her nonexistent future. At least Doc had agreed not to tell anyone for the time being, not that he could without her permission anyway.

Forty minutes later she carefully backed Tank from between two minivans and headed north on I-25. "Your timing is perfect, old girl; you missed the rush going in and now going out," she said to the aged vehicle.

Twenty minutes later she parked outside a warehouse not too far from the old Stapleton airport. The sign above the door said "Golden Lights".

Michela entered, her self-assured pace carrying her right past the reception desk. "May I help you?" a cute, blonde teenager asked from the desk.

Mich smiled back and said, "No, thanks" as she sailed on down the hall.

The receptionist jumped to her feet and nearly jogged after her. "Excuse me, but you can't go back there without an appointment." She grabbed Michela's elbow to try and slow her progress.

Michela halted and slowly turned toward the teenager. She pointedly looked at the hand on her arm and then looked stonily at the blonde child as the red-painted talons dropped from her arm.

"Excuse me, but I can. You see, I own this place." She turned on her heel and headed farther down the hall. The receptionist, jaw hanging, watched her briefly before returning to her desk and the ringing phones.

Heads turned as Mich made her way down the hall. Some old-timers came over to hug her, newcomers watched in mystification. Who is she? written on their faces. Mich noticed a lot more female employees than there had been in the past, but then it had been two years since she'd been here. Two years? Where had the time gone?

Larry's door was closed. Michela smiled to herself and took a deep breath as she firmly grasped the knob and pushed the heavy wooden door open.

"Hi, Honey, I'm home," she cheerily called into the office. Larry was seated at his desk. A buxom redhead was seated on a chair pulled cozily up to his. Her skirt was inched up her thighs and a steno pad was in her hand. *Who are they trying to kid*? Michela wondered as she glanced at Larry with one eyebrow raised. Fortunately for him, his hands were resting on the arms of his chair when Michela entered. *He still makes my heart flutter; he's so damn good looking; same rugged face and square jaw, same toned shoulders as when I first saw him on campus. And not a touch of grey in his professionally-styled hair. With those looks he should have been a politician.*

"What? No kiss for the little woman?" she said into the stunned silence. The redhead bounced up and came around the side, glancing from husband to wife in obvious confusion.

Larry rose and languidly approached Michela, totally unfazed by her sudden appearance in his office. He gave her a peck on the cheek at the same time he pinched her elbow to steer her toward a chair out of reach of the redhead. "Mich, you're out early."

"Apparently not early enough," she said sweetly as she pulled her arm from his grasp, seating herself, dropping her bag on the floor and nodding toward the lingering redhead.

"That will be all, Tina," Larry said over his shoulder. Tina scuttled passed the two of them and out the door.

Larry returned to his seat behind his mahogany desk. "To what do I owe this pleasure, Mich? You haven't been down here in a while." Mich noticed his sandy brown hair was tousled, as though he, or someone, had been running a hand through it. Larry was usually so meticulous about his looks.

"Nothing special. I finished early with Doc and thought since I haven't been down here maybe I should check up on my investment; see what changes have been made." She paused, waiting for him to ask about her doctor's appointment.

"Great. I'll get someone to show you around." Larry reached for the phone.

"I was really hoping you could find the time, Larry. We see so little of each other anymore. You're always in meetings... or something."

Larry looked hard at Michela. Did he detect an emphasis on the word "something"? He'd tried to be a little more discreet about his affairs since she'd wanted to "discuss" the last one; normally she ignored them. It wasn't his fault she'd had cancer and was only half a woman now; at least she understood that a man has needs. They'd had long conversations about his needs and she'd agreed to him having one-night stands, as long as that was all they were. And that was all they had been, until recently.

"No problem. Let me just get my appointment held at the front desk." He punched in a four-digit extension and asked Gail – Mich assumed that was the receptionist's name – to tell his ten o'clock that he'd been detained.

Coming back around the desk he motioned toward the door, "Shall we?" Mich preceded Larry out the door.

Side by side, not touching at any point, Larry escorted Michela through the administration section, introducing her to the newcomers as they went. Mich couldn't understand the shocked looks on everyone's faces until the boy in the mail room blurted out "I thought you were dead!" Mich was caught up short, then she laughed and patted his shoulder, "No, not yet, Matt, not yet." She gave Larry a quizzical look.

Larry, always concerned with appearances, put his arm around Michela's shoulder and pulled her close. "It was close there for a while, but Mich's doing much better now." Mich realized he believed it; he hadn't even noticed her recent major weight loss.

They stopped for a few minutes so Mich could chat with the company's president and her father's best friend, Grant Hailey. Having known Michela all her life, he scrutinized her closely. "Are you feeling okay, Mich, you look a bit peaked. Have you lost more weight?" Mich laughed and patted his hand, "Just getting ready for bathing suit season, Grant, nothing to worry about." She glanced at Larry for his reaction to Grant's words; nothing.

"Mich wanted a quick tour since she hasn't been here in a while,"

Larry explained as he steered her away from Hailey's office and toward the factory floor. This had always been Mich's favorite part. After her father died, Doc had let her come here whenever she wanted, to learn about the company she now owned. She'd worked in all phases of the business, but the design area had been her favorite. Even as a youngster her artistic talent had begun to blossom. It wasn't until college, though, that she nurtured it.

The main warehouse floor was divided into five sections. On the right were offices and art tables for the three designers. Here they drew up sketches of new commercial designs or custom designs for lighting fixtures ordered by clients. The next area made models of the designs, sometimes out of metal, sometimes out of wood. They used inexpensive copper or gold plating to simulate the finished product, so they had something to show potential clients.

Farther into the large expanse of floor space, the actual production occurred. Because they were a specialty lighting company, they never made too many of any one design; they did not want to get the reputation of mass-producing their work. Each light, whether a table lamp, wall sconce, floor lamp, or chandelier, was hand –hammered and molded by hand. Then 18k gold or copper or silver was melted and shaped to create the intricate designs that overlaid the light's basic shape. After each lamp was created, it went to the assembly area where the final cleaning and appropriate wiring and electrical fixtures were attached before the lamp was packaged for shipping. The company had grown so much since Mich's dad's day, they now had 20 full time craftsmen creating the lights, and just as many doing the final assembly. Mich knew Grant had worked hard to hire talented Mexican natives to help promote their work and to better the company.

The tour ended back at the hall leading to the front desk. "I wish I could take you to lunch, Mich, but I already have a lunch scheduled." He glanced pointedly at his watch.

"Not a problem, Larry, I have some errands to run anyway. I'll see you later." Without so much as a pat or a kiss goodbye, Michela watched Larry scuttle back toward the rear of the building. *Must be going out to lunch*, she thought, knowing that the employees parked behind the building. Reaching the reception area she waved to the receptionist as she turned back in the direction of Larry's office, "I left my purse in Larry's office, be right back." A few minutes later she returned to the empty reception area, wondering what had happened to Larry's ten o'clock appointment. She headed out to her car, no longer trying to hide her disappointment. "Well, Tank, some things never change. He didn't even ask me how the doctor's visit went." She put the big car in gear and headed home.

Chapter 5

February, present year

The initial discussion with Doc had been a little over three months ago. The two months of heavier chemo hadn't worked. Radiation had slowed it briefly, and then it came back with a vengeance. The cancer kept growing and spreading. Michela kept losing weight and hair. For a while she got better, but that didn't last long. Off and on she had regained enough strength to paint, her one comfort. The worst of it was Larry's reaction, his absences, as though by ignoring "it" and her he could believe it wasn't happening. But she had reassured him, as always.

She had saved her strength all week so she could make the sixty mile drive to Colorado Springs today. It was something she had to do, just in case.

"So, Ms. Merritt, what can I do for you?"

Michela studied the tall, gangly attorney with an artist's eye; good bones, curly brown hair, penetrating grey eyes, strong hands. He looked like he probably ran for fun, not that she had ever understood anyone getting sweaty for fun...unless it was sex and it had been a long time since she'd had that experience. Michela extended her hand and shook that of the young lawyer before her. She had gotten Gordon Mansfield's name as a recommendation from her lawyer neighbor; Chip had thought she needed the name for a friend who was moving to Colorado Springs.

"I'd like you to draft a will for me, Mr. Mansfield."

"Please, call me Gordon. A will is an excellent idea and fairly simple to draft unless you're making lots of strange bequests or have a complicated estate, especially if its value is over one million dollars." He smiled comfortably at the young woman seated across from him; nice smile, about his own age, blonde, but too thin for his liking; he preferred women with some meat on their bones and a few more curves. This lady was all angles, like an early Picasso.

"No, Gordon, nothing strange. I want to leave everything to one person except for one thing."

"Well, that's fairly easy to do." Glancing at her left hand he said, "Your husband, I assume?"

"Quite the contrary, Gordon. I want no more to go to my husband than the law insists." Michela smiled sweetly at the lawyer's confusion.

"Nothing? That's a bit...unusual, Mrs. Merritt."

Michela smiled her most winsome smile. "Does that mean it's more complicated? Or that it can't be done?"

"Well, yes. Complicated that is. Colorado recognizes the rights of a surviving spouse. That means everything you own jointly automatically goes to your spouse. May I ask why you're doing this?"

"You may ask," Michela replied with a smile as she stared silently at the attorney.

Gordon Mansfield squirmed under her scrutiny. He had never met anyone quite like this lady. So self-assured. She looked as fragile as a porcelain doll, but apparently there was a steel rod supporting that delicate exterior.

"Okay, how about if we start with you telling me the extent of the estate you are planning on leaving?"

"It's about eight million dollars' worth of paintings. My husband will get the house and its furnishings because they're in both our names. I'd like to eliminate him from our stock holdings, too, but I haven't figured out a way to do it. Any ideas?" she again flirted with the young man.

Mansfield was mystified by the matter-of-fact way the lady was talking about screwing her husband out of a fortune.

"Excuse me, Mrs. Merritt, it appears you are not overly fond of your husband. Why don't you just divorce him?"

"Well, Gordon, you see, I don't have the time. The doctors tell me I have less than a year to live. I don't agree with them, of course, but if they're right, there's no time for a divorce and...I don't want to die alone." The woman's eyes misted and she barely whispered the last words, but then she collected herself and continued in her former strong voice, "Besides, with a divorce, he may get half of *everything*. I want to be sure he gets as little as possible. If I'm right and the doctors are wrong, then I can rethink this whole thing next year. On the other hand, my husband is planning to kill me if I don't 'go quietly into that dark night' and soon. It's all really quite a crap shoot." She smiled engagingly at the man across the desk from her.

The young attorney marveled again at her composure. And then it hit him: Merritt, paintings.

"You're Michela Merritt, the artist? Sorry to be so slow putting it all together. I saw your exhibit at the Denver Art Museum last year. You really set the castle on its ear!"

"Thank you.... So. Can you help me?"

Gordon had been jotting notes during their conversation. "Let me make sure I understand you. Basically, you want to leave as little as possible to your husband in the event of your untimely death. Is that it?"

"Unlikely and untimely. Yes, that's it."

"Can we go back to the part where your husband wants to kill you? I'm confused. Have you gone to the police?"

"Now, Gordon, that is not part of this discussion. Let's just deal with the will, please." Michela confidently looked over Gordon Mansfield's shoulder and out the window. Mansfield paid extra for the view of snow-covered Pikes Peak; it was the one luxury in the office. The rest of the space was pure young-attorney-on-the-rise, matching cherry furniture and bookshelves that looked like he'd probably refinished them himself. Michela felt very comfortable in the office and with the man across from her.

Gordon studied her silently for several seconds and then gave up. He could tell she would not discuss anything she did not want to. "Who do you want to inherit?"

"My best friend, Cassie Kirkland, gets all my paintings; she'll know what to do with them. Here's her address, e-mail address, and phone number." Michela opened her obviously expensive brown leather shoulder bag and withdrew an index card. A name, address, e-mail, and phone number were neatly typed on it, obviously computer-generated.

"Cassandra Kirkland. It'll take me a couple days to work this out. Shall I call you when it's ready?"

"No, I'll call you early next week. And there's something else, that 'one thing' I mentioned. I own a company in Denver, Golden Lights. When I'm gone, I want it sold and the proceeds split among the employees of record as of the first day of the month in which I die. And I want it divided proportionally based on length of employment; someone who has worked there twenty years should get considerably more than someone who has worked there only twenty days, don't you agree?" She smiled her engaging smile at the perplexed look on the lawyers face. "However, the employees get first refusal on whether they want to buy the company and keep it open, or sell it and possibly be unemployed."

"That's very generous of you. Obviously you have given this a lot of thought, Mrs. Merritt. It will take me a while to get it all in order and written up. Perhaps call me in two weeks."

"Thank you, Gordon. Of course, time is of the essence. I'm sure I can count on your discretion; I would hate to read about my medical situation – or marital situation – in the local paper or online. Facebook and Twitter and all those other quasi-social things are not for me."

Gordon bristled at the comment, but maintained his professional demeanor. "Mrs. Merritt, I take attorney-client confidences very seriously."

Michela reached across the glass-topped desk and gently patted his hand. Her hand was like ice. "I knew I could count on you, Gordon. There's one other thing."

Gordon raised an eyebrow as he looked into her deep blue eyes, a hint of humor lurked in their depths.

Again she reached into her voluminous purse. This time she pulled out two small packages... padded envelopes like people use to mail photos.

"I am sure that my 'untimely' death will rate a mention somewhere. After all, there aren't that many world-renowned artists in Denver." Her self-mocking tone amazed Gordon. It was as though she didn't believe she was worth all the acclaim.

"Two months after you hear of my death, please mail this package," she said as she handed him the smaller of the two. "It's already addressed and here's cash to cover the postage. I would have gone ahead and put the stamps on, but we never know when the rates will go up, do we?"

Accepting the package, Gordon said, "No, we don't." The package was addressed to the same name as on the card he'd been given: Cassie Kirkland in Lexington, Virginia. "I've never heard of Lexington, Virginia," was all he could think to say.

"Nobody has unless you've been there. Once you've been there, you never want to leave, according to Cassie, who was born there. She calls it heaven on earth; but the streets are so narrow you have to hold your breath when two SUVs are passing. And it can take half an hour to buy a loaf of bread because the checker has to know how you're doing, how your parents are, she probably lives next door to them, and what your plans are for the weekend. I'm a big-city girl myself; give me purgatory and anonymity any time." Michela laughed a deep throaty laugh, not at all in keeping with her delicate appearance. The lawyer was completely entranced.

She handed him the second package. He held it up with a quizzical look on his face. It was not addressed. He looked questioningly at the woman before him.

"Oh, that's for you, but you don't get to open it until six months after my death. It's all explained inside," she said with her infectious giggle. "But don't tell anyone about it; it's our little secret."

Gordon Mansfield was completely confused. "As long as it isn't anything illegal, Mrs. Merritt."

"Oh, no! I promise, there's nothing illegal in there. Just some papers."

"Well, then, Mrs. Merritt, I guess I'll hear from you in two weeks."

"Thank you, Gordon. Oh, one more little thing. Sorry, I feel like that TV detective Columbo, the way he kept saying 'one more thing'."

Gordon smiled. "Anything I can do."

"If anyone should ask you about our business dealings after I'm gone, dead that is, you have my permission to discuss any aspect of our conversation, except of course those packages, but not before." With that she rose to her almost six foot height and regally walked out, leaving the attorney speechless and bewildered. Now what the hell did she mean by that?

Chapter 6

May, Present day

Sunday evening. Cassie was glad the weekend was over. End-of-the school-year at a public library was always a busy time, but this year was especially so for some as-yet-undefined reason. After only four years on staff she felt like an old-timer...actually she was the youngest librarian they had. The other two librarians felt like they had been there since before General Lee had joined W&L as president in 1865, and the staff members were like Wanda, widowed or spinster women, and one retired professor with plenty of time on their hands. Just one week until graduation and then things would slow down a bit over the summer...once the five book trucks full of last minute returns were processed and shelved. The library was open year round, but the summer was only busy for getting beach books and audio books and for the tourists to use the computer.

Children came in for story time and the summer reading program, but rarely to linger among the stacks as Cassie had as a child. Right now her ordinary 9-to-5 job looked very attractive, though. *Too bad,* Cassie thought, *they don't know what their missing; that special moment when you find a book that will be just right for your next read; can't do that with a Kindle but maybe the book really is a thing of the past, at least for the younger generations.*

She took another sip of her white wine and opened the refrigerator, Rosie joined her at the open door. Nothing appealed tonight. *Maybe I'll just scramble some eggs* she thought as she wandered barefoot back to her mini-office, Rosie padding softly at her heels. She'd been so busy at the library yesterday – checking in last minute returns, compiling late notices for mailing, and checking on lost books – she'd been too pooped recently to check her personal e-mail and had forgotten her cell phone all day today. *You party animal,* she thought to herself. *A small-town library job wears you out so much you were in bed by 8:30 on a Saturday night. What a wimp!* She glanced at her reflection in the mirror over the parlor fireplace on her way to the office. *A far cry from your days in Chicago,* she said to the bright-eyed reflection she saw there. *Thank God.*

Continuing her monologue, *Okay, Cass, check e-mail, check for phone messages, then a long hot soak in the tub, some eggs, and a good night's sleep. Maybe tonight you can set a new record for early to bed.*

She flipped on her Dell desktop PC with her right hand as she hit the overhead light switch with her left. *You're tiny but you're mine*, she smiled at her euphemistically-named office. It was really a converted sun porch, with white wicker furniture and her PC and files. The PC sat on a small knee-hole wicker dressing table with the HP all-in-one printer/copier/scanner and a phone on a small two-shelf bathroom cupboard next to it. The dressing table top had just enough room for the keyboard and mouse, the monitor set at an angle on top of a small two-shelf bookshelf. She used a two-drawer file cabinet to store all her supplies, pencils, scrap paper, and her bills. *Maybe next time I'll get a tablet computer*, she mused as she surveyed the small space. Across the room were the remnants of the sun porch furniture: two white wicker chairs and a wicker sofa with a wicker glass-topped coffee table in front of them. The room was surrounded on three sides by glass that let in light and the neighbor's stares.

She clicked on the e-mail icon and waited while her high-speed connection kicked in. Her in-box showed four new messages, nothing critical. Cassie smiled to herself, glad she had decided to check messages, but wondering why she hadn't heard from Mich in a while. Mich was just what she needed right now, a breath of fresh Colorado air to blow the cobwebs away.

Cassie and Michela had met their first week as freshmen at Vanderbilt University in Nashville, twelve years before. For reasons unknown to either of them they hit it off and had been best friends ever since. "I guess it's true that opposites attract," Cassie said to the screen as she clicked off and reached for her cell phone, charging on the windowsill. Her thoughts continued on Mich.

Michela was the effervescent, talented one. She was wonderful at everything she tried, as long as it didn't involve studying. She wrote for the school paper, starred in school plays, and played piano by ear. And then there were her paintings. When she discovered landscape art her junior year, everything else went by the wayside. Of course she had a natural talent for that, too.

Cassie, on the other hand, was more quiet and studious. She loved learning for the excitement of it. She always had her nose in a book – *no wonder you ended up a librarian* she muttered to herself as the Missed Call message displayed.

She'd been worried about Mich lately, ever since the second cancer prognosis over six months ago. She'd flown to Denver to be with her friend right after Doc had delivered the news. Mich was full of her usual spunk and stubbornness, determined she'd beat it this time just like she had before. Cassie had talked to Doc, though, and he wasn't as positive this one could be beaten; the cancer just kept spreading. Mich just wouldn't accept that she couldn't do what she wanted. "Spoiled brat," Cassie said to the phone as Mich's name and number displayed on the screen. She punched in the code to retrieve her voice mails and listened to Mich's brief cry for help from earlier this morning. Thoughts of a long bath were no longer in Cassie's head.

"Cass, can you come out Wednesday? Larry's leaving town early Wednesday and I really need to talk to you. Please come. Don't call me back, Larry checks my Recent Calls list when I'm not around and he reads my e-mails; I don't want him to know you're coming. If you're not here by supper time Wednesday, I'll know you can't make it. Please try, it's important."

What is that sleaze you're married to up to now? Cassie muttered to the inanimate phone shaking in her hand. Rosie's head rose off her paws as she stared with concern at the angry tone in Cassie's voice.

Cassie punched the speed-dial for Michela. Then she hung up. Michela's message sounded more panicked than she'd ever heard her, and Mich could be the queen of panic, a veritable drama diva.

Cassie was accustomed to her best friend's melodramatic moods. And the phone calls and e-mails over the years had run the gamut. But there had never been anything like this, at least not since her current illness hit. All her correspondence was full of enthusiasm and determination to beat "the big C", as she referred to it.

Mich had regaled Cassie with stories from the hospital and its staff, especially the lab tech she referred to as Dracula. "Maybe I'll write a book about all this when it's over," she had written once. "But who would believe it?"

Lately, though, her e-mails were less frequent, down to one every couple weeks instead of the almost daily ones she used to send. Maybe something really was going on, maybe "the sleaze", as Cassie thought of her best friend's husband, was up to his old tricks –pun intended – or maybe he'd thought up a new way to make Mich's life miserable.

Staring at the screen she vowed, "Yeah, Mich, I'll be there. I don't know what Ben will say, but I'll work it out. See you Wednesday." Cassie returned to her computer and started researching flights to Denver from either Roanoke or Washington D.C.

Chapter 7

As it turned out, Benjamin, the library's director, was very understanding. Since all the late notices were done and things would slack off a bit once school was out, he agreed to Cassie's request to take some of her vacation time earlier than she'd planned. Cassie assured him this wasn't some ploy to get out of inventory. "I promise I'll be back in just a few days, Ben. It's just something I have to do."

"Go ahead, Cassie, I'm kidding. I know I can always count on you. I hope your friend is okay."

Even with Ben's blessing it took Cassie all of Monday and Tuesday to get ready. She arranged for grey-haired Maggie to take over her Circulation and periodical duties; Maggie was her usual grumbling self, but she agreed; *good thing she loves being a martyr.* Betsy said she'd get volunteers to do shelving and shelf-reading and she'd take care of any last minute fines and late notices. Roger, the retired history professor, offered to handle any interlibrary loan requests that came up.

In between all these library arrangements she made her plane reservations. Since the only airline with semi-convenient direct flights to Denver was United, it meant she'd drive to Dulles three and a half hours away to get her flight. She wished there had been a good connection out of Roanoke, only an hour away, but nothing out of Roanoke had good connections into Denver. "Just another joy of rural life," she mumbled to Kayak as she rechecked her flight schedule.

Dulles added another item to her to-do list – make hotel reservations – and shortened her prep time. She needed to go to D.C. Tuesday night for her morning flight to Denver; it was a lot easier than trying to make the drive before sunup Wednesday morning.

It wasn't pretty, but she got it all done. Tuesday afternoon she checked items off her lengthy to-do list: the Fitzgeralds next door agreed to get her mail and newspaper, the Wallaces will keep Rosie out at their farm,

Rosie loved running around out there; the frig is empty of perishables, the thermostat is set to 65 (so mildew doesn't start in the rising May heat), and the suitcase is packed, just shirts, jeans, and slacks. *Got to love Denver* she rejoiced.

Early Wednesday morning she was on board and on her way. The flight to Denver took only a little longer than her drive to her Dulles hotel, and it was just the way she liked them: uneventful. She hadn't slept well at the Marriott Courtyard the night before, too worried about Michela, so she tried to nap on the plane. The early, midweek flight was only half full and she was able to grab an empty row and one of the four blankets on the plane and stretch out. She hadn't actually slept much, but she felt more rested.

She liked everything about Denver except the airport's location. The other times she'd been to DIA she'd been really impressed with its efficiency. She and Mich tried to get together at least once a year. One year it had been a week in Aspen just eating, sleeping, shopping, and enjoying the winter; no skiing, too energetic for either of them, they were both better ski-bunnies than skiers. But no matter how efficient things were at the airport, it was still going to be over an hour's drive to Mich's.

Forty minutes after landing she had her bags and was in her rental car and on her way. At least it's not rush hour, she thought. When they had done their Aspen trip a few years before, Mich had suggested that Cassie schedule her flight "to avoid the misnomer. 'Rush' hour it isn't. You'll just sit on I-25 if you get here before 10 a.m." Cassie had remembered and made this trip's arrangements accordingly. It was 10:45 when she pulled out of the Hertz lot.

Even the beauty of her surroundings couldn't get her mind off her friend and the great mystery. *What could be so bad? What could be worse than the cancer she is already fighting? Mich should be used to the misery Larry could cause by now. If she's not going to divorce him, then I'm not going to argue about it anymore,* she vowed as she turned off I-25 onto southbound E-470, paralleling the foothills of the Rockies, then C-470 heading west.

It was an easy drive, all super-highway until the last few miles up to

Mich's front door, no traffic and very few stoplights. Cassie hadn't noticed; her driving was on autopilot as she thought about her friend.

She pulled into the driveway at the Ken Caryl Ranch subdivision in time for an early lunch. Leaving her bag in the car, she hustled up the slate walkway to the high front entrance. Mich's artistic talent showed in the house's wood and stone façade; it looked like a piece of the mountain had broken away and somebody had attached a hanging porch light and front door to it.

Cassie rang the bell. No answer. She tried the knob. The door was unlocked so she went in. The soaring entrance was nothing compared to the sweeping vista in front of Cassie. Even though she knew the whole back of the house was glass and opened onto a view of Colorado's red rocks, she had forgotten how breathtaking it was.

"Mich?" Cassie called to the stillness. The distant red rocks outside the window and the furniture inside maintained their silence. *It's not like Mich to leave the door unlocked; it's okay for me in Lexington, but not here in the big city.* "Mich?" she called again, almost afraid to raise her voice.

She thought she heard a noise upstairs. Cassie quickly climbed the thickly carpeted curved staircase to the second floor. Stopping at the top of the stairs she surveyed the long hall ahead of her, guest bedrooms on each side, master bedroom at the end of the hall. Cassie listened intently for any sounds, wondering if she should have found a weapon of some kind to take upstairs with her. No sounds assailed her ears. It was eerily quiet. If Mich wasn't here, why was the front door unlocked?

She heard a faint rustling as she approached the master bedroom. Not knowing what to expect, Cassie hesitantly approached the open French door leading into the room. She held her breath, pushed the door a bit wider and walked in. She quickly spied the king-size bed, it was hard to miss, and the nightstand covered with prescription bottles, but her eyes were drawn immediately to the body.

There was Mich, long skinny legs splayed on the floor, black lace

Karin Rose O'Callaghan
bikini underpants, a teal sweater and... headless.

Chapter 8

Cassie let out her breath in a gale of laughter. Her friend's bald head popped out of the sweater's turtleneck, like a beach ball held under water too long. Surveying the sweaters strewn across the bed Cassie asked, "What are you doing, Mich; it's May for crying out loud!"

"Cassie! You're here!" Mich used the bed to help herself up and loped to her friend, pulling the sweater down to her too-narrow hips.

Hugging her ebullient friend, Cassie replied, "I rang the bell. Why didn't you answer? I didn't know what to expect after that phone message."

"I must have been in the closet," Mich said as she dragged Cassie across the room to the cavernous space lined with blouses, slacks, and shoes. Very few dresses 'cause Mich had always complained they weren't made for long-waisted girls like herself.

"Well, I can see if you were here in the great-beyond you call a closet you might not have heard me."

"I'm so glad you're here...you can help me decide. Blonde, brunette, or red head?" she questioned as she pointed to a shelf in the closet with six wig heads, modeling six different shades and styles of hairdos.

"Mich, you didn't leave me that panic-stricken message because you couldn't decide on a wig. What's the big problem?"

"Oh, that. Let's not talk about it now. I'm in too good a mood to spoil it. I'm so glad you're here! Have you had lunch? How 'bout a sandwich and glass of wine and we'll chat. You get wine, I don't, but I can live vicariously watching you drink it."

Cassie knew it would do no good to nag her stubborn friend; Mich wouldn't say anything until she was good and ready. *But what's with the high spirits after that panicked phone call?*

Cassie chuckled, "A sandwich sounds great. You might want to put on some pants, too." Pointing at the wigs, "Don't feel you have to dress up for me; I've seen your perfect pate before, remember? I kind of like the bristly look you've got going there, kind of makes you look like a tall chia pet."

Mich hugged her friend again. "Oh, good. Those wigs get hot and itchy. Once the radiation was over I thought my hair would come back like it did last time, but it's taking longer this time." She grabbed a pair of jeans and sat on the bed to pull them on.

Cassie surveyed her former roommate; she hadn't changed all that much since their trip to Malta the preceding fall, just before Mich's latest diagnosis and their last time together. A little thinner and bald, of course, but these were to be expected with the treatments she'd received. Mich had been through it all the first time five years ago. Cassie knew all about the trial treatments she had gone through this time and everything else because they e-mailed or talked every week; at least they had until the last month. She hadn't heard from her friend in almost a month until the mysterious message that had put her on a plane that morning.

Walking downstairs to the kitchen, Cassie broached the concern uppermost in her mind. "So where's Larry off to this week?" She tried to hide the disgust from her voice. Cassie loathed her best friend's husband for the way he treated Mich and for how he hit on *her* every time they were together. For Mich's sake she tried to be civil about him.

"I don't know and I don't care. I'm just glad he's gone for a while."

Cassie's eyebrows shot up in disbelief. *Could Mich finally be coming to her senses?*

"Of course, I'll be glad when he gets home, too, but I think it's good for a marriage if the husband and wife spend some time apart." *Nope. Guess not* Cassie thought to herself as they entered the sunny kitchen.

"What'll it be, Cass? I've got cold cuts, egg salad, or PB &J. I'll even fix a grilled cheese if you prefer."

"Let's not mess with heating the stove. I'll just have egg salad. What can I do?"

"You pour the wine. Glasses are over there." Mich pointed half a mile away to a glass-fronted cabinet. "Wine's in the wine frig in the butler's pantry; pick anything you want; I'll have just a taste of yours."

"Corkscrew?" Mich shouted from the pantry.

"Second drawer on the left."

Cassie returned with the wine and corkscrew. Cassie poured her Pinot Grigio and they settled in on the barstools at the green granite island. Cassie took a bite of her egg salad on pumpernickel and mumbled around the mouthful, "What are we going to do about dinner?" It was a running joke between them that they always talked about the next meal while eating an earlier one. They both broke into fits of laughter that didn't subside for the whole afternoon except when Mich got serious for a few minutes asking about Cassie's well-being.

"Now, Cassie, tell me truly. How are you doing? You've really been through the ringer. First the divorce and then your folks dying. You've never talked about any of it, not even on our girls' trips. Isn't there something I can do to help? That's what friends are for." Mich stared wide-eyed and teary at the best friend she had ever had. When they were together they looked like Mutt and Jeff, one tall, the other shorter. Mich had straight long brown hair when she had hair, Cassie had short blonde ringlets. Mich blue-eyed, Cassie's brown, like a fawn, or "a cow" as she referred to them.

Cassie looked back at her friend and smiled, trying to decide how much to tell without sounding like a guest on the Dr. Phil show. She had never talked about her "troubles" as she referred to them, she figured Mich had enough on her plate without adding Cassie's issues; now she tried to decide how much to burden her cancer-ridden friend. She took a sip of her wine.

"Hey, I'm fine. I think I'm finally over Kevin. The short version is he was a mistake from the start, I knew it. It was all my fault. I fell for Kevin like a ton of bricks. Big. Strong. All that Marine Corps marketing about honor and integrity. He *was* amazing. And smart. Seemed so much more mature than any of the guys I'd been dating. He'd been working at WGN five years already when I got there; had moved up to senior editor in next to no time. He could work magic with the AVID.

"We started dating about a month after I got there. He drank. A lot. But I just thought it was his way of relaxing after a long day." Cassie looked at Mich and grinned, "The sex was good, too, really good."

Mich grinned back, "It's okay, Cass, I have a vague recollection of good sex. So why the divorce? He seems perfect to me!"

"You remember we married within a year of meeting; you were so surprised! But living together is a whole different experience than dating. Things really changed once we settled into our place back in Chicago. Turns out it was just lust on both our parts. I had had some misgivings before the wedding, wasn't sure I was "in love" with him, but not sure enough to call everything off and embarrass my parents. I just sucked it up and went ahead with the wedding."

"Maybe he was just another of your foundlings," Mich said with a chortle, "like that mourning dove you found on the sidewalk and kept in our room. I remember you sitting up all night, feeding it with an eye dropper. You were desolated when it died that second morning."

Cassie grinned sheepishly, "That was me, the keeper of lost souls, champion of the underdog. I really tried with Kevin, Mich, I really did. I read up on PTSD and wondered if that was his problem – quick to anger, drinking, bad dreams, the whole bit. I went to counseling. Went to Al-Anon. I nagged. I praised. I shouted. I cajoled." She stopped and grinned. "I remember my counselor telling me 'praising a thirty year old for controlling his drinking made as much sense as praising a teenager for giving up his pacifier.' He *should* control his drinking, it's not something praiseworthy." Cassie took another sip of her wine. "So I drank more than usual. Took anti-depressants and Ambien. Everything. I had about decided PTSD is contagious; too bad the VA doesn't pay for help to spouses of PTSD victims." Cassie tried to grin. "But whenever I tried talking to him about his drinking or his anger it threw him into a rage. So I just tip-toed around him."

Mich was horrified, "Did he hit you?"

Cassie was taken aback by the question and quick to reply, "No, no, never. Physical abuse wasn't his style; at least only one time. But there are all kinds of abuse. Physical abuse is just the most obvious and the one people talk about the most. His style was more emotional and psychological; passive aggressive type stuff. I remember one time we were taking a bunch of stuff to Goodwill and he asked me which car we should take. I told him I didn't care; it was up to him, that everything would fit in either car. So he loaded *his* car with everything and as we drove out he started complaining about how stuffed the trunk was and 'I knew we should have taken your car.' Like it was my decision on the car selection. He always made me feel so worthless, like everything I did was wrong or designed to make him unhappy. He even told me once that marrying me was the biggest mistake he had ever made."

"What a jerk! I hope you told him off?!"

"Oh, no, that was the worst part. The rule for me was, don't upset him. His rages were of earthquake proportions and almost always worse when he drank. I never did anything that I knew would make him mad, and the worst thing I could do was disagree with him. Everybody kept telling me what a great guy he was, how lucky I was. If they only knew! He was a functioning alcoholic, only drank at home, never at work. Everybody at work loved him, Mister Personality, he could charm your socks off, and in many cases other pieces of apparel." Cassie sounded defeated.

Mich grabbed Cassie's hand next to her on the sofa, where they had moved when Cassie had poured her second glass of wine. "I'm sorry, Cass, you never said anything. Why didn't you tell me? I would have been there for you, shot him or something." Cassie grinned back.

"I know you would have, Mich. Well, maybe not shot him, but if I had known that was a possibility..." They both giggled again and Cassie's mood lightened.

"I just couldn't add to your troubles, you had enough to deal with – you were just getting over your first bout with cancer and then the loss of the baby. No way I was going to involve you. And somehow it seemed like I was being disloyal, to my marriage if not to Kevin. I never talked to anybody, except my therapist. She helped, but not enough I guess.

Besides, I thought I was strong, I could either deal with it or get him to stop drinking."

"I guess neither of those plans worked?" Mich asked with tears in her eyes.

Cassie noticed the tears. "Hey, Mich, it's okay. I'm over him, the scars are healing. I'm even considering getting a tattoo – I survived the big K – to go with your 'I survived the Big C' one." Cassie gripped Mich's hand harder as small smiles returned to both their faces.

"That's us. The great survivors. So what was the last straw? Why divorce after three years?"

"I just got tired of living in fear, walking on eggshells. Wondering when the next explosion would occur. Would the next time be worse? Was physical harm in him?"

Mich interrupted, "Well, now I'm mad. You never told me, never even let on that there were any problems. I'm so surprised, shocked, and furious! I thought between the two of us I was the actress, but maybe you should get an Oscar." Mich grinned widely at her best friend. "You dope!"

Cassie grinned back.

"I was okay for a while, you can get used to anything. I was young and naive. I finally just got tired of walking on eggshells. I never knew what was going to set him off; I was a nervous wreck. There was no place I could find peace. When I was at work I worried about what would happen at home; at home I tried really hard not to aggravate him. I kept thinking if I did everything I could to please him, maybe he wouldn't drink so much and we'd be happy. I tried talking to him, but I sure couldn't talk to him when he was drinking, and by morning he'd sobered up and never believed he'd done the things I said he'd done. He had an amazingly high tolerance for booze, too!" Cassie's eyes grew wide at the memory. "And he'd drink anything, whatever we had in the house; he could drink a whole bottle of wine or booze in an evening, 12 beers, it didn't matter. So I stopped suggesting we have friends over because that would require stocking up on booze, and then he'd have the leftovers to drink. I finally woke up to the fact that nothing was going to change. Since he never believed me when I told him about the things he did or said when he was drunk, he saw no need to get help.

"That's what finally decided me, that he was not interested in our marriage, that my feelings meant nothing to him, the alcohol meant more to him than I did. I just started planning. And then one day I called in sick to work, packed up my things and moved out. I had even managed to collect empty boxes to pack stuff in without Kevin getting suspicious."

"How stupid can he be? He sees packing boxes and doesn't ask any questions?"

"Not stupid, just too self-involved to want to take the time with something so common. I told him they were for shipping Christmas presents." Cassie shrugged, "That's it. Nothing else to tell."

"But where did you go? What about work? You both still worked at the same place."

"I had already taken my money out of our savings account, talked to an attorney, and rented an apartment. That's one of the joys of technology – if you don't have a landline for your phone, and you pay all your bills online, you can virtually disappear, especially in a big city. I just walked out and never looked back. Filed for divorce later that afternoon. I bit the bullet and put an end to it before it got any worse, or we had kids. I want kids someday, but I sure didn't want them with him!" All this came out in a rush, words Cassie had held in too long, grateful for the chance to finally talk to someone who cared, and Mich was the best listener in the world.

"What about his ego? I can't imagine a man like that just sitting by and letting you walk out on him."

"I worried about it, too. I really didn't know what he'd do. I just knew I couldn't continue to live under the same roof with him."

"But you worked together. What happened when you went back to work?"

"The day I moved out was a Friday so I figured he had time to calm down a bit."

"Did he try to find you?"

"Over the weekend? I don't know. If he had wanted to spend some time and his money he could have found me. All I know is he didn't find me that weekend. Best sleep I'd had in years!"

"Did he make a scene at work?"

"No, and that surprised me at first. I was prepared to get a restraining order if I had to, but I didn't even see him. We worked on different floors and our paths didn't cross that much in the normal course of the day, so everything was as normal as could be. But by late Monday I found out why. He was telling everyone he'd kicked me out because I was frigid."

"Oh, my God! You didn't have sex with him for three years? Way to go!"

"Oh, we had sex, I was too scared not to; but there was no romance, no love on either side. I just felt dead inside, like a large block of lead had been implanted between my neck and my knees. But I even faked orgasms a few times to try to keep him satisfied; I wasn't really involved in the sex process, and he didn't care. As long as he had sex on a regular basis that was enough for him. He even kept track of how many times a week we had sex and quoted national statistics to me if we were 'below average'".

"You're kidding!"

"Oh, no, he was a piece of work. But I stuck it out, blaming myself, made my plans, and finally got out. As soon as the divorce was final I quit my job and got the hell out of town, as they say."

"And are you happy? Are you convinced you made the right decision?"

"Happy? I don't know. I'm unhappy that my marriage didn't work out, that I failed. I still feel guilty about leaving him with PTSD, but I know for sure the divorce was the right decision." Cassie gave a sardonic grin, lifted her glass in a mock toast, and took a long swallow. Mich looked at her mournfully.

"I'm so sorry, Cass. I had no idea it was that bad. You never told me!"

"Never told anyone, didn't even tell my therapist the full story; it was just too embarrassing. Goodness knows you had enough to deal with, but it sure is wonderful to be able to talk to you now!' Cassie reached over and hugged her friend.

"Phew! That's more than I've talked about my marriage EVER. You certainly opened the floodgates." She paused and looked at her best friend, "I'm really over him. I promise. Life's good. And he taught me some valuable lessons; I sure don't trust my judgment about men. Who needs them anyway? Generally, I just don't trust people as easily as I used to." She grinned and lifted her glass again, this time in a serious toast, "Except for you, my friend. With the folks gone you're the only one I have left, the only one I do trust anymore." Mich grinned back and allowed herself to believe her friend was over the jerk, because she wanted to believe her. "I learned it's a lot easier to forgive than to forget, too. I forgave Kevin a long time ago, but the memories are still with me." Cassie paused and then looked mischievously at her friend.

"And, I learned another very important lesson once I came home from Chicago," Cassie said with a twinkle in her eyes. Mich raised a questioning eyebrow.

"You know how people always say life is so slow in the south, and southern women move so gracefully? We have to move slowly! It's the humidity!! Since I grew up in the south, and Lexington isn't nearly as humid as a lot of places, I never knew what humidity was 'cause I lived in it. Once I lived in Chicago for a while, which is less humid than the South even though it's on the lake, and then returned home, I really felt the humidity. Good grief! You have to move slowly or you break out in a sweat – although in the South we 'glow' – and you can't move without wrinkling your clothes. Believe me, the South isn't for sissies!"

The friends broke into laughter again. Mich hated to end it by bringing up another sore point, but felt she had to get a feel for how Cassie was doing.

"And your folks? I'm sorry I couldn't make the funeral."

"That's okay, you needed to take care of yourself, not worry about me. It wasn't much of a funeral anyway. There wasn't much left of them after the car fire and they had wanted to be cremated anyway, they just cut out the middleman so to speak, so we had a brief memorial service, lots of the other professors and their wives came, then we all went out to the Palms and got roaring drunk. I think Mom and Dad would have enjoyed the party, they were always a couple of party animals." Cassie hesitated and looked at Mich's doubting face, "I'm fine, Mich, really. Now, back to you and the reason for my trip?"

Mich promptly changed the subject again and brought back the hilarity by reminding Cassie of her college nickname, MS, short for Mother Superior because she always did the "right thing", no matter what she had to forego to do it. She'd gotten the nickname when half their dorm was going sledding the first big snowfall of the year and Cassie had stayed behind to study for the next day's Art History exam.

"Boy! Was I dumb!" Cassie said now. "A B would not have been the end of the world!"

"Well, I'm glad you've finally learned that! Here, have some more wine and we can drink to your epiphany!" Mich reached for the bottle in the wine cooler they'd brought to the coffee table. She poured Cassie a half glass, over her objections, and they clinked glasses again. "Dated any ugly guys lately?" Mich asked Cassie with a sly grin.

"They weren't ugly, Mich." Cassie grinned and gently slapped her friend on the thigh. "They just weren't outrageously handsome."

"Outrageously handsome! Some of them were so homely their mothers probably cried at the birth!" Mich rocked with hilarity at her comment.

"Oh, come on, Mich, they weren't that bad."

"I never understood why you went out with them in the first place. You could have had any guy on campus."

"I don't know. They were nice and interesting and they asked me out. Why not? I had my share of the good looking guys and they were okay, too, but most of them were pretty wrapped up in themselves. At least these other guys were more interested in me than in themselves."

"Okay, I get it, you were in your Mother Teresa mode again, watching out for the poor and downtrodden." They had had this conversation multiple times. As much as she loved Mich, Cassie knew she would never understand.

"Yep, maybe that was it. What about your date with the football captain? That wasn't a mistake?" And so it went.

Chapter 9

In the late afternoon Mich went to her room for a nap. Cassie brought in her suitcase and unpacked. Then she explored the house, noting the small changes Mich had made since her last visit; a couple new paintings – Mich's of course – the upholstery in the den had been changed to a forest green leather with bright yellow linen throw pillows. But the atmosphere hadn't changed, still that sense of light and elegance that Mich had in all her art and brought to her life. Cassie sat in the den and admired the view, thanking her lucky stars she still had Mich in her life; despite everything that had happened to her, and continued to happen, Mich was as stable as they came. Just like those rocks out there.

Having finished her inventory of the house, Cassie luxuriated in the deep bubbles of her bathtub and grinned at the thought of their lazy, fun afternoon. They'd relived their week in Malta; caught up on gossip about college friends. And, of course, discussed the pros and cons of various restaurants for their next meal.

At last they'd decided on The Fort for dinner since it was a nice day and they could sit on the terrace, at least until the sun set and the temperature dropped rapidly. Cassie blew bubbles off her hands and could almost taste the elk medallions, one of her favorites.

But nothing had been said about the reason for her trip. Mich was trying too hard to be bright and bubbly...until it was time for her nap. Then the bubble burst and Mich sat there and cussed the illness that sapped her energy. Cassie had always marveled at Mich's repertoire of four-letter words. She must have known a lot of Marines, Cassie chuckled to herself.

They were going to an early dinner so they'd have time for Cassie to have a drink outside. I'll get her to talk over dinner, she vowed as she toweled off.

And she did. In the quiet and relative privacy of The Fort's terrace, with the city of Denver laid at their feet, Mich finally opened up. She had decided on one of the straight blonde wigs and Cassie had to fight the urge to giggle each time she looked at her.

"Larry's going to kill me." Mich said it so matter-of-factly as she raised her glass for a sip of tonic water and lime, Cassie wasn't sure she'd heard her right.

"What did you say?" she choked.

Mich repeated the ominous words without a hint of fear or anger or regret, just like she had ordered her dinner. Cassie stared at her friend incredulously. This was a new low, even for Larry.

"Oh, get real, Mich. Larry may be a..." Cassie paused. She'd never referred to him as "a sleaze" in front of her friend, "a little inattentive, but isn't this a bit much?"

"I know it's unbelievable, but I have proof."

"Proof?! You have proof and you still let him live in the same house?"

"Of course. He's my husband."

Those last three words had always made Cassie see red. Mich, for all her talent and intelligence, refused to see Larry as abusive. He ridiculed her, treated her like dirt, had had numerous affairs and she always overlooked everything because of those three words.

"This makes no sense. You say you know he's going to kill you and you still keep him around. I give up. Obviously you don't trust him."

"Oh, Cass, there are different levels of trust. I trust Larry to be Larry, predictable Larry. That's my ace. I know Larry will cheat, he'll lie, and he'll always come back to me. Didn't you find that with Kevin?"

Cassie grimaced. "Hardly. He lied all the time...told me he would quit drinking and that lasted about 24 hours. Just got sneaky, drank straight out of the bottle when he thought I couldn't see him. Told me he loved me every morning after one of his binges. I kept forgiving him his lapses. I finally decided if he would lie about little things, he'd lie about big ones, too, so I never knew what to believe. Trust is so hard to regain once it's lost, and the worst of it is he killed my sense of trust about everything. I'll never be that trusting, that stupid again. I just don't see how you can continue with Larry, especially now that you think he's going to kill you!"

Cassie tried to tone down her incredulity and keep her rising hysteria in check, but sometimes Mich drove her to distraction.

"Oh, Cass, you've never understood Larry. He's like a little kid; he just wants somebody to love him, to put him first.

Cassie took the opportunity to jump in. "Oh, come on, Mich, you're not going to excuse him for trying to kill you because he had a rotten childhood?! Lots of people had rotten childhoods and don't grow up to kill people, especially people they claim to love!"

"Oh, he loves me, Cass, he just isn't very demonstrative; his parents aren't either; nobody hugs anybody; no kisses; no pats. Watch him some time. He rarely smiles, not a real smile that reaches his eyes. I've given this a lot of thought since I found out about his plans and I know he loves me; he just doesn't know why, or how to show it. He's never experienced real love except from me, so he doesn't recognize it. He thinks he married me for my money, but he really married me because he knows I love him better than anyone else on earth; he's finally number one to someone. I bring him happiness; I make him REALLY smile, twinkly eyes and all."

Cassie stared at her friend, unbelieving. "Oh, for God's sake, Mich, are you nuts? You're sitting here telling me Larry is going to kill you and you understand him! How can you be so calm, so, so dispassionate about this?"

"Well, I'm not going to let him succeed, of course. I'm going to beat him, just like I'm going to beat the cancer. And you're going to help me. Let's go inside, it's getting chilly out here." Pulling her sweater tighter around her thin shoulders, Mich led the way to their table by the fireplace. Cassie was chilled, too, but not by the climate.

"How am I going to help you? Tie him up and throw in Chatfield Reservoir?" *Actually, that doesn't sound like such a bad idea* Cassie thought gleefully.

"We can talk about that later; there's no rush. I don't think he's going to do anything until he's sure I'm going to survive the cancer. Right now he's convinced my prognosis isn't all that great. After all, if I die of these so-called natural causes he won't have to kill me. I'm guessing he'll give it a few more months and see how I'm doing. Larry has never been one to work harder than necessary."

Cassie stared in disbelief at her friend. "How 'bout if we start at the beginning? Why do you think he's going to kill you?"

"For the money, of course. You know Larry has always liked the high life; that's why he thinks he married me, as he's told me many times; so I could keep him in the lifestyle to which he felt entitled. But my medical treatments have been expensive. Even though it's not putting much of a dent in our net worth, he still resents the expenditures. He has this fear of being poor again."

"I haven't noticed any change in his life," Cassie commented sarcastically.

"There hasn't been. He still has his cars, his trips, and his honey-du-jour. Don't look surprised; I've known about his affairs all along; we have an agreement: he can have sex with as many women as he wants as long as he is discreet. Hell, he was hitting on girls at Vandy while we were engaged. I'm surprised he didn't try to get in your pants."

He did and still does, Cassie thought to herself. *That's why I loathe him.* That he could do these things to her best friend was enough to make her want to scratch his eyes out. She hoped her face didn't betray any of her feelings, she'd spent eleven years hiding how much she disliked Larry.

For the umpteenth time over the last few years she asked the same question, "Why do you put up with this? Why don't you divorce him?"

For the umpteenth time she got the same answer, "Because I love him and he needs me, or, to paraphrase the baroness in *Sound of Music*, "at least he needs my money."

"Sure has a strange way of showing it," Cassie muttered to herself, or thought she had.

"I know he doesn't appear to be very caring, but he is. He just hates to see me like this, that's why he travels so much."

Oh brother. "And the girlfriends? The affairs? Cheating is just another form of lying except it strikes at your very core, makes you feel less of a woman, less desirable. Trust me, I know."

Mich grinned at her friend as though she was a not-too-bright child in need of enlightenment. "Well, that's just sex, purely physical. I've been so sick and tired and he has to have some sexual relief. I've always understood...and since my illnesses make it hard for me to participate, we worked out our agreement. These affairs don't mean anything. He doesn't *love* them; he loves me."

How could her friend be so blind? Cassie wanted to rage at her and wake her up, but she knew from past experience it was a lost cause. Mich had blinders on when it came to Larry.

Cassie took a deep breath and a sip of her wine while she gathered her thoughts and her temper. "Okay, so you know he wants the money and you think he's going to kill you to get it if you don't hurry up and die. And you think you've got lots of time because he won't do anything until he's sure you're going to survive, which of course you will because you've set your mind to it and, being stubborn, you always get what you set your mind to. And you keep him around because you love him and he needs you, even though you think he's going to kill you. What am I missing here?" Cassie took another long swallow of her Kendall Jackson Reserve chardonnay, looking at her friend like a deer in headlights, her elk medallions growing cold on her plate.

"I know it sounds ridiculous, but that pretty well sums it up."

"Ignoring the ridiculousness of the whole situation, what makes you think he's going to kill you?"

"He ordered books about poisons from Amazon. Larry is not a great reader, so when I saw the charge on our credit card bill and I knew I hadn't ordered anything, I called to verify the purchase. Four books about poisons and drug interactions."

"It doesn't sound as though he's being too secretive if he charged them and let you see the charges."

"Well, Larry has never been one for thinking things through too completely. I have always paid the bills; he doesn't know that I thoroughly check every itemized charge on our credit card statements. I'm not even sure he's ever seen a credit card statement. That's how I always find out about his affairs; he charges flowers and gifts and thousands of dollars' worth of LaPerla lingerie and has them sent to his 'ladies'. I know I've never gotten them."

"For God's sake, Mich, why do you put up with this?" Cassie was beside herself with grief for her friend and anger at her for being so compliant. Cassie's voice rose as she marveled at her friend's...stupidity? She knew she would never have put up with this kind of treatment...and hadn't, at least not for long. Did she really have any case to charge her best friend with stupidity when she had done the same thing?

Mich just stared calmly at her friend. "I know you don't understand, Cass, but my wedding vows mean a lot to me."

Cassie was hurt. The words stung as she thought of her own divorce. She knew that Mich did not mean to hurt her; Mich would never intentionally hurt anyone.

"Okay, he ordered some books. Anything else? Did you call the police?"

"No, I didn't call the police. I don't think they can do anything until there's an actual wrong-doing. So far it's just bits and pieces. And it would just be my word against his." Mich hesitated.

"I'm getting a little tired, Cass. Can we continue this tomorrow? I thought we'd go to Cherry Creek; I need to get some new scarves to decorate my bristly head! And then we can go to Brio's for lunch. I remember you really liked it last time." The two stood, Cassie's elk medallions and Mich's soup-and-salad grown cold and lonely too.

Mich grabbed the check and put two hundred dollar bills with it; Cassie was accustomed to her friend's extravagances with cash. They left and drove the thirty minutes back to the house in Ken Caryl. It was very silent in the car.

Chapter 10

Thursday was a gorgeous, still star-lit morning. Cassie awoke even earlier than usual; her usual time in Virginia, but two hours earlier in Colorado. She put on a warm robe she found in the closet and a pair of wool socks that she used as slippers when she traveled. She tiptoed downstairs.

She fixed her tea and took it to the rustic redwood table on the deck. From her observation point she watched the sun come up with the other early birds: black and white magpies, Rocky Mountain Jays, and two different types of swallows. Below her she could see prairie dogs bustling in and out amongst the red rocks.

Cassie finished her tea feeling very relaxed, but still mystified by her friend. *Today I'll get the full story* she vowed as she headed for the shower.

By the time she got back downstairs Mich was munching a piece of cinnamon toast and all dressed for the day. She looked more herself in the brown wig that had been styled in her usual "do".

"Like it?" she asked as she caught Cassie looking at her head.

"Well, it certainly looks more like you. I was having a hard time with the blonde one. Mich – about..." She never got to finish.

"Not now, Cassie, I'm having too good a time with you here. I'll explain everything, I promise, but this is the first I've felt so good in months. Come on, I have something to show you."

Mich led Cassie to her studio on the far side of the den. The south wall was all glass and had the same view as Cassie had enjoyed with her tea: Colorado in all its early- morning glory.

All around the room was Colorado, too; Colorado landscapes, some hung, some resting against the wall, some lying flat on tables. Most of them were huge; all of them were spectacular. Mich had experimented with a variety of media: oils, acrylics, watercolors, even some pen and ink.

"Is there any part of Colorado you haven't painted?" she asked incredulously.

"Oh, lots. The wonderful thing is seeing the same expanse in different conditions, sunrise, rain, twilight, snow, whatever. Every minute of every day is different. It can change so rapidly. We can have 40 degree temperature changes in a couple hours.

"I feel like Monet. You know how he painted the same scene at different times of the day? I like to paint under different weather conditions. I could just sit here in my studio for the rest of my life and paint the view out those windows. I'd never get tired of it and never run out of something new and exciting to paint. But I still get out into the wilds when I can. I've painted from Grand Junction to Mesa Verde; Cheyenne, even though it's in Wyoming, to Pueblo and all sorts of places in between."

Cassie was encouraged by her friend's passion; the old fire had returned. "So what are you working on now?"

Mich led Cassie over to her easel standing in the middle of the room. A much smaller painting was resting on the easel, apparently completed. It showed Mich's characteristic brightness with daffodils coming up amongst the red rocks and prairie dogs; a postcard-blue sky with white cotton- ball clouds enveloped the scene.

"You've captured it!" Cassie exclaimed. "I've always said the sky is so blue that the clouds look like they've been pinned up there with thumb tacks. That's exactly how it looks."

"I remembered you saying that once and I tried to paint it. I'm glad you think I got it. It's taken me a long time because the brushes get too heavy sometimes and my hands shake, but my strength has been much better the last couple weeks and I got it finished. It's for you, Cass."

"What? No, I couldn't. It's too expensive."

"You can and you will. But you can't take it with you. It has to finish drying completely so I'll send it to you in a couple weeks."

Cassie hugged Mich tightly. "I love it. Thank you, Mich, you know how much it means to me."

Mich leaned back and looked at her friend with tears welling in her eyes. She shook her head, "Enough of this emotion. Come on. Let's get you some breakfast and head to the mall for some knock-em-dead scarves. Ooops, poor choice of words I guess." The depressing mood broke as the friends chortled and headed for the kitchen.

The day at Cherry Creek was fun. They poked along admiring the shops, had a spinach Margherita flatbread pizza at Brio's, and found three bright scarves that Mich could wear in the summer when her wigs got too hot. The salesgirl showed her new ways to tie them to add some pizzazz. Cassie picked up a Rockies baseball hat, too. It'd be a novelty back in Virginia where everyone supported the Braves or the Nationals.

As they waited to cross the street for the Tattered Cover, a stranger approached Cassie and asked directions. Cassie politely explained that she was from out of town and was sorry she couldn't help, and then asked Mich to help him out, being a native and all. The two of them had a hard time getting across the busy street they were laughing so hard. "Well, it's good to know some things never change," Mich cackled to Cassie amidst a barrage of giggles. "Remember that time in London? We were at dinner at Cheshire Cheese and those older ladies at the next table decided to ask you, "that nice English girl", for recommendations on other restaurants. And people still are asking you for directions!"

"I know, and I can't figure out why. Do I have a sign on my forehead that says 'ask here' or what? It happens no matter where I go, people are always asking me things."

As they stepped up on the curb, Mich turned to her dearest friend and eyed her quizzically. "You really don't know? It's because you're you."

"Oh, well, that helps a lot. These people don't know me, they're strangers!"

"No, I mean you're just so ....so...approachable. You go through life like a little kid, those big brown eyes wide open and looking for life's excitement; and you always greet people, even strangers, with a smile and eye contact. You are about as nonthreatening as a person can be, so people feel free to ask you things. Add to that you look so competent, people just assume you know answers. Must make you an amazing librarian!"

"So the answer is to wear a frown and keep my head down?"

"Works for me," Mich answered as they swung into Tattered Cover to browse for books before heading home.

It seemed to Cassie her friend had forgotten the threats hanging over her as they laughed and goofed around. Or maybe Mich had just imagined that Larry was up to no good.

They returned home in mid-afternoon so Mich could nap. The mood changed dramatically when they walked in; Larry was there.

"Hello, Michela, I'm home. Surprised?" Larry pecked his wife on the cheek. "You're looking well, having Cassie here has done wonders." He was obviously not surprised to see Cassie. "Hi, Cass, it's always a pleasure to see you." Cassie was able to turn her cheek to receive the kiss he had intended for her lips.

"Hello, Larry, I thought you were going to be out of town for the week," Cassie commented politely.

"Well, I was, but when Magdelena told me Mich was expecting company I decided to rush home, hoping it was you."

"Magdelena? Is she still with you?" Cassie inquired toward Mich.

"Yes, but she's cut back on her hours. Only comes in a couple mornings a week and helps with the heavy stuff, making up the beds, vacuuming, dusting. She said to tell you she's sorry she won't get to see you this trip," Mich explained.

Cassie bristled at the thought of Larry using Mich's long-time housekeeper to spy on her; maybe it wasn't Mich's imagination.

"Michela, isn't it your nap time? You run along. I'll entertain Cassie," Larry said smugly to his wife.

Mich trudged up the stairs without a word, defeat written in the slump of her whole body.

"It's okay, Larry, you don't have to entertain me. I'm still recovering from the time difference so I'm going to nap also." Cassie turned on her heel and headed up the stairs behind her friend.

Larry covered his displeasure with a big insipid grin; his eyes were not smiling however. "Fine. I guess I'll have to wait until later to find out what my two favorite girls have been up to."

Cassie hid out in her room reading until she heard Mich go downstairs. She followed shortly after.

"Cassie, it's after five, what can Mich get you to drink? Still drinking white wine?" Larry inquired as she entered the den.

"Yes, thanks, Larry, but I can get it myself." She headed for the kitchen. She came back with her glass of wine and some water with bubbles for Mich; Cassie seated herself in the Blackwatch plaid chair across from Mich. Mich looked stronger after her nap. "Feel better?" Cassie asked solicitously.

"Yep, much. I just get so tired doing simple things. It's really annoying, but at least I'm getting less tired than I used to."

"What does Doc say?"

"That old goat?" Larry interrupted. "He hasn't kept up with the times. I keep telling Mich she should find a doctor who knows what he's doing, but she remains loyal. That's our Mich, always loyal." He sat next to his wife and patted her knee as he said this.

Mich smiled at his praise; sarcastic though it was. Cassie wanted to throw something at him. How dare he talk about Doc that way? Not only was he a highly respected doctor, he was the only family Mich had.

"So how's business, Larry? Must be going well if you can cut a sales trip short." Cassie knew that was all it would take to get Larry onto his favorite subject: the wonders of Larry. As he went on about all the sales contracts he'd written and the millions of dollars he'd brought in for the specialty lighting company, Cassie thought if he was shorter he'd be accused of having a Napoleon complex. But at over six feet it was just pure ego. Too bad, because he could be really successful; he's good looking, personable, and smart. If he just took an interest in something other than himself.

He casually took Mich's hand in his, saying, "Don't spill that water, Mich, you know how clumsy you've been lately." Then he turned back to Cassie, "Yeah, it's been a great year and we're not even half into it. I don't know where the company would be without me. I write 80% of all the contracts. Seems those wives and divorcees just love to have me discuss lighting with them. I get twenty, thirty calls a week for appointments. Lots of night calls." He said this last with a smug grin that reminded Cassie of a former U.S. president.

"Are you still *vice* president, Larry?" Cassie didn't mean the pun and it went right over Larry's head. She had asked the question with an innocent look belying the fact that she knew his not being president of the company was a sore point with him. Mich's father had left the company to her with a very successful management team in place. Mich had made Larry a vice president when they married, and she refused to give him the reins of the company.

Larry's eyes narrowed and he tightened his grip on Mich's hand. Cassie saw her wince; she was immediately sorry she had brought up the subject. "Just for now. That's going to change soon, isn't it, Michela?" He pressed harder on Mich's ringed fingers.

"No, Larry, I don't think so. Unless you know something I don't." Mich smiled sweetly at her husband, despite the pain in her hand; her fingers had gone white.

"You never know," Larry said snidely. "Refills anyone?" Larry tossed Mich's hand aside and headed for the kitchen. Mich's eyes glittered at him in defiance.

"No, thanks, we need to change for dinner. We've got a 7:30 reservation at Elway's."

"I know, I checked your calendar. I made it for three instead of two. It's not often I get to take two beautiful women to dinner. I'll just have another drink while you get ready." Mich and Cassie glanced at each other and shrugged simultaneously, then walked together upstairs to change.

As they prepared to leave for dinner, Larry yelled belligerently at Mich, "Where are my keys? What have you done with them?"

Mich immediately moved to his side at the hall table and started searching for them. "I didn't do anything with them, I haven't even seen them." Her hands moved carefully across the marble surface, lifting objects, moving papers. "You usually leave them here on the table on your way upstairs."

"I know what I 'usually' do. They aren't here. Where did you put them?"

"I went up for a nap as soon as we got home. I didn't see them." Cassie bristled at the fearful tone in Mich's voice, so unlike her.

Cassie tried to intercede. "Have you checked your dresser, Larry? Maybe you put them there when you emptied your pockets?"

"Butt out, Cassie. And yes, of course I checked my dresser. I'm not stupid."

"I didn't say you were stupid, but since they aren't where they normally are I was just suggesting an alternative. You went up to change shortly after Mich and I went upstairs, so I thought that was a logical place for them to be. Just retrace your steps; that's how I find things that go missing."

Larry glared at her as he ascended the steps. "Just to show you, I'll check again."

A few minutes later he came back down the stairs, "Okay, let's go. Don't want to miss our reservation."

The ride into town was very quiet. Cassie, in the back seat, tried really hard not to grin for fear Larry would see her in the rearview mirror.

Elway's was its usual trendy self. Wonderful steaks, great selection of seafood, an expansive wine list, and sometimes a few Denver Broncos to gawk at, even in the off season. It would have been a perfect evening if Larry hadn't been there. Fortunately, Larry managed to maintain enough talk about himself that Mich and Cassie could enjoy their food uninterrupted. Cassie tried to keep her eye-rolling focused on her roasted Rocky Mountain trout.

After dessert and a mostly-silent forty minute drive Larry dropped Mich and Cassie at the front door and left for his 10 p.m. appointment. Cassie looked at Mich with a raised eyebrow. Mich shrugged and waved goodbye. The two friends went in for cups of hot chocolate and bed. Mich's only comment as they climbed the stairs was, "It's okay, Cass, it's not about 'us'; it's just physical."

Across town, in Westminster, Larry opened the front door of an expansive ranch style home. A buxom woman ran to meet him; their kiss was long and passionate, with lots of touching and groping by both of them. "I'm so glad you came," the woman groaned against his lips. "I thought you were going to be out of town for the week?"

"Something came up at work and I had to get back."

"No complaints from me. Come with me and I'll show you how glad I am to see you." She took his hand and led him into the bedroom.

Chapter 11

Friday was a rare rainy day in Denver. Mich suggested they stay in; she didn't want to take a chance of getting a chill which was highly possible running from wet parking lots to air conditioned stores multiple times. Larry had come in late and then left early that morning for the office. The two friends sat around the house all day, catching up some more. Cassie was just ready to try to get more out of Mich when she asked, "So how are you really doing, Cass? I know what you said Wednesday, but this is me, remember; I know you better than anyone. I can imagine what you've been going through and I don't think I'd be as 'fine' as you say you are."

The question took Cassie's breath away, *with all her problems she's still worried about me.* Almost too overcome by her friend's thoughtfulness, Cassie pulled herself together and answered with a wavering grin, "I'm hanging in there. The divorce was hard but something I had to do. Mom and Dad's deaths were much harder, because they were so unexpected. I'm okay. Really."

"Wednesday was the first you ever talked to me about the marriage. I have the feeling there's something more. Anything else you want to share? I've turned to you so many times, I don't feel I'm being much of a friend when you can't talk to me about anything."

Cassie reached across the sofa and patted her best friend's thin hand. "Don't ever think that, Mich, you're the most important person I have left in my life. It's just, oh, you know me, I'm not one for talking about personal things a whole lot, not to anybody. I never even talked to my mom about Kevin."

"Didn't she like him?

"For limited time frames she could keep up the facade, but if they were together too long, she got testy and sarcastic, and so did he. I think I always knew it wouldn't work out, but when we met he seemed so perfect: big strong man, vet of the Iraqi war, smart, good job, good looking. The strong silent type.

"Over time I decided he was dull and boring, not strong and silent.

As you know, I didn't date a lot in college, unless you count 'the uglies', as you called them." They both laughed. "When Kevin came along he made me feel so sexy, so desirable. But once we were married I found out it was just physical, no romance. If I didn't wear what he thought of as sexy, he wouldn't come near me. When we did have sex, it was just mechanical on his part; he never cared whether I enjoyed it or not. I tried to explain to him that sex for me was more than physical; that I needed some affection, some attention before we went to bed. He just didn't care; he'd just sit there, drinking, and watching whatever sports were on TV and then expect me to perform at bedtime. In three years we never made love, it was just sex.

"But I didn't want to be a quitter so I tried to stick it out. After three years and growing depression, though, I decided I didn't want it for a lifetime; I knew I'd never leave if we had kids. So I got up my courage and filed the papers; it was both a relief and the hardest thing I've ever done. I don't know which was more depressing, the marriage or the divorce," she laughed ruefully. "The move back to Lexington helped; out of sight, out of mind, I guess."

Mich grabbed Cassie's hand and held it tightly. Cassie smiled dejectedly.

"But then Mom and Dad died so suddenly, just a few months after I got back to town. Again, a blessing in disguise. I was so busy with the funeral and then all the paperwork I didn't have time to think about Kevin. I woke up one morning and realized I was over him, if not over the guilt of the divorce."

"But why do you feel guilty? He was miserable to you!"

"Oh, I know. I'm just so anal, I hate to fail at anything, and this was a BIG failure."

"Yep, that's you, Miss Overachiever. What was it, one B in four years at Vandy?"

They both started to smile at the reminiscences of their years in Tennessee. "Well, what about you, Miss Gothic Novel governess?"

"Can I help it if my parents named me Michela Ferncliff? You have to agree it's a perfect governess name for one of those bodice-ripping novels."

"Come on, Mich, I've bared my soul, now it's your turn. How are you doing truly? Aside from the fact that your husband wants you dead, of course?"

Mich smiled at Cassie, "Aside from that, I'm fine. Doc is turning into an old maid. I keep telling him I can beat it again, but he's not so sure. So I guess I just have to show him, and everybody else! I plan to dance at your next wedding, since I missed the first one, and it sounds like a good thing or I might have stomped on the groom!"

The mood lifted once again and they spent the rest of the morning and lunch giggling like a couple teenagers. But still Mich got tired. Cassie had noticed over lunch how her hands shook, too, she almost dropped her fork into her lap. Cassie was determined to call Doc and find out the truth of Mich's condition. Cassie had known Doc almost as long as she had known Mich. As Mich's surrogate parent he was always around when Cassie visited. Maybe tomorrow morning she'd give him a call, he wouldn't have office hours on Saturday.

Waiting for Mich to get up from her nap, Cassie was lost in thought standing at the stove waiting for her tea water to heat. *Every time I bring up the subject of her call she says "Later." How can I keep Larry from killing her if that's what he has in mind?*

She didn't hear the stealthy footsteps behind her as she mentally wrestled with her friend. But she felt his mouth on the side of her neck. She tried to push away from him, but his arms on either side of her pinned her to the granite island. Gritting her teeth she reached for the kettle, "Larry, if you don't get away from me I'll dump this boiling water on you."

Larry backed off a little, allowing Cassie to turn around and face him, but still too close for her comfort. She held tightly to the heavy yellow kettle's wooden handle.

"Come on, Cassie, let's have a little fun. You probably haven't had good sex since you moved to the hills of Virginia."

"And where would I find 'good sex' around here, Larry?" She

moved aside and poured the hot water over the cherry blackberry tea bag in a mug that said "Love Ya" in bright red letters. She smiled sweetly at him as she seated herself at the kitchen table, her back to the wide windows.

"Why don't you give it a rest, Larry, you're not my type; never have been."

"I'm not sure anyone is, Cassie; even Kevin wasn't your type was he? Maybe you prefer females?"

Cassie was not going to let him bait her. Even opening the still-smarting wound of her failed marriage wasn't going to rile her, letting it out to Mich had helped a lot.

"You know, Larry, you're right. Lots of times I prefer women to men, not sexually as your one-track mind thinks, but because many of the women I know are better people than some of the men I could name."

"Oh, Mich's been telling stories again, has she? All about what a terrible husband I am, how mistreated she is. Look around, does this look mistreated?"

Cassie almost choked on her tea. "Mich could have all this without you, Larry; I seem to recall she's the one with the money."

Larry's eyes narrowed as the slight hit home. "Well it hasn't been easy for me either. She's sick all the time; for years she's been sick. First it was those migraines. And then the first bout with cancer; that took years out of our lives. Then she lost her baby, not that I wanted it anyway. Now she's got cancer again; that quack said she'd be dead in two years tops, but she's still here. If she's gonna die I wish she'd get it over with so I can get on with my life."

Cassie couldn't believe even Larry could be so callous. She was speechless, then "You're disgusting. What a selfish pig! Do you think she's enjoyed being sick all the time? Unable to keep food down, too weak to paint, running back and forth to hospitals. And all with no support from you. You're a self-centered bastard; all you can think of is yourself. This is a new low, Larry, even for you. If your life is so miserable, why don't you divorce her?"

"Because she won't. I've asked her for one, but she says she loves me. If she fights me on a divorce, I'll lose everything. I like my lifestyle and I'd hate to have to start over with nothing. A divorce means I lose my job, which isn't much but it pays really well and I don't have to work too hard. All her big important friends would turn against me, too. I'd probably have to leave Denver and start over somewhere else without her fame or money. No, I think I'll just bide my time; even Doc can't be that far off in his prognosis."

Cassie stared coldly at her best friend's husband. Without another word she picked up her mug and went resolutely upstairs. The solitude of her room was much preferable to the rantings of a spoiled brat. She locked her door.

The evening was spent quietly at home, reminiscing more about their college days and the annual trips they'd taken. The friends ordered a Domino's pizza after Larry left for his regular Friday night "appointment". "If you want to entertain me, Cassie, I'd be happy to stay home," he'd said maliciously from the front door. He smirked at her as he headed out the door.

"Are you sure he's worth it, Mich?"

"Oh, yes. He has his little flings and then he comes right back. We'll have several months of happiness before it starts over. Most of his bimbos only last a couple weeks, although this one has been several months. Maybe he's trying her out as my replacement. Too bad, I don't plan on being replaced."

Cassie bit her tongue before she hurt her friend by telling her what a fool she was. Instead she changed the subject. "Larry mentioned your migraines, still having them?" Cassie remembered her roommate spending days curled up on the bed in their darkened dorm room, moaning at the pain, only getting up to stagger across the room to throw up in the bathroom.

"Yeah, I still get them. Fortunately they've been less frequent lately, maybe all the cancer meds have knocked them out. That would be a good thing 'cause I can't take anything for the headaches. Remember how I used to pop anything I could find? Tylenol, Advil, Aleve, I didn't care as long as it dulled the pain. Took 'em every two hours just so I could get to class. Doc says analgesics like NSAIDs and ibuprofen could be lethal if mixed with the other drugs; and the stronger migraine drugs never worked on my brand of headache. When the migraines come I just have to wait them out, not fun, but it beats the alternative I guess. I'm just glad they're less frequent."

"I'm sorry, Mich. You've been through so much, you'd think it was about time for something to go right for you."

"Hey, it's not so bad. I've got my painting and I've got you. And I'm feeling better; the Big C is almost licked again. So don't *you* get down. Let's plan our next trip. I was thinking about Ireland, what do you say?"

Cassie marveled at her friend's resiliency, even as she wasn't sure of the truth of any of it. Mich didn't look like she was getting better; she was so frail. She made a mental note again to call Doc tomorrow while Mich took her nap.

"Before we talk about Ireland, how 'bout we talk about why you brought me here with that panicked message and how I can help you. Were Larry's poison books the whole of it?""

"Oh, all right, but I feel kind of silly about it now. I think I was just feeling depressed and I blew everything out of proportion. I had just discovered the purchase of the books, Larry is spending more time than usual on this bimbo, and she's hanging around longer, and I couldn't paint...not to mention the cancer. My life seemed to be over, figuratively if not literally. I just put myself in Larry's place and decided I'd kill me if I was him. Once you got here, saying things out loud made me realize how ridiculous it all was. Sorry to bring you out on a wild goose chase. But you have helped. You've given me a reason to live...if only to be a shoulder for you to lean on."

Mich looked so contrite, Cassie had to laugh. "Well, I'm glad you're feeling better about it. You know I'm not overly fond of Larry, but I really can't see him plotting your murder; it'd take too much energy. He's just not the subtle type. Hell, he couldn't even order poison books without you finding out!"

The two friends laughed together; the relief each felt sending them into paroxysms of giggles.

"Oh, the books. I even figured those out once I started thinking rationally. They use lots of poisons down at the plant to work with the metals in the lamps, so he probably got the books for the office."

Cassie knew "the plant" was the company Cassie had inherited. "Makes sense to me, Mich. Phew! Let's stop worrying then and enjoy the weekend; I have to be back to the grind on Monday."

"I know. I wish you could stay longer. We'll go back to Tattered Cover tomorrow and shop for guide books about Ireland; then we can get serious about planning our trip. Larry has an early golf game on Saturdays and then he spends the day at the club. We'll have all day to ourselves. How about we go to Ireland a year from now? Late May? Should be beautiful!"

The friends spent the rest of the evening eating popcorn and discussing dates for their trip and planning a side trip to London for shopping. They went to bed about one. Mich gave Cassie a big hug outside her bedroom door, "Thanks for coming at my call, Cass. I knew I could count on you. I guess I just needed someone to talk to and you're the best listener I know. I can always count on you when I need you."

"Any time I get to see you is okay with me, Mich. You know that. And it's a two-way street; talking about Kevin and my folks helped me too. Now get a good night's sleep so we can get this trip up and running; I'm getting excited about it!" The two friends parted with hugs and smiles on their faces. Larry still wasn't home.

Chapter 12

Cassie stretched like a contented cat under the cozy warmth of the down comforter. Then she looked at the clock. "6:18 on a Saturday morning! Just once in my life I'd like to sleep past 7," she moaned as she flipped over in bed, bunching the pillow into a bolster for her head.

Staring at the ceiling through the early light filtering through the wood blinds she decided she was glad she had come, even if it turned out to be pointless. She should have come to see Mich sooner; she didn't look good. She reminded herself to call Doc today.

She'd known Doc since he had brought Mich to Nashville twelve years ago when they'd started at Vanderbilt. Who would have thought that freshmen roommates would hit it off so well? What were the odds on that? Through the years Cassie had gotten to know Doc better whenever she came to Denver. She liked him; he was the perfect Dad for Mich, especially after her real one had...

There was a slight noise at the door. Cassie looked across the room to see the doorknob quietly turning, but not very far. Cassie had locked her door every night, just in case. "Sleaze" she muttered with a grimace at the door.

She plumped up her pillows again and grabbed her book. "I think I'll just read a while and give you time to head off for golf," she muttered to the closed door.

A bit after seven, desperate for a cup of tea, Cassie decided Larry must be gone. She quietly opened her door and glanced across the hall toward Larry's room.

Since Mich's latest illness Larry had moved to the room next to Mich's "so she'd be more comfortable," he said. *And so he could come and go more conveniently*, Cassie thought. He had awakened Cassie briefly when he came in around 2. Right now his door was standing open and there was no noise of anyone moving about.

Pulling the heavy flannel robe more tightly around her she quietly headed down the carpeted stairs. Just as she reached the floor she heard the car being gunned down the driveway. *Wonder if the neighbors appreciate all his noise?*

Expelling her held breath she headed into the kitchen more relaxed. She fixed a pot of Earl Grey. It was going to be a good day, after all. They'd have fun shopping for Ireland stuff – she'd make sure of it. She grabbed the morning paper from where Larry had left it on the counter and resumed her place at the table on the deck.

By eleven Cassie had read the papers, finished the pot of tea and a bagel, put her dishes in the dishwasher, walked around the block twice, showered and dressed in the requisite jeans and a long sleeve blouse for their shopping trip. She grabbed a navy cotton sweater, too, as she left her bedroom. I don't care if it's going to be 82 today; it's still chilly to this humidity-reared girl. *It's a dry heat* she reminded herself.

She went downstairs ready to discuss the day with Michela. No sign of her yet. She must have been really tired last night; she's usually up by nine.

Cassie heated some more water and fixed a cup of decaf Lady Grey for Michela. *This'll get her going even if it is decaf* she said to herself as she approached the closed door at the end of the upstairs hall.

Just as she was ready to issue a resounding "Get up, Sleepyhead!" accompanied by a hearty knock on the door she thought better of it. Maybe Mich really was feeling worse and needed her sleep. She'd just go in quietly and check on her.

Softly she opened the door and tiptoed into the room. Uh oh. The room was pitch black and very warm, a sure sign of one of Mich's migraines. Normally Mich slept with the windows open, even if it was snowing. That had been about the only thing they argued about in college. The only time Mich closed up tight was when she had a migraine and got the chills with it.

Cassie closed the door most of the way so the light from the hall wouldn't bother Mich. She left just enough light so she could see where she was going. She remembered how the least little light could be a stabbing pain. As her eyes adjusted to the dimness she approached the bed. There was just the top of a bald head peeking out from under the covers. An ice bag soaked into what had once been Larry's pillow. She set the cup and saucer onto the nightstand, marveling again at the array of medicines; everything from jars of Vicks and hand lotion to what seemed like fifty prescription bottles. There was also a water carafe and half-empty glass.

Cassie gently touched Mich's shoulder through the quilt covering her.

"Mich, I know you can't eat when you've got one of these, but do you want some tea?" she whispered. "I brought you some Lady Grey, but I can get you another flavor if it sounds good to you."

Cassie waited for a response. Nothing. She nudged her friend again. Nothing. A chill started to climb up Cassie's spine, even in the over-heated room. Then she noticed the eerie silence of the room. The only noise was Cassie's breathing. Cassie's. Nothing else.

"Mich? Come on, Mich." She was afraid to pull back the covers. Hesitantly she reached out her quivering hand and pulled the quilt down to Michela's shoulder.

The frozen grimace of pain and the staring eyes told Cassie more than she wanted to know. Cassie knew her best friend was dead; no one could hold that look intentionally. Cassie started to retch and backed away from the bed. "That bastard," she moaned, tears starting to fall silently down her cheeks.

Help. Have to get help. She couldn't stay in the room another second. She raced to her room and dialed 9-1-1 from the phone beside her bed.

"Please send help. My friend's been murdered."

Chapter 13

Cassie stood at her bedroom window hugging herself. The sweater she had put on wasn't helping. It was only a few minutes until she heard the ambulance and then watched it pull up the driveway. Two Jefferson County sheriff's cars were right behind.

Cassie made her way downstairs and opened the front door just as the paramedics arrived on the front porch. "Upstairs. Room at the end," she directed them, pointing.

The paramedics brushed past her, taking the stairs two at a time, their cumbersome equipment boxes banging against hips and the banister, not slowing them down in the least. One of the deputies followed up the stairs. The other stayed with Cassie.

"M'am?" He tried to get her to focus on him, not on the stairs. "M'am, I'm Deputy Wilson. Can you tell me what happened?"

Slowly Cassie met his eyes. Cal Wilson had never seen such pain in the eighteen years he had been attending crime scenes. "Let's go sit down, okay?" he suggested.

Cassie woodenly let him lead her into the den. He held her elbow. She curled herself into one corner of the green sofa and pulled an afghan around her. *Would this nightmare never end? Why couldn't she just wake up and make it go away?* Cassie squeezed her eyes tightly shut. When she opened them the khaki shirt and brown pants with all the black leather trappings were still seated across from her.

"M'am? Can you tell me your name?" he urged. Usually something familiar was a way to get someone to start talking.

"Cassie Kirkland." Cassie's voice was a bare whisper.

"Cassie – may I call you Cassie?" he continued at her slight nod. "Are you hurt, Cassie?"

"No," she whispered. *Just hurting*, she thought to herself. *I didn't believe her.*

"Whose house is this?"

"Michela Merritt, the artist."

"Are you related to her?"

"No, we're best friends." *Some friend you are,* she slapped herself mentally.

"Do you live here?"

"Just visiting."

"Where are you from?"

"Virginia."

"Do you think you can tell me what happened?"

"She's dead. He killed her," Cassie hiccupped at the deputy. "I guess that pretty well sums it up."

"'He' who, Cassie?"

"Larry, her husband." Cal noticed the narrowing of Cassie's eyes and the sneer in her voice when she said "husband".

"Is he here now?"

"No. He's playing golf. Won't be back until later today."

"Are you telling me this man killed his wife and then went out to play golf?" Cal asked incredulously. *That's a first.*

Cassie shook her head and tried to concentrate. When the deputy said it like that it didn't make any sense, even for Larry.

Cassie nodded, but Cal could see the uncertainty in the gesture.

"Maybe you'd better start at the beginning. Did you find the body?"

"Yes. We were supposed to go shopping. Michela was sleeping really late and I was worried she was feeling worse, she has cancer. I fixed her a cup of tea and took it up to the bedroom. The room was all dark and hot so I figured she had one of her migraines. I shook her shoulder and tried to wake her. She wouldn't wake up." Cassie swallowed several times to get over the lump in her throat; the tears falling silently down her face. "She wasn't moving; she looked horrible. I went to my room and dialed 9-1-1."

Cal was writing furiously in a small green notepad. "When did you last speak to her?"

"Last night. We were planning a trip. That's why we were going shopping, to buy guide books about Ireland."

"Okay, Cassie, that's enough for now. A detective will be here in a little while to ask some more questions. Can I get you anything? Glass of water? Maybe a drink?"

"No, thank you. I'll make myself some tea in a little while." Cassie's voice was a little stronger, but still just above a whisper.

"I have to go upstairs. Are you going to be okay here?"

"Yes, I'll be fine," she smiled weakly at the deputy. "I'm sure you have lots to do; I'll be fine."

"Is there anyone I can call for you?"

"Oh, please call Doc; Dr. Bill Harper. He's Mich's doctor and family friend. He'd better know; I don't think I can tell him; his heart will be broken."

"I'll have someone contact him and ask him to come here."

Cal Wilson walked out of the den reaching for his shoulder-talkie to call Dispatch. She heard him stop by the front door and talk briefly with someone, then his steps disappeared as he hit the carpeted stairs.

Seconds later she felt someone come into the room. She opened her eyes and saw a new man sitting in the chair Deputy Wilson had vacated. He had on a blue blazer with khaki pants and a dark green and gold striped tie. Cassie thought he looked Hispanic with his dark hair and dark eyes. She thought she smelled the aroma of pipe tobacco about him. He stared sympathetically at Cassie. Cassie stared back with a question in her eyes, but no fear.

"I'm Detective Armijo. Deputy Wilson has brought me up to date. I've got a few more questions if you feel up to it."

There was a clatter at the front door and several voices were shouting back and forth from upstairs to the front door. Cassie turned her head toward the noise.

"That's the CSI team – Crime Scene Investigation. They do fingerprinting and take pictures, that sort of thing."

"Why is all that necessary? Just go and arrest him. He did it." Cassie was starting to get angry, mostly at herself she realized.

"Who?"

"Larry for God's sake." Cassie hissed at the new man.

"Why do you think he did it?"

"Because she told me he was going to kill her and I didn't believe her," Cassie whispered the last as tears started falling again.

"Are you saying Mrs. Merritt told you her husband wanted her dead?"

"Yes, that's what I'm saying. That's why I'm here. She called me last Sunday and asked me to come. She said she couldn't explain over the phone, but she insisted I had to come. So I did. I got here Wednesday; Larry was supposed to be out of town for a week. When I got here she said he was going to kill her to get her money."

Gilberto Armijo was elated. The DA was going to have an easy time with this one.

"So why didn't you believe her?"

Cassie looked startled. "What?"

"Why didn't you believe her?" the detective calmly repeated.

"Well, it was just too outlandish, even for him. You don't expect someone you've known for over ten years to kill someone. Not even someone as despicable as Larry. Even Michela had changed her mind."

Oooooops. Maybe it wasn't going to be so easy after all.

"Do you know where Mr. Merritt is now?"

"Playing golf."

"Do you know where, which course?"

"Probably Denver Country Club or Cherry Hills, maybe Castle Pines. I doubt his ego would let him play at a lesser course. With Mich's money and connections I'm sure he would have had no trouble getting a membership. She told me once he wanted to play Sanctuary but couldn't get on the course." Cassie grinned maliciously. Gil knew Sanctuary was a very private course just south of the Merritt home and restricted to use only by people the owners allowed on.

Gil was impressed with Cassie's concise explanation. It was obvious the young woman was hurting, but just the mention of the husband's name sent an anger into her posture; it seemed to emanate from every pore. He wouldn't want to be the husband when this lady caught up with him. Gil left the room and came back with a glass of water. "Here, drink this; it'll help," he said sympathetically.

"Michela? Cassie?" a male voice called from the entrance.

"Oh, Doc!" Cassie jumped up from the sofa and ran to the older man as he entered the den. The distinguished man hugged her tightly, even as he held out his hand to the detective.

"Bill Harper," he said. "I'm Michela's godfather and doctor. What's going on?"

"Gil Armijo, Jeffco." The men shook hands, one professional to another.

Doc maneuvered Cassie back to the sofa and pulled the afghan back around her. "You rest, Cassie. I'm just going out into the hall to talk with the detective."

Cassie could hear their voices murmuring outside the den. She saw Doc's shoulders sag as he got the news. Then the two men turned and their voices seemed to fade away. Cassie knew they had gone upstairs. "Oh, poor Doc," she sobbed into the throw pillow she held tightly against her chest. "Please don't let him see her like that."

The men returned a few minutes later. Doc appeared to have aged ten years. His shoulders slumped and the light was gone from his eyes.

He sat next to Cassie and took her hand. "You know, Cass, it's almost better this way. A few seconds of pain, instead of the weeks of pain and decline she was facing."

"Excuse me, Doctor, what pain was she facing?" the tall, dark-haired detective asked.

"Michela had breast cancer. It had metastasized to her bones and lungs and was just starting on her brain. She only had a few months left to live."

Oh, lordy. This one wasn't going to be easy at all Armijo thought to himself.

"How do you know it was just a few seconds, Doc? Are you sure?" Cassie asked hopefully.

"Cyanide, Cassie. All the signs are there: blue tinge to her lips and nails, and the grimace of pain from the poison. Cyanide quickly shuts down the body's systems; lack of oxygen causes the blue tinge. It's a very quick poison, extremely painful, but quick."

"Well, at least we can thank him for that," Cassie muttered sarcastically.

"Excuse me, Doctor, but are you a forensic specialist? What makes you think it's cyanide?"

Before Doc could answer, there were the sounds of stomping feet and shouts from the front door.

"What the hell is going on here? What are all you people doing in my house?" Larry was back from golf dressed in a yellow golf shirt, khaki pants, and tassled loafers without socks...not quite the picture of a grieving widower.

Doc and Detective Armijo rose to meet him. Cassie flew off the sofa before Doc had a chance to restrain her. She ran to Larry Merritt and slapped his jaw as hard as she could. "How could you? How could you?" she shrieked at him as Doc pulled her away.

Doc pulled her back to the den and got her back under the afghan.

"Do what? What is that lunatic going on about?"

Armijo looked at Doc. Doc gave a slight nod to the detective.

"Mr. Merritt, I'm afraid your wife is dead."

Although Larry tried to school his features into one of shock, he wasn't quite fast enough. Everyone saw the fleeting glint of speculation in his eyes before he covered them and the smirk with his hands. You could almost hear the wheels turning as he plotted how to handle this.

"Dead? How? The cancer?"

"No, Larry, not the cancer," Doc assured him

"Suicide?"

"Why would you think that, Mr. Merritt?" the detective asked.

"She was crazy enough to do it. Just to get even with me, make extra work for me."

Cassie started off the sofa again, but Doc held her firmly in place.

"Suicide is a possibility, Mr. Merritt, but not many people kill themselves with cyanide."

"Suicide! Not likely. Don't you even suggest it, Larry Merritt. You know as well as I do Mich was optimistic about her illness. The only reason she could have had for killing herself was because she finally decided to get away from you," Cassie whipped at Larry.

The dejected-husband mask didn't stay in place too long. "You know so much, don't you? You're the big marriage expert. How long were you married? Two years? Then you went running home to mommy and daddy. Try being married eleven years to someone who doesn't care about your needs, someone who's sick all the time and only thinks of herself. Never gave a thought to anyone but herself. It hasn't been easy on me you know."

"Maybe not. But it just got a whole lot easier and more lucrative, didn't it, you bastard."

The leaden silence in the room was broken by a new voice from the doorway. "Excuse me, Detective Armijo, may I see you a moment?" Everyone turned toward the voice. They saw a tall, dark haired man with a square jaw. No one knew how long he had been standing there.

Armijo followed the stranger out to the front porch. Doc could just hear their whispered conversation over Cassie's sobbing and Larry's pacing. Larry flopped down into the chair vacated by Armijo.

"So, Doc, do *you* think I killed my wife? Obviously Cassie does," Larry inquired sardonically.

Doc looked across at the younger man. He had never thought he was right for Mich, but he had held his tongue and tried to get along with him for Mich's sake. Fortunately Armijo came back before he had to answer.

"Mr. Merritt, we need you to identify your wife, please. If you'll come upstairs with me." A look of panic crossed Larry's face; that looking at dead bodies was not something he had planned on was plainly written on his face. "Why can't Cassie do it? She's known her longer than I have."

"We prefer a relative when possible, Sir. If you'd just come along; it'll only take a few moments."

"Oh, all right, but then I'm taking a shower." No one knew if he meant the shower was a result of the viewing or the golf.

As Larry slowly headed up the stairs, the stranger walked up to Doc. "Dr. Harper, I'm Sam Chambers, assistant D.A. I'm sorry for your loss." Cassie watched him through teary eyes from her position on the sofa. Taller than the detective, light brown hair, navy polo shirt with khakis as though he had just come from golf himself. *Great! Male bonding.* But he looked sincerely sympathetic. From her seated position Cassie could see a funny scar under his chin.

"Ms. Kirkland, are you up to a few more questions?"

Cassie nodded.

"How 'bout if we go sit on the deck?" He looked at the woman and saw intelligence and pain. Her short curly blonde hair was fashionably cut; the tears magnified her big brown eyes. Even with the puffy face he could tell she was very attractive, if not a real beauty. No mascara was running down her face so either she was naturally pretty or she used a waterproof type. She had eyeglasses hanging on a braided colored cord around her neck, reminded him of his grandmother except *her* glasses had been on slender gold-plated links.

"You look like a tea-drinker to me. Can I fix you a cup?"

The thought of tea made Cassie look at her watch: four o'clock. Tea time. "I'll get it. Would you like some?" Getting a nod she turned to Doc. "No, I think I'll just go upstairs a minute," he replied to her silent query.

Cassie and Sam Chambers went into the kitchen. Sam watched as Cassie mechanically took out the cups and saucers, a yellow Fiesta ware tea pot and some loose tea – a purist. She put water on to heat. He also watched as she prepared herself mentally for his questions. She wiped her face with a damp paper towel, her back straightened, and she ran cold water over her wrists.

Cassie poured the hot, not boiled, water over the loose tea in the pot and put on the lid. "It'll just be a minute," she said to him as she retrieved sugar and cream. "Lemon?" Sam shook his head.

She gave the attorney a watery smile as she handed him a purple Fiesta mug. "So what's an assistant D.A. doing here? Is this normal procedure?" She strained tea into the attorney's mug and then repeated the process for her own.

They walked to the outside table where Cassie had watched the birds a lifetime ago. She put the tea tray onto the table. The deck was warm from the afternoon sun. Cassie sat down with her back to the glass doors and raised her face to the sun. When she opened her eyes and looked at the attorney she was calmer, her fingers tightly wrapped around her yellow mug; she pointed to the sugar bowl and creamer with a question in her eyes. Sam Chambers shook his head.

"So? You haven't answered my question? Is this standard procedure?" she asked as she emptied a green packet into her mug.

"Only on high-profile cases. Mrs. Merritt ranks as one of those. Plus, she was a friend of the D.A. so he had me come over. He can't appear to be directly involved because of their friendship."

Cassie sipped her tea and appeared to gain strength from it. "I don't know what I can tell you that I haven't already told the sheriff's people."

"When you called 9-1-1 you said it was 'a murder'. Did you recognize the cyanosis?"

"No, Mich thought Larry was going to kill her. When I found her, I just assumed he had. Suicide never crossed my mind, so it had to be something else. She's been so happy since I got here. We were planning a trip for next year. We were going shopping today. And she just wouldn't do it, she loved him in spite of everything. If she wouldn't divorce him, why would she leave him this way? It just doesn't make sense."

"Sometimes suicides don't make sense."

"You didn't know Mich. She was always very logical. Everything made sense...except her staying married to him. I asked her why she didn't divorce him, with everything she knew about him. She said she loved him and took her marriage vows seriously. I guess it made sense to her if not to me."

"What do you mean? What did she know about him?"

"Oh, Larry could never keep his pants zipped. He's had affairs practically since the day they met. Mich told me his latest had lasted longer than most."

"She knew about the affairs?"

"Oh, yeah, they had some kind of a pact. But Larry had to rub it in, flaunt his affairs. Mich said he charged flowers and gifts to their credit cards. Even expensive lingerie. She paid the bills, so she saw the charges."

"Sounds like you two were pretty close if she told you these kinds of things."

Cassie's eyes filled again. "We were closer than sisters. We were both only children and ..." she lowered her head as the tears fell. Sam let her cry. He drank his tea and watched her; if this was an act it was the greatest job since Meryl Streep in *Sophie's Choice.*

"Sorry. I'm okay now. Where was I?"

"Talking about the credit card bills."

"That's right. That's how she found out about the books."

"Books?" Sam was getting lost.

"The books about poisons and drug interactions. Mich said there had been Amazon charges on their credit card. She had called to verify the charges 'cause she knew she hadn't ordered anything. They gave her the titles and the shipping address: Larry at the office."

"Anything else?"

"You want more? Aren't multiple affairs and poison books enough?"

"If she thought he was trying to kill her why didn't she go to the police?"

"I asked her the same question after she told me all this. She said it was pointless; they couldn't - or wouldn't – do anything until a crime had been committed. After we talked she said she'd decided it was a tempest in a teapot, that maybe he needed the books for work; they use poisons at the plant in the metal-working."

"That's possible for poison books, but doesn't explain books about drug interactions."

"I don't know." Cassie rubbed her head, something was bothering her, scratching at the back of her brain. "She told me something about drugs, had to do with her migraines."

Sam could see her practically reaching into her brain and physically pulling the memory forward. "Aleve! That's it. She said she couldn't take NSAIDs or ibuprofen any more for her migraines because they could have bad interactions with her cancer medicines. There was a bottle of Aleve on her nightstand when I went in there."

"We'll check it out. The CSI team will bag everything and check. I'll tell them to watch that bottle especially. Anything else you can think of that I should know?"

"No, I've probably said too much already. Guess you caught me at a weak moment." She gave the attorney another watery smile. "I don't want to get Larry into trouble just because he's a miserable person; that's not a crime. But if he killed Mich, I want him punished."

"Well, we won't know anything for sure for a few days. We'll need you to stay around. Do you have someplace to stay?"

The shocked look told Sam she hadn't gotten that far in her thinking. "No, I guess not. I'm sure I can find a hotel room somewhere."

"The sheriff's office will need to get statements from you and others today. We'll need you to come to the office for that. Is that okay?"

"I'll have to talk to Doc, he shouldn't be alone right now, but I guess I can stay."

"Fine. We'll set something up with you and the doctor before we leave today. A deputy will be with you while you pack; the house is a crime scene until we know otherwise." Sam handed her his card. "Well, let me know where I can reach you. My cell number is on the back. Now I think I'll go talk to the bereaved husband." He left Cassie nursing her tea in the warmth of the late afternoon sun reflected off the red rocks below.

Cassie stopped him with another question, "Wait. I just thought of something. Was there a suicide note? I didn't see anything that looked like a note, but I didn't search either. Once I saw Mich was dead I hurried out of the room."

"I don't know yet, but I certainly plan to find out. Just because there is or isn't one, though, doesn't mean it was or wasn't a suicide. I assure you, Miss Kirkland, we will get to the bottom of this."

Sam Chambers turned and headed inside.

Chapter 14

When he got to the foyer, Sam turned back and saw Cassie huddled into herself, staring at the red rocks. He couldn't quite figure her out, weepy one minute, hard as steel when she talked about the husband. Woman scorned?

As he went upstairs he admired the warmth and comfort of the house. Expensive, yes, but not obnoxious. He felt he could move into all this glass, leather, soft fabric, and wood and feel right at home. He immediately felt in tune with the owners...*or at least with the decorator*, he thought to himself.

Larry was still in the master bedroom, hovering off to the side while the Medical Examiner's attendants zipped Michela into a black bag for transport. Sam saw Armijo talking with the ME. Larry's eyes kept darting away from the activity at the bed, but he was constantly drawn back to it, fascination and horror mirrored on his face in repeating sequences. The CSI team was busy dusting everything in sight. Once dusted and scanned for fingerprints, each item was placed into a bag with a zip-close top. Each tech then wrote the date and time on the bag with his or her initials. Larry was disinterested in all the activity around him, other than as a distraction from the activity at the bed.

Sam studied him before speaking. Larry appeared to be about Sam's age, maybe a year or two younger. Same height. But there any similarity ended. Larry cast an air of superiority and aggression that Sam hoped he didn't have. Sam recognized that these qualities were not unusual for a man who made his living as a salesman. Of course, being married to one of the most famous women in Colorado, maybe he didn't really have to work. *Interesting thought.*

As the body passed him in the doorway, Sam spoke," Mr. Merritt, may I have a couple minutes?"

"What do you want? Can't you see how upset I am? Who are you anyway?"

Actually Sam could see no signs of grief on the other man. Sam introduced himself. "I understand, Mr. Merritt, but I'd appreciate it."

"Make it quick. I have a lot to do. The newspapers have to be notified, our lawyer, call the insurance company, and a real estate agent. Finally I can move into an appropriate house."

Guess he didn't do the decorating, Sam mused. *Score one for Michela.*

Masking his disgust, Sam continued, "When was the last time you saw your wife alive?"

"Early this morning. I stopped in to tell her I was leaving, room was black as a cave. I knew that meant she had one of her damned headaches. After all these years I know the signs; I can tell you I've suffered from those damn things."

"What time was that?"

"My tee time was 8:15, I was meeting the guys at the club for breakfast; must have been around 6, 6:15."

"Besides the room being dark, did anything else strike you, anything seem different?"

"She asked me to fill her water carafe and get her some Aleve. When she opened the pills she spilled them all over. I had to hunt around for them; almost made me late."

"Anything else?"

"No, I finally left for golf about 7 and didn't know anything else until I got back home. Had one of my best rounds ever. Now she's taken the joy out of that, too."

"Do you know the contents of her will?"

"Basically. I inherit everything. We had our wills drawn up at the same time. We each left everything to the other."

"When was this?"

"Oh, about four years ago, at the time of her first bout with cancer."

"Had the wills been changed?"

"No."

"Who is your lawyer?"

"Stan Culpeper of Culpeper, Lane and Weaver." Larry preened as he gave the name of the most prestigious law firm in Denver. "Why?"

"Just need to cover all the bases. What do you think happened here?"

"Isn't it obvious? Mich got tired of the pain and decided to do herself in."

Sam could believe Michela might have gotten tired of *this* pain, but wasn't sure about the medical one.

"But Ms. Kirkland says your wife was very optimistic about her chances, that they were planning a trip for next year."

"Well, then maybe Cassie killed her."

Sam's schooled features didn't reveal his incredulity at this comment. "Why would she have done this?"

Larry winked at the other man. "Just between us, she's always had a thing for me. She was really upset when I asked Mich to marry me instead of her. Why do you think she comes to visit so often? To see me."

Sam could not believe the man's ego.

"Of course she probably thought she was doing Mich a favor, putting her out of her misery. Cass has always been a sucker for stray cats and underdogs. I'm sure she knew I'd inherit, too; probably figured with Mich out of the way she'd have me and all the money. But I'm not that easy a catch; I have other ideas and opportunities, if you know what I mean."

"Not exactly, Mr. Merritt, what do you mean?"

But Larry realized he might be talking too much. "Why are you asking all these questions?"

"Just trying to get a clear picture of what happened. Any information or suppositions you can provide help us in our investigations."

"Who are you again?"

"Sam Chambers, assistant D.A. for Jefferson County."

"D.A. That means you are looking for someone to pin it on. Well it won't be me. I'm not saying another word until I talk to my lawyer."

"I understand, Mr. Merritt. You've been very helpful. I'm afraid there are just a couple other things."

"Like what?" Larry asked suspiciously.

"You'll have to stay somewhere else until we finish processing the house. It's a potential crime scene and we can't have you living here, possibly contaminating any evidence." Sam had specifically chosen the word "contaminating"; the man made Sam feel dirty. "A deputy will be with you when you pack. I'll need you to give me a contact number once you relocate."

"Anything else?" Larry asked with a sneer.

"You know that list of things you have to do?"

Larry looked quizzically at the serious attorney.

"You might want to put 'plan a funeral' on the list. The medical examiner will let you know when your wife's body will be available."

Sam turned on his heel and left the room. Larry knew he'd made a tactical error.

Half an hour later a small parade left the house, Cassie, Doc, Larry, and Sam Chambers. The techs were still processing the bedroom, then they'd move to the rest of the house, looking for means of entry, traces of an intruder, anything that might help explain the death. Some deputies had begun their search of the premises and grounds while others were talking to the neighbors to see if they had seen or heard anything.

The media had arrived, too. News crews and print reporters encircled the front drive. Suddenly it hit Cassie that Mich was more than her best friend, she was a 'name', too. Doc and Cassie hurried to his car; Cassie had to leave her rented car in the driveway at Mich's until it was released by the deputies. Doc slowly made their way out the driveway and headed for the Sheriff's department. The newsies ignored them. "Nobody knows about our relationships with Mich yet, Cass, so we're safe from them for now."

Sam Chambers was recognized and the reporters pushed closer to him, shouting questions. Sam politely but firmly repeated "no comment" as he steered Larry to his car in the still open garage. Larry kept trying to pull away from Sam's insistent grip to garner his fifteen minutes of fame.

As Sam pushed Larry into the driver's seat, he cautioned, "For your own good, do not talk to the press. This is an on-going investigation. If I find out you have talked to anyone I will charge you with obstruction of justice and lock you up. Do I make myself clear?" Sam glowered at the seated man.

"Perfectly," Larry glowered back. He turned the key of his Corvette, put the car into reverse, and slammed his foot on the gas, forcing Sam and two reporters to jump for their lives, or at least their feet.

Chapter 15

From the time he was about eight, Sam Chambers was determined to be a lawyer. All his efforts through high school were focused on getting into a good pre-law college. He took the right college-prep courses and excelled in them. He was president of his high school's student council, a national merit scholar, and an Eagle Scout. It worked; he attended Duke for undergrad and a lot of excellent basketball. Although he decided he liked the south, and especially North Carolina, he knew he would never leave Colorado, so he went back to University of Denver for law school.

In his youth he had pictured lawyers as modern day Don Quixotes, tilting at the windmills of injustice. In college his vision had changed to one of a briefcase-toting Superman, fighting for "truth, justice, and the American way". By law school he knew he wanted to join a Public Defenders office and litigate for the under-represented, those too poor to pay for fancier legal advice. After six years in the PD's office he had no illusions left. Law is a dirty business. He had learned there is a big difference between "legal" and "justice".

Nowadays he couldn't even remember what had prompted the lawyer decision as a child. Instead of the "huddled masses yearning to breathe free" that he had expected to defend, he got crafty drug dealers, whiney murderers, and slimy child molesters; all of whom knew more about the system than he did. They rarely showed remorse, unless there was a judge and jury present; then the tears flowed onto their newly purchased button down shirts and conservative ties. They just wanted him to fix it so they could pay as little as possible in the way of jail time for whatever crime they had committed. Sam referred to himself as a "fixer" rather than an attorney. Occasionally he got to really help someone, just enough times to keep him hanging in there, ever hopeful of doing some real good.

The final deciding factor wasn't even his case; it was John DeLacey's. Depending on your perspective, John was either the best or the worst of the lawyers in the PD's office. He was definitely the most popular with defendants. John would do anything necessary to get a client off, no matter who got hurt in the process. He had utterly no regard for anyone but his clients, and really no regard for them either. The clients were just a means to an end, a way to get his picture in the paper again. DeLacey walked a very fine line between legal and illegal, sometimes planting more than his toes over the line. When that happened, his charm got him nothing more than a slap on the wrist and more face time in the press or on evening news shows, and especially in social media. All of which enhanced his standing in the "downtrodden" community.

The case that finally drove Sam from the dark side, as he thought of it, was one of DeLacey's murder trials. A man had been accused of killing the policeman who tried to capture him after the defendant had killed four other people in a mall parking lot. It was pretty open and shut, the state had lots of credible witnesses, the killer had been captured with the murder weapon in his hand and three other guns next to him, all the forensics matched. DeLacey insisted the officer had been at fault; that he shouldn't have tried to apprehend the murderer by driving his squad car up near the bunker the shooter had set up in the parking lot, shooting at anything and anyone that moved. In short, DeLacey tried to convince the jury the killer was acting in self-defense, that they should ignore the .50 calibre rounds he had put through the windshield and the head of the now-deceased rookie police officer.

When DeLacey showed pictures of the murder scene and the dead policeman, the officer's pregnant wife, sitting in the courtroom, was visibly upset. DeLacey asked the judge to have her escorted from the courtroom "if she can't control herself."

Sam walked out of the PD's office after the verdict came in. All DeLacey's histrionics and shenanigans had convinced the jury to return a verdict of second degree murder in the death of the officer. The fact that the murderer was sentenced to life in prison for the other four murders did nothing to mitigate DeLacey's culpability in what Sam considered a miscarriage of justice. DeLacey's grand-standing to the press didn't help either.

Sam offered his services to the Jefferson County District Attorney's office that same afternoon. He felt there he would be able to fight for justice, at least for the victims and their families; the ones nobody seemed to care about any more.

Greg Lawrence, the D.A., was glad to get Sam. He knew and liked the younger man, and more importantly he respected him. In all the dealings between the DA's and PD's offices, Sam had always been a straight shooter. He had defended his clients to the best of his ability, but he was reasonable enough to recognize when it was a lost cause; then he got the best "deal" he could for his clients.

In the four years since he had become an ADA, Sam had proven himself time and again as a fair man, recognizing the duty he owed to the victims –or their families- to get them justice. Greg and Sam thought a lot alike. That's why Greg had asked him to look into the Merritt situation; it was time the young man got some press exposure for a big case. The death of a famous artist was just the way to do it. Lawrence had no way of knowing how much visibility Sam was in for.

Chapter 16

Normally all the investigative work would be left to the detective on the case; Gil Armijo this time. Gil and Sam had worked together several times before. After reviewing his notes Saturday evening, though, Sam felt he wanted to be more directly involved. He asked Gil to meet him at Applebee's on Kipling Sunday morning for a cup of coffee and an update.

The two men ignored their coffees as Gil reviewed the situation. "Sam, it looks like cyanide poisoning according to that Dr. Harper and the preliminary report from the ME. If that's the case, we've got too many possibles for doing the deed. The lady could have committed suicide. Her charming husband could have killed her. Even the doctor or friend could have done it, mercy killing."

"Mercy killings don't usually involve adding pain," Sam reminded the cop. "Who are the likely possibles, Gil? I can't see the doctor or Cassie doing it. Where's the motive? They provided unimaginable pain out of love?"

"I'm with you there; I can't see any reason behind it, unless you believe Ms. Kirkland had the hots for Mr. Merritt." Gil emphasized the titles.

"I've talked to her. I did not get the impression Larry Merritt is one of her favorite people. On the contrary, I think if he was dead we might be looking at her as the perp."

"And the doc is all broken up. I guess there's a chance for mercy killing, but he doesn't seem the type. I sure think he could have found a less painful way to help her out."

"I agree. So that leaves the happy couple. Facing a lingering death, Mrs. Merritt might have taken the quick, if not easy, way out. But Cassie is emphatic that Mrs. Merritt was planning a future. She says Mrs. Merritt talked about shipping her a painting in a couple weeks, they were planning a trip for next year and had plans to go shopping on the day Mrs. Merritt died."

"Excuse me, Counselor, but do we have any concrete proof of that or just Ms. Kirkland's say-so?" Gil again emphasized the "Ms." Kirkland; he had noticed the lady was the only one Sam referred to by a first name.

"You're right. All we have is her word, but she'll make a pretty convincing witness. Friend of over ten years, steady, reliable, intelligent."

"Plus, why would anyone choose cyanide? That's a pretty brutal way to kill yourself or anyone else. Sleeping pills would have been just as effective and a lot less painful."

"You're right there. So where does that leave us?"

"By a process of elimination, we've got the husband, a piece of work if ever I've seen one."

"You said it. Unfortunately, there's no law against being an SOB. If there was, he'd be up on multiple counts, not to mention several other people I could name. So what we got?"

Gil took a sip of his coffee and ticked off on his fingers, "So far, he's the best candidate. He's definitely got motive: dying wife, lots of money, maybe a honey on the side. He had plenty of opportunity; he even came home early from a trip. Maybe he came home early to try to frame Ms. Kirkland? No "means" yet, but cyanide isn't that hard to get; you can even order it over the Internet with the right ID. And supposedly he ordered books on poison, according to Ms. Kirkland."

"Other possibilities we're overlooking? Burglary? A stalker? Irate neighbor? Jealous lover? After the notoriety last year, we don't want to be accused of rushing to judgment.

Gil thought a moment. "Not this time. All the doors were locked from the inside, dead-bolts on each one; Ms. Kirkland had to unlock the front door to let the paramedics in. No signs of a break-in, nothing missing. Stalking is unlikely, and we haven't found a motive for any such thing yet. Besides, how many stalkers run around with cyanide in their pockets? All the neighbors spoke highly of Mrs. Merritt, not so highly of Mr. Merritt.

"We're still checking everything and talking to friends and employees. Need to find the alleged mistress, too. I'll keep you in the loop, but I'm 90% sure it's the husband."

"I'm with you, Gil, but it's all pretty much circumstantial. I wish we had something concrete to hang him with."

"Relax, it's still early on. We'll have some forensics back this week along with the tox screen, maybe they'll help. And we haven't finished searching the whole house yet. Maybe we'll find a big bottle of cyanide hiding under the kitchen sink with his prints all over it."

"Wouldn't that be nice? But I wouldn't count on it. Where are you with the search warrant?"

Looking at his watch, Gil replied, "Picking it up in about an hour. Judge Matthews said we could come by after church and get it signed. He said we really don't need one, but since there's doubt about whether it's a crime scene or a suicide, he'd sign it just to be safe; don't want any 'technicalities' blowing the case out of court. Of course we started searching last night, as soon as all you bystanders were out of the way. Posted a guard overnight in case Mr. Merritt forgot something and came back, or our friends in the press tried to snap a few photos."

"Good. Let me know how that goes. How 'bout if you follow up on Mr. Merritt? Phone records, credit cards, the works. See what you can find about the girlfriend or anything else that might help us. Check insurance policies and wills. See if you can find anything. I'll follow up with Cassie and the doctor."

Gil had to work really hard to keep the speculation off his craggy face. "So is this a high priority, Sam? I do have other cases you know."

"Greg has made it a top priority. She was a young, attractive, dying celebrity and it may be a brutal murder. Let's see where we are by end of week."

Standing up from the booth, Gil questioned, "Good enough. I'll keep you informed. You've got my cell number?"

"I keep it close to my heart," Sam said patting his shirt pocket and tossing a five onto the table. The men chuckled as they went to their cars.

Shortly before Sam and Gil arrived at Applebee's, Larry was snuggling up to his mistress in her satin-sheeted bed. Teri kept the sheets just for him, he loved the cool slipperiness of the satin, said he found it very erotic. "Come on, sleepyhead, time to wake up. Your man is hungry, and he wants breakfast, too," Larry whispered into Teri's ear.

Teri Muir opened her big blue eyes and grinned at him. She brushed her long blonde hair back off her shoulder as a cloud passed over her features and she pushed his teasing hand away.

"Larry, you didn't do anything wrong did you? Nothing to hasten her death? You know I'd wait as long as need be."

Larry flopped onto his back and stared at the ceiling. "This is not how I wanted to start the day," he growled through gritted teeth. "And, no I didn't do anything wrong." He threw the sheets back and reached for his boxer shorts.

"Okay, Larry, okay. I just wanted to be sure." Tantalizingly she lowered the sheet from her large naked breasts, "Come on back to bed, honey, I can make you forget I asked." Larry turned and leered, reaching to fondle her breast as he dropped the shorts.

While Sam and Gil discussed the case across town, Cassie and Doc were not having as pleasant a time in Doc's bachelor kitchen, although their conversation was similar. As it turned out Cassie hadn't had to move to a hotel; Doc had invited her to stay with him. Doc's house wasn't as big as Mich's, but it was just as comfortable. Three bedrooms upstairs, all good-sized and overlooking a pond in the back yard. All the furniture looked as though it had been in Doc's family for generations; she especially liked that he had given her the end room with the yellow and green Irish Chain quilt on the bed.

They were trying to figure out what had happened. Twenty-four hours later the initial shock and pain had passed. The statements at the Sheriff's office had been straightforward enough. Now a grim determination and resolve had settled in; Michela's death would not be written down as a suicide nor go unsolved.

"Doc, are you sure she didn't have a chance? She seemed so upbeat and certain she could lick it again."

"Cassie, you know as well as anyone how she could deceive herself.

If she thought it was so, it was. She could talk herself into anything and then believe it was fact."

"And bullheaded! My dad used to say that men were strong-willed and women were bull-headed," Cassie said with a grin. More slowly, "Oh, I know. I guess that's how she managed to stay married to Larry for so long. She was convinced he loved her and nothing could change her mind, not even proof of his affairs." A gleam came into her eyes as she said this. "Proof! Doc, she said she had seen the expenditures on his women. She had the credit card receipts for his gifts to his girlfriends. Do you think she kept them?"

"Who knows? I guess she might have. But where? There's no safe at the house as far as I know."

"Maybe at a bank? Safe deposit box?"

"Could be. Could be anywhere. Or maybe she didn't keep them."

"That's true," Cassie said deflated. "Do you think we should tell that detective? As much as I loathe Larry, I don't want to point a finger at him unfairly."

Doc stared silently at the young woman. Cassie was chewing her bottom lip, wordlessly wrestling with the decision.

"Cassie, do you honestly believe Larry could have killed her?"

Cassie looked up at the dejected man. He could read the determination in her eyes. "I don't know. All I know is Mich didn't kill herself and I didn't do it. Larry has never cared for anyone but himself. I think he could have killed her just to get her out of his way. At least this way he didn't have to actually DO anything, no knife or gun, that sort of thing."

"Then you should tell someone. Why don't you call that guy from the DA's office? He seemed pretty reasonable. Let him make the decision about whether it's important."

"Good idea. I've got his card up in my room. I'll call him right now. I'd better try my boss, too. I've been trying to reach him to let him know I won't be back as soon as I'd planned. He won't be happy. We've got inventory coming up and I promised I'd be back."

"I'm sure he'll understand. These are somewhat unusual

circumstances," Doc said to her retreating back.

Cassie shrugged her shoulders in an I-don't-even-care attitude as she climbed the stairs to the phone in her new home-away-from-home.

Chapter 17

Sam knocked at Doc's front door a couple hours after leaving Gil, as he had arranged with Cassie on the phone. A new Cassie opened the door. He admired the trim figure in jeans and T-shirt and the brightness in her eyes. "Hey, you look like a new person!"

"Sleep will do that for you. I slept like a log. I think Doc may have slipped me something." All this was delivered with a hesitant smile, as though she felt guilty about feeling better. "Come on in. Doc's gone to the office; he said work was the best thing for him."

Sam closed the door behind him. "I didn't really know how you'd feel about seeing me again so soon; I thought you might harbor some hard feelings."

Cassie tilted her head and looked at him with real confusion. "Why? You're just doing your job. It certainly wasn't *your* fault Michela died. And I want to help put her killer away. The way I see it, we're on the same side."

Sam visibly relaxed as he followed Cassie down the hall, admiring the rear view on her compact figure.

"I haven't had breakfast and was going to fix some lunch. Want some? It's just soup and sandwich, but my cooking hasn't killed anyone yet." Cassie caught herself as she said this and turned to the tall man, "Poor choice of words, I guess."

Sam took off his windbreaker as he looked deeply into her eyes. He saw no tricks, no manipulation, just honesty and lingering pain. "It'll get easier," he said as he hung his jacket over a bar stool at the kitchen island. "For a while everything you say, every thought you have will remind you of something about Michela. You'll feel guilty about laughing when she can't. For a while you'll feel guilty about everything, especially about being alive. But eventually it gets easier; the pains don't come as often." He looked over her head to something in his past.

"You sound like you've been there," she tried to draw him out.

"Yeah. My kid brother was killed by a drunk driver six years ago. We were supposed to go out together, but I decided to work late. If I'd gone I'd have been driving and the other car would have slammed into me instead of him."

"I'm sorry. That must have been really hard. I guess that's why this whole thing is so unreal, it was so sudden, so unexpected. I knew she had cancer and was probably not going to be around too much longer, but I didn't expect to lose her now, not now when we were having so much fun, when she was so upbeat. It must have been like that for you. I hope this isn't bringing it all back for you."

Sam mentally shook himself and smiled down at her. "Hey, it's in the past. I can handle it now and you'll be better too. How 'bout that lunch? I didn't have breakfast either."

Cassie looked at him another long minute and then, "Tomato soup okay? My favorite lunch is tomato soup and a grilled cheese sandwich, the original comfort food."

"Perfect, we'll talk while you fix it if that's okay?"

"Sure." Cassie opened the frig and took out a tub of soft butter, a package of mozzarella cheese, and some skim milk. As she turned to reach for the bread she found Sam leaning against the island watching her movements.

"Trust me, you'll love grilled mozzarella." They smiled at each other like old friends.

"I trust you," Sam replied.

Cassie hesitated briefly as she put the ingredients on the counter. *Better not go there* she thought. "So what do you need to know?"

"On the phone this morning you said Michela had told you she had seen credit card receipts for her husband's purchases for his girlfriends."

"That's what she said – flowers, jewelry, high-end lingerie. Since she hadn't received any of the purchases and Larry's mom is dead and who knows where his sister is, she figured they weren't for a family member. Mich said all this sort of sarcastically; who would buy lingerie for their mom or sister anyway? I just thought you might look for the receipts; I don't know if she kept them."

"They're searching now. Even if we don't find them, we can get copies from the credit card company."

"Will that help put him away?"

"Whoa, not so fast. So far we don't know for sure that he's done anything. We don't know if anyone has done anything. Maybe the cancer got her."

Cassie pulled open a utensil drawer so forcefully it almost fell on her foot. Grabbing a soup ladle she advanced on Sam, "Michela did not kill herself. I know her. If she wouldn't divorce him because she loved him, why would she kill herself and really get away from him? That doesn't even make sense." Seeing the ladle waving around like a weapon Cassie was momentarily embarrassed by her intensity. She lowered the ladle onto the counter and picked up a spoon. She more calmly stirred the simmering soup. "Sorry. I just will not believe she took her own life. We had plans. Besides, she wouldn't lie to me." The last was almost whispered. "She knew how I felt about lying."

Picking up a table knife, she saw Sam flinch out of the corner of her eye. She sheepishly grinned at him. "Relax. I'm just going to butter the bread for the sandwiches."

Remembering the force and passion that had glinted in the young woman's eyes a moment before, Sam realized there was a lot more steel there than he thought. Had she killed her friend? He immediately put the thought from his mind. If she had, why was she trying to ruin a suicide finding? If Michela's death was ruled a suicide Cassie'd be home free. And what was her motive? He couldn't believe her hatred of the husband was all an act, that she really desired him.

"I'll fix drinks. Where are the glasses?"

Cassie pointed to a cupboard left of the sink. "I'll have ice water. There's beer or whatever you want," she said as she used the spatula to expertly flip the sandwiches in the fry pan. The now-top side was golden brown and white melted cheese was just starting to ooze between the slices.

"That milk looked good to me." Sam fixed the drinks and took them to the breakfast table. He grabbed a couple paper napkins from the holder on the island and put them on the table, too.

"You're pretty handy to have around," she said as she brought the soup bowls brimming with steaming creamy tomato soup to the table. She returned for the sandwiches as Sam replied. "My mom trained me right. Is there anything else you can remember?"

Cassie chewed her lip as she searched her memory. She took a bite of the sandwich absent- mindedly as she tried to help.

"Over the years she has sent me lots of letters and e-mails. We 'talked' all the time. She had told me about his girlfriends, his sarcasms, and his put-downs. I thought Larry was emotionally abusive. He'd do things like ask her for an opinion about something, then if she gave it, he'd shoot her down and explain why it was a stupid thing to say. He did that all the time, and he didn't care who was around. But she overlooked everything. He was Mr. Wonderful for her, even though he treated her so miserably."

Sam took a bite, "Hey this is really good!"

Cassie smiled at him. "Told you."

"The last e-mail I got was a couple weeks ago. She seemed fine, upbeat about beating her illness. Then Sunday she left me a message on my cell phone, said she needed me to come see her and not to reply by e-mail or cell phone 'cause Larry was reading her messages and checking her call list. She thought he had the house phones bugged, too. She said just to come, it was an emergency."

"So you came."

"Of course, we're – were – best friends. She was always there for me when I needed her, if only at the end of a phone. We were always there for each other."

"What did she say after you got here?"

"She told me about the poison books." Cassie stopped in mid-sentence. Her eyes got big as saucers. "The poison books! Did I tell you about them? How stupid can I be?"

"Calm down. What about them?" Sam knew about them from his talk with her the day of Mrs. Merritt's death, but he wanted to see what else Cassie might have to say.

"Mich said there had been some charges to Amazon on their credit card statements. She hadn't ordered anything so she called Amazon to verify the charges. They faxed her a printout; it was books about poisons and drug interactions. They'd been sent to Larry at the office."

"What did she say about them?"

"Initially when she told me about them she was really freaked, but the more she talked, the more she convinced herself she was wrong to suspect Larry. They use a lot of different chemicals at the plant in dealing with the metals. It made sense at the time, but now it seems to have a different meaning maybe."

Sam's cell phone rang. He listened for a minute and put it back into his pocket. "They didn't find any credit card printouts, but they did find another Aleve bottle ...hidden in the back of a drawer. It only had a couple capsules in it."

"Is that important?"

"We won't know until we test them. There was a full bottle in the bathroom, so why another bottle? And why in the back of a drawer? Right now it's just something to think about."

"What drawer?" Cassie was almost afraid to ask.

"Larry's dresser."

Cassie looked long and hard at the young attorney; he looked relaxed in his khakis and sport shirt, but determined, too. Lunch was finished in silence, each thinking the same thing: *How could he?*

Chapter 18

After Sam left, Cassie continued to sit at Doc's kitchen table, looking out the window at nothing, her thoughts miles away in the past. Back to college and the day she met Michela, their winter sledding trips with other girls from the dorm. It was hard finding enough snow in middle Tennessee, but they always managed.

Their junior year Larry came on the scene, Mr. Cool. He swept Mich off her feet. For all her talent and brains, Michela had always been terribly insecure, especially with men. The few men she had dated had always been older, if not actually father-figure types. Having one of the most popular men on campus paying attention to her just overwhelmed her.

Cassie remembered her own not-so-subtle attempts to talk Mich out of marrying him. Obviously they all failed. Cassie could never give Mich the real reason for not wanting the marriage, that Larry was a liar; it would have hurt Mich and probably ruined their friendship. Cassie didn't want to lose Mich completely, although she feared the marriage would build a barrier between them.

But the barrier had never been as high as she expected. Cassie just resolved to be around Larry as little as possible. The man could not keep his hands to himself. If he propositioned Cassie once, he'd done it a million times...while engaged and then married to Mich. He just refused to take "no" for an answer. It was inconceivable to him that Cassie or any woman was not interested in him.

At least she hadn't had to worry about him since they graduated; she only saw him once a year or so. From Mich's messages, though, it seemed he hadn't changed, just found easier prey.

Cassie's reverie was interrupted by the ringing of the kitchen phone. She shook herself and unclenched her fists; she hadn't realized how tense she had become just thinking about "the sleaze".

Picking up the phone, she heard Sam's voice.

"Cassie? I've got some news. Do you want it over the phone or shall I come back?"

Cassie was surprised at how pleasurable she found his voice; she wanted to see him again. "No. I'm okay. Just tell me." *Steady, girl.*

"Dr. Harper was right. It was cyanide poisoning. The initial tox screen came back a little while ago. And they found capsules full of cyanide in the Aleve bottle next to the bed."

"But Michela said she couldn't take any analgesics; it might have bad interactions with her cancer meds."

Sam was silent, then, "There's more, Cassie."

"What else?" Cassie was holding her breath. *What else could there be?*

"The Aleve bottle in Larry's dresser had capsules of cyanide, too."

Cassie gasped. As much as she loathed the man she still found it hard to believe someone she knew might have killed, and killed someone she loved.

She leaned her forehead against the cupboard over the phone and grasped the phone tighter.

"What does this mean? Will he be arrested?"

"Well, we have to get an indictment. Then he'll be arrested and arraigned and eventually tried."

"How long does all this take?"

"The first part is pretty quick. It'll take months, maybe even a year or more before it comes to trial though."

"Can I go home after the funeral?"

Sam hesitated. "Not yet, Cassie. We'll need you to stick around for a while yet. You're our star witness. I'm sure the defense attorney will want to talk to you. Do you have some place to stay?"

"I don't know. Doc will probably let me stay here. I'll have to ask him."

"Okay, shouldn't be more than a week, then you can go back to Virginia until the trial."

"Okay. I guess. Whatever I have to do. Thanks for letting me know."

Sam was concerned with the pain he heard in her voice. He had expected jubilation. But he didn't know Cassie; for all her worldliness and all the jolts she had received in life she still had a child-like trust in others. Learning of Larry's evil crushed her spirit, if only temporarily.

"You okay? Is Dr. Harper there?"

Cassie straightened her shoulders. "Yes, I'm fine. Anything else?"

"No, I guess that's it. If anything else comes up I'll let you know."

"Okay, thanks. I'll be here unless Doc throws me out."

"Fine. Call me if you think of anything else."

Cassie hung up and went in search of a sweater.

Chapter 19

The next few days passed in a blur. At times Cassie convinced herself she was just an eyelash away from being charged with her best friend's murder. Sam kept her informed of what was going on; she wasn't sure he was supposed to be doing this, but she appreciated his attention. At least it seemed he didn't think she was a murderess.

On Tuesday, Sam met with his boss and laid out the whole case: Larry's means, motive, and opportunity. For every point Sam made, Greg Lawrence shot it down with a corresponding point of how Mich could have committed suicide, or Cassie could have killed her or even Doc.

"But, Greg, Cassie had no motive or means, and by all accounts Michela was a fighter; she wouldn't have killed herself. Cassie is a credible witness to Mich's state of mind. By eliminating Mich as a suicide Cassie knows she's opening the door to herself as a suspect, but she maintains her stance. I'll go with Cassie."

Greg looked thoughtfully at his favorite ADA. Greg had respected Sam when he first came to the DA's office, and over the years they had become friends as well as professional colleagues. That's not to say they always agreed, but they'd learned to respect each other's opinions. Their compromises were always well thought out and well fought. Greg felt Sam might have gotten in a bit deep on this one, though. "As we all know, cyanide is too easy to get. Just because capsules were found in Merritt's drawer doesn't mean he put them there. This is a very tricky case."

"Besides, Merritt will hang himself," Sam continued. "Just put him on the stand and every one of the jurors will see him for the self-centered, grasping bastard he is. You should have heard Gil after he took the grieving husband's statement. Not once did Merritt ask about finding his wife's killer. His only concern was how soon the will could be read. He didn't even ask about getting the body for a funeral. And he's been staying with another woman since he left the house Saturday. The guy's a piece of work."

Lawrence queried, "Maybe his sister? A cousin? A friend?"

Sam hesitated. "Of course anything's possible, we're checking her out now."

"And if his attorney won't put him on the stand?"

"Then we'll call him."

"He'll just take the fifth and refuse to testify."

"Then Cassie will hang him. She's known him a long time; she's got stories about his philandering and his treatment of Michela."

"It's all hear-say. The jury will never buy it."

"Who's not going to believe a librarian for God's sake? She's warm, she's sincere, and she's obviously deeply upset about her friend's death."

"And maybe she's a great actress. Is she a stereotypical Marian-the-librarian?"

Greg watched Sam closely. Sam's face took on a softer look as his mind envisioned the trim figure, curly hair, and perky nose of his star witness. "Not by a long shot. But she does wear glasses on a Croakie around her neck," Sam said with a grin.

Greg's concern about Sam's objectivity grew; he'd noticed the change in Sam each time he mentioned Cassie's name.

"So what does your gut tell you, Sam?"

"It's Larry. No doubt about it."

"It's all circumstantial, Sam; no smoking gun."

"We've got poisons at his place of work, maybe cyanide is one of them. We've got his prints on the bottle with the capsules, Merritt stands to inherit millions from a now-dead sickly wife who he was screwing around on. What more do we need?"

"An eyewitness would be nice. Cassie was in the house at the time of death; Larry was on the golf course. Maybe she resented her friend's success while she's some small town librarian. A good defense attorney will blow us out of the water."

"I can win this one, Greg, I know it. Let's go for it. Cyanide is a terrible way to die. He deserves to be punished for what he did to her."

Greg stared a few more minutes at the younger man, his pen tapping to the rhythm of his thoughts as he mentally reviewed the pros and cons. He knew Sam was a good, maybe a great, prosecutor. If anyone could win it, Sam could. Greg just wasn't sure it was winnable. But they'd gotten convictions on less.

"Okay. We'll give it a go. But I still have reservations. If it gets sticky, we deal."

"I'll have Gil go get him as soon as we get the paperwork. I would love to see Merritt's face when he realizes he's going to jail!"

"Sam, you're sure you're not getting too involved in this one, aren't you? Not doing your knight-in-shining armor routine? This has a bit of the holy grail feel to it."

"I'm sure, Greg. If you'd seen and heard this guy, you'd be as convinced as I am."

"You know it's no crime to be selfish or egotistical."

Sam ran his hands through his hair. "Yeah, I know. But it is a crime when your ego convinces you that you can get away with murder. I'll call Gil right now."

By lunchtime Cassie was ready to download more books to her Kindle. She'd walked, done the dishes, read the paper, cooked meals for her and Doc, took Uber to retrieve her car, and paced for two and a half days. She was ready to pull her hair out from inactivity. As she fixed yet another bowl of soup, she got a call from Larry's personal attorney. She needed to be at his office later that afternoon for the reading of the will. Cassie wasn't sure she was up to it.

She showered and changed into her best pair of black slacks, a white silk blouse and a white linen blazer. She wished she'd at least brought a skirt with her. She'd have to go shopping before the funeral.

When she arrived at the office on the 30th floor of the "cash register" building, nicknamed that because its exterior shape resembled an old fashioned cash register, she was pleased to see Doc in the waiting area.

He immediately put his arms around her in a big hug. "They called me at the office," he said by way of explanation of his presence. "I gave them the home number when they asked if I knew how to reach you. You okay?"

She squeezed the big man's hand and gave him a wavering smile.

"Yeah, I guess. Just hope this isn't too bad. I suppose it's too much to hope Larry won't be here?"

The words were barely out of her mouth when Larry breezed in, all cocky and self-assured. He had on what appeared to be a brand new charcoal grey silk suit and a hearty smile for the receptionist. "Tell Stan I'm here will you?"

"I'd be happy to, Sir, your name?"

Cassie and Doc smiled at each other at the fool's fallen features.

"Larry Merritt," he groused at the young lady, "And I don't like to wait."

His red face turned toward the other two in the subdued-mahogany antechamber to see if they had heard the exchange. Cassie and Doc were deep in conversation and ignoring him. He hated to be ignored.

"Cassie, you look marvelous. You seem to be holding up well," he said as he approached her, his arms extended for an embrace.

Cassie remained seated and turned cold eyes on him.

"You seem to be recovering nicely, Larry. New suit?"

"Yeah, couldn't be seen in old rags during my bereavement now could I? Like it?"

Fortunately the receptionist called them before Cassie could tell him he looked like a hit man. *Did nothing pierce his alligator hide?*

Cassie clutched Doc's arm as Larry preceded them into the spacious office. It looked like Cassie would have expected a successful attorney's office to look if she'd given it a thought. All mahogany and leather, glass walls providing a view of Coors Field; and a tea cart with a silver coffee service and silver water pitcher.

The attorney himself looked like someone from central casting. Tall and lean and grey from head to foot, grey hair, grey suit, grey tie. His chiseled features and dark eyes made Cassie think he was not a happy man. He indicated three burgundy leather side chairs arranged across from his desk. The three seated themselves.

After introducing himself to Cassie and Doc the lawyer started, "We have a somewhat unusual situation here today."

Larry jumped up and leaned across the wide desk. "What do you mean 'unusual'? I'm the husband, I inherit everything," he glowered at the older man.

Stan Culpeper gave Larry a withering look. "If you'll sit back down and give me a moment, I'll explain." The attorney stared calmly at Larry like a teacher with a rowdy student. Larry glared at the gentleman, but reluctantly flopped himself back into his chair.

"Normally, wills are read after the funeral, but since Mr. Merritt insists, it was decided to go through the procedure today. Besides, I was contacted yesterday by Gordon Mansfield, an attorney in Colorado Springs. Highly respected. It seems Mrs. Merritt left a more recent will than the one she drafted here a few years ago. He brought it to me earlier this morning at her request."

Cassie, seated on the far side of Doc, stole a glance at Larry. His eyes had become slits and the plum color had returned to his face.

"I can read the entire will, or just give you the gist of it." He looked at the three expectantly.

"Just give me the bottom line," Larry spat at the attorney. Stan looked questioningly at the other two. They each nodded their assent.

Speaking calmly he explained. "Under Colorado law, Mr. Merritt inherits all their jointly shared property. This includes physical items such as the cars, house, and its furnishings, any other real estate, bank accounts, stocks and bonds. And there is a life insurance policy of one million dollars. The total value comes to about 2.9 million dollars."

Larry relaxed back into his chair, a smug look on his face.

"Out of that Mr. Merritt will have to pay any outstanding debts of the decedent."

Larry waved his hand in a no-big-deal motion.

"Any personal property, that is property not owned jointly, Mrs. Merritt could dispose of as she saw fit. That includes money, stocks, bonds, and..." the lawyer hesitated, "her paintings."

Larry looked less confident. Cassie and Doc looked at each other quizzically.

"According to the terms of this newer will, dated Feb. 17 of this year, all jewelry, private bank accounts, and stocks and bonds are bequeathed to Dr. Harper, for use in cancer work. A rough estimate of the value comes to about 4.7 million dollars."

Doc was torn between beaming at the thought of the difference this money would make to cancer patients and crying at Michela's generosity. "I'd rather have her alive," was all he could finally say.

Larry snorted, "Yeah. Right. Well, don't spend it yet, Doc. I'm going to fight you on this."

"Mr. Merritt, as your attorney I can only say this will was drawn up by a very competent attorney and would be difficult to overturn. Of course, I will be happy to take your money while you try."

In the silence of the room the three could hear the calculator doing its thing in Larry's brain. He squished himself farther back into his chair while he ruminated.

"May I continue?" the lawyer asked.

Larry grunted at the man.

"To her best friend Cassandra Kirkland, Mrs. Merritt has left all her paintings, both those in her studio at the residence and those displayed in galleries. A reputable appraiser informs me the expected value is something over five million dollars, of course that's just a quick guess at this point. The value may very well change once the appraiser has a chance to do a more thorough inventory." The oh-so-dignified lawyer beamed at the young woman.

The shock in Cassie's face was obvious to all in the room. Doc was happy for her. "But I don't know what to do with all that. I don't want it."

"Great. Give it back to me. It's mine anyway; you're not going to keep it, Cassie. She was my wife and those are my paintings."

At his words Cassie bristled. Her back straightened and the tears stopped. If this was what Mich wanted, she'd follow her wishes.

"Is there anything else, Mr. Culpeper?" she asked.

"No, Ms. Kirkland. You will just need to make arrangements about the paintings. I know someone at the Denver Museum of Art who can advise you if you'd like."

Directing her attention solely to the attorney and ignoring Larry's mutterings she stood, "I'd appreciate that, Mr. Culpeper; I'll call you tomorrow for the name."

Again taking Doc's arm Cassie shook hands with the attorney and left his office. Gil Armijo and a uniformed deputy were waiting.

"Detective Armijo, what are you doing here?" Doc asked him while Cassie's grip on his arm intensified.

At that moment Stan Culpeper escorted Larry from his office. "Please call me when you have calmed down, Mr. Merritt. We can discuss everything more rationally then." The two men looked over at the policemen.

Gil Armijo approached Larry who had started offering objections to the lawyer once again.

"Larry Merritt, you are under arrest for the murder of Michela Merritt." The detective proceeded to recite the Miranda warning about remaining silent and having a lawyer present. Cassie thought the whole thing seemed like a scene out of *Law and Order.*

For once Larry was speechless, but only briefly. "Are you out of your mind? I didn't kill her, she killed herself, or that hoity-toity broad over there did it."

"Mr. Merritt, I'm not a criminal attorney, but I think it would be advisable not to say anything. Do you have someone who can advise you about this?" Stan Culpeper asked.

"Oh sure, I keep a criminal defense attorney on retainer just in case I get charged with murder." The click of the handcuffs snapping shut brought Larry to his senses. "Stan, get me an attorney. Get the best one you can find. Money is no object. I'm loaded now." Larry was whisked out of the room by the burly deputy, Gil Armijo following. Stan Culpeper briefly regretted that he had not had a chance to advise his client that he was not "loaded"; that in fact he could not inherit if he was found guilty of murdering his wife.

Cassie and Doc stared at each other open-mouthed. While neither could really believe anyone could commit murder, it was obvious Larry was the most likely person.

It hadn't occurred to Cassie that she had just been given five million motives herself.

Cassie and Doc had thanked the attorney once again and took the elevator to the parking garage. The drive back to Englewood was spent discussing Larry's arrest and what it would mean. They were surprised to find a news van parked in Doc's driveway when they arrived home. Doc opened the garage door remotely and pulled in. As they exited the car, a microphone was stuck in Doc's face and he was asked, "Dr. Harper, do you think Larry Merritt killed his wife?"

Doc glared at the reporter and glaringly replied, "You are trespassing. Get out of my garage." He quickly unlocked the door leading to the kitchen and pushed Cassie through while he kept his eyes on the reporter and soundman as they scurried outside. Doc pushed the button and lowered the garage door behind them. He and Cassie spent the evening with the curtains drawn and the TV turned up. Every once in a while one or the other peeked out the windows to see if the original news van and the others that had arrived had left; they hadn't. At 10 p.m. they turned out the lights and went to bed. They both slept soundly and didn't hear the mass exodus at midnight.

Chapter 20

At 9 a.m. Wednesday morning John DeLacey, dressed in his best defense attorney finery, met with Larry Merritt at the county jail. Merritt was dressed in the requisite jump suit and flip flops. He was a most unhappy person.

"Mr. Merritt, my name is John DeLacey. Stan Culpeper asked me to come talk to you about your ...situation."

"I know who you are, John; I've seen you on TV and in the papers. You have a reputation for getting people off who might not otherwise warrant it; seems you step on a lot of official toes in the process. I guess that's why there are so many editorials about you." Larry chuckled. "I like that. Will you represent me?"

DeLacey had raised an eyebrow at the sudden familiarity his almost-client adopted, and let it show. "Mr. Merritt, I will be happy to serve as your attorney. My fees are rather high, though."

"No problem, I'm about to inherit a fortune."

"Mr. Merritt, you do understand that you cannot inherit if you are found guilty of murdering your wife?"

Larry frowned. Obviously that had not occurred to him. Then he grinned wolfishly at the attorney, "All the more reason for you to see that I don't go to prison, isn't it, John? If you don't get me off, you don't get paid."

DeLacey looked long and hard at the man across the wooden table from him. He had known a lot of alleged murderers in his day, but none with as much cockiness as this one. "My retainer in a case of this nature is $250,000 and then you will be billed the remainder at the end of the trial."

"A quarter of a million dollars? You think a lot of yourself, don't you? Okay, no problem. I have some money squirreled away that my wife never knew about. I'll get you a check as soon as you get me out of here."

"Your arraignment and bail hearing is scheduled for later today. I will expect a check in my office by the end of the day or first thing tomorrow morning if the arraignment is delayed until too late this afternoon."

"Great, you'll have it." Larry didn't like the looks of the attorney, too prissy for him, looked like a French teacher or something...but he's the best in Denver, probably in all of Colorado. "Aren't you going to ask me if I did it?"

"And if I do, what will you say?" A small smile crept to DeLacey's thin lips.

"Hell no, I didn't kill her."

"Exactly. That's what all my clients say, so I usually don't bother to ask. It makes no difference to me, really. My role is to get you "off", as you say. I cannot promise to fulfill that requirement, but I will promise to get you the best outcome possible *if* you cooperate fully with me. You have to look at me as a combination shrink, priest, and best friend. Keep no secrets from me and tell me the truth and we'll work fine together. Lie to me or hold anything back and you will find a new attorney." DeLacey paused for a reaction from Merritt. "Any questions?"

Larry was taken aback by the force coming from the skinny little man. He just shook his head. "Deal. What's the first step?"

"First, we get you out of here. As I said, that will be sometime later today. Once bail is set you are free to go about your business. I will study the police reports and prepare some questions for you. We'll get together next week and start planning our strategy; we'll probably meet about once a week up until the trial. If you cannot come up with the money for the bail I can recommend a reputable bail bondsman; you'll pay him 10% of the bail amount and he'll take care of getting your bail paid. If you run away or in any way fail to repay him, he will find you and get his reimbursement, one way or another."

"You say this guy is reputable? Sounds like a loan shark to me, or one of those wise guys on the TV."

"Bail bondsmen are businessmen. Think of him as a banker, rather like the ones who made all those bad loans. He will "foreclose" if you fail to pay him what he is due. I don't know how he is reimbursed, but I do know he has a good repayment rate. As long as you are straight with him, he'll take good care of you."

Larry mumbled, "Fine."

"Any other questions, Larry?"

Larry noticed when DeLacey switched to his first name. "No, I guess I'm set."

DeLacey stood and held out his hand, "I'll see you this afternoon, then. Be sure you dress nicely and don't say a word unless I tell you to do so. Basically, that will be repeating "Not Guilty" when the judge asks you how you plead. Otherwise, keep your mouth shut. You have no idea how many clients have sabotaged their own cases by not following this directive."

"Got it. See you this afternoon, then."

While Larry was settling his lawyer issues, Cassie and Doc were finalizing the plans for Mich's memorial service on Friday, since Larry had taken no interest in doing anything. They started by going over their checklist for the church: flowers, urn, newspaper notification, not that that was really an issue what with all the publicity, invitations to the friends and neighbors who Doc thought should get personal invitations, invitations to the few college friends Cassie thought might like to know about it even if they couldn't come. Almost everyone local had replied that they would be there. Not much else to do since Mich was being cremated, no need for pallbearers, no need for limos or a hearse, and all the other trappings that went with a casket and burial plot. They did discuss what they were going to do with her ashes, finally agreeing to hold off making a decision in case Larry wanted to be included.

Doc and Cassie agreed the church service was in pretty good shape. Doc was going to do a eulogy, "I just hope I can get through it without blubbering," he said to Cassie. She grinned at him and patted his hand on top of the kitchen table where they were working, "You'll do fine, certainly much better than I ever would! I told the priest we'd just leave the flowers for the church or to give to some of their shut-in parishoners. Are you okay with that?"

"Perfect. That saves us having to do something with them, too."

They moved on to the reception being held at Doc's house, again because Larry had no interest and because his house hadn't been cleared of the crime scene tape yet. "I checked with the caterer and he'll bring tablecloths, too, so that's one less thing to think about. He'll get here about an hour before the reception starts and use the oven in the kitchen to warm the hot canapés. I told him we'd leave the house key under the potted plant on the back porch if we're not back from the service yet. He was fine with that."

Doc nodded. "Sounds like a good plan. I've used him before and he's very trustworthy. We'll put the key out right before we leave. He's handling the booze, too, right?"

"Yep, all the paperwork is in order since he has an ABC license. He said to just leave everything to him, and I'm happy to. So all the food and drink is taken care of. I've asked Justin from next door to help with parking cars and he's happy to do it. Said every little penny goes to his college fund. My only worry is if the press shows up. Do you think they will, Doc?"

"Probably. I talked to Sam about it and he gave me the name of a couple cops who work off-duty jobs and I hired a couple to come and sort of direct traffic and be a presence if the media gets out of hand. I don't think we'll have too much to worry about there."

"What a great idea! I'm glad you were thinking ahead about that. I've just been out of it since Saturday." Cassie started to tear up, "I feel like I've failed Mich."

Now it was Doc's turn to be reassuring. He got up from his chair and went around the table and put his arm around Cassie's shoulder. "We've done this together, Cass, we're a team, and a pretty good one at that. Mich couldn't have had a better friend than you." Cassie's tears slowed and she gave him a watery smile.

"Well, it looks like everything is under control. I think I'll go shopping and get something to wear to the funeral. Anything you need while I'm out?" Cassie asked as she wiped her face.

"Not a thing. I'm going to head over to the office and get caught up on some calls. I'll see you back here for dinner. Enjoy yourself."

They went their separate ways, each thinking of Mich and missing her.

Chapter 21

On Thursday, Sam made a lunch appointment with Cassie. Doc had called him about the will and Sam was worried he might have lost his star witness.

"I know you did nothing wrong, Cassie, but your inheritance could give the defense attorney room to maneuver."

Cassie looked deeply into Sam's sea-green eyes. Then she surveyed the bright colors of YaYas. Doc had told her the restaurant had done very well in the Tech Center, much to everyone's surprise. The ultra-California-modern décor was not to Cassie's taste, but at least it was relatively convenient to where she was staying at Doc's.

She thought about Sam's words. Sounded like he was doubting her. *Figures*, she thought to herself. *Here I am, the most honest person I know, and he doesn't believe me; thinks I may have killed my best friend. Just when I was beginning to trust him, too. That'll teach you, you fool.*

Sam watched the transformation across Cassie's features. When she had walked in the restaurant, he was impressed with her femininity. She was wearing a teal silk blouse and black slacks; she had looked extremely soft and vulnerable. As he watched her now, not knowing her thoughts, he saw strength and ferocity taking over.

Cassie mentally shook herself and turned cold eyes back to Sam. "I did not kill Michela," she said in deliberate, measured tones. "I do not know how I can convince you, but I did not do it. I loved her; she was the sister I never had and my best friend. I do not want the inheritance. Mich gave me a painting when I got here; that's more than enough. I'd rather have her than any of her paintings. I'll probably donate the collection to charity. I really haven't had a chance to think about it."

Sam looked long at the woman across from him, straight spine pressed hard into the back of the booth, hands tightly clenched on the table top. He believed her, but didn't know how to convince her. He didn't know what brought the wall of mistrust up, but he could tell she was too distrusting to believe mere words.

"Cassie, I didn't ask you here to accuse you of anything. I need your help. A good defense attorney will do everything possible to implicate *anyone* else for the murder, especially you. You were there at the time of the murder and you stand to gain from Michela's death. I need to know if there's anything for him to find that can be used against us."

Again Cassie quietly sized him up. *"Us."* She liked the way he had said that.

"I don't know what I can tell you, Sam. I'm a small town librarian. I live in a quiet, wonderful town in southwest Virginia. I'm happy in my life, no major problems...other than being suspected of murder of course." Sam liked to see the twinkle returning to her brown eyes.

"Let's order, then you can tell me the story of your life."

After ordering Cassie asked, "Is it okay for you to be taking me to lunch? Is this ethical?"

Sam smiled at the question that no one ever asked, "I cleared it with Greg, the DA. He said as long as we only discuss the case and I get reimbursed by the department it shouldn't be a problem."

Cassie shrugged at the vagaries of the justice system and, over a grilled Portobello mushroom "burger", she gave Sam the abridged version of her life. "I was born in the same town where I now live. Two parents, no siblings. Went to college in Nashville, that's where I met Mich. Worked for a while in Chicago after graduation. Went back home. Parents died. End of story."

Sam studied her. There had to be more than that. An attractive woman like Cassie had to have some romance. A husband? He decided not to push right now.

"What'd you do in Chicago?"

"I was a program manager for WGN, the TV station."

"What's that mean? What was your job like?"

Cassie perked up. Her animation was infectious. "It was a great job. I and my staff did all the scheduling of the TV programs. Lots of meetings to discuss programming, what shows to run when, what to add to the line-up, what to drop. Viewers' polls. National trends. It was a crap shoot and juggling act rolled into one. Pretty intense most of the time, always trying to stay ahead of the other stations. Not everyone's cup of tea, mostly a logistics position, but I loved it."

Sam marveled at the passion in Cassie's face and voice. Her whole face glowed with her enthusiasm. No pretense.

"Were you a communications major at Vanderbilt?"

Cassie chuckled. "Nope. My time-honored, no-future English degree got me the job. My verbal skills were well-trained, but it seems I'm a natural-born organizer. I have a talent for logistics and scheduling, that's what got me into programming. That and my legs," she grinned impishly.

"Your legs?"

"It seems the HR rep from WGN who came to campus recruiting liked my legs, couldn't keep his eyes off them. Hey, it got me the job and I never had to deal with him after that."

Sam resisted the impulse to look under the table at her legs, remembering she was wearing slacks anyway. "I guess I'll take your word for the great legs," he grinned at her, "At least for now."

"I didn't say they were great, just that he liked them."

"I didn't know you could be a librarian with just an English degree."

"You're right, you can't. When I got back to Lexington I got a staff job at the public library. I could have gotten a job at the college library. My folks were both professors at W&L, and it's famous around town for its nepotism in hiring, but I wanted to work in the public library..." she grinned, "and the public library was hiring and W&L wasn't. I worked on my library science degree online for about two years and completed it. I've always loved books so it seemed a natural; it's quiet and no stress and I get to help people, I like that. All the townspeople use the library, so I get to socialize."

"W&L?"

"Sorry, local shorthand. Washington and Lee, a very prestigious college, at least in the south."

"So if Chicago was such a great job, why'd you leave?"

The lights in her eyes dimmed immediately. Cassie seemed to melt into the booth right before his eyes, like the Wicked Witch from the *Wizard of Oz*. But he knew this woman was no wicked witch.

"I'd rather not go into it. I left, that's enough," she said softly.

"I'm afraid I need to know, Cassie. I know the attorney we're up against and he'll dig up anything he can to blacken your testimony. We have to be prepared to fight."

That 'we' again. "Tell me about him, Larry's attorney," Cassie changed the subject easily.

"John DeLacey is an attorney who gives other attorneys a bad name. He isn't really interested in his clients, just his batting average. He wins most of his cases. I knew him when we were both at the Public Defender's office. He'll do anything to win so he can get publicity. About two years ago he went into private practice and he's been doing well, too well from my perspective.

"This is a big case, could make the national news. Michela was becoming a nationally famous artist. It has all the sizzle of an OJ trial. John will be playing to the cameras all the time, and playing to win. His strength is that he can create doubt in jurors' minds out of nothing. As the saying goes, if you can't impress them with your intelligence, dazzle them with bullshit. Unfortunately, he's full of both."

Silence. Cassie retreated to her food. Sam gave her time to decide while he ate his real burger with cheddar, bacon, and onions. He studied the internal battle going on across from him while he chewed.

Cassie put her fork down. "I was married while I was in Chicago. It didn't work out. We got divorced and I went back to Lexington, took back my maiden name."

"Why'd you get divorced?"

Cassie glared at him, obviously not wanting to discuss it any further.

She took a deep breath and a sip of her chardonnay. "He drank...a lot. When he did he got belligerent. His anger terrified me. Eventually I decided I didn't need this anymore. After three years I divorced him and left. He didn't care. I haven't seen him since."

"Sounds like a smart move to me."

"Easy to say. It was the hardest thing I've ever done. I'm not proud of it. I wasn't strong like Mich; I couldn't stay married because of my vows. She always hinted that she thought I ran away, but she never said it."

Sam had picked up on the comment. "Are you saying Larry beat Michela?"

"No, not that I know of. He just ran around on her and treated her like dirt, practically from the day they met. Larry's strength was in the put-down, belittling her, questioning everything she did, every decision she made. She knew about his affairs; early on he bragged about them to her. I tried to get her to divorce him, but she wouldn't. Said she loved him and he needed her, whether he knew it or not. And Michela needed to be needed, if only for her fame and money. Some whacko symbiotic relationship, I guess. She wrote me all the time. Writing was a sort of catharsis for her."

"Do you still have any of those letters?"

"Maybe. It was mostly e-mails, though, and I've deleted them."

"We still might be able to recover them. When you get home, see if you can find any letters and don't delete any more messages from Michela, okay?"

Cassie nodded.

"When are you going home, anyway?"

"Saturday. I thought I'd stay one more night with Doc, after the funeral and all. He's pretty desolate. Mich was his whole family, his life outside medicine."

Changing the subject again Cassie asked, "So, Sam, are you a native Colorodan?" Sam noticed Cassie's change of subject and decided to let it go for now.

"Yep, born and raised right here in Littleton. Only time I left was when I went to college, then back here to DU, shorthand for University of Denver, for law school. I knew I was going to practice in Colorado, so no point in going to law school any place else, needed Colorado contacts, not from some other state." He grabbed a French fry and bit off half of it.

Cassie commented, "I've been out here several times to visit. Colorado is a great place. The thing that always surprised me is how easy the winters are, at least here in Denver. I came out here one January, expecting six feet of snow and there wasn't any." Cassie forked a tiny bite of portabello.

Sam laughed. "That's because the weather reporting station is in Denver. When you hear a national broadcast they say something like 'Denver reports 87 inches of snow' and they show tape from somewhere in the mountains," Sam explained with a chuckle. "Denver used to be this country's best kept secret, but word got out years ago. Traffic has come to a standstill, literally. Denver is beginning to remind me of those big Eastern cities: lots of people, lots of sitting traffic."

Cassie replied with a spoonful of crème brulee on its way to her mouth, "I know what you mean. That was one of the reasons I left Chicago; too big and impersonal. I seemed to spend my life going to or from work or being at work. I decided that was no life. I'll take Lexington any day."

"I noticed you don't have an accent, Cassie? I thought all you southern belles had accents."

Cassie grinned at the handsome attorney as she fanned her face with her hand and in her best Scarlett O'Hara accent replied, "Why I do declare, Mr. Chambers, I think my years in Chicago must have dampened it." Sam burst into laughter and Cassie dropped the hand-fanning after her face returned to normal. "I notice it still comes out when I'm nervous. I had to give a speech to about 500 people and it was full of 'y'alls' and long a's, like in 'cain't'. I think it's a subconscious defense mechanism, even got me out of a speeding ticket once in Chicago. Doesn't work worth a flip in Virginia." They both laughed at this.

Over coffee and tea Cassie learned that Sam was the oldest of three sons. Sam learned Cassie lived alone in the house she'd grown up in; her parents had died together in a car crash two years before. "It was best that it happened that way, even though they were still young. Neither would have wanted to live without the other; they were totally devoted to each other."

Cassie looked into the distance and silence returned to the table until Sam returned the conversation to the case, "There's one more thing, Cassie."

Cassie's eyebrows raised with a questioning frown.

"John DeLacey wants to talk to you before you leave town. He wanted to do it Friday afternoon, but I reminded him of the memorial service and so he grudgingly changed it to Saturday afternoon. Can you do it Saturday and return to Lexington on Sunday?"

"I guess so. Do I *have* to talk to him?"

"No, you don't have to, but he'll talk to you at some point, might as well get it over with."

"Okay, I'll change my reservations."

Cassie returned to Doc's house and found a news van parked in front of the house. As she pulled her rental into the driveway a reporter with a microphone rushed to her door. Cassie parked and exited the car, headed for the front door, key in hand. She tried to mimic Sam's stoicism as she kept repeating "no comment". Just as she got to the door it swung open and she rushed in. Doc slammed it firmly behind her.

"Vultures," he spat as Cassie caught her breath and dropped her purse on the round hall table. "What's going on, Doc? Why won't they leave us alone?"

"Must be a slow news day. I'm sure our names were mentioned in the paperwork that got Larry arrested, and that's public domain. I'll call Sam and see if there's anything we can do to get them to stop."

"Better call his cell, he just left me at YaYas; we had lunch."

Doc looked at her questioningly for a brief moment then pulled his wallet out to retrieve Sam's card as he headed for the phone in his home office. Cassie heard him talking as she headed up the stairs to change into sweats. *What next?* she worried.

Chapter 22

Cassie and Doc had been surprised they could even have the memorial so soon, but Greg Lawrence had made the case a number one priority and that got the autopsy and the various tests moved to the top of the list. Mich's body had been released to the mortuary late Wednesday afternoon. Even though many of the tests had not been completed the Medical Examiner agreed she didn't need the body any longer.

The service Friday morning was exhausting. Although Cassie knew Mich was famous, she was astounded by the crowd that showed up. In college Mich had loved socializing, but since her cancer she had become a loner; she liked and enjoyed people but didn't socialize with them a whole lot. Recently, Mich was more the one-friend-at-a-time type; and Cassie had pretty much been that friend for a lot of years. As Mich used to say, she was often alone, but never lonely as long as she had her paints. That was the same way Cassie felt about her books.

"I'm amazed at the crowd," she whispered to Doc from the front pew at St. John's Cathedral in downtown Denver.

"Gawkers," he whispered back. "Either media types or just lookers. People think they might see someone famous at a celebrity's funeral, so they show up. Others may have known her in passing, but come to be seen, sort of reflected celebrity. Mich's probably laughing her head off right now." They smiled conspiratorially at each other.

Larry sat across the aisle from Cassie and Doc with his ever-present smirk firmly in place. Cassie was surprised he didn't work up a tear, at least for the cameras.

Doc manfully survived his very eloquent eulogy. Since Mich had been cremated, the service ended at the church. Doc and Cassie did not mingle, but hurried back to his house to be ahead of the people invited for the reception. Larry was out on one million dollars bail and had "no plans to spend his time visiting with a bunch of free-loaders," as he had told Doc.

Cassie was surprised to see Sam among the guests at Doc's. Surprised and curiously pleased. He looked very distinguished in a charcoal suit with a light blue shirt. She went over to him in a corner between the bookshelves and the door to the kitchen.

"Nice service," he said. "Would Mrs. Merritt have liked it?"

Cassie thought a moment. Sam was intrigued by the way she gave each question, even this polite one, careful consideration.

"Yes, I think she would have. Not all the people 'cause Mich preferred her friends in small batches, but she would have liked what Doc had to say. She would have liked the brevity, too; she was never one for much pomp and circumstance."

"What are you grinning about?"

"I was just remembering our college graduation. It was an especially warm May and very muggy, even by Nashville standards. There was a threat of rain so the ceremony was moved to the gym instead of outside in the stadium. Needless to say those long, black polyester robes we were supposed to wear were going to be our personal easy-bake ovens. Mich decided, since all that showed on the women were our feet and hands, she didn't need to get dressed up. She had on a bikini under the gown. She was the most comfortable person during the ceremony, but the most uncomfortable afterwards. She'd forgotten that we had to turn in the gowns *immediately* after the ceremony. There she stood in her hot pink bikini and heels with her diploma in hand. She had to walk across campus like that to get back to Larry's car. She wasn't very good at seeing the whole picture; details and Mich were never close friends."

Sam was grinning at the mental picture. "What a great story! Was she embarrassed?"

"Not a bit. But Larry was furious! He didn't like her making a spectacle of herself, worried about his image. Of course that was before she became famous."

"So you've known both of them a long time?"

"Oh, yes, Mich met Larry our junior year and fell for him like a ton of bricks. He was this BMOC, frat president, student body rep, everything except football star. She was amazed that he even looked at her, let alone asked her out. They married the August before our senior year. Needless to say we didn't room together after that, although Larry wouldn't have minded."

As he said, "Oh? Tell me about Larry" Sam pushed open the door to the kitchen and ushered Cassie into it. The caterers were scurrying about taking food out the other door and washing dishes in the deep farm-style sink. "I didn't know you'd known him that long, I guess."

"I'd really rather not talk about him, at least not right now. It just doesn't seem the right time." Cassie walked back through the swinging door into the den. Sam followed silently, a frown of confusion on his face.

Just then Doc came over and shook Sam's hand. "Glad you could make it, Sam. Didn't see you at the church."

"I was in back, sort of keeping an eye on everything. You never know who might turn up, perps have been known to visit the funeral of their victims so I thought I'd keep an eye out for any suspicious characters, anybody we might have overlooked."

"See any?"

"Nope, but I did notice Mr. Merritt did not seem too upset, even with deputies keeping an eye on him."

"Oh, nothing gets Larry down. He's always believed he can talk his way out of anything. I don't know whether it's optimism or conceit, but he's full of it," Doc opined.

"He's full of it all right," Cassie murmured as she walked back over to join them. Sam glanced at her and she knew he had heard. A blush crept up her cheeks. *Did women still blush?* Sam wondered.

"I was surprised Larry got bail," Doc commented.

"Frankly, I was, too. We argued for a high bail because we think there's a real chance of him packing it in and leaving the country. We didn't think he could swing the cost and we didn't think the judge would grant bail anyway. We guessed wrong."

"At least he came to the service, if only for appearances. How do you know he won't take off and leave, Sam?" Doc looked worried.

"Three reasons. One, if he does he loses the million dollars bail money, assuming his bail bondsman can find him to collect it. Two, we have him under 24-hour surveillance and we let him know it. We sent a couple minders along to the church and let him know it afterwards. And three, he had to turn in his passport. That won't stop someone who's really dedicated to flee, but it makes it more difficult and more expensive. We've also got a watch on his bank accounts for any large transactions." Sam surveyed the crowd that had spilled outside onto the raised desk. "I see he's not here."

"He was invited of course, but he preferred what he called 'a private time" with just a couple friends," Doc explained. Cassie snorted and blushed again.

Sam frowned. "He had said he was going to a reception after church; I just assumed it was here. Excuse me." Sam walked off a few paces and took out his smart phone. After identifying himself he asked, "What's going on? Where are you?"

Listening and scowling, he then replied, "Yeah, fine. Just keep an eye on him."

He replaced the phone in his jacket pocket. "Seems his private time is with a Ms. Teri Muir. That'll teach me to ask more questions." Turning to Cassie, "Speaking of questions, are you ready for your deposition tomorrow?"

"I don't know. I have no idea what to expect. I've never given a deposition before, never served on a jury either."

"Nothing to it. Since you live in Virginia, a deposition is the defense attorney's method of getting your testimony on record in case you can't get back for the actual trial. DeLacey will ask you questions and you'll answer, but answer only the questions, don't volunteer any information. If you don't understand a question, ask that it be rephrased or restated. A court reporter will be there creating a transcript. You'll be under oath so just tell the truth and that's it. You may ask for breaks when you need them. And don't take anything with you, not even paper and pen."

"Sounds easy enough. So why do you look so apprehensive? I thought I should be the worried one?"

Sam shrugged his shoulders and hesitated before saying, "It's DeLacey. You never know what he might ask. He's pretty slick."

"But since I will be here for the trial, what will they do with the deposition?"

Sam looked off into the distance before answering, obviously wishing she hadn't asked it. "The defense can use it to try to trip you up if your story changes on the witness stand, which it can over time. People forget things, or remember them differently, that's why both sides try to get everything documented while it's as fresh as possible."

"Will you be at the deposition?"

"Yes, I'll be there. I don't think you need a lawyer because you're not a suspect. I'll try to ensure he doesn't get too far afield."

"Well, then I guess I'll be ready. The truth part isn't hard." Cassie grinned. "I learned a long time ago that I'm a rotten liar; my face turns beet red – it's really a handicap," she said with a chuckle.

Doc spoke up, "Cassie needs to relax a bit before she goes back to Virginia, hasn't been much of a trip for her."

"I'm okay, Doc, don't be such a worrier," she said as she hugged his arm.

Sam offered, "I'll let you get back to your guests. I'd better go check on Mr. Merritt. Cassie, do you want me to get you tomorrow afternoon?"

Doc spoke up, "Won't be necessary, Sam. I'm going with her. We'll see you at the courthouse."

Chapter 23

The deposition definitely was not fun. Doc had found a voice mail from Mr. DeLacey after all the guests and catering staff had left and he and Cassie were sitting in his cozy den with their shoes off and their feet up on the coffee table. The attorney had changed their appointment to 10 a.m. instead of the afternoon.

Cassie sat silently next to him in the front seat of his Taurus. That's one thing she really liked about Doc, no pretensions. Even with his local fame and money, he didn't feel the need to spend money on flash. *Unlike someone else I know,* she thought to herself.

"This building was nicknamed the Taj Mahal," Doc said as they passed the courthouse on I-70 looking for the next exit. "It was so expensive and its design so out of touch with the expected western style."

Cassie got a glimpse of sandstone and glass with a round central tower as Doc whizzed by. His age certainly hadn't slowed him down, even behind the wheel.

Doc glanced over at Cassie. She looked very professional and very feminine at the same time. She'd bought the new navy linen pantsuit and hot pink silk blouse just for this morning. Even though he'd never married and was an only child he knew looking "right" for any occasion was important to most women. He also knew Sam would agree with his assessment of Cassie's appearance.

"You doing okay?" he queried.

Cassie took a deep breath and gave him a wavering smile. "Yes, I guess so; I'll just be glad when it's over. It's the mystery of the whole thing, not knowing what to expect. I feel like I did when I took the SATs years ago; I just hope this turns out as well. Sam says this attorney can be a real hard-nose. I just hope I'm not too tired to deal with it; I'm really wiped out; the adrenalin I've been running on all week has finally faded and I'm about to crash. I don't understand why we even have to do this. He has copies of our statements to the police, nothing has changed."

Doc knew Cassie hadn't been sleeping well over the last week, even worse than his own troubled nights. He'd heard her up in the night, fixing herself a cup of tea or turning on a light to read. He hadn't slept well himself, but at his age he required less sleep than he used to. He didn't know if Cassie was having a case of the jitters, or depression, or feeling guilty. He'd offered her a sleeping pill last night, but she said it might give her a hangover and she wouldn't be as sharp as she needed to be for the deposition.

Doc and Cassie arrived at the JeffCo Combined Courthouse ten minutes early. DeLacey had suggested they meet at the courthouse rather than his downtown office since the courthouse was easier to get to with the Rockies game going on that day. The courthouse was a forty minute drive from Doc's house in the Tech Center since it was Saturday and no rush hour to contend with.

"Thank goodness it's not a Friday afternoon or we'd have been caught in rush hour plus all the Friday escapes for the mountains," Doc commented as they gathered their things before exiting the car. "Plus we'd have had sunshine slowing to deal with, the sun right in our eyes as we headed west. Saturday morning is much easier. And parking downtown would have been a nightmare with all the baseball fans. Mr. DeLacey has done us a favor by changing it."

Doc parked in the almost empty parking lot and they climbed the entrance steps under the bright Colorado blue sky. Cassie seemed to shake off her lethargy as the sun's rays hit her. "Wow! What a gorgeous day! In Virginia we call this a Carolina blue sky; ACC you know," she laughed. "Nothing could go wrong on a day like this." Cassie took Doc's arm and gave him a radiant smile as they entered the building. Doc hoped she was right.

The office where they were to meet was on the third floor. They took the elevator just beyond the metal detectors and the guards. The glass-walled hallway gave a panoramic view of the Rocky Mountains. "Almost as beautiful as my Blue Ridge Mountains," Cassie teased Doc. "Do you really need all that height? It seems a little excessive to me."

They had big grins as they found the appointed room. It was a fairly typical government office, more of a conference room than an office really. Beige carpet, beige walls, long faux wood table in the middle of the room, with eight serviceable brown chairs surrounding it. No pictures on the walls.

A young woman sat at the far end with her court reporting machine in front of her; she was the only spot of color in the room. She was in her early twenties and appeared totally put out about working on a Saturday. Cassie was fascinated by her blue and orange fingernails, tapping on the table, ready for this to be over. *Broncos colors* Cassie knew.

Their attention was immediately drawn to the dapper man approaching them. Cassie felt chilled by his too-white smile.

John DeLacey extended his hand, first to Doc then to Cassie. "Thank you both for coming. And thank you, Cassie, may I call you Cassie?" Cassie nodded, "for postponing your trip home. Virginia must be beautiful this time of year." He motioned to two seats at the table. Cassie was astounded at what sounded like rehearsed statements, not even pausing for replies.

He was nothing like Cassie had expected, even though she hadn't known what to expect. His graying blonde hair was carefully styled to look casual, sort of like Andy Warhol. He had round glasses on his lean face, and another pair dangling from a black webbed string around his neck, what people out here called a Croakie. He had on a pink and beige cotton argyle sweater-vest with a pink tie and khakis. All in all, she thought he looked more like a college professor than a go-for-the-throat attorney.

But it was his manner that was disturbing. Even though he was thin, and Theodore Bikel had been portly as Zoltan Karpathy, the line from *My Fair Lady* came immediately to Cassie's mind, "He oiled his way around the floor."

"I know you are both busy, so let's get right to this, then I can get you back to this beautiful Colorado day."

"Shouldn't we wait for Sam?" Cassie inquired.

"Sam?" The attorney looked puzzled.

"Sam Chambers, from the DA's office. He said he'd be here."

DeLacey continued to look confused. "Why would he be here? That's most unusual."

Now it was Cassie's turn to be confused. She glanced at Doc and back at the attorney. "Maybe I misunderstood."

"Does she need an attorney to be with her?" Doc asked somewhat belligerently Cassie thought, rather like a papa bear, gruff.

"Oh, no, I'm just going to ask a few questions about what went on in the house and her relationship with the deceased. Very straight forward. Of course, If Cassie wants an attorney, we can put this off until sometime next week..."

Doc leaned back into his seat, obviously settling himself in as Cassie's protector.

"I'm afraid, Doctor Harper, I'll have to ask you to wait outside. I plan to depose you at a later date so you can't be present during Ms. Kirkland's deposition. I'm only doing hers now so she can get back to Virginia." He smiled his toothy smile at both of them as though he were verbalizing, *see what a nice guy I am*, but the smile never reached his eyes.

Cassie touched Doc's hand and smiled into his troubled face. "It's fine, Doc. Go get a cup of coffee or something; I'll come find you when I'm done." Doc rose and patted her shoulder. DeLacey firmly closed the door behind him and took a seat across the table from Cassie. They began.

After going over some ground rules, like only one person speaking at a time, and the need to answer questions aloud, rather than head motions or "uh-huhs", DeLacey nodded to the court reporter and Cassie was sworn in. The deposition went for almost three hours, DeLacey asking and Cassie answering what seemed to Cassie like very mundane questions, but there were so many of them. How long have you known the deceased? How well did you know her? What is your job? Where do you live? When did you last see Michela Merritt alive? Cassie had to review the events of the morning Mich died. And on and on. When it was finally over, Cassie read and signed the recorder's copy and couldn't wait to get out of there.

Chapter 24

As Doc and Cassie drove back to the house they talked generally about her morning but she could not give any specifics because DeLacey had told her not to, it might influence Doc's testimony later. At her insistence Doc agreed to go to his office, he'd been neglecting it for obvious reasons and Saturday was a good chance to catch up.

After Doc dropped her in the garage and avoided the press outside, Cassie let herself in and headed up the stairs to what she had begun to think of as "her" room. She couldn't wait to get out of her clothes and into a hot shower. She felt...soiled. DeLacey definitely seemed to think Larry was innocent; Cassie had the distinct feeling he was planning on her as the replacement guilty party.

Opening her bedroom door, Cassie was shocked and panicked to see Larry sitting on her bed. "Hello, Cassie, surprised?" Larry asked her.

"How did you get in here?" Cassie snarled at him.

"Seems the old codger forgot we had a key to his house, just like he has a key to ours. I just let myself in; DeLacey had said he was deposing you this morning. It's just an added treat that Doc didn't come in with you."

Cassie turned and headed back toward the stairs. Larry jumped up and grabbed her arm. Cassie tried to remain calm, but she was unsure of his purpose, unsure of what he might do. With as much steel as she could muster, she glared at him and asked, "What do you want, Larry?"

"Just come back in here a minute and I'll tell you." He led her back into the bedroom. Cassie was racking her brain for the nearest phone, one in Doc's bedroom, her cell was down on the kitchen counter. It would do no good to try and break a window, the bedroom was on the back of the house. Screaming was out for the same reason. She let Larry drag her back, trying to come up with a way to escape him. No doubt he was stronger, *but I'm smarter. Think, Cassie, think.*

Larry pulled her down next to him on the bed. "There. Now isn't this cozier?" he grinned at her.

Cassie repeated through gritted teeth, "What do you want here, Larry?"

"Just a chat, Cassie, unless of course you want something more. I just wanted to tell you that I am not going to let either you or that old goat doctor pin this on me. I did not kill Mich, but I'm thinking maybe one of you did. So back off, or you'll regret it." He gave her arm one last hard squeeze, stood and left the room.

Cassie sat stunned until she heard the back door slam. Then she ran to the front bedroom and looked out, hoping to see the "minders" Sam had told her about. No cars were parked on the street but she saw Larry's car speed down the residential street. She breathed a sigh of relief, and started shaking. She went back to her room, laid down and tried to think coherently about what she should do. Call Doc? No, he needed the break he was getting at the office. Call Sam? Maybe. Call the police? And say what? It would be her word against his. Really, what had he done? He had a key that Doc had given him and all he had done was talk. She couldn't very well accuse him of inciting terror just because she had panicked. A quick vision of Osama Bin Laden flashed across her brain and that made her laugh. Okay, back to the original plan: a shower. She did some of her best thinking in the shower.

The shower helped relax her, and she decided Larry's intrusion had eliminated her worries about the morning's deposition. *So maybe I should thank him.* She laid down to rest and think about the recent events. The next thing she knew she heard the garage door opening. There was a brief moment of panic until she was fully awake and realized it was probably Doc and not Larry returning.

She looked at the clock and headed downstairs in her fluffy robe for their now ritual before dinner drink; hers wine, his Scotch. After drinks, they both retired to their rooms to prep for dinner.

Sam. Cassie liked him. *He seemed concerned and honest.* She felt she could almost trust him. *Good thing you're leaving town tomorrow, Fool; you thought you could trust Kevin, too.*

She dressed carefully for the evening, dinner out with Doc. She wore her black slacks again and the last dressy blouse she'd brought with her, a white silk with a scoop neck. Fortunately it had long sleeves so the bruises that were starting to appear would not show. Add pearls and heels and her black cashmere shawl and she was ready to go.

At his office that afternoon Doc had called Sam and asked, "We thought you were coming to the deposition this morning, Sam?"

"I was, but when I got there this afternoon and no one was there, I figured DeLacey had pulled a fast one." Doc nodded on his end of the phone, "I guess he did. After the reception yesterday I found a voicemail from him and he said the time had been changed to 10. We just assumed you had been notified, too."

Doc looked his usual splendid self in a camel blazer and navy slacks; no tie Cassie was glad to see. "You'd look distinguished even in sweats," she complimented him with a twinkle.

"One ground rule for tonight, Doc," Cassie said as Doc opened her car door, "no legal talk."

"That's a good plan, Cassie, you're too wound up. I want you to relax a bit before you go back to Lexington. Can't have those Southerners complaining about our Western hospitality." Doc chuckled while Cassie saw her chance to bring up Larry's visit disappearing.

Cassie followed Doc's lead, "So, Doc, what's the latest on the golf front? Still trying to shoot your age?"

Doc snorted, then talked enthusiastically about his golf game, the tournaments he'd played in, and how no matter how many lessons he took, or games he played, he always wanted to do better...and didn't. "I guess that's why some golfers call it 'flog'," he chuckled, "because you keep beating yourself up about it."

The rest of the thirty minute drive was spent listening to Doc compare the attributes of various professional golfers, from Fred Couples to

Tiger Woods, to Jordan Spieth and Justin Rose, and lots of others in between. Cassie sat bewildered – and relaxing – in the comfortable seat. Obviously Doc's plan was working, and he didn't even know about Larry's visit. Maybe she'd tell him when they got back home.

Cassie loved Tables the minute they drove up. The screen door and picket fence gave it an immediate feel of comfort. The interior was wildly eclectic, yet cozy.

The hostess showed them to one of the more quiet areas. After they'd placed their drink orders Doc said to Cassie, "I know after you moved back to Virginia Michela even considered packing up and moving there, but Larry didn't want to leave Denver; likes the fast pace of a big city." Doc noticed a cloud pass across Cassie's face and assumed it was from the mention of Mich. "So what's the big attraction in a small town like Lexington?"

"There's really no 'big attraction', that's what's so nice. It's more a feel...like curling up with your favorite quilt and a cup of hot chocolate. The atmosphere sort of wraps itself around you in a big hug." Cassie blushed at her words and tried to cover them up with a grin. "Of course I may be prejudiced since I was born there."

"So there's no fast pace in Lexington?" Doc watched her face intently.

Cassie brightened. "Not hardly. We're still trying to remember Robert E. Lee and Stonewall Jackson, both former residents, are dead. It can take twenty minutes to buy a carton of orange juice at Kroger. Everybody knows everybody and their families and what you did last week, and probably what you did this morning. If they don't know you, they have to remedy that right quick by asking a million questions. When you run into someone you know out on the street or at the movies or wherever, it's time to get caught up."

"Sounds a little scary to me. Must be hard to keep a secret."

Cassie grinned again. "Next to impossible. But on the bright side, it's a great place to grow up. The whole town works to keep kids out of trouble because they're probably related to each other. There's no sense trying to get away with anything 'cause you can't. Dating during high school was a real challenge."

"What about now? Does the grocery checker have to pass approval on the men you're seeing?"

Fortunately the waiter brought their dinners and filled their wine glasses at that moment. Dinner proceeded with chit-chat about the food and the restaurant.

On the drive home Cassie felt it was okay to tell Doc about Larry's visit. Predictably he was enraged. "It's okay, Doc," Cassie said trying to calm him down. "He scared me at first, but then he was almost pitiful. You may want to get the locks changed, though, since he still has a key."

"First thing Monday morning. And I'm not letting you out of my sight until you're on the plane. Maybe I'll ask Sam about getting one of those restraining orders." He pulled into the garage, still fuming, more at himself than anybody else; he was the one who let Cassie go into the house alone.

After hasty good nights and hugs, the two went to bed and their sleepless nights.

Sunday morning Cassie returned to Lexington.

Chapter 25

Monday Larry Merritt once again took himself downtown to meet with his very expensive attorney. DeLacey greeted Larry coolly and directed him to the butter-soft leather sofa on the far side of a glass-topped coffee table. A coffee carafe and two mugs were on the table. Larry poured himself a cup without asking permission.

DeLacey seated himself in the matching chair at the head of the rectangular table. "Pour me one, too, will you? Then I want you to tell me the history of Larry Merritt. Leave nothing out."

Larry grudgingly poured the coffee and handed it to the attorney, recognizing he'd been upstaged. But he'd be damned if this prissy guy was going to beat him. "Where do I start? I was born in a log cabin in Illinois? That sort of stuff?"

"No, I know the basics. What was your childhood like? Was it happy? Did you get into trouble in school? Any trouble with the law? THAT sort of thing."

"I guess it was happy. My father didn't beat me or anything. He was a big wig with Merrill Lynch, branch manager just outside Kansas City. I guess you could say my sister and I – she's six years older - grew up very privileged, my sister did anyway. She's always been kind of flaky; when I was 12 she ran off to India to study with some guru. Then Merrill Lynch started closing branches and my dad was 'down-sized' right out of a job.

"Between the depression of the lost job and the fight to bring my sister home, my home life was not too stable for a while. My sister, Ella, finally came home after about two years; my folks bought her a condo in New York, paid all her bills, found her a job, and practically waited on her hand and foot. I got nothing.

"By the time I was 14 our life-style had changed dramatically; I had to go to public school; Mom went to work; Dad just moped around the house or spent his time on the phone with Ella. I was bullied a lot for being the new kid." Larry barely took a breath and DeLacey thought it all sounded rehearsed.

"But I was smart and good looking and by 16 I was a class leader, nobody bullied me anymore. At sixteen my folks didn't buy me a car like they did Ella, said they couldn't afford it, even though they were still spending thousands on my sister. At that point I decided I'd show them; they didn't care about me so I'd just look out for myself. I never got into trouble, but I've looked out for me ever since. I even got a golf scholarship to Vandy and worked summers to pay for my college. I knew my folks would never pay for a private school. It's all worked, I've been happy and comfortable." Larry paused for breath. "This the sort of stuff you want?" He grinned superciliously at the man across from him.

"Basically, yes. Where's your sister? Do you still see your parents?"

"Have no idea where my sister is. Haven't seen or talked to my parents in years. Why would I? They'd probably just want me to help take care of my sister, the spoiled brat."

"And what about Michela? Did you ever love her?"

Larry hesitated. "I guess, maybe a little. She was part of my master plan. Get rich by thirty. And I did. Hey, I've got a question for you?"

DeLacey's blonde eyebrows rose as he stared at his client.

Larry continued, "I don't get why there's such a big fuss. Mich was dying. So maybe somebody hurried her along, she was going to be dead either way; this way it was just a little sooner. What's the big deal?"

DeLacey thought he had heard it all, but this was a new low. He steeled his features to cover his dismay and repulsion at his client. *Surely no one could be this self-involved.*

DeLacey stood. "Thanks for coming in, Larry, I think that's enough for today." He escorted his client to the door without touching him in anyway. *This is going to be a tough one.* DeLacey's biggest concern was how he was going to contain his narcissistic client and keep him from alienating the jury. "Shit."

Chapter 26

The next few weeks passed in a blur for Cassie. The end of the school year was always super busy, with students finishing their term papers and projects, returning lots of items they'd checked out to use at home, and gearing up for the summer reading program. This year seemed especially time-consuming, but maybe that was because her mind wasn't really on her job. When she wasn't actually involved with a patron, she kept reviewing the incidents of May and the aftermath. She still couldn't believe Mich was dead. *I knew she was sick, but I guess I still always thought she'd beat it again.* At least once a day she'd start to send Mich an email, and catch herself, or she'd pick up the phone to call her on the weekend and have to put it back down before the call went through. Every time she saw a picture of somewhere they'd gone, or of Ireland where they'd talked about going, she missed Mich all over again. *They said it would get easier, but I guess I'm not there yet.* Even her boss had noticed.

"So, Cassie, how are you doing?" Ben had asked her one afternoon about two weeks after she got back from Denver. Cassie just shrugged. "I don't know, okay I guess."

"Do you need to take some vacation time, get some rest? You came straight back to work after your trip to Denver, no time to decompress or really deal with your grief." Cassie shrugged again.

"I don't know, Ben, it's just hard. We'd been best friends for twelve years, we told each other everything, we were there for each other, no matter what. I just can't seem to get over her absence. But work really is the best thing for me right now. If I had time to myself I think I'd go crazy. And the trial is still looming; they tell me sometime around November, I'll need lots of vacation time for that, too."

Ben looked surprised, "Wow! Just six months to trial. That seems awfully quick for these days."

Cassie replied, "It is. It seems the DA fast-tracked it somehow.

Ben cleared his throat. "I know you're having a really hard time, Cassie, but I have to mention it's starting to affect your work."

Cassie sat up straighter in the wooden library chair she was sitting in opposite Ben's utilitarian wooden desk; it looked like it had been there since the turn of the last century. "Are you saying I'm fired?" She could hardly get the words out.

"No, Cassie, I'm just saying you need to put this aside when you're at work. We need you focused."

Cassie nodded her understanding. "You're right, Ben, I'll do better. Thanks for pointing it out. I guess I hadn't realized how bad it was getting. You can count on me."

"I know, Cassie, that's why we're having this talk. I'm not without sympathy, but we all need your work. We operate on a short staff as it is and with vacations coming up, we need you working at full capacity. I know I can count on you." Ben smiled his turtle-lips smile and nodded his bald head toward the door, indicating the discussion was closed. Cassie returned his smile and exited wordlessly.

Snap out of it, Cassie, she told herself as she returned to her seat at the Reference desk. It might have been harder to do if she had known she was the current topic of discussion in a handsome Denver law office.

John DeLacey and Larry Merritt were having one of their weekly meetings at DeLacey's downtown office. Larry was whining, "But why can't I leave town, John? I haven't done anything wrong. And Teri wants to go to Bermuda, I sort of promised her back in the Spring."

DeLacey gave Larry a pained look, *why did I ever agree to this case?* "Larry, we've been over this many times. You are out on bail. That means you have to stay in the area. You might get away with going to Steamboat or Aspen, but you certainly can't leave the country. Besides, you no longer have a passport. This is the last time we are going to discuss this. Today I need you to tell me everything you know about Cassie Kirkland. She is our best alternate theory of what happened."

"What's to tell? She's a librarian. Lots of brains, okay on looks. She and Mich met in college, roommates their freshman year. They've been friends ever since. Mich and Cassie take a girls' trip once a year, usually some place in Europe, gone about ten days. Mich used to visit

Cassie, but she hasn't traveled much since she got sick. Cassie came running every time Mich got sick or had a hangnail or whatever."

"Do you think there was a...sexual component to their relationship?" DeLacey asked hesitantly.

"What, you mean they were lesbians? No way. I know Mich wasn't and I don't think Cassie was. They were just friends, really good friends. I asked Mich once if she liked Cassie better than me; she just said 'You wouldn't understand; girl friends are different than friendships between men.' Besides, Cassie was married for a while, too." DeLacey nodded slowly at this response and stared at his wall of fame that was just to the right of his desk, his head resting on the chair back and his long slender fingers folded calmly across his stomach.

"What do you know about Cassie's marriage?"

"Not much, she never talked about it when I was around. It only lasted a couple years, never even heard what caused the divorce. She can be kind of uppity when the mood suits her, like she's smarter than you."

"Do you think Cassie could have killed Michela?"

Larry seemed to consider the question. "Nah. She's too weak, a librarian, for God's sake. Librarians don't kill people, especially not their best friends."

"Ms. Kirkland, I hope you don't mind me calling you in the evening. This is Willamette Warrenton, curator at the Denver Museum of Art. I understand you want to talk about the distribution of the art of Michela Merritt?" Cassie had answered the phone in the kitchen, she had just poured her after-work glass of wine. She took the wine and the phone over to the kitchen table and sat down. She looked out the window onto her backyard. The redbuds were getting ready to bloom, late this year because of the larger than normal snowfall. Squirrels chased each other from tree branch to branch. Rosie wandered over and laid down at Cassie's feet.

"Oh, thanks, Ms. Warrenton. No, no trouble. I just got in from work and took off my shoes. This is a great time to talk. I don't know where to start. Maybe you can help me?"

"Of course, I'll be happy to. Please call me Willa, everybody does.

I was an admirer of Mrs. Merritt's work and we had talked several times back when we were preparing for her show and then when she donated one of her larger pieces to the museum. Let's start with you telling me what you want to do with the collection. Almost 200 pieces if I remember correctly?"

"Yes, 187. I think I want to sell the collection. Mich always talked about setting up a camp for children with cancer, someplace where they could go, have fun, and maybe learn about art. She said art, like writing, is a good way to vent, to get things off your chest. She always said it was cathartic, especially when she'd had bad news from one of her doctors."

"Wow! What a great idea. Do you know where you might want to have the camp?"

"Not really, haven't gotten that far in my thinking. I guess I have to see how much money the art will bring and then go from there. What process would you recommend for selling the paintings so we can realize the most gain from them?" Cassie was very into processes.

"Just off the top of my head, I think maybe we should have a show of all the works, create a catalog of them. With all the publicity about her death and then the trial, I'm sure we'll draw a lot of interest. Then hold a charity auction a few months later. I suggest we get Christie's or Sotheby's to work with us on the auction part. Plus they'll have their own mailings lists of potential buyers. We'll give out the catalog at the show and then mail it to others. How does this sound to you?"

"Goodness, sounds like a lot of work. I'm not sure I have the time to work on all of this."

"Not a problem," the ebullient curator replied. "I've done a lot of these type events, never one with so many art pieces by one artist, but the steps are the same. If it's okay, I'll get the ball rolling here in Denver. The paintings are stored here at DMA anyway. I'll get our photographer to start getting the pictures done and then we'll create the catalog. I'll send a proof to you for your approval before we go to press. In the meantime, I'll be looking at some dates for the show and the auction and get back with you. You'll need to attend both so we can talk up the camp idea. People love to spend money for good causes!" She laughed an infectious laugh.

"But that seems a lot for you to do, and like I'm shirking my duty to Mich, Michela. Isn't there something I can do from a distance?"

"Oh, yes, you're not getting off the hook. And don't worry the bill will come due when the sale is complete. The museum usually works on a 5% commission. Will that work for you? Of course, the auction house will have to take their cut, too. But we are all working toward the same end; the more money we make at the sale, the more money we all make."

Cassie was feeling a bit overwhelmed. "I assume there will be contracts to spell everything out? What I should expect from the Museum and from the auction house, deadlines, that sort of thing? I guess I need to get a lawyer."

"I was just getting to that. Actually, the museum has a standard contract that spells everything out. I'll get you a copy just to look over and then I'll send you the real contract once we have decided on dates. And yes, you will want a lawyer and probably an accountant going forward. You need to have a tax-deductible, charitable organization created where buyers and donors can send their money. You'll need to talk it over with the lawyer and accountant and get that set up as soon as possible so we can put the name into the contract. Have you given any thought into what you might call the camp?"

"Not a bit!" Cassie panicked. "I hadn't given the camp any detailed thought until your call. I was just thinking about it in generalities."

"Well, the name will be the first thing so you can get all the appropriate government forms and filings underway. Then talk to an architect. If you can get a rough drawing of what a camp might look like in time, we can include it in the catalog. Big money donors like to see something concrete before they write checks. Once the camp is established, you can start really talking about it. Your lawyer and accountant can advise you about withdrawals from the account, but once there is actually some money in there, you can start paying them and pay yourself a salary. Until then, you'll have to make any payments yourself.

I hope that won't be a problem?"

Cassie smiled, "No, no problem. I'll get in touch with them tomorrow. And I'll start making some concrete plans for the camp, too; this part will be fun! I can't thank you enough for your help, Willa. Just one more question: I have a painting Mich gave me years ago and another one that's in with the collection that she was going to send me as soon as it dried. Should I include those in the show even though they won't be for sale?"

"By all means! The more the better. Would you know the one that is yours if you see it? I can just send you photos of the ones in storage and you can let me know which it is."

"Easy enough. It's the one that looks like the clouds are pinned to the sky," Cassie laughed, remembering her talks about the clouds with Mich.

Willa hesitated. Cassie could hear her confusion over the phone lines. "Maybe I'll still send you the photos, just in case. Anything else?"

"No, I can see I have my work cut out for me. I'm glad, I'd feel like I was letting her down if I didn't have a hand in this."

"Believe me, you will have your hands full with the paperwork and designing the camp. Selling the paintings and raising money will be the easy part. I'll call you in a couple weeks with some potential dates. Enjoy your evening!" With that the connection was broken. Cassie pushed the END button on the phone and took a big swig of her wine. "Oh, my God, Rosie, what have we gotten ourselves into?" Cassie went in search of a legal pad and a pencil to start giving some serious thought to the camp. What would it be called?

The next week Larry Merritt received a phone call from a very irate John DeLacey. "Merritt, what were you thinking? Giving an interview to CNN? Are you out of your mind? Didn't I tell you not to talk to anybody, especially the press? Do you want to get the judge mad before the trial even starts? Are you totally stupid?" Larry kept trying to interrupt, but

DeLacey was on a roll. Finally, DeLacey had to pause for breath.

"Oh calm down, John. She was cute. It wasn't a real interview, she just caught me when I left your office last week and said she wanted to ask me a couple questions. That's all. We talked and then I bought her a drink and that was it. I was disappointed, but hey, can't win 'em all."

DeLacey gritted his teeth. "Let me say this as clearly as I can. DO... NOT... TALK... TO... ANYONE... ABOUT... THE... CASE, especially the press, no matter how 'cute' she is. And keep your pants zipped. You have to be totally saint-like until the trial is over. If you cannot follow these simple instructions, find yourself another lawyer. I cannot help you."

Larry had had about all he could stand from this pompous lawyer and was ready to tell him to go to Hell. But he thought better of it, remembering that he needed DeLacey much more than DeLacey needed him; in fact, DeLacey did not need him at all. "Okay, John, I'm sorry. Won't happen again."

"See that it doesn't." DeLacey slammed the phone. On the other end, Larry gave the phone the finger as he hung up.

Chapter 27

As June progressed, Cassie found herself thinking of Mich less and less, unless it was related to the art camp. Cassie had run through hundreds of possible names and still had not found the right one. Her library work had settled into its normal routine and she was able to handle it practically with her eyes closed. Every spare minute was spent on the camp; evenings, lunch hours, and weekends. She had quickly hired an attorney and an accountant. She waited on the architect until she had more specifics she could give him.

Willa Warrenton had called and suggested the show for the week before Thanksgiving and the sale for February, maybe tied in with Valentine's Day, but that hadn't been finalized yet.

Sam called once a week with trial-prep updates. He called even when he had nothing new to report. Each time Cassie enjoyed talking with him; he was so…involved.

At the end of June, Cassie called Sam in the middle of her Thursday, early morning for Denver. "Sam, the strangest thing just happened."

"Cassie? What's up?"

"I just got a package here at the library; it's from Mich. It came in this morning's mail. It was addressed to my house but the mailman knows I work here so he brought it to me here at the library." Sam let this post office anomaly pass, chalking it up to another small town idiosyncrasy.

"Is there a postmark? When was it mailed?" Cassie looked closely at the upper right corner. She moved it in closer and then grabbed the magnifying glass in her desk. "It's kind of blurred, but it looks like Colorado Springs, June 26. The return address is Mich's house though."

"So somebody else must have mailed it for her, somebody she left it with. Maybe that lawyer who drew up her will. He's in Colorado Springs. I'll check with him. Have you opened it?"

"No, I didn't know what to do so I called you before I did anything else."

"Good girl. Don't open it. Can you get someone there in the library to witness that it is closed and hasn't been opened? And have them seal it with tape that will make it obvious if it is opened."

"Sure, that's no problem. If there's one thing we have it's boxes and tape...all kinds. Then what?"

"Get yourself on a plane and bring it to me. Don't let it out of your sight until you get it here. When do you think you can come?"

"I'll have to check flights and talk to my boss, but I should be able to come tomorrow some time; it's a Friday and there won't be much going on here. Will you check with Doc and see if I can stay at his place?"

"Sure. Just give me your receipts and the DA's office will pay for your flight."

"Great! Does that mean I can fly first class? It's a long flight to Denver," Cassie asked with a chuckle.

"I wish. Sorry, you'll have to suffer with the rest of the tourists in coach. But you may fly from Roanoke so you don't have to drive to D.C. if that helps."

"That's a big help. I'll let you know as soon as I've made my reservations. I'll need a car, too, I guess."

"Whatever, just get that package here as fast as you can."

Twenty-four hours later Cassie hugged Doc as she entered his comfortable house once again. She had been relieved to see the media had vacated the premises. It had been only a few weeks since she'd left, but he had aged another ten years. Cassie thought he looked like a popped balloon, all folded in on himself. Cassie dropped her shoulder bag and the taped envelope on the hall table. Hugging him tightly, she asked how he was doing.

The kindly man gave her a watery smile, "I'm hanging in there. I've seen lots of death over the years, but experience hasn't helped me with this." He ran his hand through his silver hair. "It's so senseless, she was dying anyway. I just don't understand."

"Me either, Doc. Part of me can't believe he did it, but there's no other explanation. I know I didn't do it. Mich wouldn't have killed herself, she was too much of a fighter. I guess Larry's ego and his greed were just big enough to convince him he could get away with it."

Doc considered a moment then shrugged his shoulders. "I'm sure Sam will sort it all out. How are you doing, Cass? I'm glad to see you again, even if it's just for this couple days." The two walked arm-in-arm into his den. It was a cozy room, very like Mich's in feel, except where hers had been full of light, Doc's was more like an English gentlemen's club, all dark paneling, leather and books, lots of books. They sat next to each other on the green leather sofa.

Cassie wondered if he was referring to more than just the death of her best friend. She looked away from his probing eyes. "I'm fine," she feigned. Since meeting Sam she didn't know how she was any more.

"All over Kevin? No regrets?" Doc reminded her of her own father, concerned and not tooooo pushy. One late night in May over cups of hot chocolate, Cassie had told Doc all about her now-defunct marriage, or almost all. Some of it she had never told anyone, except Mich, not even her therapist.

"Oh, yeah, way over."

"Mich thought you might have gone back to Lexington to hide out. She was worried that Kevin had soured you on men."

Cassie grinned her irrepressible grin and said, "Mich was a worry-wart. She said the same thing to me last month, even suggested that I pack it in and move to Denver now that I had no ties to Lexington. She could never understand anyone preferring the 'boonies' to a big city." She laughed. "I'm really fine. Love my job. Rosie keeps me company. The house is warm and cozy. And I'm swamped with work for the art camp. Life's good!" She saw his doubtful look and said with more force, "Really!" Before he could ask anything more personal she added, "While I'm here I want your input on a name for the camp, I'm really at a loss. Maybe we can talk about it tomorrow? I'll give you time to think about it." Her ploy hadn't worked.

"Dating anyone?" he asked with fatherly concern in his voice.

"Occasionally. There aren't that many opportunities for single women in Lexington. It's pretty much a college town and retirement community, slim pickins' in the middle. VMI gets the occasional single military type, but I tend to steer clear of those. Once bitten, twice shy, you know. Although maybe career military are more reliable than the short-timers. Just not really interested in finding out.

"And I'm still finalizing my parents' estate. It's amazing how much paperwork there is even with a simple estate like theirs. Thank God they had wills, I can't imagine what it would have been like without one!"

"Cassie, you're....

"Uh oh. I know that tone of voice. You're going to lecture me," Cassie teased, hoping to stop him.

"Right. You're too young to be hidden away in a library in a small town. You should be dating, finding a new man, making a life for yourself. Move out here like Mich suggested. We have libraries and lots of single males."

Cassie knew she'd be company for Doc, too; the closest thing either of them had to family now that Mich and Cassie's parents were gone.

She smiled her most winning smile, "I'll think about it."

"And I know that tone of voice; it's the 'conversation closed' voice. Okay. I can take a hint."

"Actually, Doc, I have been giving it a lot of thought. I'm just beginning to understand how time-consuming this camp is going to be. I've been thinking I'll probably have to give up my job at the library and work for the camp full time. And that will be wherever we decide the best location for the camp is. Will that satisfy you?"

Doc grumped, "Well, it's better, but I won't be satisfied unless the camp is somewhere out here. On a new topic, Sam wants you to call him."

Cassie looked intently at the good doctor; his eyes were twinkling. *Am I that transparent?*

Doc just smiled like a big Cheshire cat and headed for the kitchen. "I'll make some tea while you call. I've got some Girl Scout mint cookies in the freezer, too."

Comfort food for both of us. Cassie pulled her legs up under her on the sofa and pushed Sam's speed dial number on her smart phone. They seemed to be having so many conversations Cassie had just added him to her quick-dials. She was put right through to him after identifying herself.

"Cassie! How was your flight?"

"Fine, got in a couple hours ago, just in time for tea here at Doc's." She felt her voice was strained, hesitant. After all, she hardly knew the man. They'd had some intense time together when Mich died and she had sensed an interest on his part. They'd talked several times in the six weeks since she'd left Denver, but it had been about the case...mostly.

"Think he could make another cup? I can be there in half an hour if I leave right now."

"I'm sure there's plenty to go around."

"Great! I'm on my way." She heard the phone click on the other end. She stared at the phone in her hand and pushed the END CALL icon. *Sam is coming. How do I feel about seeing him again?* She probed her mind and her stomach, all calm. She didn't get too close to her heart, though, the danger zone.

"What did Sam say?" Doc asked from the kitchen doorway.

Cassie shook herself. "He's on his way here. I guess he wants to see the package as soon as he can."

"Yes, I'm sure that's it. I'll get another cup out, probably need a few more cookies, too." Doc turned back to the kitchen, muttering to himself, "Sam's interested in some package for sure."

"What? Did you say something, Doc?"

"No, just mumbling to myself. I like that young man. Do you know he's called me every week, just to see how I'm doing? We've even met for lunch and dinner a couple times. Hope to play golf with him this summer. Nice guy. Smart, too." His voice trailed away as he reached the other side of the kitchen.

See, Cassie, he's nice to everybody. Wise up, girl. Cassie grabbed her bag and the package and headed up the stairs to "her" room.

In fact it took Sam only twenty-six minutes, not that anyone was counting.

Cassie answered the door. She'd had just enough time to freshen up and have a good talk with herself. *Don't put too much stock in anything he says or does.* Sam thought she looked less like a librarian every time he saw her; in fact, she was downright sexy in her jeans and hot-pink polo shirt. "Aren't your feet cold on those tiles?" he asked as his head-to-toe survey reached her bare feet.

Cassie had decided on friendly-casual for her response. "As a matter of fact, yes; let's go in on the carpet." She smiled at him as she turned for the den. Sam had forgotten how her smile lit up a room.

"Tea's ready," Doc said coming into the den and shaking Sam's hand. There was a lot of mutual respect between the two men, Cassie noted. Doc retreated to the kitchen and returned with three mugs and a plate of cookies on a tray.

Cassie picked up the brown envelope she had brought down a few minutes before Sam arrived. "Here it is," she said as she handed it to Sam. "As you said, unopened and completely sealed." *So much for small talk,* Sam thought as he took the package from Cassie's extended hand.

"You two are my witnesses," he said as he took a not-so-small pocket knife out and broke the seal.

"Good grief! Do you carry that with you everywhere you go?" Cassie asked marveling at how efficiently it opened the sealing tape.

"Yeah. Holdover from my Marine Corps training, always be prepared. I tried those Swiss Army knives, but they just don't feel like a knife, more like a toy," Sam chattered on as he pulled two smaller envelopes from the mailing envelope, missing the appalled look on Cassie's face. Doc didn't miss it; he wasn't sure if it was because of the knife or the Marine reference.

Sam opened the first envelope, "It's the credit card and phone bills. Looks like Mich even highlighted the appropriate parts and made notes next to them." Cassie tucked her feet up under her again as she watched Sam at the other end of the sofa. Doc watched both of them from his wingback chair across the dark oak coffee table.

Cassie noticed the furrow between Sam's eyes as he concentrated on the pages in his hands. "Anything else?" she asked.

"Looks like it. There was another envelope inside and a letter was between the two inner envelopes. The letter's from that lawyer in Colorado Springs, says Mich had asked him to mail it to you two months after her untimely death, if such a thing occurred. Said he's leaving for a conference overseas and had to mail it a bit earlier, but figured a day or two wouldn't matter. Says Mich assured him there was nothing illegal in the package."

Cassie shuddered and muttered, "Weird, a voice from the dead. I need a sweater." She stood up and headed for the stairs.

Sam's eyes followed every move she made, the papers ignored in his hands. Doc watched him closely. Sam felt the doctor's stare and returned a steady gaze as Cassie went out of sight.

"She's been through a lot, Sam. Don't add to her problems."

"I'll try not to, Doc." Choosing to ignore any personal meaning in Doc's words, Sam continued, "The trial will be bad for her, really bad. DeLacey is going to do everything he can to point to her as the murderer; she's the only other one who was in the house. He's not above character assassination and lethal innuendo. Truth or not, he'll work to confuse the jury and at least get it hung. From his perspective a hung jury is as good as an acquittal because he knows it's unlikely we'll pursue it again. He gets paid and lots of publicity either way. I'm just trying to figure out how best to prepare Cassie."

"Not yet, Sam. She's smart and strong, but she's not ready to hear any of this yet."

Sam nodded his understanding, then said, "Something weird happened at lunch back in May; almost everyone turned to look at Cassie when she walked into YaYas; men and women both did double-takes."

Doc grinned. "You'll get used to it. I've known Cassie almost as long as Mich did and it happens all the time. Cassie says she has a 'generic face' It's not that she's a raving beauty, but rather that she looks like somebody everybody knows, the girl next door sort of thing. So people stare trying to figure out what their friend/cousin/whoever is doing here, wherever 'here' is." The two men were chuckling like old friends when Cassie returned.

"You two look awfully chummy," Cassie said reentering the room and pushing her arm through the sleeve of a raspberry pink cardigan.

"I was just telling Doc these papers are going to be really helpful. They prove Mich knew about Larry's affairs and that he ordered the books on poison." Looking at a second letter, he handed it to Cassie as he said, "We'll get in touch with this Gordon Mansfield. He may be able to tell us more." Sam took a sip of his Earl Grey and waited while Cassie silently read the note Mich had addressed to her

February 10

Dear Cass-

If you're reading this then I guess Larry won. I'll be giving this package to Gordon Mansfield when I have him draw up the new will and I'll be asking him to mail it to you two months after my death if there is any reason to believe I died by other than the 'unnatural causes' that are already eating away at me.

I'll include the original credit card statements that show the purchases Larry made for his honeys and the books he ordered from Amazon. As much as I love him I don't want him to get away with murder – isn't that a cliché!- especially mine. Give this to the DA and ask that it be used to punish Larry for taking away the time I have left. I KNOW I could have beaten the cancer and he didn't give me a chance; that's unforgivable. I know you and Doc will do all you can to help me with this fight since I didn't get to win the other one. It's really weird to be writing this as though I'm already dead!

I suppose by now you know I have left all my paintings to you. And I know you have already decided how best to care for them. You are always so efficient. Knowing you as I do, I know you won't keep any of them for yourself, but please keep the one I'm going to give you when we are together the next time...I already know which one it will be. I'm painting it with you in mind.

You have always been a good and true friend, Cassie. Forget about Kevin and Lexington and get on with your life. There are good men out there, I hope you find one who will make you as happy as Larry has made me (up until this last bit, that is). See you on the other side; don't rush on my account!

Love,
Mich

The letter was signed with Mich's characteristic sprawling signature. Sam watched Cassie tearfully hand the letter to Doc, tears spilling down her cheeks. They both quietly watched Doc read it and then silently pass it to Sam. The only sound in the room was the ticking of the captain's clock on the mantel.

At last, Sam said, "Is that Mich's signature, Cassie?"

"Of course, whose else could it be?" She didn't mean to snap, but that was how it came out.

"Don't get your hackles up, I just have to verify. We'll have a fingerprint expert confirm it, too, and get forensics for the whole package." Cassie turned her head away and looked out the window at the Canadian geese napping by the pond.

"Thanks for making this effort, Cassie, I hope you're not in trouble at work. How long are you here?"

Cassie turned back to the two men, wiped her eyes and straightened her shoulders. "Not too much trouble. Ben was a bit miffed, but reluctantly agreed. If he hadn't, I would have quit. Mich is too important, and after this letter even more so. I think Ben noticed my determination and took the smart way out. I go home on Sunday, so I'll be back at work bright and early Monday morning. We're still short-handed at the library since it's vacation time."

"I just need you to sign this affidavit, attesting to the fact that the package hasn't been out of your control since you received it." Sam pulled a paper from his black portfolio and handed it to Cassie. "That just keeps the chain of evidence in effect." He handed Cassie a pen and she signed the paper above her typed signature. Doc signed on the witness line. Sam signed next and returned the paper to the portfolio. He rose with the brown package in his hand. Cassie and Doc rose too as he turned for the door. "Thanks to both of you." He shook hands with each. "Have a good trip back, Cassie."

"Please keep me informed of what's going on. I feel so isolated back there."

"Don't worry, I'll stay in touch. I've got your email address and all your phone numbers. And you can call me if you're feeling neglected."

The last sight of him was Sam's crooked smile as he turned and walked to his car. *Nice shoulders*, Cassie thought. She'd liked the way his big hand had held hers, too.

Chapter 28

The rest of the summer passed uneventfully. Everybody but Cassie took their vacations. She was saving hers for the trial. Sam was true to his word and called each week with updates; some weeks he'd had someone named Maria call, but at least Cassie didn't feel left in the dark. She and Doc talked a lot, too, and she came to love him as much as Mich had. Still she felt helpless, like she wasn't doing enough to avenge her best friend. She just didn't know what she *could* do.

The work on the camp was very fulfilling, but didn't give Cassie the sense of justice she was looking for for Mich. The architectural plans were coming along well; she was glad she had the money from her inheritance to cover all the monetary outlays she needed to make to get the camp going; she didn't mind one penny of it. The hardest part had been deciding what features should be included in the camp. She finally decided on a library (of course), an artists' studio, a potter's studio, a couple classrooms, a sculpture studio, an Olympic size pool, a lake with canoes and kayaks, woods, playground, dining room, sleeping cabins, management offices, clinic, movie theatre, and then she had stopped, brain fried.

When she started on staff requirements it became even more daunting: housekeepers, counselors, lifeguards, cooks, servers, doctors, nurses, office staff, art instructors of all kinds, swimming instructors, and probably more that she hadn't thought about yet.

Of course there had to be wheelchair access to everything. She decided to add two of those slings that could lower children too weak to walk into the pool or the lake, she didn't want them to miss anything.

She turned her list of requirements and dreams over to the architect and hoped for the best. She wanted to have something to send to Doc by the end of September.

Upon her return from Denver, life at the library had settled into its summer routine that ended all too quickly; inventory, repair, weeding the stacks, record updates, software upgrades, rearranging the worn furniture, and then preparing for the new school year to begin. The summer reading program was a success as always. These were all able to keep Cassie busy and her mind off Mich and Denver and the murder. But evenings and weekends were another story. She continually reviewed what she knew and what she thought. She kept trying to figure out if someone else could have killed Mich. No matter how she twisted everything in her mind, it still came back to the same thing: Larry must have killed Mich; even though Cassie found it hard to believe, she was forced to believe Larry had done it. There was no other acceptable alternative.

One piece of information she thought about might help the case. In mid-August she had called Sam. "I have the backups from my computer. Mich's messages should be on them. Do you think they could help?"

Sam's excitement was tangible even across 2000 miles of cell towers. "Good idea. I'll send someone for them. Don't touch them or your computer until I can get someone there."

"Sam, I have to use my computer. When will someone get here?"

"I don't know yet. Let me check and I'll get back to you." Then he paused. "Is this your home computer we're talking about? Not the one at work?"

"Yes, my home one."

"Just out of curiosity, why do you have backups? State secrets or something?"

"No, but all my financial records are on there, and other stuff I don't want to lose. It's just easier to back up the entire hard drive than to do it selectively."

"How often do you backup? Daily?" Sam had visions of having to go through hundreds of backup discs.

"I know I probably should do it daily to be really safe. Early on I was doing it monthly, now I just do it every three or four months. I figure if anything happens I can reconstruct that much, but I don't want to do much more than that. Besides all the CDs were starting to stack up."

"How far back do your backups go?"

"Just four years, since I got this computer."

"You didn't copy over the discs, reuse them?"

"No, I know most people do that to save the cost of new ones, but

I'm not that confident of my backup capabilities, so I just use a new disk each time. Flash drives aren't that expensive these days, so I've switched to them now. If the IRS ever comes calling I want to be sure I have everything I could possibly need."

Sam said elatedly, "I'll call you back as soon as I have someone lined up. You're wonderful, Cass, I love you!"

Sam's parting words hung in the air even after they had both hung up.

Chapter 29

It had been over two weeks since that conversation; Labor Day had come and gone. Cassie asked Sam each time they talked when she could use her computer again. His response was always the same, "soon". "That's not helpful," she muttered after his most recent call. Despite his evasive answer, Cassie had to admit to herself it was good to hear his voice each week. She assured herself it was just the case he was interested in.

Over the past few months, as their conversations veered away from the case and into more personal topics she'd learned more about him.

She liked that he had joined the DA's office to fight for the victims. She liked that he entertained his nieces and nephews on the weekends. She liked the warmth in his voice when he talked. In fact, she couldn't think of anything she didn't like about him...except his Marine Corps background. She vowed to ask him about it soon. The fact that she found him so good, she refused to use the word "perfect", worried her. She just wasn't sure she was ready to trust anyone yet. She had been too badly burned to trust again so soon. *Was five years soon?* She asked herself.

Now it was the Friday after Labor Day. The students were back in school and classes had started at the two local high schools. She'd been able to check her email from the library computer, but she was annoyed that she hadn't been able to check her financial records for over two weeks; she knew she was old-fashioned to be balancing her checkbook every week. *Or is it obsessive?* Cassie was pulled from her reverie by a volunteer standing at her door, "Cassie, can you help this guy? He insists you're holding some material for him, but I can't find it with the Holds or Reserves. Maybe it's in ILL?"

Cassie shook her head and went to the Circulation desk; she wasn't holding anything for anyone. The man had turned away, checking out the children's artwork that adorned the library's walls. It didn't matter. Cassie knew those shoulders.

"Sam? What are you doing here?"

"Some greeting. I come 2000 miles and not even a hello?

Cassie beamed at him. "Sorry. Of course. Welcome! Now,

what are you doing here?"

"You're a hard woman, Cassie Kirkland. I came for the backups."

"I thought you were sending someone."

"I did. Me. I decided I needed some time off and I thought your little town might be a good place to get away. Took me some time to convince Greg this was a business trip and that I needed to control the chain of custody for the evidence. He finally relented and I got the first plane out before he changed his mind."

Cassie looked at him speculatively. He could have sent someone, anyone else.

"Where are you staying?"

"I got a room at Col Alto. I remembered you'd said what a nice job they'd done restoring it. You're right; it doesn't look like any Hampton Inn I've ever seen before. What time do you get off here? I'll take you out to dinner if you'll pick the place."

Cassie looked at the clock over the desk. "I don't usually leave until 5, but Fridays are still slow since classes have just started, so I can probably take off a little early. Give me a minute and I'll go with you."

She returned to her desk, called Wanda over and explained her early departure, grabbed her purse and was back at Sam's side in three minutes.

"Hope you've got your walking shoes on. I walk to work on nice days like this so we'll have to walk back to my house so I can freshen up a bit."

"No problem, I've got my rental car. You navigate."

"If it's parked, it'll be easier to walk than to find a new parking space."

As they left the library they could hear a Sousa march. "What's that?" Sam asked turning his head in the direction of the music.

"VMI. Friday afternoon parade. The cadets march, the band plays, and in a minute the cannon will boom. Want to go watch?"

"Not this time. I'm getting hungry, no lunch, airplane food is non-existent as you know and I can only stand so many peanuts and pretzels."

"Did you fly into Roanoke? There are lots of places to eat between here and there."

"I saw the signs, but I was anxious to get here. How far's your house?"

"Just a couple blocks." She decided he was "anxious" to get the backups.

Cassie directed Sam down the narrow one-way streets of the eighteenth century town. "Good thing I'm not in an SUV," Sam observed. "These streets are barely wide enough for a horse and buggy let alone modern vehicles." As he spoke, a horse and carriage crossed in front of them as they waited at a light.

Cassie burst out laughing as she waved to the driver, dressed in Civil War era garb. "I couldn't have timed that better if I'd had a script!" she hooted.

"I thought you said a couple blocks," Sam scowled as they strolled up another rolling sidewalk.

"We're almost there." A minute later Cassie turned into the front yard of her three story old home with a large veranda. Cassie steered Sam around to the back door; another walkway headed toward what appeared to be a carriage house. "That's the garage, but it's full of my car and old stuff I haven't had a chance to go through since my folks died."

Cassie led him across a brick patio to a kitchen door. "We only use the front door for company," she explained. "As much time as we spent together in Denver makes you practically family."

She slipped off her shoes as soon as she entered. Cassie's cinnamon colored golden retriever came to meet them. "That's Rosie, she'll probably kill you with kindness. Make yourself at home. There's beer and wine in the fridg, some cheese and sausage in the meat drawer." She reached up into a cupboard and grabbed a box of Carr's wheat biscuits. "Crackers." Reaching into a drawer she came out with a cheese knife. "Knife. That should hold you until dinner. Anything else you need, just hunt 'til you find it. I'm going to grab a quick shower and change. Don't give Rosie any cheese, she's on a diet. She won't take anything, but she will look at you pathetically." Cassie sailed barefoot through a swinging door leading into a hall.

Sam found a plate and fixed some cheese and crackers. Then he grabbed a bottle of Yuengling, glad it wasn't Coors. Munching a cracker he followed Cassie's lead into the main part of the house, Rosie following close on his heels. The hall Cassie had taken led to a staircase and the front of the house. Sam heard water running as he passed the stairs. On the left was a living room, "probably called a parlor in this part of the country," he muttered to the dog beside him, waiting for cracker tidbits to hit the floor. The antique cherry furniture had obviously been updated with more modern fabric. Lots of family photos buried the mantel. On closer inspection they appeared to be ancestors, as well as Cassie's parents, and Cassie as a child. "Cute kid, too." A Colorado landscape held place of honor over the mantel. Sam glanced at the signature although he knew it was a Michela Merritt.

Across the hall was a formal dining room. Mahogany table and sideboard gleamed from years of love and polish. Delicate English china tea cups were visible through the mullioned glass. Another landscape was in this room, too.

Cassie interrupted Sam's ramblings, "Mich gave me that one a couple years ago. She gave me the one in the parlor when I visited in May. It wasn't quite dry and she said she'd send it on; the curators at DMA got it to me last month."

"What happened with the rest of her works?"

"They're in storage at DMA for right now. Willa Warrenton at the Denver Museum of Art is advising me. She wants to do a show of Mich's works before the collection gets split up. She's helping me with an auction, too, to fund a summer art camp for kids with cancer. The paintings are fine where they are for now while Willa and I figure things out. Besides, I can't do anything with them while Larry's new lawyer is contesting the will. Even with jail looming Larry is still a pain in the butt."

"What does your lawyer think about his chances?"

"No problem. The will is bullet-proof. Larry just hates to lose out on anything. So he'll spend lots of money, probably get some publicity out of it – although not the positive kind – and end up with nothing. He's never been known for thinking things through. And you can't tell him anything; he knows everything."

Sam could see Cassie's mood deflating with the discussion.

"Tell you what. Show me the backups and we can get that out of the way. Then we can have the rest of my time here to relax and you can show me the wonders of Lexington."

Cassie perked up immediately. "Sounds like a plan. The backups are in my office." She led him back through the hall to her sunny enclosed porch off the back of the house. "It used to be a porch, but I moved my office stuff out here so I could enjoy the sunshine, birds, and squirrels."

"I like it," Sam said as he surveyed it. A bookshelf stood to the right of the door, full of bird books, a camera, notebooks, computer manuals, disks, binoculars, and a couple flash drives. The white wicker furniture gave the room a comfy feel. The PC sat on the desk facing the window.

"The disks are in the closet," Cassie said as she started to open a door.

"Wait. May as well do this by the book, or DeLacey will have me up for tampering with evidence." Sam pulled his phone from his jacket pocket. He opened the closet door and took a picture of the stack of disks and flash drives *in situ*. He was glad to see there were less than twelve of them.

"That's all of them, four years' worth. I haven't done a backup on the current system since June or July. Will you need that, too?"

"We'll do it tomorrow. You haven't touched your PC?"

"Not since you told me not to. I've been checking my e-mail remotely at the office. I'd been using it all summer, though, since I got back from Denver. There are even a couple messages from Larry, threatening me with dire consequences if I don't give him the paintings."

Sam frowned. "That doesn't sound good."

"He's all bluff. It'd take too much thought to do something. I just ignored the messages. I told you he's not too bright sometimes. Can those messages be used against him somehow?"

Sam was impressed by her cool acceptance of the man, knowing he had already murdered once.

"I'm ready for some more crackers, then dinner. Where shall we go?" Sam adroitly changed the subject.

"I called the Bistro from upstairs. Jacqui said to come on over, they're not crowded yet. We can walk there and the food is wonderful. There's not much parking on Main Street anyway." Cassie laughed at Sam's raised eyebrows when she mentioned walking again.

"I don't walk much these days," he offered as an excuse.

"Come on, it's not that far. And besides, at least you can breathe here, none of that rarefied air like on your fourteeners." The two were laughing companionably as they headed back toward town from Jackson Avenue.

Chapter 30

The evening was idyllic and tense, all at the same time.

Dinner at the restored eclectic-cuisine restaurant had been its usual excellent fare. The crab cakes rivaled anything out of Baltimore. Sam was impressed with the art work by local artists and the two comfy rooms. Conversation flowed as smoothly as the chardonnay. As predicted, they had beaten the crowd, just one other table was occupied and a couple of individuals sat at the bar. On their walk back to Sam's car after dinner, Cassie had felt a tingle each time his hand pressed her waist as they crossed streets. Sam's light kiss on her cheek as he left her at her door was as unsettling as it was unexpected.

Sam arrived bright and early Saturday morning with hot cinnamon rolls from Blue Sky Bakery. "The receptionist at the hotel recommended these. Got orange juice to go with them?" He looked especially relaxed in his jeans and western shirt with the sleeves rolled up to his elbows.

"Boots?" Cassie hooted. "This is Virginia, not Colorado."

"Hey, these are as comfortable as bedroom slippers. Besides, with all the college students around here, I'm sure boots are nothing new to the local populace.

"After I dropped you last night I gave myself a quick tour of your town. I can't believe there's so much history in this little bitty town. I started at Stonewall Jackson's grave, driving by it of course, and didn't miss the Episcopal Church where Robert E. Lee had served on the vestry. Lee's house and chapel, the Stonewall Jackson Museum, Traveller's grave, and the downtown shops. Of course I couldn't get inside any of them, but it was really amazing.

"And you haven't even started on VMI and the George Marshall museum," Cassie teased him. Sam moaned at the thought of all that walking.

Their breakfast of scrambled eggs, bacon, fresh fruit and cinnamon rolls over, Sam asked, "Can you tell me about Michela now, Cass?"

"Let's go to my office to talk," Cassie said as she stood. Sam followed her out to the sunny office. Cassie sat in her desk chair and Sam made himself comfortable sprawled on the wicker loveseat; his legs extended over the arm, his arms crossed on his chest, his eyes closed.

Chapter 31

Cassie had known she would have to talk about Mich some time. She searched around inside herself for signs of pain; none. Just a quiet hole where Michela's warmth used to be.

"We met the first day of our freshman year at college, and they say first year roommates never get along. We just hit it off, a case of opposites attracting, I guess. She was very outgoing and flamboyant; I was more reserved. If she'd been around in the sixties she'd have been a hippie. Everybody loved her.

"For all her spontaneity, though, she was very insecure. She needed lots of attention, I guess to make up for not having a mother and father. She mostly dated upper classmen, that's how she met Larry.

"They started dating our junior year and got married the next summer. I was not enthralled with him; he was in no way good enough for her. I thought he was a fortune hunter. Too slick. And..." Cassie trailed off, unsure if she should tell Sam everything. She glanced over at him. His breathing was so steady she thought he'd fallen asleep.

From behind closed eyes Sam said, "And?"

Choosing her words carefully, Cassie replied, "He was not exactly faithful. I knew several girls he'd hit on even after they were engaged."

"Anybody I know?" Sam queried.

Cassie hesitated, then with a rush, "Yes, me. He wouldn't leave me alone. Mich and I shared an apartment the year before they married. He'd come over and be too familiar with his hands, always wanting to give me a *friendly* hug or a *brotherly* kiss. He was disgusting. Even if he hadn't been engaged to my best friend he would have been disgusting. But nothing I did convinced Mr. Superego to give up. After they married, I tried to see Mich away from their apartment."

"Did Mich know how you felt?"

Cassie snorted. "She was such an innocent. She loved him so much. He had her buffaloed, convinced he could do no wrong. She knew I didn't like to be around him, but she thought I was jealous, that I'd lost her. I let her go on thinking that; I couldn't tell her the truth: that her husband couldn't keep his hands to himself or his pants zipped."

"Did you see them often?"

"I saw Mich a lot during our last year at school, mostly at lunch or afternoons. Every now and then we'd go to a movie. Larry didn't like her to be gone in the evenings. After graduation I moved to Chicago and they went to Denver. Mich and I got together at least once a year for a week or so. I flew out to be with her after her first cancer diagnosis and then her miscarriage. Other than that we mostly communicated by phone and e-mail."

"How did Larry handle the miscarriage?"

"He never wanted children, said it'd cramp their travels. Mich called me, all upset, right after the loss; I flew out and spent ten days with her. Larry left town as soon as I got there. Told me to 'deal with Mich', he had better things to do than 'deal with a whiney wife'." Cassie saw Sam's jaw clench.

"He's quite the piece of work, isn't he?" she murmured.

From beneath lidded eyes Sam watched Cassie. He needed her to be able to speak calmly about Michela on the witness stand. But he also needed her to be seen as the loyal, passionate friend she was. He hoped getting her to talk now would make it easier for her in November, at least until DeLacey got to her.

"Doc told me this was her second bout with cancer?" he prompted.

"Yes, poor Mich. The original hard-luck kid." Cassie had pulled her knees up and wrapped her arms around them. Her chin was resting on them.

"The firs bout with cancer, she was worried because she hadn't gotten pregnant so she went to see Doc. He did a complete check-up, even a mammogram although at 24 it wasn't a typical procedure. A lump was found. They talked about it. Doc recommended a mastectomy even though it broke his heart. The cancer was too far spread for just a lumpectomy and he was worried it might spread even more.

"Mich was okay with it. That was a wonderful thing about her; she knew she wasn't beautiful, attractive yes, but not beautiful, and had no qualms about it. Everyone who knew her forgot her appearance; she was so full of life, she just electrified any room she was in. She used to joke that maybe she'd have reconstruction surgery and end up looking like Dol - that's half a Dolly Parton."

Sam smiled at the thought. He felt he would have liked Michela Merritt if he'd had the chance to know her. "How did Larry feel about the surgery?"

Cassie's face hardened. "As expected. He told her if she went through with it he'd never be able to sleep with her again, that he hadn't expected to get saddled with half a wife."

"Were you there when he said all this?" Sam hoped she was 'cause then she could testify about it, but he couldn't imagine anyone saying it in front of outsiders.

"No. Mich told me in an e-mail. She used e-mail as a catharsis. She'd rant and rave and get everything out of her system. Then she got pregnant. She was so surprised and thrilled."

"Pregnant? What happened?"

"Soon after she found out she was pregnant, she had a miscarriage. She was devastated. E-mails weren't enough so I went out to Denver; I stayed about ten days. She finally accepted it and was doing well for the next year, then the cancer came back."

"When was that?"

"About a year ago. She called me one afternoon and told me. She had developed a cough and went to Doc. The lung x-rays showed the cancer. At first they thought it was lung cancer 'cause Mich used to smoke like a fiend. But the biopsy showed it was a recurrence of the breast cancer. She took chemo treatments and radiation, but they couldn't seem to get ahead of it. She was really disappointed 'cause she was past the halfway point in remission from the first go-round and she thought she was home free.

"Earlier this year it spread to her bones. That's when Doc told her it was really serious and she'd better prepare for the worst. He said if it got into her brain there wasn't anything they could do; she had no more than six to ten months."

Sam had to strain to hear Cassie's now-whispered words. He looked over and saw silent tears running down her face. Cassie was oblivious to the wetness on her cheeks.

"Where was Larry during all this?" Sam asked quietly.

The mention of Larry's name brought a pained look to Cassie's face and a stiffness to her spine. The tears disappeared.

"Catting around somewhere. Of course he always came back to Mich, even continued having sex with her once in a while; he was afraid of losing access to all her money and her growing fame."

"I don't understand why Mich stayed with him. You said she knew of his affairs."

"Knew about them? He flaunted them in her face. That last week we were together I asked her why she stayed with him. She said originally she stayed because she loved him; she felt he needed her and she needed to be needed. The last time, though, when he was a bigger pig than usual, I think she got mad. She told me she was not going to divorce him and give him half of everything. Plus, Mich was the eternal optimist; she really believed she could lick the cancer and win back Larry's love...if there ever was any. She was a master at convincing herself that what she believed was the way it was; she must have owned the factory that made rose-colored glasses."

Sam had to smile at Cassie's depiction. He liked the way she was able to give visuals. He liked her humor, too, and her self-deprecation. He understood her loyalty to her friend and her animosity toward her friend's husband. He knew a jury would love this clever woman, too.

"Now it's my turn to ask a question," Cassie said. "So when were you in the Marines?"

"In the middle of college. All of a sudden I just got this thought that I needed to contribute more than just preparing for law school. I enlisted in the Marines because I was impressed with their *esprit de corps* attitude and the fact that every Marine is a rifleman, even cooks and supply clerks know how to shoot and how to maintain their weapons. A lot of the Marines' history goes back to how the early Scots ran their fiefdoms, everybody relied on everybody else and the ones on the next higher rung were responsible for everybody below. I went to boot camp at Pendleton, did two years in the Middle East, came back and finished college. I was still in the Reserves for four more years, but my unit was never called up. After my time was up, I got out."

"Why? It seems all that honor and integrity stuff would have been right up your alley."

Sam laughed a somewhat jaded laugh. "You see a lot in the Corps, and yes they do emphasize honor and integrity: Country, God and Family. Most of what they teach is related to the Corps. Recruits are taught that their first loyalty is to the Corps and their fellow Marines. I've seen through my law practice that those attributes don't necessarily transfer to civilian life. Some Marines have a hard time being alone or no longer part of a team. A lot of them go into law enforcement or fire-fighting; those careers have the same type of comradeship.

Sam stretched. He'd been talking enough and he felt Cassie was getting drained. Glancing at his watch he was surprised to see it was almost noon and he had an hour's drive to Roanoke for his plane. "How about those last backups? Better get to them before I have to leave for the airport." Sam stood and reached a hand down to help Cassie to her feet. His warm touch sent shivers straight through her. Without thinking Sam pulled Cassie close to his chest and looked deeply into her eyes. *It's true,* Cassie thought, *time can stand still.* She pulled away but not before Sam saw the look of panic in her eyes. "Come on, Cowboy, let's get you those discs." *A witness, Cassie girl, that's all you are to him. Keep your guard up.* But it was hard.

After the backups were packed into yet another padded envelope and sealed with heavy library tape, Sam prepared for his drive to the airport. Sam stood at the kitchen door and held the hand Cassie extended to shake. "Thanks for all your help, Cassie. Get plenty of rest before November. Trials can be grueling. And DeLacey will do everything he can to make you out to be in the wrong. He may even try to pin the murder on you."

Cassie's head snapped up and fire burned in her eyes. "Well, he can try, but it won't work."

"You and I know that. All he has to do, though, is plant a seed of doubt with the jury, just enough to let them think there's a possibility of someone other than Larry having committed the crime and Larry walks. I'm sure we've got an excellent case against him, but John is a master of misdirection. Don't worry about it, just be well-rested so he can't wear you down. We'll go over all his possible scenarios when you get to Denver."

"Will you let me know if there's anything useful on the discs?"

"Of course." Sam hesitated. Then his hand came up to push a lock of hair behind Cassie's ear. Cupping Cassie's face in his warm hands, he just looked at her. Her eyes were so big, so deep; he felt himself falling into a depth from which he might never recover. The worst of it was the trust he thought he saw there. He couldn't let this go on; but he couldn't stop it either.

His thumb rubbed her cheek. Cassie held her breath, afraid the moment would end, afraid it wouldn't. "Do you still want weekly updates, Cass?" Sam whispered tantalizingly close to her lips. Cassie couldn't move except to rest her hands on his hips, afraid her knees might betray her.

The soft pressure of Sam's lips helped the flicker inside her grow into a small flame, fueled by doubt and desire. Cassie didn't move. She just whispered, "Please."

Sam lifted his head and looked again into the depths. It took all his internal fortitude not to go up the stairs and slam a bedroom door behind them, shutting the world away and the two of them inside. But he had to be strong for Michela and for Cassie; he couldn't jeopardize the best case of his career.

He tore his eyes and hands away from Cassie's innocent face and headed out the door and across the brick porch without another word.

Cassie called after him, "I need to be there November fourth, right?"

Sam turned and replied, "No, that's when the trial starts. I need you there a week before. I'll get you a hotel room."

"No, that's okay. Doc wants me to stay with him. I think he's terribly lonely."

"Fine. Just let me know when you're arriving."

Cassie smiled at his retreating back, "I'll do that."

Cassie let out her breath as she closed the door behind her. Although his kiss had been gentle and heated, she felt bruised from head to foot. She closed the door behind her, knowing it was going to be a long afternoon, followed by a long sleepless night. She was definitely *not* looking forward to November. She and Rosie headed for the coffee pot and energizing before she got back to work on the camp.

Chapter 32

The next week Sam was called to the chambers of Judge Edward Thomas, who would be overseeing the case. All Sam was told was to be there at 10 a.m. on Thursday. At the appointed time, Sam went to the Judge's office and was escorted to the door of the actual chambers by Judge Thomas's assistant, Angela Singletary.

The judge's chambers were exactly as one would have expected; Sam had never been in Judge Thomas's chambers but he immediately recognized that the room was decorated just like all the other chambers at the Jefferson County Combined Courthouse. Dark paneling, leather furniture, mahogany desk, subdued lighting. The only personal item was a large framed yellow-and-red poster from the musical "Hair", the original from the late sixties, not the newer version.

The other jarring note was the presence of the defense attorney, John DeLacey. The three men shook hands all around and then the jurist motioned them to the blue leather guest seats across from his desk.

"Sam, John has submitted a brief to have the letter from Michela Merritt excluded from the trial." He held up a copy of the letter Cassie and Sam had reviewed in June. "Says it's prejudicial and he has no chance to cross-examine the witness. What do you have to say?"

Sam fumed as he gathered his thoughts. He had expected this, but as time had passed he had hoped DeLacey had ignored it. "Your Honor, these are the witnesses own words, written just before her death. They go directly to her state of mind and events of which she was aware."

DeLacey jumped in, "Your Honor, forgetting that I can't examine a dead person, what about the right of the accused to confront his accuser? And his wife at that?"

Sam rebutted, "The law says that a person cannot be *compelled* to testify against his or her spouse. Mrs. Merritt was obviously not compelled, she wrote the letter on her own. She is trying to ensure justice for herself, in the event she was murdered."

"Maybe, maybe not." DeLacey was adamant. "A lot could have happened after she wrote that letter. She gave it to the attorney in February. That means she wrote it sometime before then. That's practically six months! She could have decided differently, she could have forgiven Larry Merritt and reconciled. She could have decided to kill herself. Anything could have happened to change the circumstances of the letter and she just didn't do anything about it, either she forgot or felt it was no longer an issue."

Judge Thomas raised his hand to stop the tirade; he knew DeLacey could go on forever once he got started on a stage. "Okay, that's enough. I've decided. The letter is out. Too much time passed between when she wrote it and when she died." Sam started to argue but the judge shook his head, "No, Sam, that's it. It's out."

The two attorneys stood, both thanked the judge, and they turned to the door. DeLacey motioned Sam ahead of him with an ill-concealed grin. Sam went through the door and headed for his office; he was not interested in polite chatter with the opposition.

Chapter 33

The trial was scheduled to start on Monday, Nov. 4. Cassie returned to Denver on Friday, Oct. 25, a week early, wanting time to relax and get settled before the trial started. This time the trip through DIA had been a zoo – all those skiers! *Remind me not to fly into Denver on a Friday during ski season again!* The early winter snows had raised a lot of ski hopes across the country. People going to any of the "name" slopes flew into Denver and then rented a car or took a van for the one to ten hour drive, depending on the weather and the roads.

Fortunately, it was a clear day and everyone, what seemed like thousands and thousands of people – families, couples, hopeful singles – filled the concourses and the train, everyone looking for luggage trolleys at the same time. The upcoming holidays were a high point of the resort season in Colorado and Cassie could tell everyone decided to get a jump on Halloween and fly the same day she did. At least most of them were smiling.

Doc had said to meet him at carousel 12 by the pay phones, regardless of where her luggage came in. The phones were almost as crowded as the baggage waiting areas. She looked for Doc, but didn't see him. Just then a hand took her elbow.

"I offered to come instead of Doc," Sam said with his lop-sided grin.

Cassie was surprised at how pleased she was to see him. Without thinking she gave him a big hug. "Sam! It's good to see you. Is Doc okay?"

"Yep, he's fine. I just thought I'd do better in this mob scene and he not-too-reluctantly agreed."

"Is there anything I should know? Has anything happened about the trial? Did Larry confess?"

"Whoa, Cass," Sam laughed. "All in good time. Let's get your bags and get out of here, then we can talk while we sit in traffic."

Sam forged a path right up to the luggage carousel with Cassie next to him. She pointed out her two dark green Eagle Creek bags; Sam grabbed them and led the way to his car. Sam was glad she hadn't brought skis, so they didn't have to fight their way to the over-sized-packages carousel, too.

Cassie fished for her sunglasses. The sun reflecting off the remains of this week's snow was dazzling. "I guess you'll have a white Halloween."

"Yep, usually do. Kids bundle up like the Michelin man, regardless of their costume. Too bad I won't get to see much of it. Denver goes a bit nuts around Halloween, offices dress up in costumes, you go out to lunch and you're surrounded by witches and monsters, storm troopers and ninja turtles, and that's the adults! No festivities for me this year, though, we're coming down to the wire on the trial and we've been working 24/7 getting ready."

Cassie looked at Sam a bit horrified and incredulous at the same time; Halloween was her least favorite holiday. She tried to picture Sam as anything other than a lawyer, maybe a cowboy? She ignored the Halloween topic and asked, "What can I do to help?"

Sam looked at her long and hard, debating his answer. "Your being here is a help." Then he opened her door and hustled her into his car; she couldn't see his face, and thankfully he couldn't see the surprise on hers.

Cassie thought about his words while he loaded the luggage and came around. Was he trying to tell her something or just referring to the trial? She shook herself, *don't be stupid. Of course he meant the trial.*

Sam started the car and headed into traffic. "It'll take a little while longer than usual to get to Doc's 'cause of all the traffic, but once we get off 70 it should pick up."

"No problem. How's Doc doing? I've talked to him frequently since I left, but I can't really tell over the phone. I think he's a pretty good actor."

Sam considered his answer. "On the whole, he's okay. He's got his work. He and I golfed a few times. But I think he's terribly lonely. Your visit should perk him right up; it worked for me." Sam grinned at his passenger.

Cassie again tried to ignore his words; *he's just being polite*. "Is his health okay? I'd invited him to visit Virginia in September, but he said he wasn't up to it."

"He's lost a lot of weight. I think he's depressed. I'm sure he didn't let on about it. He feels guilty about not getting Mich away from Larry sooner. Maybe you can convince him she wouldn't have left; I've done what I could, but I never knew her."

"I'll try. There was no way she would leave him...no matter what he did to her."

They rode in companionable silence for ten miles; Sam thinking about the trial, Cassie remembering the last time with Mich.

"It looks like a winter scene from Currier and Ives," she murmured, without even realizing she had been looking at the snow-covered mountains.

"I don't think they ever got this far west, though," Sam replied. "That reminds me, the curator wants you to call her Monday."

"Yes, I know, she e-mailed me. She's got the exhibit ready and needs to talk about it. How did you know?"

"We were talking about when she would testify and she mentioned it."

"Is it a good idea to have this exhibit right after the trial? Won't Larry's lawyer scream about the publicity?"

"He might, but since the show isn't until the end of the month, I doubt the judge will go along with it. Might make more publicity trying to fight it. We'll see what DeLacey does."

"Do you think the trial will take that long? A whole month?"

"Maybe longer. DeLacey will do everything he can to discredit our witnesses and present alternatives for the crime. All he has to do is provide "reasonable doubt" to the jury, and Larry goes home."

Cassie shuddered. "I'm not looking forward to this." She turned her face back to the view and her thoughts back to the trial coming up in ten short days.

Sam reached over and took her hand. "It'll be okay. I promise."

Cassie enjoyed the warmth of his hand, and of his eyes when she turned back toward him. The ride to Doc's continued in comfortable silence; Sam's hand warming Cassie's. They arrived at Doc's all too soon for Cassie, she hadn't figured out her emotions yet.

Chapter 34

The next week passed too quickly and took forever. Cassie spent Monday with the curator, Willa Warrenton, fine-tuning the exhibit plans. Cassie left everything - where to hang what, who to invite, what food to serve - in Willa's capable hands. The curator had everything well in hand, she really just wanted Cassie's approval since she was the owner of the art.

Tuesday and Wednesday Cassie did a little clothes shopping at Park Meadows Mall and then picked up groceries; she cooked big dinners for Doc. Sam was right, Doc had lost too much weight. But he seemed to have recovered some of his good spirits by Wednesday dinner. They played cribbage in the evenings and tried not to talk about the upcoming events.

Doc took Thursday off; leaving his staff to celebrate Halloween as they would. He drove Cassie up to Rocky Mountain National Park where she ooohed and ahhhed over the views, the elk on the hoof instead of her plate, and the Big Horn Sheep. There was a bit more than a light dusting of snow as they left the park; snow for Halloween as Sam had predicted. They had an early supper of Cassie's "world-famous" macaroni and cheese and a salad and then Doc took her to a party at the Denver Country Club, avoiding the trick-or-treaters. Cassie wasn't really in a party mood, but she agreed to go so Doc would get out of the house and see people.

And he did! There were quite a few widows and divorcees, and even a few wives, who seemed very happy to take on the job of cheering up the distinguished doctor. Cassie had insisted he introduce her as his niece to reduce the trial conversations. As soon as women realized Cassie wasn't Doc's date, he became fair game.

"I don't think you've sat down since we got here," Cassie laughed to the doctor while they danced.

"I'm sorry. Have I been ignoring you?"

"Don't apologize! Just be careful out there. This may be Denver, but there are still sharks and barracudas in them thar hills; not to mention a few two-footed cougars."

Doc looked at her quizzically, then threw his head back and laughed.

"I guess I've been out of circulation too long. I thought they were just being friendly," he said sheepishly.

"Well, I predict your phone won't stop ringing after tonight. You'll have more 'friends' than you know what to do with." She pushed him away from herself with a grin, "Get back out there, Doc, you're still a young man...and quite a catch. Enjoy yourself. Isn't that what you'd tell your patients?"

Doc was silent a moment, looking intently at Cassie. She worried she'd overstepped her bounds as a friend of the family. Then Doc heaved a sigh. "You're right, Cassie. Mich isn't coming back. I did all I could for her, for her mother. I guess I have to face it and get on with my life."

"That's the spirit," Cassie hugged him. "Now which of tonight's beauties are you going to dance with next?" The evening continued in a light-hearted spirit. They laughed and gossiped all the way home.

Chapter 35

Sam came to the house about ten on Friday morning, November 1. He had called earlier in the week and arranged the appointment with Doc and Cassie; he wanted to explain what was going to go on during the trial. His weekend was going to be tied up with last minute trial preparations. He needed to "prep" Cassie for her testimony, too, but he hadn't mentioned that when he made the appointment. He'd prepped Doc the week before.

"Good to see you, Sam," Doc greeted the younger man with a handshake. Sam was pleasantly surprised at the change in the physician; he sounded almost chipper. Sam had seen only the morose side of Doc since the day Michela had died. His surprise must have shown.

Doc grinned sheepishly. "Cassie has brought me to my senses. I've turned over a new leaf. I'm becoming more 'social'. Two dinner invitations already this morning, from divorcees! Seems I'm suddenly eligible."

"No, a catch," Cassie corrected him from the den door. "Hi, Sam." She tried to sound casual, not sure what tack to take with him; he'd been a different person at the airport, but they hadn't spoken since. Her heart was racing as she looked at him calmly, hoping her pleasure wasn't showing on her face.

Sam studied her composure. "Well, let's get started." He led the way back into the den as Cassie's hopes fell.

Cassie and Doc seated themselves on the sofa, Sam across from them in the deep blue leather wingback. He set his briefcase on the floor next to him. He leaned forward, hands clasped between his khaki-clad knees.

"Basically, the trial will progress just like it does on television; opening statements, prosecution witnesses, defense witnesses, closing statements. All the interesting stuff usually starts with the witness cross-examinations. That's when we each try to discredit a witness or redirect the jury's thinking."

"What type questions are we likely to get, Sam," Doc asked.

"With DeLacey there's no telling. He's good and he's smart. And he wants to win. He doesn't care who gets hurt on the way to his win.

"Doc, he may not even question you. I'm calling you to discuss Mich's medical and family history. DeLacey will probably ask you about her prognosis. I'm guessing he's going to try to imply Mich committed suicide or ..." His voice trailed off as he glanced at Cassie.

"Or implicate me," Cassie said calmly; staring steadily into Sam's eyes.

"Right. He'll use your inheritance as your motive, and you were in the house alone with her."

Cassie was amazed at how they could be so analytical about Mich's death. Time *did* heal wounds?

"I didn't do it, Sam," she said forcefully. "Surely the jury will see that."

"We have to *make* them see it. DeLacey will do everything he can to muddy the water and confuse them. It's like a magician's sleight-of-hand trick: misdirection."

"And Mich didn't kill herself; she wouldn't."

"I know. That's going to be a little harder to prove since she's not here to testify. I'm counting on you to get across her state of mind. Your long-standing friendship will carry a lot of weight as to your understanding of her feelings, although John is likely to object to that part of your testimony."

The rest of the day was spent going over the trial and possible questions. Doc called out for a pizza that the three ate without tasting. Sam left, telling them to try not to think about the trial. They all knew his admonition was futile. His final words on his way out the door were, "Cassie, we need to get together tomorrow and go over your specific testimony. I can't coach you on what to say or how to say it, but we need to discuss anything DeLacey might bring up that can jeopardize your credibility. Can we meet at my office at 10?"

Cassie nodded wordlessly, already worrying about what she might have to reveal to Sam and in court.

Chapter 36

Cassie arrived at Sam's office promptly at 10 Saturday morning, Doc had given her specific directions and most of the snow was gone; the car's GPS helped too; Doc was busy fielding calls from women trying to get on his rapidly-filling social calendar so he let Cassie take his car.

Cassie stopped at the building across from the county jail. A leggy brunette met her as the doors opened. "Sam saw you coming across the parking lot and asked me to meet you. I'm Maria Donovan." The two women shook hands and headed for the office.

"It's nice to finally meet you, Maria, I appreciate your help with keeping me up to date over the summer."

"Not a problem, it's what I do. I'm Sam's go-fer and his contact with the victims. Sam is one of the best ADAs in keeping the victims in the loop; he takes really good care of them, pampers them really. Much more so than any of the other attorneys. But he says it's important to let them know they're not forgotten in this big puzzle known as the justice system."

Cassie was walking and watching Maria at the same time; she didn't even see the mountain range outside the glass walls of the corridor. It was obvious Maria had a lot of respect for Sam; *is there something more?* Maria was about the same age as Cassie, with Latina features including beautiful long straight hair that fell to her waist; she was a bit shorter than Cassie. "Here we are."

Maria made a right into a door marked Sam Chambers Assistant District Attorney. Sam's desk was just inside the door. Another desk sat opposite his. Maria closed the door behind them and took a seat at the other desk. Sam looked up and smiled that lopsided grin that made Cassie's nerves tingle. "I told Maria you would be right on time; I just assumed that librarians tend to be a bit anal." Cassie could feel her hackles rising. Apparently Sam did, too. "No offense, ADAs are the same way, aren't we Maria?" He grinned at the woman across from him.

"You can say that again, in triplicate," she teased back. It was obvious the two knew each other well and had a very cozy working relationship. *Was there more?*

Cassie decided to get things started so she could get out of there. "So, what do we do?"

Sam stood and walked around from behind his desk. He opened the door on the other side of his desk. "My office used to be in there," he said as he pointed inside the door he had just opened. "But I thought it would be more convenient and comfortable if I could talk with clients someplace away from my work. So I moved my desk out to the waiting room and moved that furniture into here; the new arrangement allows me to talk with clients in a more comfortable and discreet setting. It's a little crowded out there with two of us, but we make it work, don't we, Maria?" He included the woman as she followed them into the next room and closed the door. She had a digital voice recorder in her hand. Cassie looked at it skeptically.

"That's just so we can review our session later, make sure we haven't missed anything. Okay?" Sam queried.

Cassie shrugged and took the chair Sam indicated, putting her purse on the floor next to her. The other two sat on either side of her. Her nerves were singing, and not in a good way. She didn't know what to expect from this "session" but it sounded vaguely like the sessions she'd had with her therapist. Sam's next words did nothing to allay her anxiety.

"Cassie, I need you to think of this like a therapy session. Everything we say in here is private, confidential. I won't use any of it in court unless I have to, and I'll check everything with you before I do. Are we good?" Sam smiled and patted her hand resting on her thigh.

Cassie smiled back and nodded, afraid her voice would crack if she tried to answer.

"Okay, Cassie, from now on I need you to answer aloud so we get your answers on the recorder." He nodded to Maria who turned on the recorder.

"Are you okay with Maria being in here, it's helpful to me to have an extra pair of ears; Maria is a very good interrogator." Sam smiled his winning smile at the other woman.

Cassie straightened her back and said calmly, "It's fine. I have nothing to say that the whole world can't hear." *Depending on what you ask.* "Feels like that deposition I had with Mr. DeLacey."

Sam replied, "At first it will feel like that, but Maria and I will be delving into everything more deeply, hopefully more so than John did. Ready?" Cassie replied in the affirmative. "Let's start."

Sam started off by asking Cassie to explain about how long she'd known Mich, their friendship, their yearly trips. Sam and Maria interrupted her frequently to ask her to clarify points or elaborate about them. After what seemed like hours they got to the visit six months ago and Michela's death.

Cassie took a bite of the turkey on pumpernickel Maria had ordered for them and took a sip of her water. "Where do you want me to begin?"

"Start with the email you received asking you to come and then go through everything you two did, everything that was said. We'll interrupt when we need clarifications." Cassie looked at both of them with a raised eyebrow, "Really, I'd never expect that from you two." The three of them laughed and Cassie began.

The afternoon stretched on forever. Each had taken turns walking around the small office to stretch their backs and legs. Apparently Maria was as averse to a sedentary lifestyle as Cassie and Sam were. *Why in the world did I become a librarian?*

At six thirty Sam called it a day. "Good job, Cassie. I think we've gotten everything we need at this point. We'll cover more territory once we see where John is going with his cross examinations and we find out who his witnesses are. Plan on several late sessions after court. Maria will let you know when. How do you feel?"

Cassie stood and stretched her back. "Like I'm down for the count," she grinned. "But I'll be fine after a glass of wine and a good night's sleep."

"Lucky you. Maria and I have a few more hours tonight, then all day tomorrow working on my opening statement. The trial starts at nine Monday morning. You and Doc still planning to be there from the beginning?"

"Of course, we're doing this for Mich."

Sam squeezed her elbow, "That's my girl." He hesitated and refrained from looking at Maria. "Can you find your way back to your car or do you want Maria to go with you?"

"I'm fine. You two get to work so you can get out of here." She turned to Maria and held out her hand. "Maria, it was nice meeting you. Thanks for all your help."

Cassie turned and walked out, closing the inner office door behind her. Maria turned to Sam with a raised eyebrow, "WOW! What a cool customer. And I mean that in both definitions of 'cool'". I like her and it's obvious you do, too."

"What do you mean? And don't give me that mother-hen look you get. You're younger than I am for God's sake. She's just a witness, nothing more."

"Right, boss, you keep telling yourself that." Maria picked up the recorder and her notes and plopped into the chair Cassie had vacated. "Shall we begin? I have a life outside this office even if you don't."

Chapter 37

It was a quiet Sunday. Neither Doc nor Cassie felt like going anywhere. Doc worked in his home office, Cassie did some laundry and read. She realized just how alone she was in the world; divorced, parents dead, no siblings, best friend gone. She resolved to do something about it once the trial was over. She was only 28; she didn't intend to spend the rest of her life alone. What had she told Doc? Get out there? Just 'cause she'd failed at a relationship once didn't mean she would again. Her growing feelings for Sam proved she was still capable of ...feeling something. She refused to name, even to herself, what she might be feeling.

That evening they watched the Broncos stomp the Raiders and then they went to bed victorious. Cassie hoped it was an omen for the next day's trial.

Chapter 38

Monday the fourth dawned clear and crisp. No snow in the forecast for at least a week. Cassie knew, though, that Denver weather could change dramatically and quickly, in the 70s one day and a blizzard the next, whether it was May or November. She dressed in her new black wool pant suit, saving her black dress for her testimony. *Fortunately black is a good color for you*, she muttered to herself, *how depressing*.

On Friday Sam had explained that no witnesses would be allowed into the courtroom before they testified. Usually witnesses could sit in the gallery after their testimony, but Cassie and Doc still would need to stay outside, since they were the key witnesses, in case he or DeLacey wanted to recall them. He said they probably wouldn't be called until later in the week so they didn't even need to show up daily.

Cassie and Doc wouldn't hear of it. "We're going to be there for every minute of it," Doc said emphatically. "I haven't taken any new patients for the month and have other doctors on call for my current patients. I called each current patient personally and explained everything. And Cassie's gotten a leave of absence. We'll be there."

"Good. The jury was impaneled last week so that's out of the way. It'll do them and the other witnesses good to see your devotion. Although John will do everything he can to keep them from seeing you. All the witnesses wait in the same general area outside the courtroom; just don't talk to any of them, not about anything."

"What about the jury, Sam?" Doc asked quietly. "Are you pleased?"

"It's a good mix, seven women, five men; four black, four white; three Hispanic, one Asian. In a trial like this you'd expect the women to side with Mich, but you never know. If we got some closet bible-thumper or a country music fan who thinks it's a wife's duty to stand by her man, Mich's loyalty will win us points. Or we could get some throwback who thinks the man rules the roost and the little woman had better fall in line, that's likely to be points for Larry. Can't ask those kinds of questions during jury selection so it's a crap-shoot...just like it usually is. All we can do is present our case and hope the jury is reasonable and pays attention."

Doc looked his usual distinguished self in a charcoal suit and light blue tie. The drive to the courthouse was completed in almost total silence, each lost in thoughts of Mich.

After passing through security they found their way to the third floor courtroom. About thirty people were milling about outside the court. Cassie didn't recognize any of them. She looked a question at Doc. He shrugged a "got me" answer.

Sam came over to them, Maria following in his wake. Maria shook hands with Cassie and Doc; Cassie had filled him in about Maria over the weekend. "Maria's going to stay with you, get you anything you need, serve as a liaison," Sam said. They all smiled and made the usual polite murmurings.

"I want you to see the courtroom before they close the doors," Sam directed. Sam looked very business-like in a dark grey suit, white shirt, and blue paisley tie. The usual twinkle in his eyes was gone; now they were just focused on one thing, the trial.

He led Cassie and Doc through the double oak doors. At the front was a large oak desk, raised so the judge could look down on the scene before him. As they looked, a clerk mounted stairs on the left and placed something on the judge's desktop, next to a notebook computer. Flags stood to the left and right behind the judge's desk, U.S. and Colorado. On the right Sam pointed out the witness stand. The seal of Jefferson County was affixed to the oak-paneled wall above and behind the judge's stand. There was a door directly behind the judge's chair.

There was a table on the floor directly in front of the steps the clerk had mounted. "That's for the recorder," Sam explained. Two more large oak tables, prosecution on the left, defense on the right, with several chairs at each were directly in front of where they were standing. Beyond the defense table to the right a door went to some unknown area that Sam didn't mention. A solid oak rail with a gate in the middle stretched the width of the courtroom, just behind the attorney tables, just like on television, only warmer.

The audience sat in what appeared to be bleachers or pews, oak benches with oak backs. "Those don't look very comfortable," Cassie commented, pointing at the seating.

"They aren't. You'll see the regulars, court-watchers, bring pillows to sit on," Sam chuckled. "It keeps the number of Press down, too." The overall feel of the courtroom was modern without being cold; very no-nonsense.

The room was starting to fill. Cassie saw two young lawyers laying out papers on the prosecution table. John DeLacey was chatting with an older gentleman over in one corner of the courtroom. Spectators, some with bed pillows, started sitting in the bleachers. There were no TV cameras, but Cassie noticed several people in the front rows with note pads and one with a sketch pad. She rightly guessed they were reporters.

Sam steered them back out into the hallway, leading them to a distant oak bench. "I've got to go, tell Maria if you need anything, she's wonderful." He smiled his familiar warm smile at his assistant. Cassie felt a chill.

"Good luck, Sam," Doc said as he shook the younger man's hand.

"Yes, good luck, Sam," Cassie echoed. She offered her hand, too; she would have preferred a hug, but thought better of it.

"Thanks. We'll be fine." Sam smiled and winked at Maria, and returned to the courtroom, the doors whooshing smoothly closed behind him.

They didn't have to be there, but Doc and Cassie both felt they would be letting down Mich if they didn't represent her. But there was nothing to do. "Remind me to bring a book tomorrow," Cassie told Doc.

They sat on the hard oak benches and looked out at the snow-covered mountains. They watched others enter and leave the courtroom. "Do you think it'll snow anymore?"

"Undoubtedly," Doc answered, "but not any time soon."

They paced the halls. They got coffee from the vending machines. Maria kept them company; occasionally she'd go into the courtroom and come back with updates.

"The jury has been seated and Judge Thomas has explained what's going to occur. He's told them it's a murder trial, that the accused is presumed innocent until proven guilty beyond a reasonable doubt. He's told them they may take notes, but not to ask questions. They are to keep an open mind and not make a decision about guilt or innocence until all the evidence has been presented. It's the same schpiel they all give. I think he could give it in his sleep; I think sometimes he does," Maria tried to lighten the atmosphere.

"I've heard of him," Doc said. "He makes the TV a lot."

"That's because he gets most of the high-profile cases. He's the most senior criminal court judge and I guess he gets first refusal. The talk is that he has political aspirations; the publicity doesn't hurt."

"Is he fair?" Cassie asked. "You always hear about hanging judges and bleeding-heart judges. Is he one of those?"

Maria frowned in concentration. "I'd have to say he's pretty even-handed. He respects the rights of the accused and of the victims. It's difficult not to be on one side or the other. The Constitution says everyone is entitled to a fair trial, even the blatantly guilty. It's the definition of "fair" that seems to be the sticking point these days.

"Is it fair to completely ruin a woman's reputation to get an accused rapist acquitted? Is it fair to throw out confessions or evidence because of procedural technicalities? The big question is where does "fair" fall, on whose side? It's virtually impossible to be fair to one side without being unfair to the other. As judges go, Thomas does as well as any of them, and better than most." Maria looked sheepish. "Sorry. Didn't mean to get on my soapbox."

Cassie smiled at her. "Thanks. That helped. A little civics lecture never hurts." She hated to admit that she was beginning to like Maria. "What happens now?"

"They'll probably break for lunch in a few minutes, then start opening statements after lunch. Sam will present his side, sort of tell the jury what he's going to show them, how he's going to prove guilt. Then DeLacey will talk about his plans."

"How long does this take?"

"No way to know. Sam's are usually an hour or less. He lays everything out in a logical sequence, gets the jury primed, and sits down. He thinks most juries prefer to get to the meat of the trial – the witnesses – and don't want to listen to a monologue, so he gets it over as soon as possible. It usually helps get the jury on his side, at least they don't immediately hate him."

"Are jurors really objective?" Cassie wondered aloud.

"Yes and no. The idea behind jury selection is to try to get as many jurors as possible who are likely to be sympathetic to your side and eliminate as many as you can who might be helpful to the other side. Of course both the defense and prosecution are doing this, so neither side gets everything they want. And of course they're supposed to be a jury of 'peers', people of similar socio-economic background.

"Most jurors believe they can be objective, but in reality they all come in with some bias, some unconscious pre-disposition to one side or the other. Both lawyers just try to ensure the jury is not too heavily weighted toward 'the other side'."

"Sounds pretty chancey to me," Doc muttered.

"In many ways it is. But Sam's really good at questioning prospective jurors and does a pretty good job of getting at least a balanced jury."

"What about DeLacey?" Cassie inquired.

"He's good, too. He and Sam are pretty evenly matched, except John is one of those sneaky ones who tries to circumvent, or at least stretch, the rules as far as he can. He's a grand-stander, too. His opening statements tend to go on for a couple hours, only because he loves the sound of his own voice. Sometimes he turns the jury off, sometimes they eat it up and love him. He should have been an actor; most lawyers have a lot of the ham in them, love performing in front of an audience, especially a captive one."

Cassie looked at Maria quizzically. "Sam doesn't seem that way."

"Oh, Sam is one of the best. That's what makes him so good. His sincerity. He doesn't seem to be performing. Where DeLacey poses and dramatizes, Sam is calmly, logically, sincere. He's so warm, so caring. Who wouldn't believe him? You should see him in action."

I think I have, Cassie thought to herself.

Chapter 39

After predictable courthouse cafeteria food for Doc and Cassie, they returned to their seats outside the courtroom. Opening statements went much as Maria had predicted. Sam took 47 minutes, DeLacey right at two hours. Judge Thomas broke for the day and told the jury they would begin promptly at 9 a.m. Tuesday morning with the prosecution witnesses. His look was so intense it was guaranteed no jury member was going to be late for court.

The next morning, after everyone was seated and the doors closed, Judge Thomas gaveled for silence and the court was called to order. The clerk called to the stand Sam's first witness: Gilbert Armijo. The burly detective was sworn in.

Cassie and Doc, seated on the oak benches outside the courtroom, could only look at each other, wondering what was happening inside. Of course they recognized Detective Armijo as he left the huddled crowd and went into the courtroom. They did not recognize many more of the assembled witnesses.

The real trial began with Sam's first words. As usual, Sam asked the witness to identify himself and explain his credentials.

DeLacey immediately stood and said in a bored tone, "To speed things alone, the Defense will stipulate to the detective's experience."

Sam nodded to DeLacey and turned to the witness, "Now, Detective Armijo, please tell the court what happened on Saturday, May 17 of this year."

The sheriff's detective pulled his small green notepad from his tweed jacket pocket and flipped over the first two pages. "I was called to the residence of Larry and Michela Merritt at about 11:30 a.m. A 9-1-1 call had come in reporting a murder."

"Excuse me, Detective, don't you mean reporting a death?" Sam asked.

"No, Sir, the dispatcher told me the caller said "She's been murdered."

Looking bored already, DeLacey raised his hand like a school child, "Objection, Your Honor. If there is a dispatcher who can testify to this, we should hear from the dispatcher, not this witness."

"Granted."

Undeterred and hiding a smile, Sam continued, "Thank you, Detective. Please continue. What did you find at the home?"

"By the time I got there the local deputy had secured the area. Ms. Cassie Kirkland was in the den, practically catatonic with shock..."

"Objection, Your Honor. This Detective," DeLacey said the title with a sneer, "is not a competent medical professional able to diagnose a person's condition."

"While that's true, Your Honor, Detective Armijo is a detective with 18 years' experience dealing with grief victims and crime scenes. He does have knowledge and firsthand experience of people's reactions and this is not the first murder scene he has dealt with."

"True, Mr. Chambers, I'll allow his comment for the moment, since there was no psychiatric professional on the scene."

Sam nodded at the detective; they treated each other as total strangers, not even making eye contact. Sam's eyes were all for the jury.

"Ms. Kirkland was seated in the den, hugging a pillow, tears were running down her cheeks but she didn't seem to even know it. She just sat there staring out the windows. I talked with her a few minutes and then I went upstairs to the bedroom."

"This was the master bedroom, where Mr. and Mrs. Merritt slept?"

"Well, it was the master bedroom, but only Mrs. Merritt slept there." Gil paused to see if Sam wanted him to go on. When Sam said nothing Gil continued. DeLacey jumped right in.

"Objection, Your Honor. Seems to be a conclusion by the witness."

"Sustained."

"Do you know for a fact only Mrs. Merritt slept there, Detective?"

"Well, not by sight; I didn't spend my nights under the bed." The jury sniggered at this, as Sam had hoped. "But only her clothes were in the closet, only women's clothes in the bathroom hamper, only one side of the bed had been slept on that night. Mr. Merritt's things were next door in another room, that bed had been slept in recently. And the woman was terminally ill; in my *experience* this often leads to separate bedrooms."

"Please tell us what you saw upon entering the room."

"The victim was on the bed, her face contorted in rigors of pain. The deputy was in the room, ensuring that nothing was disturbed. Paramedics were closing their cases and writing notes. The ME's folks arrived a couple minutes later. The Crime Scene guys, too."

"Can you describe the room for us?"

"We took pictures," Gil said. Sam took an envelope off the prosecution table and handed them to the detective.

"These?"

Gil quickly flipped through them as though verifying; he already knew they were the right pictures.

"Yes, Sir. These are the scenes of the bedroom."

Sam handed them to the judge who flipped through them and handed them back. Sam then handed them to the first seated juror who carefully studied them and passed them along as he finished each one.

"Tell me, Detective, in view of your 18 years' experience attending crime scenes, what did you notice at this scene?"

"The victim died a violent death. There were no visible wounds. Mrs. Merritt may have died alone, we couldn't tell that for sure, although it is assumed if someone was with her he or she would have tried to help and there would have been evidence of that."

"Again, Detective, based on your experience, could you tell how long she had been dead?"

"Not for sure, rigor mortis hadn't set in yet and the body was still warm, so sometime in the previous ten to twelve hours."

"So, this was about noon when you were viewing the crime scene; you're suggesting she died sometime after midnight and before the 9-1-1 call came in at eleven or so?"

"Yes, that'd be about it. The ME's office gave a closer time of between five and six that morning when they did their temperature tests."

Smiling, Sam turned to the jury, "Before Mr. DeLacey can object, let me say that the ME is our next witness. She will confirm this."

"Tell us what you saw about the victim."

Gil hesitated and cleared his throat. "As I said, she died in a lot of pain. That's obvious in the pictures, too. She was still in bed. A nightstand with a water carafe and a bunch of pill bottles, a lamp and a radio alarm. A water glass was on the floor next to the bed, apparently where she dropped it.

"Tell us about her physical state. What did she look like?"

"She was an attractive woman, even bald." This evoked the expected comic relief for the jury. "Kinda thin. Twenty-nine years old."

"Were there children in the house?"

"No, she didn't have any children."

"Who else was in the house?"

"Ms. Kirkland. No one else when we got there, but Dr. Harper and Mr. Merritt arrived soon after I got there." Gil's voice tightened noticeably.

"And how was Mr. Merritt? Distraught?"

Gil snorted theatrically, "Yeah. He was upset that his golf day had been interrupted."

Sam paused, expecting an objection. Nothing from DeLacey. That worried Sam.

"What did he say?"

Gil consulted his notepad once again. "I wrote down his very words. Ms. Kirkland had told us he was playing golf and we located him, sent a deputy and asked him to come home. When he walked in he was not a happy camper. He yelled, "What the hell is going on here? Who are all these people?"

"Then what happened?"

"Ms. Kirkland attacked him. She ran across the room and slapped him hard and then started yelling at him. She was yelling 'Murderer' at him. We had to pull her off and get her back to the next room while we talked with Mr. Merritt."

"What did Mr. Merritt say when he was told of his wife's untimely death?"

Gil again looked down at the pad in his hand, "He asked 'Are you sure?'"

Sam paused to let the words sink in. "No 'Oh, no'; no 'Oh, my God'?"

"Nope, just wanted to verify that she was dead."

"In your experience, is that a normal response?"

"Objection again, Your Honor," DeLacey was still seemingly bored, "Mr. Armijo still isn't a trained psychologist. Different people react to death in different ways."

"Sustained."

"Let me rephrase that, Detective, what responses do you usually see when a loved one is told of a death?"

"Those two you mentioned are the most common. Then they want to know how it happened."

"Did Mr. Merritt ask how it happened?"

"Not of me."

"Did you see Mr. Merritt cry at any time while you were in the house? Show any expressions of sorrow at the death of his wife of ten years?"

"No, Sir."

"Now, Detective, let's turn to your investigation following the murder. Was there insurance on the deceased?"

"Yes. There was a million dollar personal life insurance policy."

"And who was the beneficiary of that policy?"

"Mr. Merritt."

"Any other insurance?"

"The company she owned, Golden Lights, had a policy on her; the company was the beneficiary."

"Was there any sign of forced entry? Broken windows? Broken locks on doors? That sort of thing?"

"No, nothing like that."

"Was anything taken? Televisions? Computers? Jewelry?"

"No, according to Mr. Merritt everything was still there."

"Was there anything that you would consider abnormal in her phone records?"

"No, nothing. Just calls to local stores, doctors, Ms. Kirkland, that sort of thing."

"Thank you, Detective Armijo. Your witness, Mr. DeLacey." Sam returned to his seat at the prosecution table and made a couple notes on a legal pad; just scribblings, really; something to make DeLacey curious and maybe off balance.

DeLacey rose to his full just-under-six-feet and approached the witness box. He buttoned his gray tattersall jacket over his periwinkle-blue shirt, smoothed his signature pink tie into place. He seemed to be choosing his words very carefully.

"Now, Mr. Armijo, you say you did not see Mr. Merritt express any emotion at the news of his wife's death. Is that uncommon?"

Armijo considered the attorney. "'Uncommon'? Not necessarily, but unusual. Most people show something, sadness, anger, disappointment even, but it's unusual to show nothing."

"What if someone is very self-contained, not accustomed to public displays of emotion?" DeLacey hesitated, waiting for an objection. None came.

Again Armijo thought carefully, apparently reviewing eighteen years' of crime scenes in his mind. "It has been my experience that family members of loved ones show something; it's only the uncaring ones who manage to maintain total control."

Score one for our side, Sam thought gleefully. *Good job, Gil.* He didn't look up from his notepad.

"Tell me, Mr. Armijo, if Ms. Kirkland was the only one in the house at the time of death, why was my client arrested? Isn't it possible that she killed Mrs. Merritt?"

Sam's head jerked up at this. He hadn't expected DeLacey to tip his hand so early.

"Our investigation found no motive for her to do so. They were best friends for twelve years. She was obviously distressed over the death. All the evidence pointed toward the husband."

Sam studied the opposing attorney, wondering where this was going so early in the trial. He didn't have long to wait.

"Is it possible, Detective," again he sneered the title, "That you may have overlooked some evidence in your rush to arrest my client?"

"Anything is possible, Mr. DeLacey, but we did a thorough investigation and found no other viable suspects."

"What about other beneficiaries of the will? I assume there were others?"

"Yes, there were. All beneficiaries were questioned and no one appeared to have a motive except Mr. Merritt."

"Has the Jefferson County Sheriff's Office ever been found negligent in a case? Ever been found to have focused on one suspect and ignored others?"

"'Ever' is a long time."

"Please answer the question."

Gil tried not to become defensive. He knew that many members of the jury were probably remembering the case from the previous year when this very thing had happened. Shoddy police work by a new detective, anxious to prove himself. He was no longer a detective.

"Yes, Mr. DeLacey, it has happened in the past, but not..."

"That is enough. I have no further questions. Thank you."

Back to square one, Sam thought.

Chapter 40

Dr. Wilson Naylor was called next, a statuesque blonde who looked more like a model than a trained medical examiner.

Sam politely asked the witness, "Dr. Naylor, please tell the jury your credentials."

DeLacey jumped to his feet, wanting to forestall any recitation of the witness's impressive biography. "We stipulate to the excellent credentials of this witness as a pathology expert, Your Honor."

"Dr. Naylor, please tell us the time and cause of death of Michela Merritt."

"The body temperature was taken at the scene and the time noted. In the event of unexplained deaths, it is normal to perform an autopsy. The body was transported to the county morgue where a full autopsy was performed. No wounds were found, although there were a few older bruises on the upper arms of the victim."

"What would these bruises indicate?"

"It appeared the victim had been grabbed around the upper arms by someone with very strong hands, probably a week or so before the death, based on the greenish yellow tinge to the bruises."

"The time of death?"

"These can never be pinned down to the exact minute, but it appears Mrs. Merritt died between five and seven in the morning of May 17."

"If the autopsy found no knife wounds, no bullet wounds, how did she die? Were there needle marks? Any indication of drugs? Strangulation? Asphyxiation?"

"No, no illegal drugs. There were needle marks, all consistent with her cancer care. The autopsy found little in her stomach other than water, a little food, and the remains of gel medicine capsules. This indicates she died very quickly after taking the capsules, or the capsules themselves would have dissolved completely. It also shows she died a good while after eating, probably the last night's dinner."

Building the suspense, leading the doctor like an orchestra conductor, Sam asked the crucial question, "What killed her, Doctor?"

"Cyanide."

Sam paused and let the answer sink in. "Cyanide. Is that easy to get?"

"I wouldn't say easy. There are specific industries that use it, gold work, metal processing, chemical research, that sort of thing. It used to be in rat poisons, but that's been discontinued. The only way for individuals to get it now is over the Internet."

"Over the Internet? You mean anyone can order it and have it delivered right to the front door or mailbox?" Sam tried to sound incredulous.

"Yes, Mr. Chambers. There was a case where a high school student ordered two ounces of it and killed one of his teachers. There are several web sites that offer it, you just fill in the screens and give them a credit card number. The screen says the FBI will check you out, but who knows? The FBI may do random checks, or look at the records if something comes up in a case."

"Thank you, Doctor." Turning to the defense table, Sam indicated that it was DeLacey's turn to question the witness.

DeLacey couldn't wait to do so. "So, Dr. Naylor, what is your theory as to *how* Mrs. Merritt died?"

"It appears she ingested some cyanide, either it was in the drinking water next to her bed or the capsules."

"And do you have a theory as to how she got the poison?"

"Objection. Calls for a conclusion."

"Your honor, this woman is an expert. She is paid to make conclusions every day, based on her experience and expertise." DeLacey smirked.

"Very well, objection overruled."

"Again, Dr. Naylor, how did the poison get into Mrs. Merritt?"

"Even with all my experience and expertise, Mr. DeLacey, I can't answer that. I wasn't there."

"So you're saying there are any number of ways she could have taken the cyanide?"

"No, not any ways she could have taken it; it appears she took it by mouth, took the capsule with water; the cyanide was in the capsule or in the water. Whether she took them willingly, knowingly, or not, I can't answer."

DeLacey let that sink in with the jury while he steepled his fingers under his chin and stared at the woman on the stand. "Thank you, Doctor, no more questions."

The trial broke for lunch and the rest of the day; Judge Thomas had a doctor's appointment that he couldn't – or wouldn't – change.

Sam left the courtroom deep in thought. He gave Carrie and Doc a thumbs-up as he sailed passed them and down the hall to the elevator. Maria excused herself from Cassie and Doc and ran to catch up to him, her heels clicking on the marble floor.

"Well, that wasn't very helpful," Cassie muttered to herself as she gathered her sweater, book and purse. Maria came back and told them court was adjourned for the day.

"I'll see you tomorrow?" Maria asked as she walked backward toward the elevator. Doc and Cassie smiled their assent and then looked at each other, stupefied at their lack of information and at the mysteries of the judicial system.

The two trudged out to his car, completely in the dark as to what had happened inside the courtroom. They both opted for a late lunch back at the house and rode in silence the whole way across town.

"Well, Sam, what do you think?" The D.A. asked his star prosecutor as he bit into his ham and Swiss sandwich at his cluttered desk.

Sam ran his hand through his already mussed hair. "I can't figure out what DeLacey's up to. It's not like him to show his cards so early."

"Probably just planting seeds of doubt at this point. He'll wait and see which ones seem to take root. Don't worry about it. Just stick to your game plan and see how things develop. It's way too early to start second-guessing ourselves or DeLacey."

"You're right," Sam smiled ruefully. "I'm going to take this afternoon and go over the testimony from today and prep for the rest of the week, lucky break to get the afternoon off." Sam rose and headed for the door.

"Get some lunch, too," Greg called after him, waving the second half of a pickle at Sam's back.

That night Cassie had just gotten into bed, her lavender flannel nightgown warming her chilled bones. She knew it wasn't the forty degree night that was causing the coldness in her bones. She and Doc had sat glued to the evening news and knew of the ME's testimony, opening the door to a variety of scenarios.

Cassie caught the phone on the first ring, hoping it wouldn't wake Doc; this was the first night that he'd gone to bed and she didn't hear him pacing his room.

"Just wanted to see how you're holding up," Sam said with a slight question in his voice.

"We're doing okay; it's so frustrating not being able to hear things first hand. Thank you for having Maria explain the process to us." She was very careful to include Doc in the conversation, not wanting to presume that he called to check just on her.

"No problem. She's great isn't she? She's one of our best victim-assistance advocates. Greg started the program for instances just like this. He felt the victims are often overlooked in the search for truth and justice; attorneys are so tied up with our own objectives that sometimes the families and loved ones of the victims become victims themselves, their interests getting trampled in all the jurisprudence. The program has been a big success and other states have copied it. The program, and Greg, are the main reasons I joined the DA's office."

"I guess we don't exactly fall into the family category, but we appreciate her help. How is everything going for you? I know you can't talk about anything in detail."

"No, I can't since you're a witness, but I can tell you it's going about as we expected. DeLacey is very good. A trial is like a chess game, you try to outthink, outguess your opponent. Sometimes you guess right on what he will do, sometimes he guesses right on what we're going to do. I think we came to a draw today. At this stage, that's acceptable. Right now it's sort of a feeling-out mode, like two boxers in the early rounds. You circle your opponent, look for openings, try to find weaknesses. It's important to get the jury on your side, too."

"Maria told us about the maneuvering. She said it was like going to a junior high school dance and hoping you're not a wallflower."

Sam snorted. "Good analogy. Don't know if it's one I would have thought of, but it works. Juries and verdicts are as much about personality as they are fact. You remember how a school teacher gave the popular kids the benefit of the doubt, but the troublemakers had to toe the line? Same thing applies here. If the jury likes an attorney or a particular witness, they're more likely to accept what is said. If they don't like them, it's harder to convince them."

"Do they like you?"

"So far. We managed to bring in a little humor, lighten the mood. Juries appreciate that. Murder trials are stressful, so anytime you can ease the tension a bit you win points. But I don't know if they like me better than John. Let's just say I haven't made them mad at me yet."

"What's next? Will I be called soon?"

"We just keep plugging away at the facts of the case. What-was-done-when stuff. Once we have a concrete foundation of irrefutable evidence then we build the case of who did it. You'll be one of our last witnesses, probably sometime next week." Sam hesitated. "You know you don't have to come to court until it's your day to testify."

"We know. We've discussed it. We still feel it's better if we're there. It's harder on Doc than on me, he knew Mich her whole life, but he says he needs to be there. I want to be there for Mich, no one seems to care about her...just about 'the case'. I want people to remember she had people who cared about her. We'll be there."

"That's my girl," Sam said unthinkingly. "See you tomorrow then."

"Thanks for the update, Sam. In the morning I'll let Doc know you called. Good night."

Cassie hung up the phone and stared into the darkness. She felt warmer than she had been a few minutes ago...and ready to sleep.

Chapter 41

"Call your next witness, Mr. Chambers."

Brianna Adamson was sworn in. The jury craned their collective necks to see the petite woman in the witness box. Sam almost wondered if he should have gotten a booster seat for her.

"Ms. Adamson, as the lead forensic analyst with Jeffco, could you please relate your findings at the Merritt home."

Without consulting her notes, the petite expert replied in a strong, confident voice. "The fingerprints on the water glass belonged to the victim and ..."

"I object, Your Honor. For all we know Mrs. Merritt committed suicide. In which case the word "victim" does not apply."

Straining to keep his exasperation under control, Judge Thomas sustained the objection. "Please rephrase your answer, Ms. Adamson."

"The only fingerprints on the glass were those of the deceased and her husband."

Sam held up the water glass for the jury. "Anything else?"

"The water in the carafe and the inside of the glass were tested, just water."

"Was the house searched?"

"Yes, a warrant was issued and the house was searched. An Aleve bottle was found at the back of Mr. Merritt's dresser drawer. His were the only fingerprints on the bottle."

"She asked me to get that bottle at the drug store for her," Larry shouted from the table next to his attorney. "You do a little favor for your wife and end up accused of murder. Stupid bitch." DeLacey grabbed Larry's arm and forced him to be quiet.

Sam had been watching the jury during the outburst. Obviously they weren't sure if "stupid bitch" referred to the witness or the wife.

Judge Thomas scowled at Larry but didn't say anything since the attorney seemed to have his client corralled.

"Was there anything in the Aleve bottle, Ms. Adamson?"

"Yes, there were four capsules. Before you ask, they were tested and found to contain cyanide, not Aleve." Sam saw the jury members turn as one and look at the defendant.

"How can that be? Is this another case of medicine tampering?" Sam was incredulous.

"Well, yes, it's medicine tampering, but not the random sort like with those Tylenol capsules years ago. Apparently someone opened these capsules, poured out the medicine and replaced the medicine with cyanide. The difference is, these weren't even Aleve capsules."

"Excuse me? You just said they came from the Aleve bottle."

"These capsules were from laetrile, a cancer supplement, not approved by the FDA."

"If laetrile is not approved by the FDA, how do people get it?"

"It can be ordered online or through the mail. For several years it appeared that the all-natural ingredients in laetrile were beneficial in slowing the progress of some cancers, but in recent years research has shown that not to be true. But when you are dying of cancer I guess anything looks good to you; you are willing to try anything."

Sam appeared stunned as he turned slightly toward the jury. "Let me see if I understand this. Someone took laetrile capsules, a cancer supplement, opened them up, dumped out the laetrile, replaced the laetrile with cyanide, and then put the capsules into an Aleve bottle. Is that correct?"

"Apparently. Yes, Sir."

"So were there fingerprints on the capsules? It seems to me it would be hard to do all this work with those tiny capsule parts while wearing gloves."

"You're right it would be hard to fill the capsules with gloves on. We did find partial prints on the capsule parts, but because the parts are so small there was not enough for a match."

"And how would the cyanide have been inserted? Could a funnel have been used?"

Brianna Adamson smiled, as though talking to a very young child, "No, Mr. Chambers, it is unlikely there is a funnel small enough. The only way would be to hold half of the capsule in one hand, or in a very tiny vise, maybe tweezers, and use a small implement, like a toothpick or a pipette, to carefully fill that half with the cyanide salts."

"So I guess it would take a steady hand?"

"Oh, yes, the person doing it would not want to get any of the salts onto their skin or inhale it. They'd probably wear a mask, too. Small batches of it are lethal, whether inhaled, absorbed through the skin, or taken by mouth."

"When you say 'small batches', have you been able to determine how much cyanide would have been needed to kill a sick woman such as Mrs. Merritt?"

"It only takes about half an ounce – one tablespoon - to kill an average size person, so I'd say less than half an ounce."

"And how much cyanide do you think one of those capsules would hold?"

Adamson paused, obviously doing mental calculations. "Maybe a teaspoon, maybe a little less."

Sam held up a teaspoon measuring spoon for the witness and the jury to see. "So your expert opinion is that two or three capsules would have been all that was required to kill someone in the weakened state of Mrs. Merritt?"

"Not more than two certainly."

"And you did say there were prints on the Aleve *bottle*, only one set of prints..."

"Yes, Sir, the prints of the defendant." The jury rustled around in their seats.

"One more question, Ms. Adamson. We heard from the medical examiner there were capsule parts found in Michela Merritt's stomach. How many capsule parts were found?"

"Five."

"Meaning she took at least three capsules. Were you asked to test them?"

"Yes. They were just like the ones in the Aleve bottle. There were traces of cyanide still on them."

"And what about the carafe and water glass and all the medicine bottles on the table next to where the deceased was found? What about the Aleve bottle on the nightstand?"

"Naturally everything was checked very thoroughly. All the bottles contained just what they were supposed to, including the Aleve bottle. The various medicine bottles had fingerprints of Mrs. Merritt, the nurse who checked on her weekly, and others we haven't identified yet, no one else in the house though. The carafe had the prints of Mr. and Mrs. Merritt only. The water glass had the prints of Mr. and Mrs. Merritt only."

"Am I understanding then that the only medicine bottle of any kind that had Larry Merritt's prints on it was the Aleve bottle found in his dresser?"

"Yes, Mr. Chambers, that is correct."

Sam stared at the witness while this sank in with the jury. "Was there anything else unusual that was found during the search?"

The young forensic specialist consulted her notes. "Yes, there was a stash of sleeping pills in a shoe box in Mrs. Merritt's closet."

"Stash? What do you mean by that?"

"Sleeping pills seemingly are the suicide method of choice for the middle-class woman. Various ones are prescribed readily and all a woman has to do is save them up until she thinks she has enough. It's becoming quite a phenomenon."

"What do you think has started this 'phenomenon', Ms. Adamson?"

"As best anyone can tell it's fear of Alzheimers. Women seem to have decided they would rather end it all than put their loved ones through the years of caretaking and expense. Some Alzheimers patients can live very long times, especially those with early onset. Some women think it is better to end it all than to put themselves and their families through it. So they save up sleeping pills." The woman gave a 'go figure' shrug of her thin shoulders.

"And how many pills did you find in this stash?"

"Hundreds. Well over five months' worth of prescriptions."

"Were there enough of these sleeping pills to kill a woman the size of Mrs. Merritt?"

"Undoubtedly. If she took them and nobody found her for quite a while, the pills would have done their work, slowing her respiratory system until it stopped." Sam stared at the young woman a moment longer, shaking his head at the ingenuity of mankind, or in this case, womankind.

"What would death by sleeping pills be like? Would it be painful?"

"Not at all. The person would just go to sleep and not wake up...unless he or she was found in time, of course." Sam paused, allowing the jury to digest this information.

"Did you find anything else significant?"

"There were several books on poisons on a closet shelf under some extra pillows."

"And whose closet was it?"

"It appeared to be Mr. Merritt's closet, his clothes were hanging in it and men's toiletries were on the dresser and in the bathroom." Sam paused, again letting this information sink in with the jurors.

"I think that's all, Ms. Adamson, thank you." Sam returned to his seat.

"Just a couple questions, Ms. Adamson," DeLacey tried to ingratiate himself with the witness and the jury. "If someone wore gloves, would their fingerprints show up on the glass or the medicine bottle?"

"No." From her clipped tone it was obvious DeLacey's warmth was not reaching the forensic scientist.

"So anyone could have handled the water carafe, the water glass, the Aleve bottle, and the other things on the table, in addition to the deceased and her husband, and we wouldn't know it, if that person wore gloves."

"That's probably true."

"Were there any fingerprints on the books in the closet?"

"No."

"Not even the housekeeper's?"

"None."

"So you found books on poison on Mr. Merritt's closet shelf, but no fingerprints on the books. Is it reasonable to assume that the books were either wiped clean or the person who put them on the shelf wore gloves?"

"Objection. Calls for a conclusion."

"Your Honor, this is an opinion, not a conclusion. An opinion based on Ms. Adamson's years of experience."

Judge Thomas hesitated then allowed the witness to answer.

"That is a reasonable assumption, but only an assumption. We did not check every page in the book. And there are all kinds of gloves, even mittens would reduce the chances of fingerprints if the books were put on the shelf in the winter."

"That's enough, Ms. Adamson." *More than enough*, DeLacey fumed. "Witness is excused."

Chapter 42

"The prosecution calls Willamette Warrenton."

The bailiff at the door repeated the name outside the courtroom. Willa had arrived just half an hour before she was called. Cassie had introduced her to Doc and the three had chatted politely until Willa heard her name called. The middle-aged woman rose to her five foot six height, straightened her grey wool skirt and jacket, picked up her purse, and headed for the solid oak doors. Cassie smiled at the curator as she walked from their seats to the courtroom doors.

Dr. Warrenton was a small, thin brunette with a noticeable accent; Sam knew from conversations with her she was originally from Brussels.

"Dr. Warrenton, please tell the jury your credentials." The jury admired the conservatively attired, middle-aged woman with grey streaks in her hair, pulled back in a chignon.

"I am an art historian with DMA, Denver Museum of Art. I have an MFA from University of Denver and a PhD in art history from Northwestern University. My specialty is modern landscape artists."

"Do you ever do art appraisals?" Sam queried.

"Yes, I am on retainer with both Sotheby's and Christie's auction houses."

"Are you familiar with the work of Michela Merritt?"

"Oh, of course. She has – had - a wonderful reputation and a growing following. Her work was really coming into its own at the time of her death."

"Was she a prolific artist? Did she have a lot of paintings, do a lot of shows?"

"Yes, she was very popular. I have seen her collection. I guess she had a couple hundred paintings that she has done over the last twelve years or so."

"Now, Dr. Warrenton, popular does not mean the same thing as good or worth anything. We all know pitiful books that end up on the best seller list. Just because something is popular or sells well doesn't mean it's any good, does it?"

"That's an excellent point, Mr. Chambers, but Michela Merritt was an accomplished artist. She expressed real emotion through her art and touched people's lives. She was able to express what other people felt about a Colorado scene. Many artists have painted the red rocks and the mountains, or the eagles, Michela Merritt painted feelings, not just scenes. Her art was a collective sigh, a universal heartbeat, a..."

"Please, Your Honor, ask the witness to save her orgasmic ramblings for her next book," DeLacey interrupted.

"Is that an objection to something, Mr. DeLacey?"

"Yes, Your Honor, to the witness's lack of objectivity."

"Your Honor, Dr. Warrenton is an art expert. Part of her expertise is in defining why a piece of art or an artist is successful. Because emotion is part of her explanation does not mean she is not being objective," Sam countered.

"Although I agree with you, Mr. Chambers, I will sustain the objection, reluctantly. Please provide facts, Dr. Warrenton, not feelings."

Dr. Warrenton nodded in the direction of the judge.

"Dr. Warrenton, could you please give the court an *objective* estimate of the value of Mrs. Merritt's collected works?"

Picking up on Sam's sarcasm, the art expert replied, "Objectively and professionally speaking, a conservative value for the works would be eight to ten million dollars." The jury gasped, for the first time hearing a possible dollar motive.

Sam let that sink in while he flipped pages on his legal pad, trying to look like he was really searching for a note in his pages.

Raising his head he stared directly at the witness. "And what would you say was the value of Michela Merritt's work a year ago, before her death?"

"Not more than one million dollars."

"WOW. That's quite a difference. To what do you attribute the increase?"

"Very often when a respected artist dies unexpectedly the value of his or her work will jump dramatically because there is a limited supply. That's what happened here. As I said, Mrs. Merritt was just coming into her own, prices for her work were starting to increase before her death. Her untimely demise just increased their value a lot sooner and a lot faster."

"You said you saw Mrs. Merritt's collected works. When was that?"

"About six months before she died."

"She had you over for tea?"

"No, Mrs. Merritt wasn't even home. Mr. Merritt had hired me to give him an appraisal of the work."

"So Mr. Merritt had the art appraised without his wife's presence and six months later she's dead. Thank you, Dr. Warrenton."

Sam turned and looked disgustedly at Larry, daring him to make another outburst.

DeLacey restrained Larry with a hand on his arm. Recognizing his client's damaged position DeLacey decided to get rid of this witness as soon as possible.

"Just one question, Your Honor."

"Ms. Warrenton, in your experience, does a lack of presence at an appraisal indicate a lack of knowledge of the appraisal or a lack of interest in it?"

The petite woman chose her words carefully. "There is no way to tell what an absent person knows or does not know."

"Thank you, Ms. Warrenton, no more questions."

"The witness is excused." Judge Thomas turned to the jury. "We will break for lunch now. The jury is reminded not to discuss the case with anyone, especially not with other members of the jury. The bailiff will take you to lunch at a nearby restaurant and stay with you. If I hear of any courtroom conversations occurring, your next lunch will be a secluded take-out affair." He paused and looked his most fierce at the jury. He turned back to the room, as a whole. "We will reconvene at 1:30." Judge Thomas and the rest of the room rose. The judge escaped out the door behind the bench, the spectators stretched and headed for the exit.

"Shit, Larry, do you think you might have told me that you'd had the art appraised?" DeLacey glowered at his client. He had finally dragged Larry Merritt from the courtroom and into one of the small interview rooms.

"Calm down, so what? I was trying to make plans, she was dying. I did it when she wasn't around so she wouldn't get upset. It's no big deal."

"And it didn't occur to you that it would make you look guilty?" DeLacey's sarcasm practically dripped onto the scarred wooden table between them.

"Well, at the time of the appraisal she was still alive wasn't she? I'd forgotten all about it until that shyster lawyer brought it up when he read the will."

With great difficulty DeLacey regained his composure, smoothed his tie, and spoke more quietly to his client, "Okay. Do you understand? I can't defend you if I don't know everything. My job is to provide you the best possible defense, regardless of your guilt or innocence. I do NOT want to know whether you did it or not, but I do need to know what the prosecution can find to use against us? Is there anything else you haven't told me?"

"Thanks for that vote of confidence, John," Larry snarled. "It seems to me Cassie has nine million more reasons than I had for killing my wife."

Chapter 43

"The court calls Lisa Muir."

Larry's girlfriend strode purposefully to the stand. She didn't look at Larry. The jury saw a "pleasingly plump" strawberry blonde in a forest green suit with sensible heels and a tailored blouse. She looked more like a school teacher than someone's idea of a mistress.

Sam turned to the judge, "Permission to treat this witness as hostile, Your Honor?"

Aware that Lisa Muir was the defendant's mistress Judge Thomas agreed.

Sam approached the stand, determined to be his most gracious.

"Ms. Muir, please tell the court how you are acquainted with the defendant."

"We're friends."

"Good friends?"

"Yes."

Sam thought, *it's like pulling teeth!* "*Very* good friends?"

"I guess you could say that."

"How long have you known Larry Merritt?"

"Three and a half years."

Using his most ingratiating smile, Sam asked, "How did you meet?"

"He came to my house to give me an estimate." The jury and audience sniggered. Lisa Muir blushed. Judge Thomas banged his gavel. "On lighting for the house I was building."

"Mr. Merritt is a Vice President at Golden Lights. Didn't you find it unusual that he was making sales calls?"

"He said he liked to handle some clients personally." She reddened again at the implication of her words.

Sam looked bemused. The jury sniggered again. "What is your occupation, Ms. Muir?"

"I'm a computer systems analyst for IBM."

"That means you write software programs, right?"

"Among other things, yes."

"Writing software programs takes a strong emphasis on logical steps, is that correct? You have to be able to put things in their proper order? This comes first, then this, then this, that sort of thing?"

"Yes."

"You have to map out a process and then follow all the steps exactly to get to the desired end?"

"Yes."

"Sort of like a military campaign would you say?"

"Your honor, I object. Is this line of questioning going somewhere?" DeLacey's annoyance was clearly visible.

"Please move on, Mr. Chambers. I see no relevance."

"Yes, your honor. Ms. Muir, how did you select Golden Lights for your lighting needs?"

"I didn't. Larry, Mr. Merritt, called me. He said he had heard from my builder that I was going to need some specialty lights and he offered to discuss the plans and give me an estimate."

"This was three and a half years ago?"

"Yes."

"Are you still seeing him?"

"Yes."

"Isn't that a long time for house construction, even with weather delays?"

Lisa squirmed on the witness stand and whispered her reply, "The house is completed." Sam had her repeat her reply a bit louder.

"And when did you move in...to the house?"

"Almost three years ago."

"So the house was completed about three years ago and you're still "friends" with the defendant?"

"Yes."

"Must give good service," Sam seemed to mumble to himself, just loud enough for the jury to hear. "Do you still see other people who worked on your house?"

"No."

"Does Mr. Merritt ever visit you at your new home?"

"Yes."

"How often?"

"Well, he came to check the lights a few times." It was obvious Lisa was trying to avoid the question. She gave Larry a look of desperation, pleading with her eyes for him to understand she had no choice in her answers.

Changing his direction, Sam asked, "How much do you make as a systems analyst for IBM, Ms. Muir?"

"Objection, Your Honor, no relevance."

"I can show relevance, Your Honor."

"Proceed."

"$190,000 a year."

"Phew, that's good money. Did you ever buy any gifts for friends with that money?"

Recognizing the trap, Lisa hesitated. Then gave an extended "yes".

"Ever give any gifts to Mr. Merritt?"

"Yes."

"Ever give gifts to anyone else who worked on your house?"

"I made some cookies for the painters."

"Could you please tell the jury some of the gifts you gave your friend Mr. Merritt."

"A wallet. A watch. Some cufflinks."

"To be exact, wasn't it a monogrammed Coach leather wallet, valued at $780, a Rolex watch valued at $19,800, and the gold and emerald cuff links he's wearing today, valued at $8,700?"

"Yes, but how did you know all this?" Lisa was getting irate.

"Now, Ms. Muir, just exactly how good a friend is Larry Merritt?"

"A very good friend."

"Are you lovers?"

"Yes."

"For how long?"

"Over three years."

"Did you know he was married when you became lovers?"

"Not at first."

"How did you find out? Did he tell you?"

"I saw his picture in the paper with his wife, I think it was at an art gallery opening."

"When was this?"

"About a year ago."

"So you were having an affair with Larry Merritt for two years, even before his wife's cancer came back, while she was still healthy, and he never told you he was married. Did you question him once you found out the truth?" Sam lingered over the word *truth*.

"Yes, I did."

"And what did he say?"

"He said it was a marriage in name only. That she was dying and with any luck she'd be gone soon and he'd have lots of money and marry me."

"Objection, Your Honor, this is obviously a fabrication of a jilted lover," DeLacey tried.

"I haven't been jilted! Larry and I are getting married as soon as this trial is over. He loves me and I love him."

"Over-ruled, Mr. DeLacey."

"When was this conversation about Mrs. Merritt?"

"About a year ago, maybe a little longer. It was when I found out he was married."

"And you continued to see the defendant, knowing he was married and expecting his wife to die?" Sam tried to appear incredulous.

"Yes," she whispered, obviously embarrassed.

"Did you see him after her death?"

"Yes, that night." Sam liked the way she was starting to volunteer information without him having to drag it out of her.

"So the bereaved husband went to see you the same day of his wife's death?"

"Yes."

"Didn't you find that a bit odd?"

"In retrospect, maybe a little. But I didn't know she was dead and he didn't mention it at the time. I didn't know she was dead until the next day when I saw it in the paper."

"He didn't even mention that his wife had died *that morning*?"

"Why should he? It made no difference to us. Why should he pretend otherwise? He brought champagne for us to celebrate, but he never told me what we were celebrating."

"And you didn't ask?"

"No. He brought champagne lots of times, to celebrate a big sale, or a new client, or a good golf game. It was excellent champagne, I didn't care the reason."

"Speaking of golf, did you ask him how his game was that morning?"

Obviously confused by the question, the witness hesitated, then, "I don't remember. He usually told me when he had a good game, and I'd learned not to ask him if he didn't volunteer information about it; golfers can be really touchy." Several members of the jury smiled, *probably golfers or golf widows* Sam decided.

"Ms. Muir, did it ever occur to you that if Mr. Merritt would lie to his wife, a woman he had promised to honor, love, and cherish, that he might lie to his mistress?"

Teri Muir obviously had not thought of it; her mouth fell open, giving her the look of a dying carp.

"Thank you, Ms. Muir. I have no more questions."

"Mr. DeLacey?" the judge prompted the defense attorney.

DeLacey held up one finger to indicate he'd have a response momentarily, while he talked animatedly with his client. Their whispered conversation continued. The courtroom could hear DeLacey hissing at his client and his client responding "bitch" and "no way" in a snarl.

"Mr. DeLacey, do you have any questions for this witness?"

"Yes, Your Honor, I'm sorry for the delay."

Approaching the witness box, DeLacey smoothed his pink tie and smiled at Lisa Muir. "Ms. Muir, did my client ever give any indication that he was planning to speed his wife's departure from this earth?"

"No. Why should he? He told me she had terminal cancer and we just had to wait it out. He said she wouldn't live more than two years."

"And were you willing to wait?"

"Oh yes. It didn't matter to me. We had a good thing going; marriage is just a piece of paper. I'm not in any hurry."

"Thank you. No more questions." Lisa Muir rose and exited the witness box, casting a pleading eye at the defense table. Larry Merritt ignored her completely, looking at the jury to avoid her gaze.

Everyone was surprised when court was adjourned following this testimony. Judge Thomas gave no explanation for the earlier-than-usual release.

Back in his office, Sam explained to Maria what had happened in court and how they'd found out about the gifts. "It was just a case of connect the dots. First we were checking Larry Merritt's financials for any strange transactions. We found a check to Lisa Muir for $5,000. So then we checked her financials and found the credit card receipts to the various stores. When we checked the stores we got copies of the purchase receipts. We saw the charge for the monogram on the wallet. Once it appeared they were lovers it was an easy leap to the idea that the other items were gifts for him, too."

"Whew! I'm glad I've got my job and not yours, too involved for me." Maria grinned at her favorite prosecutor.

"Well, I can't take the credit, Gil did all the leg work. Between us we put together the picture."

"Good for both of you, then. I'm going out to grab lunch. Bring anything back for you?"

"Sure. Whatever. I'm going to prep for tomorrow. We've got Larry's boss and a whole lot is riding on his testimony...I don't want to miss anything."

Maria waved, grabbed her heavy coat from the coat rack and headed off. Sam opened the top file on the tallest stack on his desk. He began to read.

Chapter 44

Thursday morning Grant Hailey was sworn in as the first witness.

"Mr. Hailey, please tell the court your title," Sam prompted.

"I'm president of Golden Lights."

"How long have you held that position?"

"Michela's father hired me right out of college, thirty years ago. I started out in design and then moved up through the ranks. I've been president for fifteen years."

"And the boss of Larry Merritt?"

"Technically speaking, yes. Larry is a vice president, I'm president." He glared at the defendant's snort of derision.

"Why do you say 'technically' then? It sounds pretty straightforward to me."

"Well, on the org chart it is. But since his wife owns – I guess owned – the company, he has sort of a special position."

"How do you mean 'special'"?

The witness looked a bit uncomfortable. "Well, Larry sort of does his own thing, whatever he's in the mood to do. He's really good at schmoozing the clients – especially the women – so he was made VP of sales. His major responsibility is to wine and dine clients and potential clients, keep them happy so we get new and repeat business."

"And what type business is Golden Lights?"

"We make specialty light fixtures for residential and commercial use."

"Like those at WalMart, the ones with flowers on them?" The jury snickered at what seemed to them to be a stupid question.

"No, a little more special than that. Our lamps are copper and bronze, often embellished with gold or silver."

Sam walked to a box next to the prosecution table and withdrew a table lamp. He held it up for the whole court to see. It had silver tracings in the shape of arrowheads on the base. "Lamps such as this one?"

"Yes, we made that one for a bank executive who was going through an Indian phase. He designed the lamp and we created it. Actually, we created fourteen of them for his homes in Aspen and Switzerland."

"And you use gold also?"

"Yes. We use gold more often than the silver." The fiftyish gentleman shook his head, "Some people. I guess they see their light fixtures as an investment, like putting money under the mattress, only more showy. Gives new meaning to having more dollars than sense but it keeps us in business."

"Where do you keep all this gold and silver?"

"We have a vault at the plant. It doesn't take much gold to decorate most lamps; gold is very pliable when it's heated. But we do keep a good supply on hand. Most of it is kept at the bank though."

"So what is the process? How do you work with the gold in manufacturing lamps?"

DeLacey jumped to his feet. "Your Honor, while this is very educational, I'm sure, I fail to see the relevance of this testimony."

Sam looked surprised at the defense attorney, knowing full well this testimony was among the worst for his client. "I intend to show relevance if you will allow the witness to continue."

"Continue."

The mention of gold had caught the jury's attention. They were hanging on every word.

"Gold is very soft, compared to other metals. It can be shaped and cut into whatever design
we want. It can be hammered into strips to outline other items. Basically we carve the design onto the lamp, then apply the gold – or silver – to embellish the desired design. Once the design is finished, every lamp

goes into a cyanide bath to polish it up, remove any tarnish." The jury became a bit more focused at the word "cyanide".

"Excuse me, Mr. Hailey, did you say 'cyanide'?"

"Yes, it's very commonly used when working with gold. It was even used when the gold dome was put onto the state capitol building downtown."

"So do you keep cyanide at the plant also?" Sam was playing out the testimony like a fisherman with a nibble, reeling in the jury.

"Of course, we use it all the time. It takes one ounce of cyanide per pint of water to create the water bath; for tall lamps that have to be fully immersed, it takes quite a bit of cyanide to get the bath deep enough. We use sinks that are deep, in an enclosed chamber. The people doing the bathing wear protective gear, like a HazMat suit. We are very careful. It only takes a few seconds for the cyanide to do its work and the lamp glows like it's never been touched by human hands."

"And where is the cyanide kept?"

"In the vault, except when someone gets some out to use."

"And is there a procedure for removing it from the vault for use?"

"Most definitely. We know how lethal it can be. Anyone wanting some has to get it through his or her supervisor. The supervisor goes to the vault, gets as much as needed, and logs it into the record. We keep very strict accounting of everything in the vault."

"And how often are those records reviewed?"

"At least every six months, quarterly if we have the time."

"Who is Mr. Merritt's supervisor?"

The witness hesitated. "Well, I guess I am."

"So if Mr. Merritt wanted to use some cyanide he'd come to you to get it for him?"

"No, of course not. Mr. Merritt is in sales, there'd be no reason for him to be getting cyanide. Only the designers and craftsmen actually use it."

"When was the last audit?"

"In May of this year."

"At the last audit of the vault, was everything okay?'

"Yes, except for the amount that had been found missing at the previous audit."

"So at the audit – when? A year ago? – there was a discrepancy?"

"Actually it was done in December, so we had our end of year totals. About a tablespoon of cyanide salts was missing. Since there was a shortage, we did the next audit in May, a bit sooner than usual."

"And are discrepancies normal? I would guess it's hard to keep track of such small amounts of something like this."

Hailey bristled. "No, they are NOT normal. That was the only discrepancy we've had in over ten years, ever since we instituted new tracking procedures after the last loss."

"And you checked the log?"

"Yes, nothing showed up to give us a clue as to where it had gone."

"Could someone just have spilled that small amount, kicked it under the rug, so to speak?"

Hailey spoke emphatically, "No. Everyone knows how lethal it is, that it can be deadly if it's inhaled. We keep it stored in sealed packets of one tablespoon quantities. Any supervisor who needs some just grabs the required number of packets and signs them out."

"Is it possible that someone could take cyanide out while ostensibly in the vault for another reason? Say someone went in to get gold and took cyanide at the same time?"

"Well, I guess it's possible, just no reason to do it. At least no reason to keep it secret."

"Who exactly has access to the vault?"

"Well, I do, and the design and production supervisors."

"Did Larry Merritt have access?"

"Well," he hesitated, obviously uncomfortable speaking against the man who possibly was now his boss, depending on the trial's outcome and the employees' decision about selling. "As I said, Larry is sort of a special case. He can do pretty much anything he wants since his wife owned the company."

"Thank you, Mr. Hailey. No more questions."

Grant Hailey started to rise.

"Just a moment, Mr. Hailey, I have just a couple questions," DeLacey spoke as he approached the box with his best presidential-like smirk.

"Tell me, please, who did the designs for these specialty lamps?"

"We have a design team, several people."

"Men? Women?"

"Yes, both."

"Did Mrs. Merritt, this wonderful artist, ever do designs for her own company?"

Recognizing the trap, Hailey responded, "Yes, sometimes, but not much in recent years because of her focus on her painting and her illness."

"And did Mrs. Merritt ever come to the plant? Ever visit with other designers? Ever meet with you? That sort of thing."

"Yes, of course, but not for about the last year before her death."

"And did *she* have access to the vault in her own company?"

"Yes." Hailey resigned himself to seeing this through with as little help to the defense counselor as possible.

"Did you ever see Mrs. Merritt go into the vault?"

"No. Not once. Never."

"Did you ever see *Mr*. Merritt go into the vault?"

"No."

"Let me see if I understand this: both Mr. and Mrs. Merritt had access to the vault, a tablespoon of cyanide powder went missing some time in the year prior to Mrs. Merritt's mysterious death, the last time Mrs. Merritt visited the plant was about a year prior to her death, and you never saw either Larry or Michela Merritt in the vault. Is that about it?" The attorney's sarcasm was so thick a deaf person could have recognized it.

"Yes."

"Thank you. I'm done with this witness." DeLacey turned with obvious contempt.

Chapter 45

The clerk called Gordon Mansfield to the stand.

The attorney from Colorado Springs took the stand and was sworn in. After the usual questions about his age and occupation, Sam started his real questioning.

"Mr. Mansfield, did you know the vic...the deceased, Michela Merritt?"

"I had met her, yes."

"When was that?"

"Late February of this year."

"Was this a social meeting or in your professional capacity as an attorney?"

"It was purely professional. She came to my office to consult me about a will."

"To your office in Colorado Springs? About sixty miles from her home?"

"Yes, that's correct."

"Under the rules of lawyer/client confidentiality, you cannot testify about your conversation with Mrs. Merritt, is that correct?"

"Under normal circumstances, that is correct." DeLacey was fidgeting at the defense table.

"Are you saying these are *not* normal circumstances?" Sam asked with a note of surprise in his voice.

"That is correct."

"Please explain the circumstances of your meeting with Mrs. Merritt."

"As I said, Mrs. Merritt came to my office to discuss a new will." There was a rustle of movement in the jury box as all eyes and ears strained to hear every nuance of this revelation.

"Are you saying that an accomplished, wealthy artist like Michela Merritt didn't have an attorney?"

"She said she wanted her own attorney, not someone who was loyal to her husband." Mansfield restrained himself from looking at Larry Merritt.

"Go on."

"Mrs. Merritt told me her husband wanted her dead and she wanted...."

"Objection, Your Honor, hear-say."

Sam addressed the judge. "If you will allow us to continue, Your Honor, we are prepared to offer proof of this." DeLacey looked confused.

Judge Thomas spoke to the witness, "Continue, Mr. Mansfield."

"As I was saying, she said her husband wanted her dead and she wanted to be sure he didn't get anything if he succeeded."

"How did she plan to exclude him from inheriting?"

"First she had me draw up a new will. She left it with me with the instructions to send it to Stan Culpeper, her husband's Denver lawyer, in the event of her early demise. She didn't want there to be any question about its authenticity."

"Was there anything else?"

"Yes, she left a package that I was to forward to you six months after I learned of her death."

"Did she tell you what was in the package?"

"No, only that it was evidence against her husband. The package was sealed."

"Objection again, Your Honor. We see no proof of these alleged comments by the deceased."

Turning to the witness, Sam asked, "Mr. Mansfield, do you have such proof?"

"Oh, yes. Mrs. Merritt was very thorough and very organized. She brought all her instructions written out and then signed them in my presence. My paralegal witnessed her signature."

Sam showed several plastic-enclosed sheets of typed pages to the attorney before him. "Are these the instructions you received?"

Gordon Mansfield flipped through them. "Yes, these are the same pages."

"Now, about this package you sent to me, why me?"

"As you can see in the instructions, it wasn't you specifically, it was 'the DA handling my murder'. I got your name from the Internet."

DeLacey rose to his feet, clearly agitated. "Your Honor, why was this not disclosed earlier? Why is the defense just now hearing about this evidence?"

"I'm surprised you didn't object sooner, Mr. DeLacey. Counselor, what about it?" the judge addressed Sam.

Instead the witness spoke up before Sam had a chance. "If I may, Your Honor. Mrs. Merritt saw me in February with the instructions to deliver the package six months after I heard of her death. She died in May. It is just now six months. I was out of the country from mid-October until yesterday and when I returned I saw the trial had started. I had the package delivered to Mr. Chambers late yesterday. He didn't know about it until then."

"All right, Mr. Chambers. I assume you are going to provide defense counsel with copies of everything?"

"Of course, Your Honor, as soon as we finish with this witness."

"Continue, then."

"Mr. Mansfield, to recap, Michela Merritt had you draw up a new will excluding her husband from inheriting. She gave you a package and written instructions about it in the event of her untimely death. What if she hadn't died unexpectedly?"

"She told me she was dying of cancer, and if she was still alive in two years I was to destroy the package and the will."

Picking up a large white Tyvek envelope from his table, Sam said, "Returning to the package. Is this the one you sent me?" Sam handed it to the lawyer.

Gordon Mansfield examined it. "Yes, she left it with us sealed. We used one of our office labels" – he pointed to the label – "and put your name and address on it. We sent it to you yesterday via secure courier."

"Please open the envelope, Mr. Mansfield, and tell the court what is inside."

The attorney removed several sheets of paper and flipped through them. "It looks like a letter."

"Objection, Your Honor, where's the chain of evidence? How do we know these documents actually arrived in that envelope?" DeLacey was incensed.

"Point taken, Mr. DeLacey. Mr. Chambers?"

"Your Honor, Mr. Mansfield called my office late yesterday morning and left a message that he was sending a package by courier to me and that it would arrive by the end of the day; all he said was that it was a package from Michela Merritt. As you know I expected to be in court all afternoon. I got the message during the lunch break. I left instructions at the office that the package should be received and put into the office safe until I returned after court. As soon as I got to the office I called in two witnesses and opened the package in their presence."

He picked up a couple papers from his table. "Here are their sworn statements as to the package's condition and its contents." Sam showed the documents to the judge. "This all transpired late yesterday afternoon. I did try to call Mr. DeLacey, but he did not return my calls."

"That seems to settle the question. Mr. DeLacey are you satisfied?"

DeLacey thumbed through the pages. "I'd like to take a bit of time to review these and the letter that was in the envelope."

Sam thought he was stalling but could not find a good reason to object.

Judge Thomas glanced at his watch. "Very well, we will resume with this witness at 2 p.m. Will that be enough time, Mr. DeLacey?"

DeLacey glanced at his own watch, realized that gave him a little over three hours, grimaced, and said, "Yes, Your Honor, I think we can make it." *The martyr*, Sam thought.

Everyone in the courtroom rose as the judge left the bench. Then they started gathering their pillows, purses, notepads, and pens, and headed out for a long lunch. As soon as the audience started leaving, Maria worked her way against the tide of looky-loos and got to Sam's side at the table.

"What's going on? Why the early recess?"

Sam turned to her and recapped the events of the last few minutes, "Wish we didn't have to interrupt his testimony, we were on a roll. The jury was hanging on his every word."

"Don't worry, you'll get Merritt; he'll be damned with his poor dead wife's own words."

"Let's not count our chickens, Maria. DeLacey probably has a snake up his sleeve. He's a master of twisting things. How's Cassie holding up? And Doc?," he added as an afterthought.

"They're both doing fine. It's really hard on them not knowing what's going on in here, not knowing if we're ahead or behind."

"I know. I'd like to think we're ahead, but there's still a lot of ground to cover and John's very adept at offering alternatives. He has to convince just one juror that the facts fit together just as well in a different scenario and we're screwed. I've got to beat him to the punch, take the wind out of his sails, and all those other clichés. I just wish I knew in which direction the wind was blowing! What are you seeing, Maria? What have I forgotten?"

"I haven't seen anything. It looks really solid. You're making a very logical, straightforward case built on solid evidence. The jury can't think anything else. And they like you, too," she said with a smile. "I've heard the spectators talking, they're usually a good barometer."

Sam smiled ruefully. "That and fifty cents will get us a cup of coffee."

"Not in this town!" Maria quipped back.

"We both know juries are scary. They may decide differently because they don't like the tie I have on, or because I don't smile enough, or I smile too much. And it only takes one. Save me from the self-righteous ones who know better than everybody else." Sam ran his fingers through his hair.

"Okay, Sam, calm down. You're good. You've tried lots of these cases. You win some, you lose some. All you can do is your best; we can't control the idiosyncrasies of those twelve people. Don't get uptight. It's just another case. And next month there'll be another one." She put her hand on his arm.

Sam looked into space. *Was this just another case? Why was he so hell-bent on this one?* "You're right, Maria. I just feel Michela's death is such a loss. Even though I never met her, I feel like I know her. She didn't have to die this way." He grinned his lop-sided grin and patted Maria's hand, still resting on his arm. "Come on, let's get back to the office and I'll order us lunch while we've got the time." He paused and looked sheepishly at the young lady next to him, "Thanks. You're good at this!"

They were both smiling happily, arm-in-arm as they left the courtroom and sailed passed Doc and Cassie hidden in the departing crowds, their minds on the working lunch ahead.

As Doc and Cassie looked after them, TV camera lights blinded their eyes, a bundle of microphones was shoved in their faces. Multiple shouts of "how do you think the trial is going?" and "Cassie, were you in this new will?" bombarded them as they tried to escape to the elevator.

Doc and Cassie forcefully responded "no comment" to each and counted themselves lucky when the elevator doors finally closed with the reporters on the other side.

Cassie looked quizzically at the good doctor. "I thought they were banned from this floor? I haven't seen them up here during the whole trial."

Doc shrugged, "I guess the ban is only when the trial is in session. Since we recessed early it looks like we were fair game." The doors opened to another mob of reporters, Cassie noticed a CNN logo on one of the mics.

They silently pushed their way to Doc's car and slammed the doors. "How does Wendy's sound for lunch? We don't have time to go back across town and get back again. The vultures will never look for us there," Doc said as he pointed to the reporters and started the engine. Cassie smiled her agreement and the car managed to ease out of the parking lot without hitting any reporters. *Darn it*, Cassie thought to herself.

Chapter 46

Promptly at 2 p.m. Judge Thomas turned to the attorney in the witness box and reminded him he was still under oath. "Continue, Mr. Chambers."

Sam reviewed the earlier testimony in an effort to remind the jury of their earlier emotions. "Mr. Mansfield, before the lunch break you told us Mrs. Merritt came to your office in Colorado Springs early this year, had you draw up a new will in which she excluded her husband from being a major beneficiary, gave you an envelope to mail in the event of her death from anything other than natural causes, and told you her husband wanted her dead. Is all that correct?"

DeLacey sat seething at his position, gritting his teeth at the summation provided by his opponent, pointing the finger of guilt at his client, and helpless to object. Sam's summary was factually correct according to that morning's testimony.

"Yes, Mr. Chambers, that is correct."

"And how did she seem?"

"Objection. Witness is an attorney, not a psychologist."

"Your Honor, I'm not asking for a medical opinion, just an observation from a professional who deals with people in many of life's most stressful situations."

"Over-ruled."

"Mr. Mansfield, in February of this year, how did Mrs. Merritt appear to you?"

"Well, she was blonde for one thing. I almost didn't recognize her when I saw her picture in the paper."

Sam hurried on, realizing the opening DeLacey had just received. "Was she tense? Seem nervous?"

"No, she was perfectly calm. Almost as though she saw the whole thing as an exercise, or a game. She was very composed and had everything well organized."

"What about her husband? Did she say anything about him?"

"Just that he wanted her dead."

"Did she seem upset about this?"

The thirtyish attorney considered the question. "I don't know if I'd use the word 'upset', maybe 'hurt' is a better word. Maybe 'resigned'. She was very matter-of-fact when she told me about it."

"Did she show any evidence of anger?"

"Not a bit. Like I said she was very calm. Almost like a mother talking about her petulant child."

At the defense table, Larry Merritt was berating his attorney, loud enough for everyone to hear. "Child! What does he mean? Mich thought of me as a child?! Just because she had no children of her own, and she talks about me as a child!" De Lacey tried repeatedly to shush his client, but the damage was done.

"Now, Mr. Mansfield, please read this letter from Mrs. Merritt that you sent on to me last night." Sam handed the plastic-sealed letter to the other attorney.

"Objection, Your Honor!"

Judge Thomas stood and said "Mr. Chambers, Mr. DeLacey, my office right now." The three men exited the courtroom through the door behind the judge's bench while the jury and the audience sat in stunned silence. A single thought was running through their minds, *what is in that letter?*

Judge Thomas slammed the door to his office. "Okay, Sam, what is this? We already had this conversation. No letter because John can't examine Mrs. Merritt."

"Yes, Your Honor, but this is a different letter." He handed a copy to the judge. "More of a dying declaration. John would not be able to cross-examine a person who had offered one of those, but they're accepted in courts all the time."

The judge placed the plastic-covered page on his desk and considered the argument. The two attorneys maintained their silence, although DeLacey could be heard breathing heavily.

"I hope this won't come back to bite me, but okay. This letter's in. Let's get back to court." DeLacey started to speak and the judge raised his hand, "Save it for the appeals judge, John. It's in."

Once everyone was reseated in the courtroom, Sam once again asked Gordon Mansfield to read the letter.

The attorney glanced over the letter and turned toward the jury. He cleared his throat and read

January 31

Dear Sir or Madam,

My name is Michela Merritt and if you are reading this, I am dead, and it's not from the cancer that is eating away at me. For many years my husband has treated me like nothing to him; abused me emotionally and mentally, if not physically. I know he will be the cause of my death, I just don't know when or how. I hope he waits long enough that I can get my strength back to fight him; right now I am so weak I can't even lift my paintbrushes. I don't know if this letter can serve as evidence, but I want someone to know that Larry caused my untimely death."

The attorney looked up and said to the jury, "The letter is signed Michela Merritt and dated January 31 of this year. Two witnesses have affixed their signatures, too." He turned back to Sam Chambers, "I told you she was very organized."

Sam looked at Mansfield. "Thank you, Mr. Mansfield. That's all."

DeLacey jumped to his feet, either eager to put holes in the witness's testimony or to escape his client's rantings.

"Mr. Mansfield, you said Mrs. Merritt came to your office in disguise – why do you think she did that?"

"I did NOT say she came in disguise. I said she was blonde. It could hardly be a disguise since she told me her name."

"And how many times did you meet with her?"

"Just the once. We used couriers to send paper back and forth for corrections and signatures. She had insisted I call her cell prior to any deliveries so she could be sure to be at home to receive them, told me it was so her husband wouldn't know what was going on."

DeLacey grimaced. That had not gone as he had planned. He tried again. "So you met with a blonde woman once, a woman who *claimed* to be Michela Merritt, and you accepted her story and her envelope on her say-so, is that correct?"

Mansfield hesitated, "Yes, that's correct, but..."

DeLacey interrupted him. "And then, months later, you saw a newspaper picture of Michela Merritt that you 'almost didn't recognize' and you sent the envelope to the District Attorney, is that correct?"

"Not exactly. I had seen the picture at the time she died. I read of the trial starting when I returned from overseas and *that* prompted me to mail the package," the lawyer replied defensively.

"Tell me, Mr. Mansfield, if there had been no caption to the newspaper photo identifying the woman as Michela Merritt, would you have recognized her?"

Again the young attorney hesitated. "I'm not sure. But who else could she have been? Why would anyone else claim to be her?"

"Good questions," DeLacey replied with a huge smile. "And one I hope to answer before this trial is over.

"Now, Mr. Mansfield, returning to the letter Mrs. Merritt wrote. "Does she say her husband is "going to kill her"?"

Gordon Mansfield reread the letter and looked up. "No, she doesn't."

"What did she say TWICE?"

"She says Mr. Merritt is at fault and has caused her death."

"Legally speaking, is causing a death the same thing as murder?"

Mansfield hesitated, "No, I wouldn't think so."

"No, I wouldn't either. Would you believe there have been cases where someone caused a suicide without even being in the room?"

Again, Mansfield hesitated. "Yes, I would believe that was possible."

"Now, Mr. Mansfield, please tell the jury who witnessed this letter."

"Magdelena Rostoff and Peter Sung."

"Do you know what their relationship was with the deceased? Why did she ask them to witness this letter?"

"I believe they were her housekeeper and gardener."

"Do you know if these two employees read the document or just signed where their employer told them to, on the dotted line as it were?"

"No, I do not." Mansfield felt he had let down Sam Chambers and Michela Merritt with his testimony.

"Tell me, Mr. Mansfield, since Mrs. Merritt did not want her husband to inherit, were there other beneficiaries to the will?

"Yes."

"Please tell the court who they were." DeLacey smiled his glowing white teeth smile while his eyes shot daggers at Sam.

Mansfield looked over DeLacey's head, apparently trying to recall. "Mrs. Rostoff received a bequest, Ms. Kirkland, there was a bequest to the Denver Museum of Art, and..."

DeLacey interrupted. "Thank you, that will be all for this witness then."

Judge Thomas turned to the prosecution table as Gordon Mansfield left the courtroom. "Mr. Chambers, will your next witness be lengthy?"

"Possibly, Your Honor."

"Then we will recess until tomorrow morning."

Sam calmly gathered his papers and strode purposefully out of the courtroom. He casually patted Cassie on the shoulder as he passed her in the hall, but didn't say a word. Sam grabbed Maria's arm and determinedly steered her out of the building with him. He maintained his calm, unruffled demeanor until he was seated behind the wheel of his car, Maria in the passenger seat.

"Damn it to hell!" he exploded, beating his fist on the steering wheel. "That snake! I thought he was going to try to say Michela had killed herself. Now it looks like he's going to try the 'bushy-haired man' defense."

Maria was obviously confused. "The what?"

"Back in the 50s, in Ohio; I remember studying the case in law school. Dr. Sam Sheppard was accused of killing his wife. He claimed it was a stranger, a bushy-haired man. The man was never found. Dr. Sam was convicted. And the TV series and movie, *The Fugitive*, were born."

"So how does that help DeLacey?"

"It just lets him muddy the water and confuse the jury. Enough confusion and he gets an acquittal. He's trying to show that someone, ANYONE, could have committed the murder, even if he can't point to a specific person. It's some unknown person who hasn't been caught yet. Next to impossible for us to prepare for; all we can do is use our chance to redirect and ask a few more questions after DeLacey finishes."

"But why would a stranger use cyanide? And how did he or she get into the house?" Maria asked.

"I don't know and I don't know," Sam replied with a grimace.

"So where do we go from here?"

"We have to start thinking like a predator, like DeLacey; try to predict what his devious mind might cook up, then refute his theories before he has a chance to voice them. It's going to be a late night. Better order a pizza. And call Cassie, she's going to be the key. We've got to be sure of her testimony, make sure she's prepared for any questions he may throw at her, or he'll rip her to shreds and end up pointing the finger at her. Have her come to the office right away. Offer her pizza." They drove off in a cloud of apprehension.

Chapter 47

It had been a very long night, they didn't leave the office until after three in the morning. Sam, Maria, and Cassie had been over Cassie's testimony from every angle, evaluating it, nurturing it, questioning it; trying to second guess DeLacey. Even though Cassie was Sam's last witness and he had a few more to present before her, including Doc, he wanted her prepared in case things went faster than he expected and she was called the next day. Sam had driven Cassie home in a mental fog, each lost in his or her own thoughts.

Sam was back in court at nine, ready to do battle with John DeLacey all over again. Every day it felt like the first time. Sam was a little worried, not trusting the man, but hopeful he could stay one step ahead of him.

Jim Ellis was called and sworn in. Ellis entered through the double doors at the back of the courtroom. He'd been hanging around outside with the other witnesses all week, never sure when he would be called, gradually the witness pool had gotten smaller and smaller. He was an attractive man, in his late fifties with grey hair and a long knife scar just in front of his left ear. "Detective Ellis, please tell the court your position," Sam began.

"I am a retired Denver City homicide detective. Currently I work as a special investigator for the D.A.'s office in Jefferson County."

"How long were you with Denver PD?"

"Twenty-six years."

"And why did you retire?"

Unconsciously, the detective's hand went to the scar on his face. "I was wounded, it affected my hearing."

"Isn't it true you received multiple commendations during your career and the department's medal of valor for the incident that ended your career?"

"Yes."

"Your Honor, the defense will stipulate to the stellar qualities of the witness if it will speed the process," DeLacey sighed dramatically.

"Thank you, Mr. DeLacey," Sam smiled graciously at the other man.

"Now, Mr. Ellis, in what capacity have you been involved with this case?"

"You asked me to investigate the contents of an envelope you received earlier this summer."

"Objection, Your Honor, the contents are not allowed."

"Your Honor, while the letter from this envelope was disallowed for court, the other contents were not. I do not intend to ask about the letter."

DeLacey realized his mistake as soon as he looked at the jury; they were all curious about the forbidden letter now and why the defense did not want it in court.

"Objection over-ruled. Continue, Mr. Chambers."

Sam handed the envelope to Ellis. "Is this the envelope?"

Ellis made a pretense of checking the labels though he readily knew the container. "Yes, Sir, that's it."

"And what was in the envelope?"

"Three credit card statements and two cell phone statements."

"And whose name and address are on the pages?"

"Larry Merritt."

"And what did you learn about these papers?"

"We determined that on January 4 of this year Mr. Merritt made a purchase from Amazon.com, a total of four books: a PDR, that is the *Physicians' Desk Reference*, the *Handbook of Toxic and Hazardous Chemicals*, a book just called *Toxicology* and *The Complete Drug Reference*. The phone logs show calls to his home, his business, his mis...that is Ms. Muir, and to six different pharmaceutical companies."

"I guess the home and business calls are normal. And calls to Ms. Muir are...understandable." The jury members grinned at Sam's delicacy, as he had intended. "Were you able to find out who he talked to at these pharmaceutical companies?"

"No, Sir, we weren't. They are just call centers, places people call for general information. The callers don't have to give any personal information."

"But aren't there tapes of calls? They always say something to the effect of 'these calls may be monitored for customer service'; what about those tapes?"

"The people I talked to at each company said they destroy the tapes after about a month, so there's no record left."

"So what you did find out is that Mr. Merritt ordered four books about poison and had talks with several drug houses in the months immediately preceding his wife's death, right?"

Larry jumped to his feet and pointed his finger at the witness, yelling, "You stupid dick! Why would I do that? All I had to do was wait and she'd be dead! I never called anybody. And I sure never ordered any books. Hell, I don't even read." Merritt ranted from the defense table again, pounding his fist on it in his anger. DeLacey once again attempted to rein in his client.

Sam managed to look incredulous and disgusted at the same time. Having been distracted from the witness, he returned his attention as Ellis said, "Yes, Sir, that about sums it up."

"Did you find the books that were ordered from Amazon?"

"Yes, Sir, they were in a couple Amazon boxes on Mr. Merritt's closet shelf. The forensic guys found them."

"Going back to these receipts. These pages were provided by Mrs. Merritt. How could that be?"

"According to Mr. Merritt, when I talked with him, Mrs. Merritt did the family books, paid the bills and so on. So she'd see the bills when they came in. He said he never bothered with them, left it all to her."

"Those aren't my charges on my cell phone," Merritt said loudly to his attorney as he appeared ready to lunge for the paperwork held by the witness.

Judge Thomas banged his gavel so hard Sam thought it might have broken. "Mr. Merritt," he thundered. "You will NOT speak out in my courtroom. You will sit there and be quiet. This is your last warning. Do I make myself perfectly clear?"

DeLacey shushed Merritt and got him to regain his seat. Merritt mumbled "Yes, Your Honor." Sam took a quick peek at the jury and was glad to see their disgust growing.

"How about that, Mr. Ellis? Could someone else have ordered the books and made the calls to make it look like Mr. Merritt? Could he be framed?" Sam was stealing DeLacey's thunder, asking about a possible second scenario. He was disturbed when DeLacey did not object to the conclusion- jumping required by Sam's question. *Now what is he up to? Letting me play his hand?*

"Well, sure, that's the problem with all this new technology, it's so anonymous. You go on the Internet, give them a credit card and a name, and the item you want gets sent to you wherever you want. Heck, you or I could have ordered the books if we'd had access to his credit card number. You or I could have placed the calls if we'd had access to his cell phone. The whole world is composed of numbers these days, no people, just numbers; no identities, just numbers. Credit cards, phones, computer IDs, passwords, you name it, just numbers."

"Very philosophical, Mr. Ellis, I'm sure, but could you please stick to the point," DeLacey sarcastically inquired.

Sam hesitated, knowing Judge Thomas would jump in.

"Is that an objection, Mr. DeLacey? Please refrain from addressing witnesses in my court except when it is your time to cross examine."

"Yes, Your Honor, I apologize."

"Continue, Mr. Chambers."

"So, Mr. Ellis, are you saying Mrs. Merritt had ready access to these items?"

"Yes, Sir, as Mr. Merritt's wife I would expect she did."

"Doesn't it seem strange to you that someone plotting a murder would leave such damning evidence readily available?"

"Objection. Calls for a conclusion."

"Sustained."

"In your many years as a professional law enforcement officer, had you ever seen anything like this?"

"No, Sir. It was really careless, really stupid, or he just didn't care."

DeLacey was on his feet in a shot. "Objection, Your Honor, conclusion by the witness and highly prejudicial."

"Sustained. Jury will disregard the witness's last statement."

Sam decided to quit while he was ahead, knowing the jury could not 'disregard' Ellis's statement even if they wanted to. "That's all, Mr. Ellis, thank you."

DeLacey hurried to replace Sam in front of the witness, apparently itching to get into the fray.

"As I understand it, Mr. Ellis, these credit card statements only show that someone using Mr. Merritt's card ordered these books, correct?"

"Yes." Jim Ellis's respectful tone was obviously missing.

"Could anyone have used the number to order things?"

"Yes, but the items were shipped to Mr. Merritt at his office."

"So anyone with access to the credit card could have placed the order for books on poison?"

"Yes, I've already said that." Sam could see the jury was getting as fidgety about this rehash of previous testimony as the witness.

"Mr. Merritt? Mrs. Merritt? A secretary? The housekeeper?"

"Theoretically, yes. Of course, they would have to have a reason to order them, too."

"Hmmmmmmm, yes, a reason." DeLacey paced in front of the jury, appearing to give deep thought to the witness's comment.

"And the cell phone logs? Someone would have to actually use the phone for the numbers to be recorded?"

"That's correct." Ellis looked at DeLacey as though he was in his dotage.

"And what time of day were these calls recorded?"

Ellis studied the lists still in his hands. "All times, day time, evening, even one at two a.m."

"And these calls could have been made from anywhere in the country, correct? The only thing for sure is that they were made with Mr. Merritt's phone."

"That is correct. Although roaming charges might show up if the calls were made from a different service area."

Switching gears, "Are you married, Mr. Ellis?"

Sam started to object and then decided to see where DeLacey was going.

Confused and wary of the sudden shift, Ellis replied hesitantly, waiting for the shoe to drop, "Yes..."

"Have you ever let your wife use your cell phone?"

"Objection. Relevance."

"Over-ruled. Please answer, Mr. Ellis."

"Yes."

"Have you ever left your cell phone lying around the house and not touched it for hours?"

"Once in a while, yes."

"Have you ever gone off to work and completely forgotten it, left it at home?"

"Yes." Sam cringed inwardly as one of his prime witnesses was being shot down.

"Nothing further, Your Honor." DeLacey turned away. Then he turned back. Giving his best Columbo impression, "Excuse me, Mr. Ellis, just one more question. You said anyone plotting murder who left this information so accessible was either careless, stupid, or uncaring...Isn't there another possibility? What if he was being framed?"

"Objection, calls for a conclusion." Sam knew it was too late though. The seed had been planted.

"Withdrawn. That's all I have for this witness." DeLacey smirked as he resumed his seat at the defense table.

Thankfully, they broke for lunch. Sam felt like he needed a stiff drink.

Chapter 48

Sam had skipped the drink at lunch, wouldn't do to face DeLacey with only half his wits about him. He faced the judge and said, "The prosecution calls William Harper." Out in the hall, Doc stood as the bailiff called his name, he kissed Cassie's cheek and headed into the courtroom.

Doc was duly sworn and took his seat. Sam was impressed once again with his appearance. Confidence and honesty seemed to come from every pore of the silver-haired doctor.

"Dr. Harper, what type of doctor are you? What is your specialty?"

"I'm a cancer specialist."

"And were you the doctor of Michela Merritt?"

"Yes, I had been her doctor her whole life." The kindly doctor blinked rapidly to eliminate the tears that were forming.

"She had cancer her entire life?"

"No. Her mother died of cancer shortly after Michela's birth. I had been Lily's – Michela's mother - doctor and became a family friend during her mother's ordeal. When Lily died, Tom, Michela's father, just came to rely on me whenever there was a medical question for his little girl. Fortunately there were no major concerns until five years ago."

"That's when the cancer was diagnosed the first time?"

"Yes, she had breast cancer that had metastasized into her lymph nodes. We did a radical double mastectomy." Sam saw the women on the jury cringe, one even nodded her head as she raised her hand to her chest.

Doc was continuing, "We thought we had gotten it all. She was cancer free for about three years; then it came back, this time in her lungs."

Before Sam could ask the obvious question, he continued, looking directly at the jury, "A cancer takes on certain properties, regardless of where it is located. So if a cancer is in the lungs and has the properties of breast cancer, it's still breast cancer."

Sam smiled his thanks to the doctor for his clear, easily understood explanation. Juries do not like heavy technical jargon, and they don't like to feel as though they're being talked down to. Doc had hit the middle ground perfectly.

"And what was the outlook for her situation the second time the cancer struck?"

"With care, she could have lived two, maybe three, years. It was spreading quickly. The new chemo had seemed to slow its progress a bit, but I had no real hope that it was going to go away."

"And how did Mrs. Merritt take this?"

"Objection, Your Honor. The witness has already told us he is an oncologist, not a psychologist or psychiatrist."

Sam jumped right back. "Your Honor, the witness had known the deceased her entire life, all 29 years. No one could better describe her attitude toward this disease."

Judge Thomas considered for a moment. "Over-ruled."

"Doctor?" Sam prompted.

"She took it just fine. She knew it was bad, but she never gave up hope, never thought she wouldn't get better. She told me several times 'I licked it before and I'll lick it again this time'. She was a fighter."

"As a visitor to the Merritt home, did you observe Michela and Larry Merritt together?"

The muscles in the doctor's cheeks stood out as he clenched his teeth. "Much to my displeasure, yes."

"What do you mean by that?"

"Michela waited on him hand and foot. Even when she was sick from the chemo, or recovering from the surgery the first time, she couldn't do enough for him. He never lifted a finger to help her; she was always fetching a cup of coffee, finding his keys, making dinner reservations for him, even though he usually went out in the evenings without her."

"She was too sick to do anything, old man! What was I supposed to do? Sit home and watch her puke? Clean up after her? Get real," Larry shouted from the defense table.

"Mr. Merritt, one more outburst from you and you will be removed from the courtroom." Judge Thomas had obviously had enough.

Sam continued, successfully hiding his glee at the judge's admonition as well as Larry's latest nail into his own coffin. "Did Mrs. Merritt have any other medical problems?"

"Two years ago she had a miscarriage. She had been told that a pregnancy was unlikely because of all the chemo she'd had with the first bout with cancer. When she found out she was pregnant she was elated." Doc beamed at the memory of Mich's joy. "She bubbled over with plans for the baby; Mich had already decided 'she' would be the first female president. Her enthusiasm was infectious, to everyone except her husband." Doc scowled at the defendant.

"How did Mr. Merritt react to the pregnancy?"

"Basically, he ignored it and Mich, except when he referred to her as a 'fat cow' or 'beached whale'."

Sam paused for the expected objection; again, none came. DeLacey was writing furiously on his yellow pad, though. "And the miscarriage? How did he react to it?"

"He said he was glad, he thought a child would have interfered with their time. He meant he was worried he might not get Mich's undivided attention."

"Objection, Your Honor, the witness is interpreting, not providing evidence."

"Sustained. The jury will disregard the witness's last statement."

But Sam knew again they wouldn't, couldn't. Doc had done an amazing job.

"No more questions, Your Honor."

Although it was only 11:30, the judge announced they would break for lunch.

Sam was glad Doc would have a chance to relax before what he expected to be an ordeal for the older man.

If only he had known how much of an ordeal it would prove to be, for both of them.

Chapter 49

At 2 p.m. Doc returned to the stand and the judge reminded him he was still under oath.

John DeLacey sprang to his feet, obviously anxious to interview the witness. Although today he was more somberly dressed in a navy silk suit, he still had his trademark pink tie. His graying blonde hair flopped casually across his forehead.

"Dr. Harper, would you say you are totally objective in your interpretation of the relationship between the Merritts?"

"What do you mean, Mr. DeLacey?"

"In your deposition you said that Michela was 'like a daughter' to you, that you had known her and her parents for a long time. Can you honestly say that your understanding of the interplay between husband and wife might have been prejudiced by your," he paused dramatically, "affection for the family?"

"No. I heard what I heard. I saw what I saw."

"So you don't think Larry Merritt's dismay at his wife's pregnancy, a pregnancy that could endanger her life, and his relief at the child's loss, might have been concern for his wife's health?"

"No. I do not." Doc was starting to lose his equanimity. His twinkling eyes were now glaring at the attorney.

"You say you spent a lot of time with the couple?"

"Yes."

"Did you ever see Larry Merritt strike his wife?"

"No."

"As Michela Merritt's personal physician, did you ever see bruises on her body?"

"No, but..."

"Did Mrs. Merritt have any unusual emergency room trips, broken bones, that sort of thing?"

"No, but..."

"As far as you know, were the police ever called to the residence for a domestic disturbance?"

"No, if..."

"Tell me doctor, do you have a key to the Merritt house?"

Very obviously Doc was having to restrain his temper at the lawyer's rudeness. "Yes."

"Have you ever gone there uninvited? Unexpectedly? Have you ever let yourself in when no one was home?"

Doc glared, "Which question shall I answer first?"

DeLacey waved his hand airily. "It doesn't matter. Take your pick."

"Yes."

"To which question."

Doc leaned back in his seat and replied, "It doesn't matter. Take your pick."

The jury members smiled as the tension was broken. Sam was glad to see they seemed happy that DeLacey had gotten his come-uppance.

"You're saying you have been to the Merritt home uninvited, unexpected, and alone?" DeLacey appeared incredulous.

"Yes." Doc looked at him unwaveringly, innocence beaming from him like a beacon.

"Now, Doctor, please explain how you managed to lose two women from the same family to the same disease? Are you just a slow study or incompetent?"

Sam was on his feet before DeLacey's question mark was voiced. "Serious objection, Your Honor. Defense counsel is impugning the witness's reputation."

"That is enough, Mr. DeLacey. Character assassination is not allowed in my courtroom."

"Yes, Your Honor, I withdraw the question." Turning back to the witness, DeLacey continued unabashed.

"Doctor, do you know how Mrs. Merritt had a prescription for sleeping pills?"

"Yes. I wrote it."

"And did you allow refills for it?"

"Yes." Doc was looking confused.

"Do you know how many refills were allowed?"

"Not off the top of my head, but I'm sure the records are in her file."

DeLacey changed tactics once again, "You and Mrs. Merritt had a very close relationship, isn't that right?"

"Yes." Sam watched Doc closely, his voice had changed, had taken on an edge of hesitancy.

"Would you say closer than you have with the rest of your patients?"

"Yes." Doc was sounding wary.

"Please tell the jury exactly what that relationship was, the one you and the deceased had in addition to your doctor/patient one." The jury members leaned forward, straining to hear, tense for the answer.

Doc hesitated. "I was her godfather as well." Sam and the jury started to relax at this anticlimactic response.

DeLacey was disappointed but proceeded. "And how was it that you were the godfather of a child whose mother had died while in your care?"

"On her deathbed Lily had asked me to look after Michela; Tom was beside himself with grief and didn't know what to do with a baby. He had Michela baptized right away and asked me to be godfather."

DeLacey grinned his wolfish grin. This was a fishing expedition, but based on the doctor's posture, he felt there might be something out there. He tried to reel in the good doctor. "And now, Dr. Harper, what about the other *relationship*?"

Doc was obviously agonizing. *How could DeLacey have found out? He thought he was the only one who knew.* He hesitated in answering.

"Doctor?" the defense attorney prompted.

In barely more than a whisper, Doc responded, "I am her biological father."

DeLacey was elated, not a sexual relationship as he had expected, but almost as good. An even better motive for a mercy killing! The jury was visibly shocked. DeLacey assumed a look of someone who was in on the secret as he asked, "And did Mrs. Merritt know that you were her biological father?"

"No. I only found out myself when she was diagnosed with cancer the first time, hadn't really paid attention to it before, there was no need. We were checking to be sure we had enough blood on hand for the surgery. Mich was type AB. I knew her mother and father had both been type A, so Tom couldn't have been her father. I'm type B. Lily and I had slept together one time only, but it only takes once. Lily never told me, I'm not sure she knew, and Tom never knew. I never told Michela."

"So when you said you loved her 'like a daughter', you were lying weren't you, Doctor? In fact, she *was* your daughter and you loved her, period. You would have done anything for her, wouldn't you?"

Doc could see where DeLacey was heading. "No, not anything, Mr. DeLacey. I wouldn't have killed her to end her suffering, not even if she had asked me to do so."

"And did she ask you, Doctor?"

"No, she did not. Michela was a fighter. She refused to give up." DeLacey looked skeptically at the older man.

"No more questions, Your Honor. I've had quite enough of this witness."

Considering the emotions of everyone in the court, Judge Thomas adjourned for the weekend. The print and Internet reporters scrambled for the exit, pulling their cell phones from pockets and purses as they scurried to file this breaking news. TV reporters loitered at the courtroom doors, wondering what was going on. As soon as they heard, they hoped to interview the Denver-famous doctor.

Sam escorted Doc through the side door and told him to go straight to his car. Then Sam went to the lobby through another door and told Maria to take Cassie around the back way and out to the car. Sam went back through the courtroom and provided fodder for the TV cameras, stalling them so Cassie and Doc could get away from the courthouse. "No, we did not know about this revelation and it makes no difference. Larry Merritt is on trial, not William Harper. There is no evidence to suggest anyone other than Larry Merritt committed this heinous crime. No further comments." Sam said all this while strolling casually to the elevators.

As soon as they got into the car and were on their way, Doc told Cassie what had happened in the courtroom; he knew she'd find out anyway as soon as the evening news came on. Cassie looked at him incredulously and then said, "Good. I'm glad Mich had someone around all the time who loved her." Doc looked over at the young woman seated next to him, not fully believing that she could be so accepting. "She had two of us, Cassie, two of us."

Cassie patted his hand on the console between them and lapsed into a comfortable silence broken only by, "I just wish Mich had known."

Once again reporters were waiting when they arrived at the house. Once again Doc drove straight into the garage and closed the doors. They were safe in their refuge for the weekend.

Chapter 50

Friday night was a late night in the District Attorney's office. Greg, coat off and tie thrown on his desk, called Sam in for an update. "I hear it's a stalemate, Sam. DeLacey is pulling out all the stops and using all his usual tricks to confuse the jury even before he presents his defense."

Sam was slumped in the chair across from Greg. "That's about it, Greg. But I think we're holding our own. I've seen several jurors squirm in their seats when John goes on one of his fishing expeditions. I think he's starting to wear thin, getting on their nerves because he interrupts so often. As usual, it's a crap shoot. I still think Cassie will sell it for us."

Greg tried to be casual when he asked, "And how is our star witness? She okay? Not going to fall apart on the stand is she?" He watched Sam closely to see his mood when he talked about Cassie Kirkland.

Sam grinned and sat up straighter. "Cassie fall apart? Not likely. She has this look of a little kid, all bright-eyed and trusting, but underneath she's a very determined lady. I think the jury is going to eat her up, in a good way. Who doesn't trust a librarian?" The grin never left his face. Greg worried that Sam was more passionate about the woman than the case.

"Can she withstand DeLacey's cross?"

"I'm sure she can. Maria and I have gone over every question we can think of that he might throw at her. We've warned her not to let him get to her, no matter what he asks because we can't think of everything that sneaky bastard might come up with. Cassie is a very surprising woman: smart, classy, warm, and stubborn. She'll be fine."

Greg hesitated again while he studied the younger man. "And what about you, Sam? You aren't getting too close to this case are you? Maybe taking it a bit too personally?"

Sam looked surprised by the question, then he thought about it. "Yeah, Greg, I'm beginning to think my interest isn't purely professional, but I can handle it. I promise you, absolutely nothing is going to impact my prosecution of this case. Once we win, then we'll see. Deal?"

Greg waved his gold Cross pen in Sam's direction, "Fair enough, Sam. I know I can trust your judgment on this. Keep up the good work." He smiled a fatherly smile as he said, "And good luck once it's over."

Sam grinned back as he rose from the chair beside Greg's desk and headed for the door. "I don't know which is harder, the case or the waiting for it to end. Usually I enjoy the challenge, the verbal battles of a trial. This one is so obvious and there's so much personally riding on its outcome that I just want to get it over with." He held up his hand as he saw Greg about to issue an admonishment, "Don't worry, I'm at the top of my form. I have to win this. I don't think I can face Cassie, or Doc, if we don't." He left the office with a mumbled "Back to work." Greg watched after him before shrugging his shoulders and returning to the stack of papers on his desk.

Needing a break and some relaxation for a few hours, mid-afternoon Saturday Sam drove over to his brother Jack's house. He'd spent the morning running errands to the cleaners and the grocery. He knew Doc and Cassie were closeted at Doc's house and he shouldn't see them for fear of incurring the ire of his boss. He'd talked to Doc the previous evening, who said they were both fine, enjoying books and wine by the fireplace. This weekend was Sam's mother's sixtieth birthday and her family was trying to give her a surprise party. It wasn't easy because she was hard to snooker. Back in October Sam had hoped to bring Cassie with him to the party but had decided not to since it was after the trial started.

"Hey, bro, let's get busy," his brother Jack playfully punched his shoulder as they went into the house. Sam's niece and nephews all greeted him and eight year old Abigail gave her favorite uncle a hug; they were all busy hanging streamers and blowing up balloons. Sam looked around the comfortable, cluttered living room; books, magazines, iPads, and cell phones everywhere. *More a family room than a living room*, Sam thought, *as it should be.*

"So what's the plan? How are we going to get her over here without giving it away? After all, it *is* her birthday, she'll be expecting something."

"Got that covered, big brother," Jack grinned. "We told her we want to take her out to dinner for her birthday but to come here for drinks first. See, I have been listening to you all these years. Mix the lies in with the truth and the listener will never suspect. Or just tell part of the truth, not all of it. Maybe I should be the next lawyer in the family!" Both men laughed good naturedly.

"Forget that, Denver is better off with a superb fire lieutenant rather than another attorney. How did you get off today?"

"Just switched. All we have to do is hope there isn't a fire tonight! Get over there and help with the balloons, you've got all the hot air we need." Jack grinned at his older brother as he pushed him in the direction of his sons Philip and Sam.

Just then Sam heard the kitchen door open. "Saved! I'll help Heidi with the groceries, wouldn't want you to strain your aging back." Sam rushed passed the dining room and into the kitchen just as his sister-in-law labored through the door, arms laden with two brown grocery bags. "Hey, Heid, need help? Any more in the car?"

"Bless you, big brother! Lots more. Be careful with the cake, keep it flat."

Sam headed out to the garage. He opted for the grocery bags and left the cake for Heidi's tender ministrations, he decided he'd probably trip going up the garage steps and smash the cake.

Once all the bags were on the kitchen island, Heidi reached over and hugged her much taller brother-in-law. "Where have you been all my life?" she joked. "A man who helps with the groceries."

"Right here, little sis, let's run off to Tahiti and make mad passionate love on the beach," Sam teased as his brother walked into the kitchen.

"Sorry, Sam, she's spoken for," Jack said as he grabbed his wife around the waist, bent her over his arm, and planted a resounding kiss on her giggling lips.

"Just my luck, all the good ones are taken," Sam said as he snapped his fingers and grinned back. "Just out of curiosity, what are all these groceries for? Is all of Denver coming?"

"You'd think, wouldn't you?" Heidi replied with a shrug. "When we started compiling the guest list it just kept growing. Mom's bridge club, golf buddies, book club, church friends. It was like one of your cases. We started with one group and they'd say 'but have you included so and so', and then they'd lead us to another group, and it kept going. We had to cut it off at 100 people so we could still have room for air in the house. Thank goodness it's going to be a nice evening, we'll be able to open a couple windows at the back of the house so air can circulate."

"Not my room!" Philip shouted from the other room. "It'll make my bed too cold."

The adults in the kitchen laughed. "Can't get away with a thing around here," Jack grinned ruefully. "Beer, Sam?"

The two brothers headed to Jack's den, off-limits to the rest of the family because this was where he kept his work files. Jack was a highly respected arson investigator for the city of Denver and often did his best thinking here in his home office, away from the distractions of his official office.

"So how's it going, Sam? I'm following you in the papers and on TV of course, but they don't tell what's really going on unless you tell them, and all I'm hearing from you is 'no comment'."

Sam rocked his beer-free hand back and forth in a so-so gesture. "We'll just have to see, can't tell yet." Sam hesitated. Jack could see he had something else on his mind, so he waited for Sam to take the lead.

"I've met someone, Jack. I think you'd like her." Sam looked sheepishly at his younger brother.

"Whoa! Don't tell me the mighty has fallen! Woo hoo! Who is she? Another attorney? Tell me all about her."

Sam reddened. "No, nobody I work with. She's a librarian. Short, curly blonde hair, big brown eyes. Smart. Classy. Nice."

"Sounds too good for you. Where'd you meet her?"

Sam hesitated, debating how much to tell his brother. "I met her in connection with a case I'm working on."

"So when do the rest of us get to meet her? Are you bringing her to Mom's party? Oh my God, will Mom like her? That's the big test."

"Don't I know it! No, she can't come. Maybe another time. I'm not sure we're at that stage yet. I'll just have to see."

Jack stared at his brother, knowing him well enough to know there was more to the story than he was letting on. "I'll look forward to it. Maybe we can meet for dinner some time? Heidi would love an excuse to get away from the monsters and Mom would love an excuse to keep them. Just let me know when."

"I'll do that." Sam looked at his watch. "Isn't it about time to get this shindig underway?"

With that the doorbell rang and the party had begun. Everyone had parked down the street so the guest of honor wouldn't recognize the cars. Sam's parents arrived promptly at 6:30 and everyone jumped from hidden corners and halls to surprise the birthday girl. It appeared she was truly surprised, too. The best surprise came at 7, though, when Sam's youngest brother, Chris, walked in from Afghanistan. *Everyone* was surprised at that. Chris almost stole the show from his mother. "It was just like a Hallmark moment," Eileen Chambers commented later as she again hugged her three tall sons.

Sunday Sam spent meeting his family for brunch and then reviewing his notes. The next week was going to be crucial to his case.

Cassie and Doc spent Sunday hiding from the Press and reading all the newspaper articles about the case. Various reporters – Cassie couldn't think of them as "journalists" – speculated about the guilt or innocence of Cassie, Doc, and Larry. Others wrote about the relative importance of the various witnesses and their testimonies, especially Doc's revelation.

Fortunately their biases were so blatant Doc and Cassie felt sure a blind cow could see them.

Chapter 51

Bright and early Monday morning, everyone convened once again. Doc thought he would be able to sit in the courtroom, but Sam reminded him he couldn't because one of the attorneys might want to recall him. Doc joined Cassie in the sunny arcade outside the courtroom.

"The court calls Rock Matheson." With a name like that the jury perked right up, visions of some wrestling idol swimming before their eyes.

A small, bespectacled, mousey man took the stand and was sworn in; more like a skinny Leonard from *Big Bang Theory* than a wrestler. Sam approached.

"Mr. Matheson, what is your profession?"

In a surprisingly deep voice the witness spoke, "It's Dr. Matheson. I have a PhD in toxicology. I teach at the CU Medical School here in Denver."

"Toxicology. That's the study of poisons?"

"Not in the way most people think. 'Poisons' as most people think of them comprise part of our studies; we study all poisonous substances, including plants, snake venom, and so on." The little man's obvious enthusiasm for his topic had captured the jury's interest.

"We have been told by the medical examiner that Michela Merritt died of cyanide poisoning. Are you familiar with its effects?"

"Oh, yes, cyanide is a very lethal substance. It only takes a little bit to kill an elephant, let alone a person."

"How does it work? Does it build up in the system like arsenic?"

"No, cyanide is very fast-acting. Cyanide works by paralyzing the major organs, cutting off the oxygen flow to the heart and brain. If it is ingested, that is taken into the body, it would make a person dead in a very short time. It's not like arsenic that builds up in the body and *eventually* kills a person. All those 17th and 18th century ladies who used arsenic to lighten their complexions were just looking for trouble, it's a wonder more of them didn't die of it. Of course, they may have and we just don't know it because nobody did toxicology tests back then."

Trying to rein in the witness and get him back on track, Sam asked, "How short a time period are you talking about for cyanide? A day? An hour?"

"Well, of course it depends on how much is ingested. Generally, I'd say a matter of minutes. Depending on the size of the person it could be as little as a few seconds to up to a couple minutes."

"Have you seen the ME's records on this case?"

"Yes. I entirely agree with her findings. The painful grimace on the lady's face is very typical of someone who has been poisoned with cyanide. It's a few seconds of very intense agony as the body's organs shut down, and then death occurs. Not pretty or calm, but thankfully it's quick."

"Thank you, Doctor. Your witness."

DeLacey lounged back in his chair, his left arm dangling over the back of it. The fingers of his right hand twirled a red pen. He stared thoughtfully at the witness and then casually rose to his feet and walked to the stand.

"If cyanide is so dangerous, Doctor, how is it obtained?"

"Well, I understand you've heard about its use in gold work. It's also still used as a pesticide. And, unfortunately, anyone can order it over the Internet. It really should be regulated better. Did you know..."

DeLacey cut off the witness's speech. "Thank you, Doctor. So what you're saying is that *anyone* can get their hands on a lethal amount of cyanide?"

The grey man wrinkled his forehead, causing his grey hair to rise. He pushed his glasses farther up on his nose and replied, "Unfortunately, that's true."

"They don't have to work with gold? Don't have to have some sort of license?"

The good doctor obviously was getting exasperated, "I said so, didn't I? All they need is a credit card and they can order it over the Internet."

DeLacey gave the expert a self-satisfied smile. "Thank you. That's all."

Chapter 52

The court clerk swore in Brian O'Leary.

Sam strode purposefully to the witness stand. "Dr. O'Leary, please tell the court your profession."

"I'm a board-certified psychiatrist. I specialize in forensic psychiatry; helping explain the mental whys and wherefores of crimes."

"Does that mean you're a profiler?"

"Rarely. Profilers try to define a pattern that thereby defines a perpetrator type. I work more with statistics that help to explain the crimes themselves."

"In your capacity as a crime expert, what can you tell us about poison as a weapon?"

"Poison is almost always used by someone close to the victim. It is unlikely a total stranger would use poison on another person. The nature of murder by poison..."

"Objection. No foundation. So far there is no proof a 'murder' has been committed."

"Your Honor, the witness is speaking in generalities, not addressing this case specifically."

Judge Thomas considered a moment. "Very well. Continue."

Looking displeased at the interruption, the physician continued, "By the nature of poison, it takes planning and care to kill someone this way. Most poisons meant to kill are administered over a period of time; the poison builds up in the system and then one day the victim's system can tolerate no more; death occurs."

"Doctor, generally speaking can you address the type of mentality that uses poison?"

"In general, a poisoner is cunning, probably duplicitous, because he or she is close to the person and poisoning him or her at the same time. And, because of this ability to act a part, is usually sociopathic, unfeeling, without remorse. At the same time, poison is chosen because the poisoner does not want to get too close to the victim physically, therefore no knife, no gun."

"What are the most common forms of poison used?"

"Well, of course, anything taken incorrectly and in sufficient quantity can be poisonous, hence the proliferation of warning labels. There have been cases of aspirin poisonings, bleach, lots of everyday items. But in the way I assume you mean, probably arsenic and sleeping pills."

"What about cyanide as a weapon?"

"Cyanide is a world unto itself. The user must plan ahead to get it because it's not sitting under many kitchen sinks and the user must have a serious reason to kill another person. Because of the extreme pain involved with death by cyanide, it would be given only by someone with a serious rage or desire to harm the other person; there would probably be a lot of anger."

Trying to take the wind out of DeLacey's sails, Sam asked, "Doctor, in your professional opinion, would cyanide be taken as a means of suicide?"

"Highly unlikely. As I said, it's a very agonizing death. There are easier, more comfortable ways to kill yourself. It is doubtful anyone would inflict that much pain on him or herself willingly, especially when pain-free methods are available."

Sam looked meaningfully at the jury as he said, "Thank you, Doctor" and walked back to his table. What he really wanted to do was high-five the doctor.

DeLacey jumped to his feet, not even allowing time for Sam to take his seat before launching his assault. "Just two questions, Doctor. Who is most commonly a poisoner, a man or a woman?"

Fidgeting at the question, the doctor replied, "Historically, the largest percentage of poisoners have been women. However, European studies have shown that the greatest number of cyanide suicides are men, although, as I said, suicide by cyanide is rare, in either sex."

"As I understand it, you have not talked with any of the other witnesses in this case, did not know Mrs. Merritt. My second question is whether you can really know what a person would or would not do under extreme conditions without interviewing them? Everything you have said here is hypothetical isn't it?"

"Actually, that's questions two and three, Mr. DeLacey. The answer to the first is 'no', it is next to impossible to predict someone's future behavior without having met them. And 'yes' the information I have given is hypothetical, but based on years of research into the habits of killers."

"Thank you, Doctor. You are excused." With a triumphant smirk, DeLacey resumed his seat, reaching to pat his client's shoulder as if to say "we've won".

As the psychiatrist passed in front of the bench, the judge turned to Sam. "Any more witnesses, Mr. Chambers?"

"Just one, Your Honor. Since testimony is bound to be lengthy, and it's already the lunch hour, may we call the next witness in the morning?"

The judge raised an eyebrow toward the defense attorney. DeLacey grinned, "No problem, Your Honor. If prosecution feels he needs more time to prepare, the defense has no objection."

"Very well. Court is recessed until tomorrow morning at 9 a.m."

Chapter 53

Maria had told Cassie Sam wanted to meet with her again right after lunch. Cassie and Doc ate a quiet meal in the courthouse cafeteria, then Doc went back to his office. Cassie had assured him she would get an Uber home whenever she was finished with Sam.

Once again Sam, Maria, and Cassie were closeted in Sam's office. They covered every minute of Cassie's life, of her friendship with the Merritts, of her last visit with Michela, and especially their future travel plans.

"It's those plans that are critical, Cassie. They show Mich's state of mind just hours before her death."

"I understand. I'll do my best. I'm just nervous, not knowing what to expect from Mr. DeLacey. Doc said he's pretty rough."

Sam reached over the round conference table and patted her hands folded on top. "Don't worry, you'll do great. Just be yourself. Answer truthfully and in short statements. Don't provide anything more than what was asked. Got it?"

Cassie gave them both a weak smile. "Got it."

Maria stood and started to gather the remnants of their taco dinner. "Sam, it's getting late. Cassie had better get some sleep. I'll call Uber. You walk her out while I clean up here."

Sam and Cassie rose as Sam clucked at Maria, "Yes, Mom." All three were smiling as the door closed behind Sam and Cassie.

Sam gently guided Cassie out with his hand to the small of her back. "Sometimes she acts like a mother hen, and she's younger than I am. Bet she drives her husband and son nuts." Sam was grinning while he said this, his affection for her was obvious. "Uber will take just a minute, there are usually several in the vicinity."

They exited into a cold, clear Colorado night, millions of stars shining above the dimly lit parking lot. An Uber pulled up.

Sam handed her into the back seat. "Sorry to have kept you so late."

Cassie smiled up at him, reluctant to release his hand. "It's okay, I know it's important. I probably wouldn't have slept anyway."

"I'll still be here for a couple more hours, call me when you get home so I know you got there safely." The Pakistani driver turned and glared at Sam. Sam ignored him.

Cassie gave Sam a mock salute and a smile, "Yes, Dad, will do." The door closed gently and the car headed across town.

Cassie caught the late evening news before reporting in to Sam. "I'm home, Doc is asleep. And I'm going to bed, see you in the morning."

"Thanks for calling, Cassie, good night."

The evening news had filled Cassie in on the morning's testimonies. She caught Sam before he hung up. "I don't understand. How can DeLacey get away with this? He's not proving that Larry didn't do it, he's just smearing a lot of innocent people with innuendoes. It's like a shotgun – if he puts enough shot out there he's bound to hit something."

Despite the gravity of the trial, Sam had to smile at the librarian using the shotgun metaphor. "That's exactly what he's doing, Cass. That's how the system works. The prosecution has to **prove** its case, in this case we have to convince the jury that Larry did it. The defense just has to raise enough reasonable doubt in the jury's collective mind to get them not to convict. It's defense lawyers like DeLacey who give lawyers a bad name."

"Can't DeLacey be brought up on charges or something? Can't the local Bar Association sanction him or...do something? He seems so underhanded."

"As much as it pains me to say this, he's actually a very good defense lawyer; he does whatever he has to to get his client acquitted. It's dirty and underhanded and improper, but not illegal. He comes very close to the line, but he has never done anything totally sanctionable."

"And if we lose we can't appeal. Larry can't be retried."

"Not if he's acquitted. Once a verdict is announced, that's it; he's 'not guilty' forever if he's acquitted. If it's a hung jury or if the case is dismissed for some reason, we can retry the case; but it's doubtful we will unless new evidence comes to light."

"But the defense can appeal if he's found guilty. Why do they get more chances and the prosecution doesn't?"

"It's the old double jeopardy thing. Can't be charged more than once for the same crime. It's a good law, or it was originally, but with so many appeals through the years, and when the courts bend over backwards to defend the rights of the accused, the whole system has become somewhat bastardized. You can't be completely fair to the victim **and** the accused; it's impossible.

"In recent years the tendency has been to come down on the side of the accused, rather than the victim or the victim's family. I agree that the accused has rights, and we have to do everything possible to protect those rights but lately it seems everybody's going out of their way to help the accused get off, not just protect the rights. I hate it; it's like beating your head against a brick wall. A prosecutor presents the best case, gets a unanimous verdict of guilt, and the defense lawyer can take years appealing a case; the punishment, whatever it is, may never be fulfilled. The courts are overturning verdicts on technicalities, a name misspelled on a piece of paper, or something equally stupid." Sam stopped talking abruptly. "Sorry, it's late. You're tired. I'm tired. Didn't know I had enough energy left to climb onto that soap box. Get some sleep. DeLacey starts his defense after your testimony."

"But what about the letter Mich wrote? And the backup disks and hard drive you took from my house? Aren't you going to use them?

"Unfortunately, Judge Thomas ruled the letter was inadmissible because Michela isn't here to be questioned by the defense. I knew if I tried to use the disks he'd rule the same way, or John would claim they'd been tampered with. I think we're okay without them."

"Do you know who his first witness is?" Cassie asked groggily.

Sam hesitated again, his silence deafening in Cassie's now-wide-awake ear. "Your ex." Sam waited for a response from Cassie. When none came, he just said, "Try to get some sleep. All in all, we're not doing badly." He slowly lowered the phone. On the other end, Cassie did the same, but she knew sleep would be a long time coming.

That afternoon John DeLacey had met once again with the defendant. "Tell me all you know about Cassie Kirkland," he had instructed his client. And Larry did.

Chapter 54

"The court calls Cassandra Kirkland."

A bailiff stuck his head out the door and motioned Cassie into the court room. Cassie rose from her spot on the oak bench, straightened her black dress, tugged her burgundy jacket into place, and squared her shoulders. Doc walked her to the double oak doors and patted her shoulder as she and the bailiff entered. She knew this was going to be the hardest thing she'd ever done, she just had no idea how hard.

Cassie walked down the aisle between the two sections of spectator benches. She kept her big brown eyes focused on the court clerk, not looking at Sam or the defense attorney or Larry. She tried to keep an open, calm look on her face, but she feared she was failing.

This was it. The jury could feel it. Each jury member sat up a bit straighter, eyes fixed on Cassie as she approached. Everyone in the courtroom, in the whole city of Denver, knew her testimony was critical. She was the only other person in the house at the time of the death. Did she do it? Maybe they'd soon know.

After the ritual swearing in, Sam approached Cassie, sitting erect and composed in the hard wooden chair.

"Ms. Kirkland, I know this has been a terrible time for you. Please tell the court where you live and what you do."

Cassie calmly replied, "I am a librarian at the public library in Lexington, Virginia." Her eyes twinkled at the thought.

"Now please tell the court how long you knew the deceased."

"We were best friends for 12 years. We met our freshman year in college." Cassie's voice was strong and confident.

"And where was that?"

"At Vanderbilt in Nashville, Tennessee." She pronounced it Nashvull. Sam knew the western jury would respond to her southern accent, even more pronounced now with her nervousness. He was doing his best to set her at ease and still keep the accent.

"And what was she like?"

"Objection, Your Honor, what anyone was like 12 years ago certainly has no bearing on this case before the court."

"On the contrary, Your Honor, it lays a foundation for any current change in attitude or mind-set," Sam jumped right in.

"Over-ruled. Please proceed, Ms. Kirkland."

"Mich– Michela – was fun. She loved life. She could do anything. She'd try anything. She was amazing. She was one of those people who was as good at math as she was at art. She started college planning to major in math, do something with computers. But she had to take calculus at 7:30 on Saturday mornings; she decided math was too rigid for her and switched her major. I guess it's fortunate, 'cause the world ended up with a wonderful artist instead of another programmer." Cassie was relaxing. Her depiction of her friend was joyful and loving; her eyes were shining; her lips were smiling.

"And did you know *Mr.* Merritt in Tennessee?"

Immediately the sparkle left Cassie's eyes and she clenched her teeth. "Yes," was all she could force herself to say.

"Tell us how you knew him."

"Mich and Larry met at a Sigma Chi party the first weekend of our junior year. He was a senior. He just swept her off her feet. Mich had a thing for older men."

"And what was their relationship like?"

Knowing it was futile, DeLacey objected anyway. "Over-ruled."

"Mich was ecstatic. She couldn't wait to get married; I guess you could say he pursued her until she caught him. He played hard-to-get one minute, can't-live-without-you the next. When they set the wedding date, Mich was so excited. I tried to get her to wait."

"And why was that?"

"I didn't like Larry; he was phony. He was hitting on other girls the whole time he was courting Michela."

Sam noticed several jury members smile at Cassie's use of the word "courting". *Did people do that anymore?*

"Objection, Your Honor, hear-say."

"If you will give me a moment, Your Honor," Sam requested.

Judge Thomas hesitated. "Continue."

"Ms. Kirkland, how do you know he was hitting on other women?"

"Because I was one of them. Every time he came to get Mich for a date, he'd touch me, or whisper to me. He'd make excuses to be alone with me, send Mich to get him a Coke downstairs or something. He gave me the creeps. And I didn't like him paying more attention to me than he did his supposed girlfriend."

"And what did Michela say to your suggestion to wait?"

"She said she didn't want to wait. That she had enough love for both of them. She said she thought Larry was exciting and that he would learn to love her as much as she loved him."

"And after they were married?"

"Nothing changed. Mich still adored him, he still played the field."

"Was Mrs. Merritt aware of her husband's infidelities?"

Cassie hesitated, expecting DeLacey to object. When he didn't she replied through gritted teeth, "Yes, painfully aware, most definitely. She sent me e-mails telling how hurt she was. Giving me details of his gifts for his girlfriends. She said he flaunted his affairs by charging flowers and gifts to their joint credit cards, knowing she would find them when she paid the bills."

"Why didn't she divorce him?"

"I asked her that very question the last day we were together." Cassie hesitated and cleared her throat. "She said she loved him and he needed her, whether he knew it or not. She said her wedding vows meant a lot to her." Sam saw several male jurors nodding in agreement.

"That last time you were together, what was her mood?"

Cassie grinned, remembering the fun they'd had. "She was very upbeat, even the cancer couldn't defeat her. We usually take a vacation together each year. She insisted we start planning our next one. We were planning to go to Tattered Cover that Saturday and buy guide books for Ireland. She had a painting she had done just for me, said she would send it to me in a couple weeks, as soon as it was completely dry. She was very positive; she was sure she was going to beat the cancer again. She even joked about her hair loss and her shaky hands; she showed me her wig collection. She wore a different wig every time we went out."

Sam looked pointedly at the jury. "Was she trying to disguise herself when she wore the wigs?"

Cassie looked perplexed, not having heard the other lawyer's testimony and cross examination. "Disguise? No. Why would she? She wore the wigs so other people wouldn't be uncomfortable by her bald head; she was like that, always thinking of others. Around the house she went 'natural', as she called it; bald as could be."

"Please tell the jury, Ms. Kirkland, why you were visiting Mrs. Merritt last May."

Cassie hadn't expected the question, what was she supposed to say? When all else fails, tell the truth. "She left me a voice mail and asked me to come, said it was an emergency."

"Objection, Your Honor, counsel knows the deceased's communications are excluded."

Sam smiled. He'd already won a point even if the judge sustained the objection: the jury was now wondering why the exclusions and what was in them. "Your Honor, this is a communication of the witness, too, she can attest to its veracity."

Judge Thomas hesitated briefly, looked once at Cassie and said, "Objection over-ruled."

Sam hid his exultation as best he could. Turning back to Cassie, "Was it easy for you to get away from your job?"

"Yes and no. May is one of our busiest times of the year, students are finishing up their last papers and projects, getting ready for summer and graduation. Fortunately I have a very understanding boss and he let me go. I would have gone anyway, though, even if it meant my job."

"You would have given up your job, a job you love, for a trip to Denver?"

"No, Mr. Chambers, not for a trip to Denver; for Michela, she needed me."

"And did she ever tell you why she needed you? Why you had to drop everything and rush to Denver?"

"I had to drag it out of her, but she told me. I started asking her the minute I walked in the door but she kept saying 'not now, I'm enjoying your visit too much'. Finally at dinner Wednesday night she told me; she said Larry was going to kill her."

"Just like that?"

"Exactly like that. Just very matter of fact, said Larry was going to kill her."

"And what was your reaction?"

Cassie paused. "I was stunned at first, that wasn't what I was expecting. I thought she'd gotten more bad news about the cancer. Then I got mad. I asked her if she had gone to the police, why she hadn't left him, what she expected me to do? I don't remember what else. I was furious!"

Sam smiled at the passion in Cassie's fury. She was visibly shaking on the witness stand.

"And her reply? Or maybe that's replies?"

"She said she wasn't going to let him get away with it. She just needed somebody to talk to so she could marshal her thoughts to outwit him, that's why she had called me. Then she stopped talking and wouldn't talk about it anymore."

"And how was she the remaining two days of your visit, before you found her dead Saturday morning?"

"She was fine, we had a good time, went shopping, talked about old times, went out to eat, talked about our next trip."

"And how was Larry Merritt on that last visit?"

"The same. At one point he followed me into the kitchen and tried to kiss me. I was even more uncomfortable around him than usual, I felt I had to lock my bedroom door at night."

"And how was he with Michela?"

"He pretended to be the devoted husband, patting her hand, offering to get her something to drink. But it was all an act..."

"Objection, Your Honor."

"Sustained. Ms. Kirkland, please refrain from giving opinions."

Cassie looked ashamed. "Yes, Sir, I'm sorry."

Sam quickly continued, "Did Mr. Merritt do or say anything else that upset you?"

"Yes, the night he followed me into the kitchen he said, 'She's not going to live forever; she can't. I just hope she hurries up so I can get on with my life."

Sam carefully reviewed his notes, giving the statement time to sink in with the jury...and for Cassie to dry her eyes and regain her composure. He decided it was time to get the jump on the other side. "Now, Ms. Kirkland, were you a benefactor of Mrs. Merritt's will?"

"Yes."

"In what way?"

"She left all her paintings to me." The jury gasped at the largesse, knowing the collection was worth millions of dollars.

"When did you find out you were becoming a millionaire?"

"Just before the funeral, at Larry's lawyer's office. He read the will and explained that she'd left her art to me."

"Now, considering how much she loved her husband, didn't you find it strange that she left the majority of her fortune to you?"

Cassie smiled. "Yes and no. Mich was very mercurial, but she was always a realist. No matter how much she loved Larry, she knew he wouldn't take care of her legacy, he'd just sell them to the highest bidder. She knew I would do what she would have wanted, so I guess that's why she left all the paintings to me."

"And what are you doing with this inheritance?"

"A select few of the paintings are being donated to the Denver Museum of Art. Most are being sold to museums; the proceeds are being used to create and sustain a summer art camp for children with cancer. This was something Mich had talked about doing but she never got the chance." Cassie whispered the last words as tears started to flow again.

"And how much money are **you** getting out of this?"

Again Cassie looked confused. "Money? None. I'm sure she left me the art so I could complete her dream and ensure that her beautiful paintings of Colorado and the Southwest would be available to the public forever. I have a couple paintings she has given me. I treasure them because she painted them and gave them to me, not for any monetary value. To me they're priceless."

As if on cue, Larry snorted in derision and muttered, "Dumb, really dumb."

"That's all the questions I have for this witness, Your Honor," Sam said and smiled at Cassie.

Judge Thomas turned to the defense table, "Mr. DeLacey?"

"Yes, Your Honor, just a few questions." He was practically bouncing in his excitement to get to his cross examination.

"Ms. Kirkland, it sounds like you and Mrs. Merritt were," he paused, "shall we say close?"

"Yes."

"*Very* close?"

"Yes."

"Would you say you *loved* Mrs. Merritt?" Sam immediately sensed where DeLacey was going with his questioning, up to his old tricks of smearing a witness when he didn't have enough evidence to clear his client. He hoped Cassie figured it out, too.

Cassie maintained her composure and replied calmly, "Yes, Mr. DeLacey, we were closer than some sisters."

Good girl, Cass, Sam thought. She caught it.

"Have you ever been married, Ms. Kirkland?"

"Objection, Your Honor, relevance."

"I will show relevance, Your Honor," DeLacey replied gleefully.

"Over-ruled. Please answer the question, Ms. Kirkland."

Cassie looked stonily at the defense attorney. "Yes."

"Are you divorced? Widowed?"

"Divorced."

"And the reason for that divorce?"

"Irreconcilable differences." Cassie was doing a great job of following Sam's instructions to keep her answers short and to the point, he just hoped she wasn't annoying the jury.

DeLacey was obviously annoyed. "Could you be more specific?"

"My former husband and I had a difference of opinion. He thought it was all right to abuse me, I disagreed. Every time I disagreed, he drank more, abused me more. After three years I'd had enough terror. I didn't want to wait around for his abuse to turn physical."

"And this failed marriage had nothing to do with your '*love*' of Mrs. Merritt?'

Cassie bristled at the implication, but kept her cool, except for the coldness that settled in her eyes, turning them from warm brown to deepest black. "No, it did not. Mich didn't even know I was getting a divorce until it was a done deal."

"In your earlier testimony you said Mr. Merritt was attentive to you and other friends of Mrs. Merritt and that you did not like his attentions, is that correct?"

"Yes, since he was engaged, I thought he should be faithful to Mich, not trying to seduce anyone around."

"Is it possible that Mr. Merritt was just being friendly, trying to be nice to the friends of his fiancée?"

"No, it is not. Man-handling other women is more than being *friendly*." Sam glanced at the jury and saw the women nodding in agreement. The men looked less convinced.

"So you do not like being handled by men, Ms. Kirkland, is that correct?"

Cassie glared at the innuendo and the pompous attorney who was getting away with asking it. "That is NOT correct, Mr. DeLacey. I do not like men who cheat on their wives and girlfriends. It's the supreme form of lying and abuse."

"Other than his attentions to you, how did you feel about Mr. Merritt?"

"He could be quite charming and fun when he wanted to be."

"So, if he wasn't married to your best friend, you might have been interested in him?"

Cassie thought about her answer just a little too long for Sam's comfort.

Cassie replied forcefully, "No, Mr. DeLacey, Larry Merritt would never be my type under any circumstances."

"Are you currently involved romantically with anyone, Ms. Kirkland?"

Cassie forced herself to avoid looking at Sam. "No, Mr. DeLacey."

"Have you had sex with a *man* since your divorce?"

Sam jumped to his feet. "Your Honor, this is really too much. Defense Counsel is asking totally irrelevant questions and impugning the witness's character."

Before the judge could respond, Cassie jumped in, ice dripping from her words, "No, Mr. DeLacey I have not had sex since my divorce, period."

DeLacey looked elated. "Were you jealous of your friend's happy marriage?"

"Hardly. It wasn't all that happy."

"How so?"

"Mich knew of Larry's infidelities, his extravagant gifts and expenditures on other women. The way he treated her hurt her deeply." Again, Cassie teared up.

"You really cared about her, didn't you?" Cassie was confused by DeLacey's sudden change of mood to one of sympathy.

"Yes," Cassie whispered through her tears.

"Did you know about the pain she could expect as the cancer progressed?"

"Yes, she and Doc both told me about her prognosis. There was going to be pain and drugs to control the pain, probably a loss of consciousness, and then she'd die."

"You didn't want your friend to go through all that pain and suffering, did you?"

"No, of course not. I wouldn't want anyone to go through it, not even you." Sam was pleased at Cassie's response and the jury's smiles.

Once again DeLacey changed directions. "In your career in Chicago I understand you were a program director for WGN, the television station. Is that correct?"

"Yes," Cassie answered wondering where this was going.

"And what qualifications does someone need to be a program director for a major station?"

Sam was on his feet again. "Objection, Your Honor. Relevance?"

"Please give me some latitude, Your Honor, and I can show relevance."

Judge Thomas said somewhat wearily, "Over-ruled. Please show relevance soon, Mr. DeLacey." Turning to Cassie, Judge Thomas said, "Please answer the question Ms. Kirkland."

Cassie thought a second before answering, "It takes someone with a talent for logistics, statistics, and planning."

"And would you say that Mr. Merritt possesses any of these qualities?"

Sam fumed, suddenly aware of DeLacey's new trap. Cassie again hesitated, apparently recognizing the trap, too. But she had to answer truthfully. "No."

"Tell me, Ms. Kirkland, what sort of hobbies do you have?"

"Objection, Your Honor, relevance again?"

DeLacey smiled ingratiatingly at the judge, "If you'll allow me, Judge, I'll show relevance."

"Continue."

DeLacey turned back to Cassie, crooking an eyebrow, waiting for her response.

"Hobbies?" Cassie's confusion at the question was obvious.

"Yes. Back in Virginia. I understand it's beautiful, lush foliage, lots of green, unlike our Colorado that's too dry for very many plants to flourish. Do you garden?"

Cassie perked up, she took great pride in her flowers, as did most every gardener in Lexington. "Yes, most of us in Lexington have some kind of garden, either flowers, or veg..."

DeLacey interrupted her. "And in that garden, do you have pests? Mice? Snakes? Bugs?"

Cassie immediately recognized the trap he was setting, she replied quietly and warily in the affirmative.

"And how do you control these vermin?"

Cassie chose her words carefully, "With a variety of insecticides and mice traps."

DeLacey looked suggestively toward the jury. Then he turned back to Cassie.

"Did you know Mrs. Merritt took pills to help her sleep?"

"Yes, she told me over lunch when I was visiting last May."

"Did you know where she kept the sleeping pills?"

Cassie hesitated, wrinkling her brow. "I never thought about it. I guess in the medicine cabinet or on the bedside table with the rest of her medicines."

"Please tell the court, Ms. Kirkland, why you waited five hours after your friend's death to call the police?"

Cassie bristled. "I did NOT wait five hours. I called them as soon as I found her. She went to bed the night before happy and smiling. I didn't worry about her not getting up when I did because she had slept late every morning since I'd been there. I just poked around the house that morning, had breakfast, read the paper, that sort of thing. About eleven I thought I'd see if she was okay, see if she wanted a cup of tea. When I went into the dark room she didn't say anything. I guessed she must have one of her migraines. She'd suffered from them as long as I knew her. She'd learned that the best recourse was a dark, warm room and silence. The only light in the room now was from the door I had opened; it shown directly on her bed.

"I tiptoed over to her bed and tapped her shoulder." Cassie paused, took a deep breath, and willed herself not to cry again in front of this boor. "As soon as I saw her face I knew she was dead. It was ghastly. I ran to my room and called 9-1-1."

DeLacey looked theatrically skeptical. "So let me get this straight. Your deathly ill, almost invalid friend went to bed the night before happy as a clam. She left you and her husband alone in the house. The next morning you're wandering around in your bedclothes for hours before you think to check on your 'best friend'. And then, miracle of miracles, she's dead."

"Objection, Your Honor, counselor is presenting facts not in evidence and making outrageous innuendoes."

Having created a mental image for the jury, DeLacey stated, "withdrawn" before Judge Thomas could rule.

Cassie jumped in. "She did not leave me alone with Larry, I went to bed, my own bed, at the same time Mich did and Larry went out for the evening; I don't know when he got back."

DeLacey looked askance for just a beat then asked his most important question, "Now, Ms. Kirkland, just a couple more quick questions. Having known the defendant for over ten years, would you say he is capable of murder?"

Cassie blanched at the question, immediately recognizing the trap. If she said "yes", would it be the truth? If she said "no", it as much as ruled him out as a suspect.

"Ms. Kirkland, did you understand the question?"

"Yes, Mr. DeLacey, I understand it. It's hard for me to imagine that Larry would have done it, but yes, I think he could." DeLacey obviously did not like her response so he rushed on.

"Isn't it true Ms. Kirkland that you loved your friend? That if you could not have her, you didn't want her with anyone else? That, loving her, you couldn't see her suffer. And, her death made you a very wealthy woman? Isn't all that true?"

"Your Honor, badgering the witness." Sam glowered.

Cassie's shocked face told the whole story, but she managed to stammer, "No, none of it is true."

"What part isn't true, Ms. Kirkland? You didn't love your friend? You did want her to suffer? That you did not inherit a fortune on her death?" DeLacey turned his back on Cassie. "I'm confused, Ms. Kirkland."

"Yes, it's true, but you make it sound..."

DeLacey interrupted again with his characteristic smirk, "Thank you for clearing that up, Ms. Kirkland. That's all."

He turned with a disgusted look to the judge, “No further questions of this witness, Your Honor.” Turning to Cassie, Judge Thomas said, “You are excused, Ms. Kirkland.”

Chapter 55

Cassie expelled a breath she hadn't known she was holding and shakily stepped down from the witness stand. As she did so, Sam rose to his full height and said, "The prosecution rests, Your Honor."

Reporters jumped to their feet and began to head for Cassie. Judge Thomas pounded his gavel to return order and announced that the trial would reconvene at 2 p.m. Everyone stood silently while the judge exited the courtroom, then pandemonium broke out again. Cassie had gotten only as far as Sam's table before court was dismissed. He grabbed her, turned her around, and propelled her to one of the small conference rooms in the back hall. Only lawyers and their invited personnel were allowed back there. Sam closed the door behind them.

"Great job, Cassie, you were super!"

Cassie slumped into the wooden chair closest to her, she was completely drained. She just looked up at Sam and gave him a wan smile. She rubbed her hands against the rough wool of her skirt, trying to dry the sweat that seemed to be dripping from every pore.

"You okay? Want some water? Can I do anything for you?"

Cassie smiled again and shook her head. "I'll be fine, just give me a minute." She paused, then looked deeply into Sam's eyes, her own eyes reflecting the shock of what she had just been through.

"How can he do that?" she whispered brokenly. "How can he get away with it? He tried to say Mich and I were lovers, then he hinted I had killed her so I could get Larry, then he tried to point the finger at me as a mercy killer. For God's sake, ME?" She was practically shrieking now, her whole body shaking, her hands pounding the graffiti-covered table in front of her. "Of course I did not want her to suffer, but I never would have killed her! Hell, I have a hard time killing ants in my kitchen. How can he say such things? Did the jury believe any of that? Can't I say something, make them understand I did none of those things?" She choked on the injustice of it all. She looked at Sam with tear-filled eyes. "Sam, what can we do?"

Sam pulled the other chair around next to hers and seated himself. He reached over and stilled Cassie's shaking hands by covering them with one of his big ones. Slowly he shook his head. "I know, Cassie, it's not fair and it's not right, but it is legal. A defense attorney can do almost anything short of slander to try and convince a jury of his client's innocence. And DeLacey is one of the best, from a defendant's viewpoint. All I can say is to the people who know you it won't matter and the people who don't know you don't matter." He shifted one hand from Cassie's to her shoulder and pulled her close; she rested her head on his shoulder and gave in to his supporting warmth.

A knock and Maria's head around the side of the door brought Sam's head up inquiringly, Cassie didn't move. "Do you want me to pick up lunch for you two," she asked, managing to keep the sisterly smile from her lips if not her eyes. "Yeah, that'd be great," Sam replied. "We still have to prep for John's witnesses." A small groan escaped Cassie's throat; she just wanted to stay where she was, forever if possible.

"Do you want me or Doc to sit in with you?" Maria asked.

Sam shook his head. "No, I think it will be better with just the two of us. Tell him he can go home if he wants, I'll get Cassie home after the afternoon session." His tone was completely professional but Maria wasn't sure his thoughts were. "Got it. Be back in a bit with lunch. I'll tell Doc, but you know he'll stay."

She quietly closed the door. Sam leaned back a bit and gazed at the ceiling, his hand still rubbing Cassie's now relaxing back. How long should he give her before he ruined the rest of her day? He waited and rubbed until he felt her sigh against his chest, her right hand now clasping his waist.

His thumb reached down and turned her face up to his. She looked trustingly into his eyes. "Hey, don't go to sleep, we've got a lot of work to do." Cassie nodded groggily, her eyes never wavering from his.

Sam took a deep breath. "What do I need to know about your ex-husband?"

Cassie's eyes turned to ice. She pushed herself up straight and forcibly shook herself back to the present. "Just when I thought this day couldn't get any worse. What do you want to know?"

"Whatever you think I need to know. I'm sure DeLacey is calling him as a means of discrediting your testimony, but I don't know what he can say to do that. Now's the time for you to be completely honest with me. Tell me what you think Kevin might say."

Cassie pulled herself together and stared icily at Sam. "I've always been honest with you, Sam. I have no idea what Kevin will say. I never knew what Kevin would say. He has PTSD. That makes him unpredictable. He can be sweet as candy one minute, mad as a tiger the next. There is no telling what will set him off. That's why I divorced him; I couldn't stand living in fear any more. I tried to stay with him; like Mich I believed in my marriage vows, but when he didn't care enough about me to get help for his PTSD, I left. I refused to live that way any longer. It made me sick to do it, physically, mentally, and psychologically sick, but I did it. I felt guilty for a long time. I mean he was a war veteran, he gave up his sanity for this country, but there was help available for him and he refused to take it. If he had just stopped drinking things would have been a lot better, but it was like he was happy the way things were and he didn't care whether I was happy or not." She paused for a breath.

"Did he ever get physically abusive with you?" Sam had to force the words out.

Cassie hesitated, then made her decision. She took a deep breath and forged on, "Just once. "I'd been sick in bed for four days with the flu, a really bad case. Fever. Chills. Nausea. The works. I had finally fallen into a restful sleep. Must have been about two in the morning. Kevin yanked the covers back, so drunk he could barely stand, grabbed my shoulder and flipped me onto my back. I was hardly awake and dopey from the meds I'd been taking; couldn't figure out what was going on. Then he was on top of me, muttering filth at me and forcing his way inside me. It was so dark I wasn't even sure it was Kevin until I heard his voice, and then I wished I hadn't. He kept calling me names, saying he hated me,

I'd ruined his life, and then more filth about what he was going to do to me. I tried to push him off, but he was too big and I was too weak. I beat at him and yelled his name over and over. Nothing worked. At least it was fairly quick, although it seemed an eternity. When he was done he just rolled off me and fell into a drunken stupor. I went out to the living room for the rest of the night, no more sleep for me."

Sam's hands clenched on the scarred tabletop. "Is that when you decided to leave?

"No, that was just two months after the wedding. As it turned out I was the poster child for abused women, even with all my education. I figured the rape was a one-time thing, and it was. I learned to get away from him when he got to his fourth or fifth drink of the night and never do or say anything that would upset him. Of course it was hard to tell what that might be; it could be me, something on TV, something in the paper, or just something that occurred to him. For two years I tried to talk him into counseling, to go to the VA for treatment for the PTSD. But he refused, said he didn't need any help. That I imagined everything." Cassie paused again, the worst of the telling over. "After another year, I just gave up, swallowed my pride, and left him. I just couldn't live in fear any more. I quit, and I've never been a quitter." She hung her head, afraid to look at Sam, afraid to see the disgust in his eyes.

Just then Maria sailed in with two box lunches and a two-liter bottle of Diet Coke. She took one look at Sam's angry face and Cassie's downtrodden head, and she said, "I'll stay. There's enough for all of us." She pulled out the other chair, started serving food onto the paper plates she'd brought and pouring Coke into plastic cups, all the while chattering about her toddler's latest fall.

Too soon it was time for Sam to return to court and Cassie to return to the lobby and Doc. Maria noticed the lack of conversation between them. Something had happened while she was getting lunch. Damn! She knew she should have stayed with them.

Chapter 56

Judge Thomas sat a bit straighter in his chair, glanced at his watch, and turned to the defense table, "Mr. DeLacey, call your first witness."

"The defense calls Kevin Alexander." A bailiff called for Kevin outside the courtroom.

Cassie, seated outside the courtroom felt herself tense as her ex-husband walked down the corridor from a small room down the hall and entered the courtroom without so much as a look at her. It was like all the air had suddenly been sucked out of the building. Doc reached over and patted her tightly gripped hands in her lap. Cassie wondered how she ever could have been taken in by his pretty-boy looks.

Just as the doors started to close, Kevin's head came around one of them and he gave her a smug, I've-got-you-now grin. Cassie's blood pressure was approaching overdrive, she could feel it mounting as her heart raced. It had NOT been an amicable divorce; Kevin could not believe *anyone*, let alone his calm, submissive wife, would want to leave him; he was a catch. Nonetheless, what could DeLacey hope to gain by calling Kevin? Kevin had never even met the Merritts.

A buzz started in the courtroom. Since the names were different it was unlikely the court-watchers knew who he was. But his striking appearance set them twittering, it had always been like that for him. Tall, blonde and tan, even this late in the year, he strode confidently to the witness stand, fully aware of the effect he had on casual acquaintances.

As if reading Cassie's thoughts through the courtroom walls, DeLacey asked Kevin to identify himself and then, "Mr. Alexander, how well did you know Mr. and Mrs. Merritt?"

"Not at all. I never met them." The jury rustled its confusion.

"Did you know ABOUT them?"

"Oh, yeah, I heard about them. ALL the time."

"How?"

"From my wife, my ex-wife, Cassie Kirkland."

Every spectator in the courtroom turned, sat a little straighter, as Sam leapt to his feet.

"Objection, Your Honor. The witness has just said he did not even know the Merritts, I fail to see what purpose there can be in his hear-say testimony."

DeLacey gave his characteristic smirk to Sam and wiped it off his face as he turned to the judge. "This witness goes to the credibility of the previous witness Cassie Kirkland, Your Honor."

"Very well, Mr. DeLacey. Please stay on point."

"Thank you, Judge."

Turning back to the witness, "How long were you and Ms. Kirkland married, Mr. Alexander?"

"Three years."

"And where did you live?"

"Chicago."

"So let me get this straight, you were married to Ms. Kirkland for three years, she claims she and Mrs. Merritt were best friends for twelve years, and yet you never met Mrs. Merritt or her husband?" His voice dripped incredulity.

"Wasn't Mrs. Merritt in your wedding? After all she and your ex-wife were best friends. Since you say you never met the Merritts, are you saying neither of them came to your wedding?"

Kevin Alexander appeared startled by the question, apparently it was one for which he had not been prepped. "Yeah, that's right, neither of them could take the time to hop a flight to Chicago; there are direct flights between Denver and Chicago every day, but no, not for them, her rich friends," he sneered, sounding like a spoiled child.

DeLacey decided his last minute question may not have been a good idea and tried to bring Alexander back on track. "How often did your ex-wife see the Merritts without you?"

"She and Michela got together once a year, but it was girls only. Cassie said it was their private time, no men allowed. And Cassie flew out to Denver every time Mich called, said she was sick, or had a hang-nail, whatever."

DeLacey looked askance at the witness, silently willing the jury to pick up on the implication he was trying to give. "What about Mr. Merritt. You two didn't get together, have a guys' weekend?"

"No, never met him. But I know all about him. He was the reason our marriage broke up. He was all Cassie could talk about. Larry this, Larry that. She drove me crazy, it was like she was obsessed by him or something."

Seated next to Sam now that Doc's and Cassie's testimonies were over, Maria wondered *Why didn't Sam object?* Kevin was twisting everything. He made it sound like Cassie was in love with Larry rather than that she loathed him as Maria was sure was the case from the conversations she had had with Cassie. Sure Cassie probably talked – more likely ranted – about him. Maria could only see the side of Sam's head, a pulse pounding in his neck, bent over his legal pad, making notes...or doodling for all she knew. Was he even paying attention? And then in an offhand manner...

"Objection, Your Honor. Witness is not qualified to give a professional clinical opinion." Sam did not even rise to voice his objection, subtly pointing out that Alexander's testimony wasn't worth the effort.

"Sustained."

"How was your marriage, Mr. Alexander? Was it a happy one?"

"Objection again, Your Honor. Relevance."

"If I may, Your Honor, the relevance will be apparent momentarily."

"All right. Over-ruled. You may answer the question, Mr. Alexander."

"Most of the time we were happy. Except when she'd get back from one of her trips with Michela; then she'd turn real frigid, wouldn't have anything to do with me for weeks. But then she'd get over it."

"By this you mean your sexual relations were strained?"

"Objection!" Sam shouted.

DeLacey jumped in, "Goes to motive, Your Honor."

"Over-ruled. Continue."

"Strained? I'll say. Non-existent is more like it. I guess she used it all up while she was away. But I got her straightened out right quick."

DeLacey hurried to cut off his words before his demeanor jeopardized the advantage won by his words. "Thank you, Mr. Alexander, that will be all.' He turned, "Your witness, Mr. Chambers."

Sam rose slowly and approached the witness. He hoped the loathing he felt did not show on his face...too much.

"Tell me, Mr. Alexander, do you ever have a night out with the boys? Poker? Bowling? The bar? That sort of thing?"

"Yeah, sure, every week. A couple of us go out for a few drinks, some laughs."

"Ever take a trip with the guys? Fishing? Hunting? Maybe Vegas?"

Kevin's eyes lit up and he grinned whole-heartedly, "Yeah, we went to Vegas a couple times, Atlantic City a couple times. I got lucky on all those trips, if you know what I mean," he smugly turned to the jury.

"I take it the wives did not go on these trips?"

"What? You gotta be kidding. This is for guys."

"And from your previous comment there was sex on these trips?"

"Objection. Relevance." DeLacey was trying his hardest to shut up his client.

"The defense opened the door, Your Honor, when he solicited information about Ms. Kirkland's sexual behavior."

"That's right, Mr. DeLacey, you did. Over-ruled. Proceed, Mr. Chambers."

"So, Mr. Alexander, did you ever have sex on these trips?"

"Well, sure. We were gone from home a week." Two male spectators sniggered; the women were glaringly silent.

"Did you have sex with any of the guys on these trips?

Alexander sat up straighter and pointed his finger directly at Sam's nose, "Hey! I'm no fag. We just picked up some broads in the bars. It was just sex, we weren't going to marry them or anything."

"Of course not. You were already married weren't you?"

The audience realized Sam was ridiculing the witness, but the realization hadn't quite hit Kevin Alexander yet. And then it did.

"Hey! I'm a guy. Guys have needs."

Switching tactics, Sam slid the next question in very softly, "So how did you 'straighten out' your wife when she failed to satisfy these needs, Mr. Alexander? Did you hit her?"

"NO! I'd never hit a woman." Kevin was obviously affronted by the question.

"Did you rape her?"

"Rape, of course not, she's my wife. Wives are supposed to provide for their husband's needs. Sometimes she forgot that part of her vows, so I had to remind her." Sam could see the questioning look on the faces of the jury. Here was this well-spoken, good looking, educated man, talking like someone from the turn of the last century.

"Did she need reminding any times other than when she returned from these trips with Michela?" Sam was working very hard to keep the disgust out of his voice.

"Sometimes. She was real stubborn, she'd get her back up, call me names. And she cried; I hated it when she cried."

"So let me get this straight. Your wife – whom you vowed to love and cherish – didn't appreciate your educational efforts, she took a trip once a year, just like you and the guys, after a week of fun and relaxation she came home ready for a fight. And you re-educated her again, and again. Is that about right?"

Kevin looked steadily at the attorney before him. "It wasn't like you're making it sound, you've got it all twisted."

"And you think she was having an affair with Larry Merritt? You think she was interested in sex with *anyone* after the way you treated her? You think the Merritts broke up your marriage? Wherever did you get such an idea?"

"Mr. DeLacey said it sounded like it to him." The jury laughed out loud at that. DeLacey looked stricken.

"While we're talking about weddings, Mr. Alexander, did the Merritts ever give a reason for not attending yours?"

"They had some lame excuse about Michela being too sick to travel, but I know lots of people who travel even when they're sick."

"I understand you and your former wife met at work. Where was that?"

"WGN, in Chicago. She was a newbie in scheduling and I was an editor, been there a few years already. I sort of took her under my wing, taught her the ropes, who to kiss up to, who to ignore, that sort of thing."

"Do you enjoy editing?"

"Oh, yes. Love it. You get to see everyone the way they really are and then take out all the bad stuff and make them come off like angels, or the other way around, depending on the story's slant."

"And do you still work at WGN?"

Kevin visibly squirmed in his chair and gave his briefest answer yet, "No."

"And why is that, Mr. Alexander. I thought you liked the work."

"Objection, your honor, relevance."

"Goes to the witness's credibility, Your Honor."

"Over-ruled. Please answer the question, Mr. Alexander."

Kevin gave a quick, nervous glance toward DeLacey. DeLacey returned it with a confused look of his own. It was obvious to Sam that DeLacey had no idea where he was going with this. Kevin licked his lips and replied, "Down-sizing."

"So you're saying, under threat of being accused of perjury, that you were let go because of budget problems at WGN. Is that correct?"

"Well, partially, and some new hire accused me of sexual harassment, said I made inappropriate comments to her and touched her inappropriately."

"Which of course you didn't do, did you?"

"Hell, I don't know what is appropriate these days! Some women get pissed if you hold the door for them, some get pissed if you don't! Maybe I did, but it was her word against mine. WGN couldn't afford any bad publicity so they gave me a nice severance and showed me the door."

"No more questions, Your Honor." Sam didn't even try to hide his disgust this time.

"You are excused, Mr. Alexander." Judge Thomas quickly surveyed the jury and realized the last two witnesses had worn them to a frazzle. "Court will reconvene at 9 a.m. tomorrow morning. I remind the members of the jury not to discuss this trial or any of the testimonies with anyone." Judge Thomas appeared to be in a hurry to get away himself.

Chapter 57

Wednesday was another bright and sunny day; one in which the dry cold of Denver's high desert made it feel warmer than the thermometer's 38 degrees said. Court reconvened promptly at 9 a.m. At this point, Cassie and Doc were the only ones left on the benches outside the courtroom, although they were sure there were other witnesses secreted in the small rooms down the hall, as Kevin had been.

As soon as the preliminary procedures were completed, DeLacey bounced to his feet, once again eager to enter the fray. His likeness to Andy Warhol was even more pronounced with his addition of round glasses and his hair more tousled than usual. "The defense calls Patrick Marshall." A bailiff went to the center doors and called the name into the empty hallway.

A man about fifty approached the center doors. He had a short haircut and military bearing. There was no doubt in Cassie's mind he was a Marine in civilian clothes; they all had the same erect, confident stature, but without the swagger of insecure people. Who he was was another question. She'd never seen him before although there was something familiar about him. Patrick Marshall ignored the heavy swoosh the doors made as they swung closed behind him.

"Mr. Marshall, state your profession please." Even DeLacey seemed impressed by the quiet confidence of his own witness.

"I'm a security consultant."

"And what exactly do you do as a security consultant?"

"Pretty much whatever the client wants. My company follows people, does background checks, serves as bodyguards, does credit checks. We're full service."

"What are your credentials for being a security consultant?"

"I was in the Marine Corps security forces for ten years, then a Treasury agent for twenty years. I had a lot of experience in all phases of security, from identity theft to terrorism. After I retired I decided to put my skills to work and augment my meager government retirement pay." He looked at the jury with clear blue eyes and said, "The government doesn't pay its employees very well, at least not as compared to private industry. You have to be pretty dedicated to work for the government 'cause you'll never get rich, at least not if you're honest." A few jurors nodded their heads in agreement or commiseration. A few chuckled, seemingly in agreement.

"And you were hired by me to do what?"

"You asked me to check out Ms. Kirkland."

"What reason did I give you for wanting this investigation?"

"You said she was the only other person around when Mrs. Merritt died, other than your client of course."

DeLacey gamely ignored the last part of the consultant's statement.

"And how did you perform this investigation?"

"I sent people to her home town, Lexington, Virginia and to her last place of employment, WGN in Chicago. We checked her credit history and her credit card charges. We got her phone logs. We talked to friends, coworkers, and her neighbors, in both Chicago and Virginia."

"And what did you discover?"

"Not much. She worked at WGN in Chicago for almost five years, right out of college. Everybody we talked to thought highly of her. After her divorce she moved back to her home town. Her parents still lived there, but they died two years ago in a car accident; Ms. Kirkland inherited the house and some money. She works as a librarian at the public library. Been there a little over three years. Again, highly thought of. Doesn't seem to date. Seems to enjoy books – which I guess is a good thing for a librarian." He chuckled at his humor and the jury did too.

"What about her credit? Anything unusual there?"

"Well, yes, there was. She doesn't carry any credit card balances. Has what bankers refer to as a solid gold credit rating. Her house's mortgage was paid off by her parents, she has one year left on a car loan, other than that nothing. Now that's really unusual these days...someone who lives within her means."

Sam was beginning to wonder where this was going. Why was DeLacey setting Cassie up as such a great person when she was one of the possible escapes for his client? This wasn't like him at all.

"Were you able to get her phone logs?"

The witness hesitated. "Yeah, I found a guy who had a cousin who worked at the local phone company; he got them for me." Knowing he was on a slippery legal surface he hurried on.

"Ms. Kirkland spent a lot of time on calls to the Merritts' home in Colorado, several times a week. She called there more than calls came from there."

"And how long were these calls?"

"Some were real quick, less than a minute, others were as long as an hour."

"And who did she talk to?"

Marshall looked rueful. "I'm good, Mr. DeLacey, but there's no way to know that. Technology only tells us where the call went and where it came from, we can't tell who was on the phone without recording the conversation."

"So anyone could have called the Merritt house from Ms. Kirkland's house?"

"Technically, yes. But since Ms. Kirkland lives alone, except for her dog, it's a pretty safe conclusion that she made the calls."

"But you can tell who owned the phone she called, can't you?"

"Oh, sure, she called the house phone and the cell phone of Mrs. Merritt."

"In your investigations did you find any indication of a romantic interest on the part of Ms. Kirkland?"

"Objection, Your Honor. Relevance?"

"Your Honor, Ms. Kirkland stated she has had no romantic life since her divorce."

"Agreed. You may answer the question, Mr. Marshall."

"No, nothing on a regular basis. Although she did have one interesting visitor the week we watched her back in September."

"Interesting how?"

"It was ADA Chambers. He arrived on Friday afternoon and left mid-afternoon Saturday."

DeLacey turned and stared at Sam, a feral gleam in his eye. "Are you saying he spent the night?"

"Nope, he spent one evening and part of the next day with Ms. Kirkland. He slept at a hotel."

DeLacey paused and let this latest bit of news sink in with the jury. He knew it meant next to nothing, but you never knew what little tidbit would turn a juror's mind and verdict.

Moving on, DeLacey asked, "Did you see any evidence of any kind of poison at Ms. Kirkland's house?"

"Just in with her gardening stuff. Rat poison."

"No books on poison on her nightstand?" DeLacey chuckled, showing that he too had a sense of humor. Marshall joined him.

"Well, no, we didn't search her house, but she does work in a library. She doesn't need to own books to use them."

"Objection. Conclusion by the witness."

"Sustained."

DeLacey grinned. "That's all, Mr. Marshall, thank you."

Sam obviously couldn't wait to get to his questioning.

"Mr. Marshall, in your professional opinion, do you find it unusual to find poison in a gardening shed?"

Marshall hesitated, aware of the trap Sam had set. There was no way he could answer that would not get him into trouble, either with DeLacey, his best client, or with the jury. "No, Mr. Chambers, plant poison is not unusual, but rat poison might be."

"And did you interview Ms. Kirkland? Did she have a rat problem at her house, maybe mice in her garden?"

"No, we did not talk with Ms. Kirkland."

"Then you did not ask her the purpose of the rat poison?

"No."

"And since you didn't speak to her you did not ask her the purpose of my visit either, did you?"

Marshall blanched at the unexpected shift in questioning. "No."

"So, as far as you or your men know, I could have been there on official business or on a vacation or a job interview or any number of reasons could have taken me to Lexington, Virginia over a weekend. Is that true?"

Marshall had decided monosyllabic replies were the best course. "Yes."

"Mr. Marshall, in your work as a security consultant, are you aware of the TSA rules for carrying "lethal weapons" onto an airplane?"

"Yes."

"According to the TSA, would rat poison be a 'lethal weapon'?"

"Yes."

"Is it against the law for anyone to carry rat poison onto an airplane?"

"Yes."

"And are there severe punishments for doing so?"

"Yes."

"So, Mr. Marshall, in your background checking of Ms. Kirkland, did you check for police records?"

"Yes." At this point it was obvious to everyone where Sam was going and Marshall was resigned to his fate. He'd just lost DeLacey as a client.

"And in your professional check of Ms. Kirkland's police record, what did you find?"

"Nothing."

"Nothing, Mr. Marshall? No parking tickets? No speeding tickets? No burglary charges? No assault charges? Nothing?"

"Just one call in Chicago where she called 9-1-1, recorded as a domestic disturbance." Marshall squirmed in his seat, knowing what he was doing to DeLacey's star witness.

"So, Mr. Marshall, in your professional opinion, would Ms. Kirkland, a librarian with not so much as a parking ticket, a rule-follower, and a dedicated helper to the students and faculty in the town where she works, would she have taken rat poison from her gardening shed to Colorado on an airplane? When she must have known it was illegal?"

Marshall hesitated again, trying to come up with an answer that would be honest and keep him out of further hot water with DeLacey.

DeLacey tried to forestall his answer. "Objection, Your Honor, calls for a conclusion by the witness."

"Objection over-ruled."

Marshall gave up. "No, but she didn't have to take it on the plane, she could have bought it here or she could have packed it into her checked luggage."

Sam tried a new tack, ""How old was the rat poison in the gardening shed? Newer versions do not have cyanide."

"It was pretty old. Looked like it hadn't been used in a while." Marshall did a mental *phew*, maybe he could save the day with DeLacey after all.

"Just one more question, Mr. Marshall. How did you get into the locked gardening shed? Wouldn't you need some kind of legal form to enter private property?"

Marshall looked sheepish. "I looked through the windows, saw the stuff on the counter."

"I take it then you didn't actually hold the box of rat poison, you just surmised its age by looking through the window?

Marshall quietly agreed.

Sam continued in an incredulous tone of voice. "So let me see if I'm understanding you correctly. You looked through a window into a dark gardening shed and saw a container of rat poison on a counter. Was the counter under the window or across the room?"

Marshall tried to ignore the beads of sweat forming under his armpits and on his forehead. He looked to the ceiling, apparently trying to review the layout in his mind. "Sort of at a right angle to the window, on a side wall. It was a tall, thin box. Said Rat Killer in big red letters across the front."

"And please explain to the jury how you knew there was rat poison in the box if you did not touch it. Could it have been an empty box?"

"No, there was poison in it."

"I repeat, how did you know? Maybe the box was kept as a reminder to buy more, or as a reminder of a brand that didn't work?"

Marshall knew he was screwed. "I found the door unlocked and went in and looked around. The box was half full."

"And did you do this looking around without a warrant?"

"Yes, no warrant."

Sam stared at the witness in disgust. "Your Honor, I move to strike this witness's testimony as fruit of the poisoned tree."

DeLacey bounded to his feet, his face turning red. "I object, Your Honor. People wander in and out of other people's garages all the time. The lack of a warrant does not change the fact that Ms. Kirkland had ready-access to poison containing cyanide."

"Mr. Chambers' objection is sustained. Mr. Marshall, you are excused but please keep yourself available. The jury will ignore the testimony of this witness. Court will reconvene at 2 p.m. this afternoon. I will confer with both attorneys in my chambers, **now**."

Judge Thomas stood in obvious fury and exited through the door behind his desk, his black robe swirling like an angry cloud behind him.

Sam and DeLacey glanced at each other then followed the judge through the same door. The spectators and reporters stood and stretched then headed for the courthouse cafeteria, glad of the early recess. Maria hurried out to the lobby to explain to Doc and Cassie what was going on, realizing they would hear the hubbub of voices from the usually silent courtroom and seeing everyone leaving so early, before the normal lunch break.

Judge Thomas flung his robe onto the back of one of the chairs surrounding his small conference table. With hands on hips, he glared at the two attorneys as they entered.

"Listen, you two, and listen well. I don't know what's going on between you, but I've had enough. No more sniping at each other. No more nit-picking at witnesses. No more getting witnesses on the stand when you know their testimony will be disallowed. I won't have it. I want everything to be up front and above-board. Do I make myself clear?"

Both men sheepishly nodded their agreement.

"All right. Remember it. I'll see you after lunch."

Sam and DeLacey left the judge's chambers without another word to him or each other.

Doc, Cassie and Maria approached a much-chastened Sam as he left the courtroom. "Sam, how's it going?"

"We may have won some points today, Doc. We won't know for sure until the verdict comes in and we're a ways away from that."

"Does DeLacey have a lot more witnesses?"

"I doubt it, probably some rebuttal witnesses to try and refute what our experts said. Most of the primary testimony was covered by my witnesses and his cross."

"Is Larry scheduled to testify?" Doc asked hopefully, realizing how much damage Larry could do to himself on the witness stand.

"Not right now. I think DeLacey would be nuts to put him on the stand. Larry is a ticking bomb, no telling what he'll say or do. Right now I think we're pretty even on points, but Larry could tip it way over in our favor. Ultimately it's Larry's decision, and he's got enough ego to think he can win the case on the stand. We'll just have to see." Sam grabbed Maria's arm, nodded at Cassie and headed off, "We have to prepare for this afternoon, Doc, excuse us." Sam barely looked in Cassie's direction.

Chapter 58

Promptly at 2 p.m., the court came to order and DeLacey had Andrew Crockett called to the stand.

"Please state your name and profession for the jury."

Crockett was obviously at ease on the stand, and probably everywhere else. His six foot four frame barely fit in the box and yet he looked very comfortable. He smiled graciously at DeLacey and the jury. His deep voice resonated, "Andrew Crockett, Chief of Surgery at the CU Medical Center and chair of the Colorado Medical Association."

"Dr. Crockett, as chair of the Medical Association, what is your role?"

The elegant surgeon smiled in self-deprecation. "Like the chair of any committee or group, I facilitate meetings and oversee the function of the organization."

"And what *is* the function of the Colorado Medical Association?" DeLacey looked very intent, despite his blonde hair flopping into his eyes, leaning close to his witness in apparent interest.

"In a nutshell and without getting too technical, the purpose of any medical association is to oversee the licensing of physicians, to ensure doctors act ethically, and to handle any inappropriate ethical, medical, or licensing actions."

"Sounds like a big order. Aren't ethics hard to judge? It seems they would be rather subjective."

Sam was on his feet, trying to close off the line of questioning, even though he knew he would not succeed. "Your Honor, where is defense going with this line of questioning? I see no relevance to this trial." In fact, Sam saw all too well the impending relevance, and didn't like it a bit.

"My next question will show its relevance, Your Honor."

"Very well. Over-ruled. Please answer the question, Dr. Crockett."

"All physicians take an oath when they become licensed, vowing to do no harm. That forms the basis of all ethical questions. There is also a code of conduct defined by the American Medical Association and generally accepted practices that regulate what a doctor can, cannot, should, should not do. All these together guide us in determining whether a doctor has overstepped his or her proper functions."

"And in all those guidelines, is there anything that says a doctor should not treat family members?"

"Most certainly. Of course it does not apply to minor things, like applying bandaids or giving out aspirins or even providing treatment in an emergency, but doctors are not supposed to treat family members because of the emotional involvements that could cloud their decisions. They most definitely are precluded from writing prescriptions for family members."

DeLacey hesitated, letting the comments sink in with the jury. "In other words, no doctor should treat a blood relative, is that correct?"

"Blood or not, no member of the immediate family, that includes adopted children and step-children."

"And by 'immediate family' you mean spouse, parents, children?"

"Exactly."

"And is there a penalty for such an infraction?"

"Of course. It depends on the exact nature of the treatment and the length of time it went on."

"Hypothetically speaking, if a doctor treated his daughter for cancer for five years, would that be something the Colorado Medical Association would look into?"

Dr. Crockett sat a bit straighter in the chair and looked directly at the jury, "This is something we would take very seriously."

"Thank you, Dr. Crockett, that will be all." DeLacey tried in vain to hide the smirk lurking at the corners of his mouth.

Sam stood fully erect behind the prosecution table and faced the doctor. "Just two questions, Dr. Crockett. Are there ever extenuating circumstances in how you handle cases that come before the ethics committee?"

"Of course. Each case is handled on its own merits. When dealing with medicine and people, there are no hard and fast rules or judgments. We must treat each occurrence as it is presented."

"So, Doctor, hypothetically speaking in the case Mr. DeLacey presented to you a few minutes ago, if the woman did not know the doctor was her father, and if he was the best oncologist in Colorado and therefore the best doctor to treat her, would that have a bearing on your decision?"

Dr. Crockett took a moment before he answered. "I cannot give you a direct answer without knowing all the facts in your hypothetical case, but I can reiterate that extenuating circumstances would be considered in any case brought before the ethics committee or the licensing board."

"Thank you for your candor, Doctor. That's all I have."

"You are excused, Dr. Crockett."

DeLacey stood up to forestall the judge's next words. "Your Honor, my next witness may be lengthy. I'd like to ask that we adjourn until tomorrow?"

Judge Thomas glanced at his watch. "Very well, Mr. DeLacey. Is that all right with you, Mr. Chambers?"

"No problem, Your Honor."

Judge Thomas banged his wooden gavel against its wooden block, "Court is adjourned until 9 a.m. tomorrow." Everyone rose as the judge exited through the door behind his bench. Spectators started gathering their belongings, and slowly made their way out to the lobby and the bright Colorado sunshine. DeLacey patted Larry Merritt on the shoulder and smiled a winning smile. *Grandstanding to the crowd*, Sam thought to himself.

Cassie and Doc made their way to Sam and Maria at the prosecution table. Doc said, "Sam, I saw Andy Crockett go in. I can guess what he was here for; revoking my license will make me look guilty. I can handle it," Doc spoke without preamble, "I'll even plead guilty; better I go to jail than Cassie."

Sam, Maria and Cassie were obviously shocked by his comment. All three started talking at once. Sam overrode the two women. "Whoa, let's not get carried away. We're still a long way from this being over. All DeLacey is trying to do is muddy the waters, and I have to admit he's doing a damn good job of it. But that's all, he hasn't proven anything, just hinted. He doesn't HAVE to prove anything. I'd like a bit more confidence from you three. I think I proved that Larry did it, even if we don't have a smoking gun; I proved that he had means, motive, and opportunity which is more than either of you two had. So let's all settle down and wait it out. You two go home and get some sleep. Maria and I are going to prep for DeLacey's next witness and closing arguments. See you in the morning."

Cassie spoke for the first time. "Is it Larry?"

Sam nodded and looked directly in her eyes, "DeLacey says Larry's going to testify, but I don't know when. I can't believe he's taking the stand, but he is. That's why Maria and I have to be ready for tomorrow."

Maria spoke up for the first time, "Sam, Greg wants to see you as soon as we're done here, too." Sam scowled and headed off muttering to himself. *Great! Just what I need, second-guessing from the coach.*

Half an hour later, having gulped a Coke and pack of peanut butter crackers, Sam strolled into Greg Lawrence's office down the street from the courthouse. Without any pleasantries, Greg jumped right in.

"How's it going, Sam?"

"About like I expected. John is pointing his polished fingers at anyone and everyone who could have been in contact with Michela Merritt. Sometimes the shotgun approach works, sometimes it doesn't."

"What's your gut telling you?"

"I think we're a bit ahead. It's a seemingly smart jury, they tested well at least. I don't think John's innuendoes are having as big an impact as he hoped. On the other hand Cassie was a very compelling witness. Especially a librarian who comes across like she does, all soft and sweet and competent, and a fierce friend. Everybody who looks at her feels like they know her, that she's someone they can trust. I've seen it happen. Men and women both do a double-take, like they can't believe that they're seeing someone they know; it's weird. I could understand men staring at her, she's very attractive, but women do it too."

"I'm glad you brought that up, Sam. As we discussed before, I think you're getting in over your head here. If you weren't so far into the case, I'd assign someone else to take over. It feels like you're too emotionally involved."

"Why do you say that, Greg? What have you heard? I am not *too* involved."

"I haven't *heard* anything. I sat in the courtroom yesterday, when that detective was testifying. What were you thinking? You went all the way to Virginia and spent the weekend with a witness? At the very least it could lead to disciplinary action. At the worst it could jeopardize the case!"

"Just a damn minute, Greg! I cleared it with you. Someone had to go get the hard drive and backups from her computer, what difference did it make whether it was me or someone else? Cassie has no one. Her best friend had just been killed. She's halfway across the country with no one to talk to, no one to tell her what's going on. I felt sorry for her; sue me, fire me. Yes, we spent time together, but nothing happened that would not have happened regardless of who went to get the flash drives; we talked, we walked, we ate, I gave myself a tour of her hometown. Alone. I was trying to console a very lonely woman. But she's also a very nice, very friendly woman; she would have been nice to anyone who showed up."

Greg's fingers were steepled under his chin as he silently studied his protégé. Sam was right, on the surface there was nothing wrong. But Greg could feel that *he* was right too, Sam was too close to this case, too close to 'Cassie'. "You assure me it was purely in the line of duty that you went out there?"

Sam hesitated, he didn't know what his feelings were now, but at the time he went to Virginia, "Yes, purely professional."

"Okay, just stay away from her until this case is over. No phone calls, no contact of any kind where you are alone with her. Her testimony is over so there should be no reason for you to be contacting her other than to be 'nice'. If something needs to be said to her, let Maria do it. We cannot take a chance on losing this one on appeal because of any glimmer of inappropriate contact between a DA and a witness. Is that clear?"

Sam glared at his boss, but agreed and changed the subject. "Do you think they'll appeal?"

"Why not? What have they got to lose? All they have to do is find grounds for an appeal, and I don't want it to be this office. Of course, that assumes they lose the verdict in the first place. Right now I think it can go either way. It will depend on Larry Merritt's testimony and your summation." He paused. "Don't blow it. I knew Michela and Larry socially; I liked her. And I liked her art; she will be missed."

Sam grinned his lopsided grin and assured the Jefferson County DA that he was ready and eager to finish the trial and with a positive outcome for their side.

Sam rose and left the office. Out in the hall he took in a deep breath and stared at the beige wall in front of him. *What **are** my feelings for Cassie? Is Greg right? Am I too close to her and this case?* Sam closed his eyes and leaned back against the wall, taking another deep breath. *Guess I'll have to wait until the trial is over to find out.*

Across town, John DeLacey was holding a similar conversation with his client. "I think it can go either way at this point, Larry. But it can swing in their favor if you blow it on the witness stand. I still don't think you should testify."

Larry shrugged his shoulders and glared at his attorney. "John, I'm going to testify. I have to tell everyone I did not kill my wife. How can I blow it? You are getting paid very highly to ensure I don't get blind-sided on the witness stand. We've gone over the DA's potential questions. I know the answers backward and forward."

"As I've told you repeatedly, Larry, we cannot foresee every possible question Chambers might throw at you. If you elaborate on your answers, or get off on a tangent, you may give him an opening to new avenues that we can't predict." The blonde attorney wondered not for the first time why he had ever taken on this egotistical client; he certainly didn't need the money and right now it looked like the publicity he was hoping for might not be the kind he wanted.

"If you don't keep your answers short and direct, you can blow this whole case and end up going to prison for the rest of your life. I'm not sure you are capable of doing this, Larry." He stared at his client like a chastising headmaster.

"Don't worry, John, I can handle it. I'll put that pompous attorney in his place and get my freedom at the same time. Piece of cake."

"It's NOT a piece of cake, Larry. Sam Chambers is an excellent DA and he'll take advantage of any opening you give him. Forget about putting him in his place and just answer his questions." He paused. "Better yet, take my advice and don't testify."

Larry rose and stared down at his prestigious attorney, he balanced his fists on the desk between them and said, "I'm going to testify, John, end of discussion." He straightened and gave a cocky grin to his attorney as he turned for the door. "Right now I've got a buxom blonde waiting for me. See you in court tomorrow, counselor." He turned breezily and left the office. John DeLacey stared after him, a worried frown on his tanned face. *Shit! This is going to be a disaster.*

Chapter 59

The usual routine was followed at 9 a.m. Thursday morning when DeLacey asked that Magdelena Rostoff be sworn in.

The bailiff escorted a small, Hispanic woman in her mid-fifties to the stand. Magdelena Rostoff was dutifully sworn and DeLacey approached her.

"Ms. Rostoff, please tell the court your relationship with Michela Merritt."

Tears immediately welled in the woman's brown eyes. "I was her housekeeper and friend for twenty years, since she was a little girl. I cared for her when she was home from boarding school" she said in strong, unaccented English.

"So you spent a lot of time in the house?"

"Yes, during the day, but not in the evenings, not since she got married."

"Did you ever see Mr. and Mrs. Merritt together?"

The little woman sat up straighter in the hard wooden chair. "Sometimes, but not often; he was gone during the day."

Even though she was DeLacey's witness, it was like pulling teeth to get to the answers he wanted.

"When you did see them together, how would you describe their relationship?"

"Okay."

"Let me rephrase my question, Ms. Rostoff. Did you see them argue, fight? Were they affectionate, friendly, loving? Do any of those words apply to what you saw?"

"No."

"What do you mean 'no'?" DeLacey was at his wit's end.

"I would say they were distant. Miss Mich tried to be affectionate, friendly, but Mr. Larry ignored her. Mostly he just stayed away, from the house and from her."

"So you did not see them fight, is that correct?"

Elena hesitated, she knew what the lawyer was trying to get her to say and she did not want to give it to him. Resignedly she replied, "That is correct, I never saw them fight."

DeLacey smirked and turned to the prosecution table, "Your witness."

Sam stood tall and approached the witness with a smile. "Ms. Rostoff, you say you were 'housekeeper and friend' to Michela Merritt. Does that mean she confided in you?"

The round little witness sat taller but continued to look fearful, not knowing where this other attorney was going. "Yes, she did."

"What types of things did she tell you?"

Softly, Elena replied, "She told me she loved her husband and would never divorce him, even if he asked."

"To your knowledge, Ms. Rostoff, had Mr. Merritt asked for a divorce?"

"No. Miss Mich said he never would because he wanted **all** her money."

"Thank you, Ms. Rostoff. That is all we needed to hear."

At the same time that Sam was smiling at Elena, DeLacey shouted "OBJECTION, Your Honor. Hear-say evidence of the worst kind. Extremely prejudicial."

Judge Thomas leaned over to the witness stand and told Elena Rostoff she could leave. He turned back to the courtroom and the jury. "Sustained. Jury will disregard the witness's last statement."

"Call your next witness, Mr. DeLacey."

"The defense calls Larry Merritt to the stand." The jury and spectators straightened in their chairs and stopped rustling their papers and clothes.

Merritt strolled to the stand as though he had no cares in the world. He looked like the Big Man On Campus he had been thirteen years previously: sandy blonde hair carefully styled, dark blue suit, Ben Silver striped tie. He forcefully affirmed that he would tell the truth and took his seat. DeLacey approached him with a legal pad dangling from his long, tapered fingers. His head rose like a lion sniffing the air for dinner. His eyes bored into his client's.

"Mr. Merritt, did you kill your wife?" DeLacey surprised everyone with his opening question. The jury perked up. Sam Chambers looked startled. The spectators stopped wriggling on the hard benches. Only Judge Thomas managed to maintain his impartial demeanor. It was as though everyone in the courtroom was holding their collective breaths to hear the answer to the ultimate question.

"No, I most certainly did not." DeLacey started to speak but Larry continued, "Why would I? She was dying anyway. A couple more months, a year tops, and I would have been rid of her." DeLacey forcefully interrupted his over-talkative witness.

"Did you love your wife, Mr. Merritt?"

"Yes, once I did." Again DeLacey tried to keep Larry to short answers and again Larry kept going. Sam was delighted! "But then she became obsessed with having children and when her daughter died you would have thought she was the only one who had ever lost a child." DeLacey cut him off, wanting to do it literally. He had stressed to Larry the need to keep his answers short, without elaboration.

"How was your sex life?"

"What sex life? She was usually too sick and definitely not interested. So I found comfort elsewhere. Michela knew about it, she didn't care, as long as I didn't bother her."

"Did you order books about poison?"

"No, not my style. I'm more the sports type, magazines mainly."

"Please tell the court what happened in the days before your wife died."

"Not much to tell. I was out of town, got back the day after Cassie got to town, so Cassie had 24 hours to continue lying about me to Mich."

"Objection, Your Honor, supposition, no basis in fact."

"Sustained. Please keep to the facts, Mr. Merritt, not things you think may have happened."

"Anyway, the three of us got along fine. Friday night we sat around talking, having a few drinks, then I went to see Lisa and got home about two a.m. The house was dark, they hadn't even left a light on for me. I went upstairs. Just as I was passing Mich's door, she called me in and asked me to get her a glass of water and some pills from the bathroom, said she was getting one of her damned migraines. I did; she asked me to open the bottle because the lid was too tight for her shaky hands to manage. I opened it and put a couple pills on the nightstand for her next to the water glass. I asked her if there was anything else she needed. She said no and I went on to my room and went to sleep.

"I got up about five-thirty, showered and shaved, and headed for the golf club. Had an early tee time, 7:15. I left the house about 6:30. The rest of the guys were there, we had a quick breakfast, warmed up with a bucket of balls, and headed out to the course. Had one of my best rounds ever, shot 84; the course played really fast, too; no slowpokes ahead of us for a change. Came back in, changed our shoes and were just getting ready to go to the bar when the deputy arrived and said I needed to come home.

"I got home about 11:30, maybe a bit after, and they told me Mich was dead. Way to ruin a good round of golf."

"Did you know your wife had changed her will, virtually cutting you out and leaving everything to her *friend* Cassandra Kirkland?"

"Well, it's not like she cut me off completely, couldn't do that. I still get a couple million. But Cassie gets the bulk of the art and that's where the real money is. I could have sold those for a mint, especially after her 'untimely death", as the papers call it. And no, I didn't know about the change in the will."

"Was anyone else in the house when you weren't there?"

"Objection, Your Honor. If he wasn't there how could he know?" The jury giggled at the obvious stupidity of the question.

DeLacey glowered, "I'll rephrase."

He turned back to the witness, smoothing his features into a look acceptable for the jury to see. "Mr. Merritt, of your own knowledge do you know of anyone else who was at the house either while you were away or while you were sleeping?"

"The only one I know of was Cassie. She was there the night before and she was there the next morning when I left for golf."

"Does anyone else have a key to the house?"

"The housekeeper, of course, and Doc. And we keep a spare key outside the house for emergencies."

"So anyone could have gotten into the house in the night?"

"Sure, anybody could have killed Mich."

"Mr. Merritt, I ask you again, did you kill your wife? Please answer yes or no."

Larry Merritt turned to the jury and forcefully said, "No."

DeLacey let the drama sink in for a few seconds, then "Thank you, that will be all." DeLacey returned to his seat with a silent prayer that Larry would shut up. This was always the danger of putting the defendant on the stand, the prosecution got a chance to ask questions in open court with the defendant under oath, not that John DeLacey had any illusions about Larry being concerned with a little thing like an oath. In fact, John DeLacey had no illusions about his client whatsoever.

Larry straightened his blue and gold striped tie, smoothed his suit coat, sitting on it like news anchors do, and flicked an imaginary piece of lint from his sleeve. He also developed a light sheen of sweat on his forehead. His right hand combed his carefully casual hair back from his forehead with a nervous motion. *Keep your answers short*, he thought to himself. *Just do what John told you, don't talk so much!*

"Mr. Merritt, we are all sorry for your loss."

Larry had expected a hardball question right off the bat. Sam's sympathy disconcerted him. "Thank you," he mumbled.

"If I may, I'd like to follow up on a couple questions Mr. DeLacey had for you. How do you know Ms. Kirkland was in her room when you left for golf?" Sam asked the question very softly.

"What do you mean, how do I know? Where else would she have been at six o'clock in the morning?"

"Couldn't she have been downstairs reading a book? Or making tea in the kitchen, or even gone out for a walk? Or maybe left the house while you were gone the night before and never came back?"

Larry Merritt appeared confused and more sweat appeared above his lip. "Of course Cassie was there."

"And my question is, how do you know? Did you search for her? Were you looking for her? Did you go into her room?"

Larry shouted at Sam, "NO, I didn't go into her room. The damn door was locked."

Sam feigned a look of consternation. "I take it then you did TRY to go into her room? Why else would you have been testing the door?"

Larry was shaken and visibly forced himself under control. He hesitated and then mumbled, "Yes, I was going to let her know I was leaving. Ask her to look in on Mich since she was feeling worse again."

"And what did you do when you discovered the door locked?"

Again, Larry looked confused, like he couldn't understand why Sam would ask that. "Nothing, I just left for golf."

"No note to Ms. Kirkland asking her to check on your terminally ill wife, no message slipped under her door?"

"Nothing. Cassie'd figure it out when she got up. Either Mich would be up or she wouldn't. Cassie had more experience dealing with Mich's sick headaches than I did, Mich had them all through college. When she got them after we were married and still lived in Nashville, I'd call Cassie to come take care of her, I got tired of Mich being sick and tired all the time."

"And the extra keys to the house? Of the 'anybody' who could have gotten into the house, can you think of anyone who would have had a motive to kill your wife?"

Larry appeared to be really thinking about the question and an answer that the jury would accept. He finally gave up, his shoulders slumped and he whispered. "No. Mich was nice to everybody, didn't have an enemy in the world. We had our differences, and I'm not the most patient man in the world, but I really can't think of anyone who would have wanted her dead. She was dying already, her friends knew it, Mich was the only one who couldn't accept it. Maybe it was a burglar, I don't know." His whole body gave evidence of resignation and defeat. "I just know I didn't do it."

Sam didn't like this new sympathetic Larry Merritt. He had to find a way to leave the jury with the earlier impression. "What about your mistress, Mr. Merritt? Didn't she have a motive?"

"Hardly. I give Lisa everything she wants and all she really wants is me. She'd have had me, too, in a few months, a year at the most. Makes no sense for her to kill my wife. Mich didn't care about my women; she'd always known about them. Hell, we talked about them; I had the affairs to take the pressure off her. I knew she wasn't up to sex, not physically, not emotionally. Until Lisa, that's all they were, sex. When Lisa came along I already knew it was just a matter of time before Mich died; I guess I was ready for someone else in my life."

"So you're saying you loved your wife and would have given up Ms. Muir if your wife survived the cancer?"

Larry hesitated. Lisa was sitting at the back of the courtroom. "I don't know what I would have done if she survived; but that's not a riddle I have to solve now, is it?" The self-confident grin returned.

That's what Sam wanted to hear. "Thank you, Mr. Merritt, you've been very helpful." That's NOT what Larry Merritt wanted to hear.

"Mr. DeLacey, call your next witness." Judge Thomas spoke to the defense attorney as Larry exited the witness box and returned to his seat at the Defense table.

"No more witnesses, Your Honor, the Defense rests."

"Any rebuttal witnesses, Mr. Chambers?"

"No, Your Honor."

"Then we will proceed with closing arguments after lunch. Court is adjourned until 2 p.m."

Doc and Cassie rose from the oak bench as the spectators wandered out. *What was going on?* It was too early for lunch and most of the spectators were feeling lost with nothing to do for the next few hours. Doc and Cassie looked at each other in dismay as they overheard some of the comments passing them, "Well, I never expected that", "I've been coming to trials a lot of years and that's the first time a defense attorney gave up after only five witnesses". Once again Doc and Cassie worked against the tide of spectators and headed into the courtroom to query Sam.

Sam felt as stunned as Doc and Cassie looked. He couldn't believe DeLacey had rested the defense after so few witnesses. He turned and looked at Maria; she shrugged her shoulders and started to gather their papers. Keeping in mind Greg's admonition, Sam turned to Doc and Cassie, and said to Doc, "Well, I guess that's it. Closing arguments this afternoon. Maria and I are going to work on it, good thing we started last night, just need the finishing touches today. That was a surprise, wasn't it? Thank goodness for Judge Thomas. He always likes the jury to hear both sides of the closing arguments at the same time, no breaks between, says it's more fair that way." Sam's left eyebrow went up a fraction, "You and Cassie okay?" They both nodded, still stupefied. It was almost over.

"But why, Sam? Why so few defense witnesses. Isn't this a bit unusual, especially in a first degree murder trial?" Doc asked the question they were all wondering.

"I really have no idea, Doc. My only guess is that he's trying to give the impression that he doesn't need any more witnesses, that it's an open and shut case in favor of his client." He grabbed his briefcase and Maria's elbow and then turned back, "We really have to go; lots to do and not as much time as we expected to do it." The two headed out of the courtroom. Doc and Cassie looked at each other, more stupefied by Sam's curtness than the defense attorney's actions.

Chapter 60

Larry Merritt paced his holding cell. He'd removed his suit jacket and tie and ignored the boxed lunch the court had provided; no more dry turkey sandwiches for him. DeLacey had stopped by briefly when court was dismissed; he had chastised Larry for not following his instructions. "There's nothing we can do about it now. I'll have to rewrite part of my closing argument to try and buy you some sympathy. You had the jury in your hands at one point, then you blew it with your wisecracks. If we lose, just remember it was you who insisted on testifying."

Larry grimaced at the memory of DeLacey stalking out of the cell, his floppy blonde hair rising and falling with each heavy step. *I really don't like that guy, pompous little ass. But he's supposed to be the best. At the prices he's charging me he'd better get me off, or I won't pay him the rest of his fee.* This thought cheered Larry briefly. Then he looked at the stark nature of his ten-by-ten cell and suddenly realized he could spend the rest of his life in a cell just as Spartan, and maybe with a roommate – *cellmate-* he corrected himself. His bravado left him all of a sudden as the reality of his situation sank in. Fear sent silent tears running down his tanned cheeks.

Once everyone was seated and the rustling of papers, tissues, and fabric-covered butts settled down, Judge Thomas turned to the jury. "Ladies and Gentlemen of the jury, you have heard the witnesses and the evidence for both the Prosecution and the Defense. In a few minutes you will hear the closing arguments from each. Please try to keep an open mind until they have both finished."

"Mr. Chambers, please proceed."

At 2:15 Sam began his closing argument. "Ladies and Gentlemen, this is a tough one. You have to decide the guilt or innocence of Larry Merritt. Did he kill his wife? If so, did he plan to kill her or was it in a fit of pique? In making your decision, you must look at whether Larry Merritt had means, motive, and the opportunity to have committed this crime.

"Let's look at the solid evidence of this case. First, did Larry Merritt have the means to poison his wife? You have heard from his own lips that he handled the medicine bottle, carafe, and glass that had his fingerprints on them. He certainly had access to cyanide at the company where he worked. Books on poison and drug interactions were shipped to Larry Merritt at his office from Amazon. Capsules full of cyanide were found in his dresser with only his fingerprints on the bottle.

"Did Larry Merritt have a motive to kill his wife? He told us he did not know his wife had changed her will, as far as he knew he was set to inherit her art work that sky-rocketed in value after her death, worth millions of dollars. He had a new woman already waiting in the wings, waiting for his wife to die so they could be married and enjoy the fruits of Michela's artistic talent. Larry Merritt himself said his wife didn't have any enemies.

"And finally, did Larry Merritt have the opportunity to kill his wife? He had full access to the house where she died. He had full access to her at any time, day or night. His were the only fingerprints on the carafe and water glass besides Michela Merritt's. He was in no hurry, he could kill her when the time suited him, whenever his patience with her illness ran out.

On the morning of May 17 Larry Merritt arose at 5:30 a.m. and left the house around 6:30, plenty of time to give fake pills to his sick wife. We know he was in the hall before 6:30 because he tried to enter Ms. Kirkland's room at approximately 6:20. It could not have taken more than five minutes to pour the water and give the fake pills to his wife. The Medical Examiner says Mrs. Merritt died between 5 a.m. and 7 a.m. Mr. Merritt has sworn under oath that he was in the upstairs hall during that time. His were the only prints on the water glass and the carafe.

"Yes, ladies and gentleman, Larry Merritt DID kill his wife, and he did it with premeditation. The forensic psychiatrist explained that poisoning is not a sudden decision, it takes time. In this case, the capsules had to be prepared with cyanide before they could be given to Michela Merritt. Filling the capsules took a lot of precision and a steady hand, it wasn't something to be done whimsically.

"The defense has tried to confuse the issue by showing that other people could have done the deed also. Let's look logically at the other possible suspects. Recognize that there has been no evidence brought forth to implicate any of them, only suggestions and innuendoes from the defense attorney.

"Bill Harper, the family doctor, and now we know the father of Michela Merritt. Is it logical to assume that this man, who has devoted his whole life to helping cancer patients, who has loved one woman his whole life, who was grief-stricken at the death of Michela Merritt, and who wasn't in the house at the time of her death, would pick this particular time to kill her? Why? If it was a mercy killing, as the defense has suggested, why not sooner? Why put her through all the pain and suffering she had already experienced?

"And Cassie Kirkland, the best friend. What motive did she have? She didn't know about the will. It was plain that she wasn't after Michela's husband." The jury sniggered at this suggestion as Sam had hoped they would. "Yes, she was in the house at the time of the death, because Michela had asked her to come for a visit. Larry Merritt testified she was locked in her bedroom at the time he left for golf; the ME testified the death occurred at some point before he left for golf. There's no evidence that Ms. Kirkland was in Michela Merritt's room the day of Michela's death until after Mrs. Merritt was already dead. Maybe she and the good doctor were in it together? He mixed up the poison pills and she delivered them. I'm sure that either of these people, who loved Michela Merritt, could have come up with a less painful way to help her die.

"And finally, did Michela Merritt commit suicide? By all accounts, she was a fighter, she had big plans for the future; she loved painting; she planned to go to Ireland next year; she wanted to open an art camp for children with cancer. Both Larry Merritt and Cassie Kirkland testified to how Michela's hands shook; the toxicologist testified that it would take a very steady hand to fill those tiny capsules without poisoning yourself in the process. Again, there were less painful ways to die. Michela Merritt could have just taken sleeping pills, there were hundreds of them in her closet. There was no need to put herself through the pain of a cyanide death."

Sam stopped directly in front of the jury and slowly looked at each juror in turn. "Ladies and gentlemen, when you look at the facts of this case, not the innuendoes and *possibilities*, you will see that there is only one person with the means, motive, and opportunity to have killed Michela Merritt. And that someone is Larry Merritt. You have heard several witnesses attest to the fact that he was cold and uncaring toward his wife. He now has a replacement for his wife waiting in the wings. Logically, rationally Larry Merritt is the only person who could have, would have killed this young, vibrant, talented woman. You do not need to worry about any other possible suspects. You just need to look at all the facts and decide if you think Larry Merritt is guilty or innocent. I'm sure you will do the right thing and find him guilty of murder in the first degree. Thank you."

Sam looked at each juror again and then turned and returned to his seat at the prosecution table. Maria gave him a small smile and a pat from her seat next to him. He did not look toward the spectators where Doc and Cassie sat with their hands clasped.

Chapter 61

Immediately following, Judge Thomas directed, "You may begin, Mr. DeLacey."

John DeLacey pulled himself to his full five foot ten height, buttoned his blue suit jacket, smoothed his pink and blue tie and approached the jury. He stopped just short of the jury rail and carefully made eye contact with each juror.

"Ladies and Gentlemen, this is a very sad case. A caring, talented, young woman has died in a very painful manner. Notice that I say 'died' rather than that she was murdered, because at this point in time there is no evidence that she was murdered. The prosecution has proven HOW she died, but not who gave her the poisoned capsules. She may have given them to herself. It is your sworn duty to wade through the evidence and determine BEYOND A REASONABLE DOUBT that my client, Larry Merritt, did or did not, kill his wife. And there is a lot of evidence to consider.

"The prosecution has a lot of circumstantial evidence, the books ordered from Amazon with Larry Merritt's credit card; but his wife handled the household accounting, she could have ordered the books and used his credit card number. The cyanide was possibly taken from the vault at Golden Lights; again, no fact of who took it. Larry Merritt's fingerprints on the water glass and pill bottle. He explained that, Michela Merritt asked him to get them for her. Yes, there was a bottle of pills hidden in Larry Merritt's dresser, but he says he had no knowledge of it; maybe someone else placed it there. Anyone with a key to the house could have put the bottle in that drawer.

"And of course there is the fact that Mr. and Mrs. Merritt had a very unusual marriage. She was sick a lot and he had affairs; even according to her best friend, Cassie Kirkland, Mrs. Merritt knew about these affairs and refused, REFUSED, to divorce Larry Merritt.

"But if not Larry Merritt, who killed Michela Merritt? There are plenty of options and the defense does not have to prove who did it; we just have to present the possibilities for you to consider. First, there's the kindly, lying family doctor, who in fact, was Michela Merritt's father AND her doctor. After having loved and lost Michela's mother, and then taken care of the daughter her whole life, is it possible that he refused to see his daughter suffer the final stages of the horrible cancer that was not-so-slowly eating away at her body? He had a key to the house. He knew all about poison; for heaven's sake, he's a doctor. He loved her. He was a doctor and committed to sparing people pain and suffering. Means, motive, opportunity. They're all there.

"And of course there is the best friend, Cassie Kirkland. She was present in the house at the time of the death. She stands to inherit a LOT of money. And, by her own words, she 'hated' that Michela would not divorce Larry...her reasons for this hate have not been made clear. Cassie Kirkland, an avid gardener, was familiar with poisons. She could have brought poison from her tool shed to kill her friend, or bought some after she arrived in Denver. She could have filled the capsules in Virginia and packed them in her suitcase; her hands don't shake. Means, motive, opportunity. They're all there.

There's even the mistress, Lisa Muir. Maybe she got tired of waiting for the wife to die. Had Larry Merritt told her about the key hidden outside? Maybe. Had she borrowed his house key while he slept? Maybe. There are a lot of possibilities.

"Of course, there's the chance that Michela Merritt committed suicide. Spare herself the pain that was undeniable with the cancer. She had the same access to the cyanide as her husband. No one had a better opportunity. Facing a slow and painful cancer death, no one had a better motive.

"Finally, what about the defendant? He had means, motive, and opportunity, too. But why? Michela Merritt was dying. All Larry Merritt had to do was wait a few more months and she would have been gone. Is it *logical* to assume that Larry Merritt had more motive than anyone else? Is it *reasonable* to think that Larry Merritt, rather than someone else, killed Michela Merritt?

"Ladies and Gentlemen, your deliberations will begin shortly. You don't have to like the defendant; you can even loathe him. But if you find there is **reasonable doubt** to find Larry Merritt guilty of the death of Michela Merritt, you MUST acquit him. We thank you for your attention and your sense of duty."

DeLacey made a small bow to the jury and returned to his seat. Larry was still fidgeting at the table. He shook hands with his lawyer and tried to look positive, but he just looked like he was going to throw up.

Once again John DeLacey had shocked Sam Chambers. This time it was the brevity of his summation. DeLacey was noted for his long summations, taking every opportunity to hold center stage. Sam looked down at his notes and shook his head. He had no idea how the jury would figure this one out.

Judge Thomas directed his attention and words to the jury, "Ladies and Gentlemen of the jury, it is time to perform your civic duty and determine the verdict in the case of the State of Colorado versus Larry Merritt. Mr. Merritt has been charged with first degree murder; that means that he killed Michela Merritt and he planned to do it; it was not a spur-of-the-moment action. He planned it and he carried it out. It was not an act of passion, it was a reasoned, logical act on the part of Mr. Merritt."

Judge Thomas paused and looked at each member of the jury in turn.

"When you go into that jury room you must confer and come to a unanimous decision of guilty or not guilty. No other verdict is possible. The court will ask you to appoint one person as the spokesperson, for the jury. You may ask for records or evidence from the trial. A bailiff will be just outside the jury room; just ask him or her for whatever you need. Meals will be brought to you on a regular schedule.

"You may NOT confer with anyone outside the jury room; not family, not friends, not any members of the trial. If it is determined that any of you have done so it will be brought to my attention. Depending on the severity of the exchange, I will make a ruling at that time. I hope it will not come to that." The graying judge looked solemnly at each jury member again.

Judge Thomas looked at his watch, 3:40. "Ladies and Gentlemen, I know the hour is late, but I think it is to your advantage to gather for a little while and start your deliberations. You may decide as a group how long you want to work today. Dinner will be brought in if you request it. You will be allowed to go home and come back Monday to resume your deliberations. AGAIN, you may not discuss this case with anyone outside the jury room. If anyone does, the jury will have to be moved to a hotel for the duration of your deliberations. So far I have heard of no infractions; I hope it continues.

"Please ask the bailiff for anything you need. When a verdict has been reached or if you find yourselves hopelessly deadlocked, please inform the bailiff who will inform me. You are excused."

Judge Thomas turned to the bailiff closest to the side door, "Bailiff, please escort the jury to the jury room." You could have heard a pin drop.

Twelve average citizens stood. The women grabbed their purses. No one looked at either attorney, nor at the defendant. No one smiled. They seemed absorbed in their civic responsibility. Silently they left the room through the door to the right of the defense table. Both attorneys tried to read the faces, but all they saw were twelve blank expressions, no hint of what anyone was thinking.

As the door closed behind the last juror, Judge Thomas banged his gavel, "Court is adjourned." He stood and exited for the next-to-last time through the door behind the bench.

A bailiff came and took Larry out through the same door the jury had used. The attorneys just looked tired and stressed, the hardest part of the trial for them was the waiting for the verdict. Sam couldn't help turning to look for Cassie and giving her a weak smile.

Chapter 62

Like the jurors, the spectators, reporters, and witnesses stood and gathered their belongings. Unlike the jury, they weren't quiet. Babbling immediately broke out, everybody trying to second guess the jury. Would it take long? If it did, was that a good sign or bad sign for the defendant? The reporters stood still and opened their various smartphones to let their respective editors or station managers know what was going on. From what Cassie and Doc were hearing, it was a toss-up between "he did it" and "Nah, he didn't do it." But nobody seemed sure of who did it if Larry hadn't; or maybe they just didn't want to talk about it with Cassie and Doc within hearing range.

Michela's "family" waited quietly at their places in the spectator seats, hoping for a chance to talk to Sam. As the courtroom emptied, Sam and Maria walked over to them. At their unasked question, Sam replied, "I don't know. It can go either way. DeLacey was his usual persuasive self. I've said it all along, it's a crap shoot. I've never met a totally impartial juror; it just depends on what their personal biases and experiences are. We did the best we could in jury selection, but there's no telling." Sam paused and ran his hand through his hair, looking carefully at the witnesses who had become friends, and more. "Come on, let's get out of the building and get something to eat. They'll call me if the jury comes back; I'm not expecting anything this late in the day." He lightly grabbed Cassie's elbow and propelled her out of the courtroom, leaving Doc and Maria in their wake.

Their early dinner at the convenient Jose's Fajitas was a quiet affair, each of them too exhausted to talk and each subconsciously listening for the buzz of Sam's cell phone. They left their food mostly untouched and Sam drove them back to the courthouse. Sam had said it was unlikely the jury would reach a decision this late in the day. He dropped Doc and Cassie at Doc's car and the two drove home in silence. Sam and Maria went back to Sam's office to clean up some loose ends and rehash the trial.

"I never knew how tiring doing nothing could be," Cassie said as she hugged Doc and kissed his cheek as they came in from the garage. "Try to get some sleep, Doc, I'll see you in the morning." Doc hugged her back and trudged upstairs to his room. Cassie fixed herself a cup of tea and carried it up to her room. They both slept fitfully and awoke several times to memories of the trial.

Once again it was a long, quiet weekend, confined to the house as they were by the television and newspaper people camped on the front yard. They were not constrained from discussing the trial and the witnesses. Doc and Cassie spent the weekend reviewing, rehashing, and rethinking every witness and every facet of the trial. Even they could not determine which way the jury would decide.

Monday morning Cassie fixed them a ham and cheese omelet with corn bread, coffee and tea for breakfast. Sam hadn't called to say the jury was back, but they still wanted to be near the courthouse when the jury returned; it was too long a drive to wait for Sam's call. They rode quietly to the courthouse, arriving at eleven. Cassie texted Sam to let him know they would be in the cafeteria. They headed downstairs for more watery coffee, responding "No Comment" to the shouted questions from the lingering reporters.

The jury had started deliberating again at 8 a.m.

Chapter 63

It only took until 3:17 that afternoon. Maria had found them chatting and drinking cold coffee in the cafeteria. Maria told them the jury would deliver their verdict in, she glanced at her watch, twenty minutes. Doc and Cassie gathered their reading materials and trailed after her. They took the elevator four floors to courtroom 3B. All seats were taken when they arrived, but the second row of spectators skooched together to make room for them. Sam and Maria were seated at the oak table on the left, just ahead of where Cassie and Doc were sitting; DeLacey and Larry Merritt at their matching table on the right.

The jury silently filed back into the packed courtroom, again avoiding the eyes of everyone. They resumed their seats and looked at Judge Thomas.

"Madam Foreperson, has the jury reached a verdict?" The tall brunette accountant on the end of the first row stood and faced the bench. "We have, Your Honor." The resounding inhalation of breaths throughout the courtroom was deafening. She handed a folded piece of paper to the bailiff. The bailiff walked seventeen steps across the floor and handed it to the judge. Judge Thomas looked at it impassively and laid it on his desk. "The defendant will please rise." John DeLacey and Larry Merritt stood and faced the jury box. Merritt's hands were tightly clenched at his sides. Judge Thomas turned back to the jury, "Ladies and Gentlemen of the jury, in the matter of the State of Colorado vs. Larry Merritt, how do you find?"

The brunette opened the remaining piece of paper in her hand and read, "We, the members of the jury find Larry Merritt..."

Epilogue

It has been almost six months since the trial and a year since Michela's death. Lexington is in full bloom, the azaleas, red buds, and dogwoods are displaying their spring glory for all the world to see. Cassie too feels like she is coming back to life, she still cannot believe the verdict, cannot believe that she knows a murderer! How could Larry have done it? She never liked him but she never considered him capable of something so inhuman. How would he ever survive life in prison?

The six months had been hard, every time she opened her e-mail she expected to find a message from Mich. She'd read something about Ireland or one of the places they'd visited and she wanted to call her and tell her about it. Sam and Doc had been wonderful, staying in touch, trying to lift her spirits.

Cassie had stayed through the opening of the Michela Ferncliff Merritt Exhibit the week after the trial ended and then flew home in time for Thanksgiving. The Exhibit grand opening was a smashing success and the February auction raised a lot of money for the summer camp, over 12 million dollars. Cassie had gone to Denver for the auction and stayed with Doc. She saw Sam briefly at the auction but was too busy to spend time with him. She flew home the day after.

A large part of Cassie's time was now taken up with making decisions about the camp. At least she and Doc had finally decided on a name: Mich's Kids' Camp. She knew she would have to leave her job soon and devote her full time to the camp. Doc had agreed to be chief doctor in residence in the summers.

She remembered her departure from Denver. Doc hugged her on his front porch and told her to come back for the holidays. Sam drove her to the airport, seemingly lost in his own thoughts, quiet as the mountains to their west. At the airport Cassie asked him just to drop her and her bag at the curb, she hated airport good-byes. As the skycap headed off with her bag, Sam took her hand and looked deeply into her eyes. "You were great, Cassie. I know we haven't had a lot of time to talk except about the case, but I hope we will soon." Cassie returned his look, not knowing what to say, what was *he* saying? "Cass, I don't know...I can't...I'll call you."

Cassie was confused and disappointed. Sam took both Cassie's shoulders in his strong hands and pulled her to him. "I hate to see you go," he whispered against her hair. Cassie leaned back and again looked into his eyes, questioning him. Sam leaned forward and gave her a warm kiss, almost crushing her to him. Cassie surprised herself and responded, clinging to his leather jacket like a lifeline. Sam recovered first. "Hey, don't want you to catch cold, even if it is a dry cold," he chuckled as he gently pushed her to the warmth of the airport terminal. "I'll call, Cassie, I promise." Cassie was more confused than ever as she headed through the automatic glass doors.

True to his word, Sam had called. He kept her up to date on his job, he told her when Larry was sent to prison, they laughed together about Doc's romantic escapades. Sam invited Doc to share Christmas with his family and Doc had enchanted everyone. By choice, Cassie spent a quiet holiday with Rosie in Lexington.

In January Doc had to go before an ethics review board of the medical association; he'd gotten off with a reprimand due to extenuating circumstances.

Now it was spring and Cassie was feeling restless. The doorbell rang. She padded over to it in her bare feet, Rosie fast on her heels. When she opened it, Sam was on the front porch. He reached for her and pulled her to him, "I've really missed you, Cassie." He gave her a long, lingering kiss.

Cassie beamed, "Sam, what are you doing here? You didn't tell me you were coming."

Sam threw his arm around her shoulders and propelled her into the house, closing the front door behind them. "It's a long story, Cassie, one

I've been working on for a while. But first, I have to give you something. Let's sit down." Sam led Cassie to the butter yellow sofa in the back parlor cum TV room.

He pulled a flash drive from his shirt pocket. "Cassie, this came to the office last week, for you. I got one, too, so I sort of know what's in it, but not everything." He handed the flash drive to Cassie. She immediately recognized Mich's handwriting on the tiny label. She looked up quizzically at Sam.

"Just watch it, Cass, then we'll talk."

Cassie carefully plugged the drive into her TV and turned it on. She punched a few buttons on the remote and suddenly Mich was alive again.

Hi, Cass, it's me, back from the dead, so to speak.

I wish I could be with you, taking another trip to...anywhere. We had so much fun together, didn't we? But since you're watching this, I'm dead. WOW! That's weird. Mich smiled her irrepressible grin.

Ever since Doc gave me the news that the cancer is back and it's unlikely I'll survive it this time, I've tried to be strong and positive, I really have. I didn't want to bring anybody else down.

But now I'm tired, I'm just so tired. And I'm sick and tired of being sick and tired. Tired of being strong. Tired of being the giver. But mostly, I'm tired of being lonely...I think I've always been lonely, even as a child. Not alone necessarily, but lonely. Even my art couldn't fully fill the void, although it helped me hide a lot of the pain.

My whole life I've wanted to be "special" to someone. I've given this a lot of thought, had lots of time to do it lately! I guess I mean I want to be the one person who means more than anything or anyone else to somebody. To be first to somebody. And I haven't experienced that; it doesn't look like I'm going to either.

Lord knows I was never special to my dad; he never got over losing my mom. I was a little special to Doc, but only because I was Lily's daughter, not for myself." Cassie caught her breath at these words; if only Mich had known.

Larry fooled me into thinking I was special to him, but that was only for my money. My sickness was quite a shock to him and definitely not something he had signed on for. My sickness brought out his true colors. Whatever happened to people sticking to their wedding vows? I guess "cherish" and "in sickness and in health" are out of style. I just wanted to be cherished but nobody has ever meant more to Larry than Larry. He is so self-involved he even admires himself in every mirror or reflective window he passes! He doesn't talk to me. He's out almost every night. What I would give for just an occasional hug or have him hold me at night, but if we touch in bed that means sex to him, and I'm just not up to it. So I spend my nights alone and most of my days, too. Like I said, I've had a lot of time to think.

I think I would have been special to my baby girl, but she died before I had a chance to find out.

And then there's you, my dearest friend, the best friend anyone could wish for. I know I'm special to you and that you love me, but it's not the same. I know you'd do anything for me. But I also know that while you were married, Kevin came first, and he should have, he was your husband. I don't know what caused the divorce, but I know you'll marry again and then I'll move to second place again. That's not a complaint, just a fact.

I am glad to have had you in my life.

Sam watched Cassie, watched the silent tears spill over and run down her cheeks.

Most of the twelve plus years, that I have known you, you have provided the only real happiness I have known. That's why it hurts me to use you the way I'm going to.

Cassie looked up at Sam, questions in her watery eyes.

I have decided to kill myself and frame Larry for it. I want to punish him for hurting me so terribly, for not sticking to his wedding vow to "cherish" me, for not putting me above all others, even himself. I trusted him! He lied to me, our very marriage was a lie. I hate liars, both lying by commission and omission, and here I am turning into the biggest liar of all.

But I trust you to help me, even though you won't know you're helping me. I hate to use you like this, but you are so open and honest, brutally honest sometimes, that everyone will believe you. Remember that time a bunch of us were going to Chicago for the weekend and we didn't invite Alice? You were so worried she'd be hurt about not being invited, since she'd always been part of our "gang", that you told her we didn't invite her because she was a scholarship student and we didn't think she could afford it. That was the truth, but I'm not sure which hurt more; the truth or the missed invitation?

I haven't decided when I'm going to do it, but I have all the details worked out. I changed my will last month. I'm doing this video, even had to learn how to do it! You'd be so proud of me, you know details are not really my thing. I've explained everything in a separate letter and video to the DA's office. And Elena has agreed to handle the delivery of these.

Cassie looked at Sam and hit Pause on the remote. "But Elena didn't say anything about it when she testified?"

Sam looked sheepish. "She said nobody asked her if Mich had given her anything. Mich told her if she left too many mailings with the attorney in Colorado Springs he might be compelled to turn them over during the trial, so she left these last ones with Elena, just in case."

Cassie punched Play and Mich sprang to life again.

Because, despite everything, I can't let Larry suffer too long. I want him punished, but not forever. I'm sure with you as a witness, and the evidence I'm going to provide, not to mention his ego, he will be convicted of my murder. But it's just not in me to leave him in prison forever; loss of my paintings and the life insurance money will be as big a punishment as prison: insurance won't pay out since I'm going to be a suicide. Maybe he'll get it after this? Who knows?

But back to you, my almost-sister. I don't know when I'll do this, but I know I'll have to see you one last time. And I know you'll come when I call. Please don't hate me. Always know I love you and I'll see you on the other side.

Mich waved good-bye with a smile on her face. The TV screen went black.

Cassie smiled through her tears as she hit Stop on the remote. She looked up questioningly at Sam. "She says she sent stuff to the DA's office, too?"

Sam nodded and pulled another letter from his jacket pocket. Cassie reached for it, but he held it back. "The video was a duplicate of the one you've just seen. You can read the letter later, I'll just tell you the details. Sam explained.

"Mich said she'd made her decision shortly after the talk with Doc in January when he told her the chemo hadn't worked and she only had six to twelve months left. She said she took a page from your book and went to the public library, different branches each time, and researched poisons.

"She decided on cyanide because it was quick and she had ready access to it at the plant without leaving a trail. She said she thought the momentary pain was better than an extended period of morphine and unconsciousness. She said she felt like she had some control over her life for the first time in a long time." Sam watched Cassie's tears silently spill again. He put his arm around Cassie's shoulder and pulled her close to his chest. Her hand came up to rest comfortably on his shirtfront. He squeezed her gently. Rosie rested her head on Cassie's knee and watched them both, her eyebrows twitching.

"Ready?"

Cassie sniffed and nodded against him.

"She ordered all the books, using his name and credit card, just like it was brought out in court. I feel like such a jerk! To think DeLacey was right all along, that's what really hurts. It was a combo, suicide and a frame job."

He felt Cassie smile against his chest.

"Mich said she was already filling capsules with the cyanide – this was January when she wrote the letter we got – because she was afraid she wouldn't have the strength later. She was going to fill about ten of them and leave some hidden in the back of Larry's sweater drawer; she figured he'd never notice it since he rarely wore sweaters and she wasn't going to put them there until the last minute."

Sam looked down at the top of Cassie's head. "She really thought this through, didn't she?"

"Not really like her," Cassie mumbled, still snuggled up against his warmth. "I guess I didn't know her as well as I thought. Although she was quite the actress at Vandy." The tears and sniffles started again. Sam squeezed her shoulder and Rosie adjusted her chin on Cassie's knee, carefully keeping an eye on both of them.

"She ended by explaining that she would call you for one last visit whenever she decided the time was right. It wasn't plain from her letter though whether she planned to kill herself while you were there or if that was a last minute decision. She said you knew nothing about her plans, that it was all her doing. In her letter to us she said she just wanted to punish Larry and she hoped this letter would be enough evidence to free him; she wanted us to be sure he knew that she had done this to him and why."

Cassie sighed. "Poor Mich. I wish I had known. I wish I could have helped her so she didn't feel this was the only way out."

Sam grabbed Cassie by both shoulders and sat her up straight to face him. He pulled her chin up so her watery eyes were looking into his. "No, Cass, there was nothing you could have done. Mich even wrote that you would blame yourself, but that this was what she wanted; she wanted to go out in control of her life and ending her loneliness."

"But I should have been a better friend so she didn't feel so lonely."

"Cassie, you did the best you could. You had your own life to live and you lived across the country. In the long run, we can't be responsible for another person's happiness; it's up to each of us to find our own. You were the best friend anyone could have wanted and Mich knew that. Hey! You even invited her to move out here to Lexington. You can't live another person's life, you can just be there for them when they need you. And you were there for Mich, always."

"Boy, that's for sure! I even helped her kill herself with me as the chief witness!"

Sam gently shook Cassie. "No! She was determined to kill herself, you just helped frame Larry."

They looked at each other and broke out laughing at the silliness of what Sam had just said.

"Well, that makes me feel a lot better," Cassie replied sarcastically with a grin.

"It's okay. They were starting the process to get him out of prison as I drove to the airport. He'll be out in a day or two. The way I see it, he deserved what he got. Six months in the state pen isn't so bad for the way he treated Michela; he should just be glad there was no death penalty involved."

"Is this the defender of the people talking?"

"No, this is Sam Chambers, defender of the downtrodden...and Mich was." Sam paused, "How about if I fix us some tea? I think I remember my way around your kitchen. Or maybe something stronger?" Sam rose, Rosie at his heels and Cassie following, a frown on her face.

While the water heated Sam arranged the cups on the breakfast room table, Cassie asked, "Did she explain how she got the poison books out of his office without Larry finding out? That's the piece I'm missing."

"Nope. But it wouldn't have been too hard." Sam poured the water into the yellow Fiesta ware teapot and brought the pot to the table. "Amazon is pretty quick with their deliveries, or she could have paid for express delivery and known exactly which day the shipment would arrive. All she had to do was wait for a week when Larry was out of town, then waltz into his office with a big purse or briefcase and waltz right back out. If anyone saw the Amazon box or the books she could just say she was picking them up for Larry. No questions asked. She could have gone in on a weekend when no one was around."

"But what about getting the cyanide? Did she take it from the vault?" Cassie was stricken.

"We guess so. She didn't say anything about it in the stuff she sent us. But she could have done it the same way, just waltz in when nobody was around."

Cassie sipped her Lady Grey and looked at Sam across the rim, her big brown eyes even bigger than usual. "This has to have been a blow for you, Sam. How are you doing?"

Sam put on his lop-sided grin. "Recovering. The hardest part was having to call DeLacey and tell him he was right. He couldn't wait to call a press conference. But win some, lose some; that's the legal game. I'm really impressed and more than a little mortified that Michela out-smarted some of the best legal and investigative minds in Colorado! She would have made a great lawyer."

They smiled companionably across the table at each other, Rosie lying with her head under the table between them.

"Thanks for bringing the video, Sam. I know you didn't have to do that. You could have mailed it or had someone else bring it."

Sam looked sheepish. "Well, Greg suggested I needed a vacation, some time off to 'get my head back on straight' as he put it. He was really mad about the DA's office being put in this light, made us look really incompetent. So I decided since I haven't had a vacation since I joined the

DA's office to make it a really good one. So here I am. Maybe I can get you to show me around some this time? I didn't have a real tour guide the last time I was here." He looked hopefully at Cassie. "I've got six weeks of semi-enforced vacation. Think you can get some time off and show me the wonders of springtime in the Blue Ridge?"

Cassie looked long and hard at Sam, took another sip of her tea, debating whether to trust him or not. Between Kevin and now Mich, her track record with people wasn't all that good. She finally decided. "I'm sure I can, Sam, I'd like that. It's time for me to quit the library anyway. Mich's camp needs me full time."

Sam visibly relaxed. "Know any place a poor government employee can get a room cheap?"

Cassie smiled at him as she said, "I think I can find a place for you."

He refilled their cups and asked, "Shall I call the Bistro for a dinner reservation?"

Acknowledgments

As a fledgling author I have to acknowledge my husband of 50 years who has put up with my challenges to write; his patience has been as helpful as it has been surprising.

Our children Mike and Brian and our DIL Janet have been supportive, too, by reading my books and offering helpful critiques.

A BIG thank you to my wonderful editors, Merrily E. Taylor and Shenoa L. Herlinger. You two make a great tag-team. I think I took care of most of the split-infinitives this time, Merrily!

Brother (in-law) Bill Marshall has been my legal eagle, reviewing the lawyers' parts and correcting my many errors.

To my many readers, I never thought I would have any readers other than friends and family. Thank you so much for giving me a chance.

Please feel free to contact me at
Amazon.com/author/KarinRoseOCallaghan Or visit my web site **KarinRoseOCallaghan.com**. I'd love to hear from you!